Linda Gillard lives on tl   D0509845   ghlands and has been an actre.., ,...........ne's the author of six novels, including STAR GAZING which was short-listed in 2009 for *Romantic Novel of the Year* and *The Robin Jenkins Literary Award* (for writing that promotes the Scottish landscape.)

HOUSE OF SILENCE became a Kindle bestseller and was selected by Amazon as one of their Top Ten *Best of 2011* in the Indie Author category.

Also by Linda Gillard

Emotional Geology
A Lifetime Burning
Star Gazing
House of Silence
The Glass Guardian

www.lindagillard.co.uk

UNTYING THE KNOT

Linda Gillard

First published as a Kindle e-book in 2011
This paperback edition 2013

*All characters and events in this publication
are fictitious and any resemblance to real persons,
living or dead, is purely coincidental.*

ISBN 978-1484824795

Cover design by Nicola Coffield

For Philip

Good knots have no rope
But cannot be untied.

Lao Tzu

Chapter 1

Fay

I stitch memories. That's what I do. Not mine, other people's. I capture them in cloth, thread and ink. I fix them, like insects in amber. The moment, imprinted on the memory, is printed on the cloth, then embellished and decorated.

That's what we do.

Embellish.

Decorate.

Unvarnished truth has only limited appeal. Some events are a joy to recall, but others are best modified, even forgotten. They live in some lumber-room of the mind, housed somewhere you wouldn't want to go alone and never after dark.

If I make a mistake in my work or if I change my mind, I can unpick. Undo what I've done. I can make good my errors and no one is the wiser. If they looked, even through a magnifying glass, all observers would see would be the tiny holes where my needle had travelled. I can erase even that evidence by scratching carefully at the weave of the linen with my needle, until the holes are no longer visible.

But life isn't like that.

Mistakes once made are rarely reversible. The holes they leave in the fabric of life aren't tiny and they can't be scratched away. You have to live with them as best you can. Work round them. That's why you have to come to terms with memory. You can't obliterate the past or eradicate it from the mind, even when, for our own good, memory enfolds us in a blanket of forgetfulness. There are always traces left, marks where time gripped us and left its telltale fingerprint.

~

1

Fay looked round the brightly lit gallery. It was a good turnout, better than she'd hoped. Not bad for a wet Wednesday in Glasgow. The punters were mostly female, but that was always the case with textiles, an essentially female art and, in the opinion of some, only a craft. In their quietly sensuous and tactile way, textiles appealed more to women than men, so the man standing alone in front of one of her wall hangings might have caught Fay's eye anyway, even if he hadn't been a head taller than most of the women milling round him; even if that head had not been crowned by an untidy mane of dark, greying curls.

He'd been standing for some minutes now, regarding a large work depicting an oak tree that in turn represented a family tree, festooned with portraits. The man didn't approach the work, but even when someone walked between him and the textile picture, his concentration didn't appear to falter. Out of the corner of her eye, Fay registered a journalist making his way toward her, his wine glass empty, his expression irritable. Since she regarded journalists as no more than a necessary evil, Fay set down her own glass, picked up a catalogue and approached the man who was studying her work so intently.

She strode across the polished wooden floor, a diminutive figure, confident in her high heels, a hint of challenge in her intelligent grey eyes. Fay was of an age difficult to determine from a distance, but at close quarters her hands, laden with chunky rings, betrayed her as being in her forties. She was dressed in neutral shades of linen and silk and wore heavy ceramic jewellery. Rust-coloured earrings swung from small, neat ears, drawing attention to elfin features and a stark, uncompromising cap of auburn hair. Standing at the man's side, she lifted her chin and said, 'Good evening. Would you like a catalogue?'

It was a second or two before he turned to acknowledge her presence. He looked down at the catalogue, extended toward him. 'Och, no thanks. I don't like being told what to think,' he added amiably.

Fay was distracted by the pale blue eyes, large and unsettling. The hair – so much of it! – obviously once black, was now brindled with grey, but the artist in her couldn't help admiring the classical regularity of feature that might once – twenty years ago perhaps – have betokened beauty.

'It isn't that sort of catalogue,' she explained. 'This is just titles, dates, methods of construction, that sort of thing. And prices of course.'

He inclined his leonine head. 'Of course.' He returned to his examination of the piece. 'The likenesses... They're very good.'

'They would be. They're transferred from photographs. But the likeness isn't the point.'

'I didn't say it was. The *feeling's* the point, is it not?'

She hesitated, suddenly thrown. 'Yes. That *is* the point.'

He shot her a sidelong glance, suspicious. 'Will your catalogue tell me what to feel?'

She ignored the question and said, 'You like *Root and Branch* then?'

'That's what it's called? This piece? "Like" isn't the word.'

'What is?'

'It... disturbs me.'

'Oh, good. You must like being disturbed.'

'Not at all. Why d'you assume that?'

'You've been standing here for some time now.'

'You've been watching me?'

She faltered, caught off-guard. Keeping her voice even, but avoiding his eye, she said, 'No, I haven't been watching you, but I'd registered you hadn't moved. On average people spend about thirty seconds in front of a piece before moving on to the next, so you tend to notice if anyone stops for longer. And you were very noticeable because – well, because you obscure so much of the piece.'

His eyebrows shot up under the curling fringe. Very Charles II, she thought. Or was it more Brian May? Either way, at his age, quite ridiculous. Were good-looking men always vain, she wondered?

'I'm obscuring your piece?'

'Yes. Your height. And – and your hair.' She tried to keep the note of disapproval out of her voice and failed.

'I'd better move on then.'

3

As he turned away, she blurted out, 'You don't want to buy it then?'

'No, thanks. Much as I like it. I'll wait till they turn it into a book jacket. Or a greetings card.'

Stung, she replied sharply, 'This one isn't for sale anyway. It was made as a gift.'

'And who is to be the lucky recipient?'

'My mother-in-law. My *ex*-mother-in-law, I should say.'

He nodded and she watched as the preposterous curls bobbed. 'She'll love it, no doubt. The wee boys look bonny...Well, I hope you manage to sell a few of the others,' he said, sounding doubtful.

'If you cared to look in the catalogue, you'd see quite a few are already sold.'

The eyebrows rose again. 'Congratulations.' He said nothing more and turned away to scrutinise another picture.

She glared at his shabby corduroy back. 'You know, only one of my pieces has been turned into a book jacket. And as for greetings cards, *everybody* does it now. Vettriano made that quite respectable.'

He turned mocking blue eyes toward her. 'We can look forward to a calendar then?'

She arranged her features in a gracious and, she hoped, condescending smile. 'Perhaps if you'd ever tried to earn a living from selling art, your attitude might be rather different.'

'*Do* you earn a living?'

'Yes, I do. Though that's none of your business.'

'Indeed, it's not. But I was interested. I'm glad you do. You deserve to. Your work is...'

'Disturbing?'

'Deeply felt. And moving.'

She blushed and felt immediately foolish. 'Thank you.'

'You're welcome.'

She put her fingers to her temple and rubbed. 'I'm sorry. Sorry I was so — so touchy. It's been a long day. And I've taken a lot of flak about that wretched book jacket. But I thought it was a perfectly appropriate use of my work. It was a memoir after all.'

'And it can't have done you any harm that it turned out to

be a best-selling memoir.'

'Apparently some readers bought it for the jacket. Interest in that was what made my work take off.'

'Aye, I read all about it in *The Herald*. It was a good photograph.'

'Of the jacket?'

'Of you.' He regarded her steadily.

Nonplussed, she thrust the catalogue toward him. 'Here, take this. I don't think there's any chance of it telling *you* what to think. Or feel.'

'How much—'

She waved a hand. 'Forget it.'

'I won't forget the piece,' he said, taking the catalogue. 'Thank you.'

As Fay turned away, she came face to face with a smiling young woman, juggling wine glass, catalogue and a battered bunch of lilies.

'Hi, Mum! Sorry I'm late. I got held up in traffic. These are for you.'

'Emily! Lovely to see you!' Fay embraced her daughter gingerly, careful to avoid both wineglass and lily pollen. 'I'm so glad you could make it. I wasn't really expecting you.'

Over her mother's shoulder, Emily registered the tall man regarding them both quizzically. As her eyes widened, his smile became a grin. She straightened up suddenly, spilling white wine and scattering lily petals.

'Dad! Fancy seeing *you* here!'

Fay

Magnus McGillivray doesn't look like anyone's idea of a hero, even if he does live in a castle with everyone's idea of a princess. When we divorced, he got the ruin and I got the garret. We were both happy with this division of spoils, in so far as one is ever happy after a divorce. There had been no infidelities, but as far as I was concerned, the other women in my husband's life were the Army and – when he finally dumped the Army – Tullibardine Tower.

Tullibardine Tower drained my husband's love, energy

and money for years. No mistress could have been more demanding, more all-consuming. In the end I stopped trying to compete. I knew my limitations. Given a choice between a romantic ruin, crumbling away on a Perthshire hillside and a struggling artist, crumbling away – not quite so romantically – in a Glasgow tenement, which do you think a war hero with an over-developed sense of duty and an irrational desire to atone would choose?

And he did.

So I said I was leaving.

And I did.

It was the best thing that could have happened to me. (Well, that's what people said. Perhaps they say that to all new divorcées.) I was able to pursue my new-found career as a textile artist and I rediscovered what it was to live in a small but comfortable, permanent home, after years in Army accommodation, then a caravan on site beside the ruinous Tully Tower, as it came to be not very affectionately known.

I suppose if Magnus had had any real aspiration to creature comforts, he would never have joined the Army in the first place, let alone thrived on postings to the Falklands, Belfast and the Gulf. He understood, but didn't share my craving for warmth, light and colour. For peace. It was a good day for Magnus if nobody was trying to kill him. (His exasperatingly sunny personality needs to be seen in that appalling context.)

I understood Magnus. I loved him. But in the end, I just couldn't live with him. A familiar story, you might think, but some friends and family saw things differently. Wives are meant to stand by their man – Army wives particularly. And I didn't. I walked away. I walked away from a war hero.

It was a long, at times agonising walk. It wasn't as if I was walking into the arms of a new love. I couldn't even persuade my teenage daughter to come with me. I felt like the loneliest woman in the world. I think I was only able to do it because Magnus understood exactly why I was going. That was possibly the hardest part. The lack of recriminations.

But Magnus knew all about The Long Walk. And feeling like the loneliest man in the world.

~

In the dream he's walking. He's walking as if he has all the time in the world; as if he's out for a stroll on a Sunday afternoon. Except there's nobody else out on the streets. No one at all. And there's no sound, just his own footsteps on the tarmac as he approaches a parked car. And he's not dressed for a Sunday stroll. He's wearing an armoured suit. A suit that stinks of sweat and fear.

In the dream, the car never gets any nearer. He just keeps walking and thinks about mercury tilt switches and tremblers and pressure plates. Booby traps. He thinks in clichés, about how this time his number might be up, it might be his turn, he's had a good run for his money. In the dream he thinks of Fay and wee Emily and that's how he knows it's a dream. He never used to think of them. You stayed focused. You just thought about the job. So he knows there's nothing at all to worry about, it's just a bloody dream.

He approaches the car, calmer now, the adrenalin subsiding, his breathing finally steady. But as he lays his hand on the car door handle and starts to open it, he realises this isn't a dream, this is for real. And it's a trap.

The last thing he feels is moving air, the shock as it perforates his eardrums and collapses his lungs; the waves of energy as they enter his mouth, his nostrils, his eyes and his ears, destroying his body even before his limbs are torn off and flung across the street, before his already dead flesh is stripped from his bones and tossed into the air. His last thought before annihilation is not for his wife and child, but for the poor bastards who'll have to clean up the mess.

Chapter 2

The gallery was crowded now. Fay took the bunch of lilies from Emily and stood aside to let Magnus kiss his daughter on the cheek. Emily McGillivray had inherited the long, elegant frame of her father and even in flat shoes, she dwarfed her mother. Not long out of university and living in Perth on a limited budget, Emily's sartorial style was still Oxfam, but Oxfam-with-panache. She shared her mother's talent for transformation and knew how to make an impression with her vintage buys. Fay approved and admired, but rarely felt at ease with her daughter.

'I didn't know Mum had invited you, Dad,' said Emily, smiling. 'This is quite an occasion, isn't it? All three of us in the same room – and nobody's started shouting yet.'

'Well, *you* only just got here,' Magnus replied. 'And your mother's on her best behaviour on account of the Press. But the night is young.'

Fay sighed. 'Oh, do shut up, Magnus.'

He spread his hands and looked at Emily. 'See what I mean?'

'Is Nina here too?' Fay asked, scanning the gallery.

'No, she's at home,' Magnus replied. 'She has no interest in textiles. Not unless you're talking about remnants of an Egyptian shroud, or the sole of a Roman sandal. The present isn't really Nina's period.'

'It's not really Mum's either,' said Emily.

'Oh, I don't know,' Fay replied. 'My work is as much concerned with the present as the past. I try to say something *about* the present by looking at the past. And by looking at it *through* the past.'

'Which is pretty much the historian's view too,' Magnus added.

'Yes, but a historian and I would part company over

boundaries. They see the past as something that has – well, *passed*. They see it as a timeline, with the past receding year by year. I don't see it like that at all. I see the past and present as layers, one on top of the other. So the past is present *in* the present.'

'Only in memory, surely?' said Emily who'd begun to glance round the room, as if looking for someone.

'No, it's there in a physical sense too. Let me show you what I mean.' Fay walked up to *Root and Branch*, the hanging Magnus had been studying, and pointed. 'This piece of linen is over a hundred years old. And this lace,' she said, stroking the cloth. 'This came from a seventy-year old christening gown.'

'Was it Granny's?' said Emily.

'Yes. The tree trunk was pieced from neckties belonging to your grandfather and your great-uncle Lachlan. And these pieces here...' Fay indicated green cotton fabric that had been cut into leaf shapes. 'These were originally a pair of shorts your father wore as a small boy. So what you have here is a picture of the past, made from *pieces* of the past. But it was made for the present.'

'And *as* a present,' Magnus added.

'For Granny?' Emily asked.

'Yes. I made it for her seventieth birthday.'

'Brilliant! Has she seen it yet?'

'I showed it to her before we hung it for the exhibition. I asked if she'd mind it going on display before I gave it to her.'

'Was she pleased with it?'

'Yes, I think so. It was hard to tell. She didn't say much. She just kept touching it. Touching the faces. She cried a bit.'

'Poor Jessie,' said Magnus. 'She hates to lose it like that. All that messy emotion...' He shook his head. 'It's bad for your health.'

Fay recognised the bait from long experience, but still rose to it. 'You know, I don't know how the English got lumbered with their reputation for stiff upper lips. You Scots make the English seem positively Latin in temperament.'

'Ah! *There* he is!' Emily exclaimed. She laid her hand on her father's arm. 'Don't go away. I'll be right back.'

Fay watched as Emily hurried across the gallery. 'Now

what? She sounded very excited.'

'I suspect we're about to meet her young man.'

'Is this one serious?'

'Possibly.'

'You've met him?'

'Aye, a couple of times.'

'Do you approve?'

Magnus shrugged. 'Would Emily care? Do you, for that matter?'

'No, not really. Is that him over there? He looks older than her.'

'That wouldn't be difficult. She's twenty-two.'

'He looks smart at least.' Fay craned her neck. 'His suit actually fits.'

'You should see him in a tux.'

'You have?' Fay abandoned her scrutiny of Emily's new man and turned to Magnus. 'Where?'

'Em dragged me to a concert in Perth. She met him there when he was rehearsing at the Concert Hall. He's a post-grad student here in Glasgow. Training to be a singer. A *classical* singer. Funny way to earn a living, if you ask me.'

'Not as funny as being blown up for a living. And nobody did ask you.'

'I see age has not yet begun to mellow you, Fay,' Magnus replied, gazing at his ex-wife with a gratified smile. 'Brace yourself, now. You're about to meet the man who may become your future son-in-law.'

She turned to him, aghast. 'You're joking! Emily's twenty-two!'

'At which age you were married to a soldier and had a wee bairn.'

'You're saying a capacity for disaster is passed down through the genes?' Fay snapped.

Magnus folded his arms and sighed. 'You know, there are times when I miss your douce tones and calm reasonableness.'

'Like hell you do. Look, tell me this is just an example of your macabre sense of humour. She isn't really talking marriage, is she?'

10

'Hinting, certainly.'

'She's *twenty-two*!'

'Aye, so you said. Maybe she's in love. It happens, I gather... Here they come, now. Look pleasant. You can do it if you try.'

'Magnus, did anyone actually *invite* you to this event?'

'No. In fact the blonde Amazon on the door informed me my name was on a blacklist.'

'Morag? She said that?'

'Well, no, she didn't, but she wouldn't let me in without an invitation, so I went round the back and found an unlocked door. Smile, Fay. You're on camera.'

Emily approached her parents, her arm linked through that of a fair young man, solidly built and of upright bearing. As he stood facing Emily's parents, his colour became heightened and his confidence seemed to ebb. He glanced at Fay, who wasn't smiling, then looked anxiously at Magnus, who was. The men exchanged a hearty handshake. Still clutching the young man's arm, Emily said, 'Mum, I'd like you to meet Rick. Rick, this is my mother, Fay Austin.'

Rick extended a large hand and murmured something polite without meeting Fay's eyes. As if dazed, she let go of the empty wine glass in her right hand and Magnus (whose lightning reflexes had preserved his life on more than one occasion) caught it as it fell. Ignoring Rick, Fay stared for a moment at the two glasses in Magnus' hands, then looked up into his eyes. He frowned at her and jerked his head slightly in Rick's direction. She drew herself up to her full height, turned and offered her hand with a gracious, if fixed smile.

'Rick, delighted to meet you! Have you come far?'

The empty gallery echoed with the tap of Fay's heels as she collected up the last few wine glasses. She placed them on a tray and carried them into a tiny kitchen where a tall, fair woman was washing up.

Fay set down the tray. 'That's the lot, Morag. Thanks for staying to clear up. It's very good of you.'

'Och, no bother,' Morag replied comfortably. 'I don't have

11

to be in again until lunchtime tomorrow. And it's good to wind down after all the buzz.' She tossed her improbably blonde locks, grey at the roots, and added wistfully, 'It's not as if I'm keeping George Clooney waiting.'

'Some day, Morag. Some day your prince will come.'

'It's not so much the prince I'm waiting for, more his gold Amex card. *Much* more reliable.' She turned on the tap and began to rinse glasses. 'It went really well tonight, Fay. You must be feeling pleased with yourself.'

'I am rather. We didn't sell that much, but there was a lot of interest.'

'That's what you want. It leads to commissions.' Morag submerged more glasses in the washing up bowl. 'Who was the tall guy? He seemed *very* interested.'

'Tall?... Possibly my daughter's boyfriend.'

'No. Different generation. The good-looking guy with all the crazy hair.'

'Oh, *him*.'

'He tried to charm his way in at the start of the evening. He didn't have an invite, so I said a firm but polite "No", but it fair broke my heart to turn him away. Did you let him in?'

'No. I think he sneaked in round the back.'

'Is he a fan of yours?'

Fay smiled, picked up a glass from the draining board and started to dry it. 'Not exactly.'

'Did he buy anything?'

'No. He's family. Well, he *was*. Magnus is my ex.'

Morag turned to Fay, her eyes wide. 'So *that's* Magnus? Och, if I'd known, I wouldn't have turned him away! He told me he'd lost his invitation, but I thought that was just a line.'

'It was. I didn't send him one.'

Morag shot Fay a sidelong glance and said, 'I *see*... That bad, huh?'

'Yes. Well, no, not really. Not any more. But we don't see each other socially. We both have our separate lives now.'

'But he still takes an interest in your work? That's nice.'

'Yes, I suppose so,' Fay replied, polishing the glass and peering at it for smears.

Morag, twice divorced herself, was not deceived by Fay's

air of preoccupation. She said gently, 'But you'd rather he hadn't come.'

'Afraid so. I don't know quite how he does it, but Magnus always brings out the worst in me. And I really didn't need any more distractions tonight.'

'Aye, he looked like a pretty distracting kind of guy,' Morag said, shaking her head. 'Was there trouble?'

'No, not really. I descended into Queen Bitch mode, but Magnus always goads me until I do. My daughter turned up out of the blue and I hadn't seen her for ages, so that was nice. But... well, she brought her new boyfriend along too. So there were introductions to be made. It was all a bit strained.'

'Well, it's over now,' Morag said, emptying the washing up bowl. 'And you were a big success! How about sharing a taxi home? It's late. And we're worth it.'

'Good idea. I was going to get the bus, but I'm dead on my feet. Can't wait to get these shoes off.'

'They were worth suffering for,' said Morag, admiring Fay's small feet, encased in beaded and embroidered satin. 'They're *gorgeous*.'

Fay looked down and pointed a sparkly toe. 'Shoe porn from Helen Bateman in Edinburgh. My secret vice. When I'm not wearing them they live in a glass case, locked and burglar-alarmed to protect them from envious girlfriends.'

Morag laughed and shook her head. 'If *I* wore those, I'd be taller than most of the guys in Glasgow. And that would be kind of counter-productive.' She looked thoughtful for a moment, then said, 'Is Magnus single?'

'You're too late, I'm afraid. He lives with a primary teacher in a Perthshire castle. The kind with running water. It runs down the walls. I don't know how she puts up with it. Or him for that matter.'

'Well, teachers have a lot of patience, don't they?'

'She'd need it,' Fay replied, putting the last of the glasses away in a cupboard.

Morag removed her apron and flung it over a hook on the back of the door. 'Ready then?'

'Will you lock up while I order the taxi? Ten minutes?'

'Make it five. I need my bed. And for once,' Morag added,

stifling a yawn, 'I'm glad it'll be empty. I'm *jiggered*.'

Some time after midnight Fay turned the key to the door of her flat. As she entered, she paused on the threshold and thought of Freddie. He'd not been far from her thoughts all evening. She closed the door behind her, kicked off her high-heeled shoes and padded toward the kitchen area where, out of habit still, she filled the kettle for two. She turned away from the worktop and faced the large, open-plan living space where she lived, worked and ate. Visible through floor-to-ceiling windows, the city lights winked and sparkled like Christmas decorations, their number doubled by their reflection in the River Clyde. Light pollution meant that city dwellers rarely saw stars, but Fay never felt deprived when she looked out at the illuminated cityscape that formed the fourth wall of her flat.

The kettle switched itself off and she decided to make herself a pot of camomile tea. She only wanted one cup, but whenever she made the mistake of boiling water for two, she dealt with the resultant sense of loneliness by making a pot, as if this were a special treat, instead of yet another reminder that she was a middle-aged woman living alone and – mostly – sleeping alone.

Freddie…

Freddie had been another of Fay's famous mistakes. A humdinger. Freddie was a very enjoyable mistake, a mistake that did her a power of good at the time, but a mistake nonetheless. She could see that now. Pushing Freddie's image to the back of her mind, Fay poured hot water into the teapot and took out a blue and white Japanese mug, her favourite. She arranged teapot and mug on a tray and carried them over to the sofa, positioned to face the view of the Govan shipyard on the opposite bank of the river. Fay always sat at one end of the enormous sofa, as if someone else might sit at the other. This habit of hers irritated her so much, she'd considered getting a pet to share the sofa, but she was allergic to cats and travelled too much to keep a dog. She also feared that if she had one, she might actually start talking to it.

Fay stared out at the river, its surface quilted by waves and now stippled by the heavy rain that had begun to fall. The ship opposite was almost finished. She'd observed its construction, a process so slow as to seem imperceptible, like the growth of stalactites. Every day the great hulk of the ship looked exactly the same, as if nothing had been achieved in the previous twenty-four hours, despite the efforts of a hundred men in hard hats and boiler suits. But now there it was, almost finished, looking like a proper ship, not a metal skeleton. When had it happened? Fay only ever noticed progress if she went away for a week. It was like that children's game, except in *Kim's Game*, you took something away. In Fay's version, she would study the ship-in-progress and try to spot what had been added. She rarely could, but the ship grew nonetheless.

The scene before her was like a spectacular stage show, something performed for an audience of one. At times men swarmed like insects up and down scaffolding staircases, spot lit beneath long, sinister shadows cast by four gigantic cranes. Even through double-glazed windows, she could hear the agonised shrieks of sheet metal being tortured into submission. Mighty crashes and clangs conjured up armoured dragons engaged in mortal combat, their death throes the eerie whine and rhythmic boom that accompanied the invisible work of the shipyard, which went on twenty-four hours a day, seven days a week.

It was a noisy place to live, but the sounds of creation bothered Fay less than rowdy neighbours or traffic. The noise was stimulating, a clamour that heralded the birth of something tremendous: a steel Leviathan that would slip into the river, then glide on out to sea. Fay would never see the ship again, a ship she'd watched being built from the ground up, a ship she felt was partly hers. When it was gone, she knew she'd miss it. The riverbank would look empty and she'd feel a sense of loss, of loneliness almost.

Ships that pass in the night...

Freddie.

She leaned forward and pulled the tea tray toward her, in need of something soothing, something to smooth away the irritations and fears she always experienced around Magnus. Why had he shown up at the gallery? Why hadn't he asked her if he could come? Presumably because she hadn't sent him an invitation. And why *hadn't* she invited him? Because she'd supposed he wouldn't come. And did that matter? Yes, dammit, it did. She wanted Magnus to see she was successful now, that she'd been right to leave him and go her own way. She wanted him to know she was a person in her own right, not just somebody's mother and somebody's wife. She wanted Magnus to see that.

Or maybe she just wanted to see Magnus.

Fay tilted the teapot and a stream of clear water flowed into her mug. She'd forgotten the teabag. She banged the pot down on the tray and flung herself back on the sofa, suddenly close to tears. Couldn't she do *anything* right?

She got to her feet and, leaving the tray where it was, turned off all the lights and headed for the bedroom. As she undressed, she thought of Freddie again. It was too late now. What's done is done. She would just have to live with the consequences. Livid with herself, she scrubbed at her face with cleanser and cotton wool and brushed her teeth until her gums bled. As she tossed about in the middle of her defiantly king-sized bed, Fay thought again of Freddie as she wrestled with two questions.

Should she tell Magnus?

And, even supposing she could, *would* she?

Fay

Everyone makes mistakes, but I sometimes think I've made more than most; that when it comes to making big life decisions, I'm what you might call emotionally accident-prone. Perhaps that's why I take such care with my work. To compensate. (Being prone to error *and* a perfectionist doesn't make for an easy life, either professionally or personally.) I will re-arrange fine, woven threads to conceal my mistakes from the casual observer, but I don't know – have never known – how to re-arrange the threads of my life to mitigate domestic disasters. People aren't as resilient as antique linen.

When life needles us, the puncture holes remain. They might be small, but they're there. A disturbance in the weave. A distortion of the threads. A weakness.

When I work, I sometimes subject the cloth to processes that fade or discolour it. The fabric might be torn or frayed, even burned. This manipulation of the cloth is called "distressing". What life did to Magnus was distressing. It left a trail of holes in his mind and some in his body. What Magnus did to me was also distressing. It too left a hole. Not in my life. That was easily filled with work. (Magnus had always been more of an absence than a presence anyway.) The hole that couldn't be filled was in my heart.

I've made a lot of mistakes in my time and marrying Magnus was one of them. I suppose the biggest mistake I ever made was divorcing him. That didn't leave a hole, it left a crater. A bloody great bomb crater.

Chapter 3

Wind and weather made little impression on Nina Buchanan. She was a hardy young woman, the product of an affluent Anglo-Scottish upbringing that had inured her to damp and discomfort and discouraged any tendency to complain. A fondness for sport and keeping herself busy meant that, despite a perpetually ravenous appetite, her figure remained firm, even a little muscular. This was not immediately apparent to an observer since she tended to dress in bulky, oversized jumpers and fleece-lined trousers. Personal vanity wasn't an option if you lived, as Nina had done for the past year, in Tullibardine Tower. Of necessity, you dressed for warmth.

Summer was over and it would soon be time to don the woollen hat she wore on winter days, even indoors. Her long blonde hair hung down in an unbecoming but practical plait. Magnus liked to unwind it, marvelling at the soft, kinked cascade of hair as it spread over Nina's shoulders. In jest, he'd called her "Rapunzel" and the name had stuck.

They'd met at a meeting of the local history society. Nina, an archaeology graduate, unable to find a job on a dig, had moved back home to Perthshire to live with her parents. She'd finally trained as a primary teacher, relegating her love of history to her spare time. It was in that spare time she'd gone to hear Magnus give a talk about the restoration of Tullibardine Tower, a project to which he'd dedicated six years of his life.

Nina was already in love with the idea of Tully Tower, which she'd known as a ruin for as long as she could remember. She'd dreamed of what it must have been like in the sixteenth century, had wished it could be rescued and restored, but locals said Tully was beyond repair and totally uninhabitable. Only a madman would take it on. An *English* madman, they added with a wink.

But Magnus McGillivray had proved them wrong, living with his family on site while he and a small army of local builders and craftsmen set about turning what appeared to be a pile of rubble into a family home. Predictions were confidently made that the McGillivrays wouldn't last a winter, then that they wouldn't last a second winter. Some took satisfaction in the fact that Mrs McGillivray didn't last a third, but others claimed to be shocked when she left, especially since her teenage daughter stayed behind.

It was Emily McGillivray who'd suggested her father try to raise much needed cash by giving talks about the restoration of the tower house. These proved popular. Nina had attended one and, entranced, approached Magnus to ask if he'd consider giving a talk in school. Magnus, equally entranced, suggested they discuss it in the pub. By the end of the evening, he'd agreed to give a talk on *Life in a Sixteenth-century Tower House* and Nina had agreed to dinner and a tour of Tully Tower. It was as she leaned out of an upstairs window, her long golden hair spilling over the edge, that Magnus had smiled and called her "Rapunzel". Nina, at twenty-five not an overly sophisticated young woman, had been impressed by the romance of this; had been even more impressed by the romance of Magnus, who resolutely refused to discuss his former career, although his partial deafness and a variety of scars on his body (with which Nina soon became familiar) told their own story, albeit an incomplete one.

A year later, Magnus invited Nina to move into Tully. To her mother's dismay, she agreed. Nina reassured her that the tower was perfectly habitable; that Magnus was divorced; that he wasn't mad, merely eccentric and that an age gap of seventeen years was nothing these days. What if his daughter was only a few years younger than Nina? He'd been very young when she was born.

Another year later, Mrs Buchanan, mother of an only daughter, despaired of ever being able to shop for a Mother of the Bride outfit. She despaired too of having a proper son-in-law and now dreaded the appearance of longed-for grandchildren before Nina had walked up the aisle. Mrs

Buchanan took some comfort from the fact that, lately, she detected a certain restlessness in her daughter. She suspected Nina was waiting for a marriage proposal and that, as thirty loomed on the horizon, biological panic might finally have set in. Mrs Buchanan saw a faint glimmer of hope.

Magnus had no idea his girlfriend and her mother cherished ambitions in his direction. He assumed Nina found teaching fulfilling; that she was happy in her ancient home; that his prowess as a lover (or at least his enthusiasm) didn't leave her hankering for a younger man. Magnus was in many respects a simple soul. His life had long ago been pared down to basics. Home or abroad. Friend or foe. Dead or alive. He was by nature cheerful and inclined to optimism. These characteristics plus his army training ensured he never met trouble halfway. So it hadn't occurred to him to mention, either to Nina or her mother, that having a second shot at marriage and fatherhood was something that never entered his thoughts.

Nina poured two mugs of tea and set one beside Magnus, who was stirring porridge. She turned and leaned back against the shiny red Aga, glad of the warmth as it penetrated her buttocks and thighs. It was only September but the Tower was cold. Sunlight barely penetrated many of the windows, some of which were little more than narrow defensive slits. Despite a rudimentary form of central heating, the air remained chilly until they lit one or more of the big fires. Cradling the hot mug in her hands, Nina started to speak, then remembered to move round to Magnus' other side. His hearing loss wasn't great, but Nina knew he would sometimes pretend that being deaf in one ear prevented him hearing something he preferred to ignore.

'You were calling out in your sleep last night. And flailing around.'

'Was I?' He didn't look up but gazed into the porridge pan, as if hypnotised, and continued to stir. 'Sorry.'

'No need to apologise. I'm used to it now. I just don't know how you manage to *sleep* through it. How is it possible?'

'Years of practice. And industrial-strength Ovaltine before bed.' He poured porridge into two bowls and placed them on a round oak table that would have comfortably seated all King Arthur's knights. 'You could always sleep in one of the other rooms. We could have conjugal visits. By appointment.'

As she joined him at the enormous table, Nina lifted her hand and ruffled his untidy hair. 'But I want to sleep with you. Especially if you're going to wake up screaming.'

Magnus frowned. 'I don't follow.'

'Well, I wouldn't want you to wake up in that state and realise you were alone.'

'Och, I'm never alone,' he replied, dragging a heavy wooden chair out from under the table. 'I've my ghosts to keep me company,' he added cheerfully as Nina sat down.

'Ghosts?'

'Aye. Absent friends. Old enemies. The dear departed. My ex-wife. They all drop in to say "Hi, how's yourself?" '

As Magnus took his seat opposite her, Nina's placid brown eyes narrowed. 'You dream about *Fay*?'

He looked up from his porridge. 'No, of course not! Just kidding.' He smiled and changed the subject before Nina could reply.

Fay

I think Nina's good for Magnus. She's uncomplicated, steady and devoted. Like a Labrador. And of course she's very pretty, with all that long blonde hair. There's something very wholesome about Nina. You could imagine her presenting *Blue Peter*.

Perhaps it's surprising that I approve of her, but why wouldn't I? I walked away from Magnus. It's not as if I resent him finding happiness with someone else. I'm relieved he did. It makes me feel slightly less guilty to know they're happy together. At least, I assume they're happy. It's difficult to tell. Nina is relentlessly upbeat and Magnus acts happy even when he's completely miserable. But you're not telling me his ego isn't boosted by having a young and gorgeous girlfriend. And

Nina ought to be happy, assuming she can cope with the spartan living conditions at Tully Tower and, as she hasn't succumbed yet to pneumonia or hypothermia, it would seem she can. But I do sometimes wonder. And occasionally, I think I hear a clock ticking...

Nina strikes me as the maternal type. She certainly tries to mother Magnus (which he isn't used to and doesn't actually like. His mother said, even as a small boy, he was fiercely independent.) I imagine Nina has visions of a family, but no mother in her right mind would consider raising children at Tully. Not babies and toddlers. You can't keep that place warm without lighting enormous fires and all the fireplaces would require a fireguard the size of a single bed. (When we had visiting toddlers, Magnus used to rig up a Heath Robinson contraption made from rusty iron railings that he'd salvaged from a skip.) Since Magnus has never got around to turning the deeply rutted track that leads up the hill to Tully into a proper road, I wouldn't rate Nina's chances of being on time for the school run. In winter the duckboards used to go down and Emily and I would trudge down the hill in wellingtons to where the Land Rover had been parked. Well, abandoned, really. Magnus still tends to drive as if he's at the wheel of a jeep in the Iraqi desert. King of the Road.

No, if Nina has her sights set on miniature McGillivrays, she'll doubtless be dreaming of a des. res. on a smart new estate, a stone's throw from a top-notch primary school. Instinct tells me Nina probably hasn't mentioned any of this to Magnus. Experience tells me, when she does, he won't hear, whichever ear she speaks into.

Emily wasn't one of my mistakes. The pregnancy was planned. I never meant her to be an only child, things just turned out that way. Magnus was an only child himself and he was never convinced by my arguments that she needed a playmate. After we'd been married for a year, a baby seemed like the next step, so we were both still very young when Emily was born.

When Magnus came home from tours of duty in Northern

Ireland, he was remote, oddly detached. It took him days to adjust to civilian life and he was never really able to relax. He'd fought in the Falklands when he was only eighteen and, for a young man, he'd seen a lot of death, all of it pretty pointless. Almost worse than the deaths were the terrible injuries. He wouldn't talk about it, any of it, not for years.

In my naiveté (I was only twenty-two) I'd thought a baby might bring Magnus back to life. She did for a while, then, when Emily was three, he was posted to the Gulf. I was eaten up with worry, but Magnus was happy. There was none of the "What's the point?" soul-searching of the Falklands. He had a job to do and he got on with it.

Magnus appeared to thrive and so did little Emily, but I didn't. The odds were stacked against him, you see. As an army wife, you learn to live with the idea that your husband might die in combat, or even accidentally, as a result of handling ordnance or so-called friendly fire. You know he might pay the ultimate price. What you don't reckon with – how can you, until you actually live with it? – is the daily toll that knowledge takes on a marriage, on your happiness, even your sanity.

That's how it is for a regular soldier's wife, but Magnus' job was in EOD. Explosive Ordnance Disposal. Bomb squad, in layman's terms. The initials also stand for "Everyone's divorced", referring to the fate of many of the marriages. The cracks began to show in ours. I told Magnus if he wanted us to stay together, he'd have to leave the army. I said I couldn't cope any more with the long separations, his moods, the terrifying flashbacks, the his'n'hers nightmares. It was easier for me to say all that than admit the real reason I wanted him to quit. Magnus deserved the truth and probably could have handled it, but I couldn't bring myself to tell him that I wasn't prepared to spend any more of my life waiting to become a widow.

In the end it was taken out of our hands. In 1994 he was blown up by a booby-trapped bomb in Londonderry. Surgeons and psychiatrists pieced him back together again, but Magnus said the bastards had had eight of his nine lives, so he was quitting while he was ahead. Once he'd recovered from his injuries, he began training men to do the job he used to do. He stuck it for a couple of years, then resigned. I was relieved he'd finally made the break, but he became profoundly depressed and his nightmares (which we now knew were symptoms of post-traumatic stress disorder) got worse. The doctors knew what was wrong with him and the cause, but they appeared to have no idea how to treat it. (Magnus used to joke that the military had in fact made great strides in their understanding of PTSD. Now when a soldier went to pieces, they no longer took him out and shot him.)

9/11 changed the world and it changed Magnus. He sat for days watching the same footage of the catastrophe, saying nothing, his face completely impassive. I feared the worst. Then some of his old army mates got in touch and told him they were off to Afghanistan. They asked him what he was doing with himself. He said he was going to find a ruined castle and restore it. I suppose his friends must have assumed his condition was much worse than they'd imagined. They got off the phone quickly, with promises to stay in touch.

I assumed Magnus was joking but he wasn't. In a last attempt to save my marriage, I gave in to his pleas and allowed him to put our flat on the market. With the proceeds he bought a heap of rubble with a romantic name and told me it was going to be our new home. He was going to restore it and it was going to restore him. In a way, it did.

People often used to ask Magnus why he went into bomb disposal. Then later, when we lived at Tully Tower and he refused to talk about the army, they'd ask why he'd decided to restore a castle. I don't think Magnus knew the answer to either of these questions, although over the years, he gave a variety of facetious answers. Sometimes he'd admit he had no idea. But I always thought the answer to both questions was probably the same.

Donald McGillivray.

His father.

~

Afterwards, as the billowing cloud of dust begins to settle, revealing a mountainous pile of rubble, there is silence. Bystanders are still, as if posing for yet another photograph. A small boy wriggles in his mother's arms and gazes up at the clear blue sky. He didn't know it was so big.

He turns his head to ask her a question. His mouth forms the words, he feels the vibrations in his throat and chest, but hears no sound. He frowns and his mother smiles, squeezing him. She mouths a reply. The silence begins to frighten him and his lower lip trembles. She shifts him onto her hip and touches his ear, still mouthing words. He hears faint noises, but still he cannot understand. His mother points to the remains of the building and the boy jerks his head round to look, rubbing at both ears with plump little fingers, perplexed.

Now there's a hum and distant sounds of voices shouting. Looking past the bobbing heads in front of him, he sees a man running, then more men running. One of them is his father. The boy laughs and, reassured by a sound he recognises, points at the men, then turns to look at his mother. She doesn't return his look but presses him to her, squeezing the breath from his body. Her lips form a single word. She sets him down abruptly and he stands, lost in a forest of legs, his world suddenly dark.

His hand is taken by another, female and familiar. He leans against the woman's skirt, wrapping himself in the soft folds of fabric, trying to hide, for he knows something is wrong. As the shuffling legs and feet disperse, he sees daylight, then the sky swoops down toward him as he's lifted off his feet and swung into the air again. He inhales a familiar scent. Gardenia, but he doesn't yet know the word. Relieved and tired, he lays his head down on his grandmother's shoulder and closes his eyes.

Sounds are clearer now. There's a buzzing in his ears but he can hear a distant siren, coming closer. He opens his eyes again, looking for a fire engine. He likes fire engines. All around him voices are asking questions. Women sound anxious, men puzzled, then someone starts to cry. He lifts his head to look at his grandmother's face. She isn't crying, but nor is she smiling and his grandmother always smiles. Her eyes are moving rapidly back and forth, as if looking for someone. There are more shouts, then she begins to elbow her way through the crowd. He throws his arms round her neck and clings on, frightened. As they move forward, the air becomes dense and grey and he starts to cough. His grandmother sets him down, then grasps him by the shoulders. She looks into his face, her eyes wild.

'Don't move! D'you hear me, Magnus? You're not to move!'

Her words are too loud. They hurt his ears. But he understands and folds his hands in front of him, squeezing soft little fingers, as if his own hands might comfort him. He feels the hot urine begin to trickle down his legs, soaking his shorts, the new green shorts his mother made for him. He starts to cry, but he doesn't move, not even when a woman starts to scream.

Dust... Fear... People running...

Death.

His first memory.

Chapter 4

Fay

I prefer my materials to come to me with a history, so I hoard all kinds of fabric for my work, none of it new. I have boxes of old photographs, postcards, letters, diaries – all sources of words and images that I can transfer on to cloth using special paper and a photocopier.

Clients think they're buying art. They're also buying therapy. There's usually unfinished business somewhere, although often they don't have much idea what that business is. Nor do I. It can be a journey into the unknown for both of us. My work is always about family and has much to do with birth, death and marriage, but details are sometimes hazy, even unknown. Clients come to me to talk about filling in the gaps in their knowledge, even gaps in their family: the father they never knew; the illegitimate child given up for adoption fifty years ago; the grandfather who emigrated and was never heard of again. My work gives their memories solid form, something tangible.

I've had cause to think about memory and the harm it can do; the way it also heals and consoles. I spend my working life preserving other people's memories, trying to capture them in a form of textile "still life", but I spent much of my marriage watching the man I loved being tortured – all but destroyed – by the demons of memory. His memories weren't like yours or mine, destined to fade with the passage of time. If anything, they seemed to become more intense as the years went by. Very little is known about post-traumatic stress disorder, but there's a theory that each traumatic flashback releases stress hormones that "engrave" the remembered event deeper in the memory. It may be true that time heals even psychological wounds, but it isn't true in the case of PTSD. The healing is only temporary. Time can open up old wounds and a wounded memory festers, poisoning an otherwise healthy mind.

We know so little about memory and how it works, but my marriage and work have taught me that memory is something to be treated with caution and respect. It's a form of energy and, like all forms of energy, it can both nurture and destroy. I've seen the peace my work can bring, the closure. I've seen memories of grief, betrayal, hatred and death neutralised in the creation and contemplation of one of my pieces. Clients can touch and contain what they feared to behold in their mind's eye. Or they can put it safely behind glass, the unfinished business now finished. People react differently, but what I always see in their faces is a mixture of gratitude and relief, a sense that, *now*, they can move forward.

My thoughts on this subject were vague to begin with. (My medium is cloth and thread, not words.) But when I talked to Magnus about it, long after I'd left him and the dust had settled between us, he understood exactly what I was doing. He knew its importance. He said, 'You're defusing bombs, Fay. Memory bombs, full of nails and ball bearings, stuff that could rip a mind to pieces. You neutralise them. You stop the clock and remove the detonator. You make memory a safe place to go.'

I thought this speech was just more evidence of Magnus' self-absorption, his crippling inability to move on from his own horrific past, but the more I thought about what he'd said, the more I felt he was right. It *is* what I do.

I had a commission recently from a Polish Jew who wanted to commemorate the extermination of a branch of his family he'd hardly known. Sometimes, when I work on a difficult subject like that, I feel as if I'm guiding the client through memory's labyrinth. When the threads of time seem fragile or stretched to breaking point, I know what the client and I both need is courage, courage to take that long walk back into the past.

~

Jessie McGillivray put the black and white photograph, brittle now with age, back into its wooden frame and restored the picture to its usual position on the mantelpiece, between two other photographs: one of her husband, Donald, taken in his sixties, toward the end of his life; the other of her son, Magnus, in uniform, old enough to fight, not yet old enough to vote, taken in 1982, just before he left for the Falklands.

Jessie dabbed at her eyes with a tissue, then stood for a moment, regarding the wedding photo of her younger self. Plump and pretty despite a shapeless sack-dress and a pillbox hat perched precariously on her helmet of dark curls, Jessie smiled self-consciously as she clung to Donald, awkward in an ill-fitting suit, his eyes veiled by ferocious horn-rim spectacles.

She sighed, picked up the telephone and dialled Fay's number.

Jessie was not inclined to view the occasion of her seventieth birthday as an excuse to look back over an uneventful life with a nostalgic or regretful eye. Brisk and energetic, she chose not to dwell on what might have been. Instead, she preferred to count her blessings, chief among them that her only child, Magnus was (despite his best efforts and those of terrorists of all creeds and colours) still alive.

She'd married Donald McGillivray in 1963 and, barely seven months later, her son had been born. In an earlier age, Jessie might have found it hard to convince anyone that her strapping eight-pounder had been premature, but in the sixties, it was enough to have a gold band on your finger. Doubts might be entertained privately, but if the niceties were observed, no questions would be asked.

Jessie had been a popular girl. It was assumed she'd take her pick from her many admirers, but she took her time about it. As her twenty-fifth birthday loomed, Jessie surprised her family and friends by settling on Donald McGillivray. At thirty-seven, Donald was thirteen years Jessie's senior and many had thought him a confirmed bachelor. Though a self-made man with a successful demolition business, it was generally agreed that Donald possessed neither the looks nor charm of his younger brother and business partner, Lachlan, who had (to the regret of many hopeful young women and their mothers) married some years earlier.

Jessie and Donald enjoyed what her mother described as "a whirlwind romance", followed by a brief engagement. When Jessie announced she was expecting "a honeymoon baby", the whirlwind nature of the romance was accounted for. If some eyebrows were raised, it was because no one saw Donald McGillivray as an ardent lover, let alone one who couldn't be denied. "But you have to watch the quiet ones," was the general consensus, and few were quieter than Donald.

When Donald contracted lung cancer, Magnus was serving in the Gulf, so it fell to Fay to support her mother-in-law through Donald's long illness. The experience drew them closer together and they found they had much in common, not least a troubled marriage. When Donald died in 1991, Jessie struggled on, doing battle with the faded rural grandeur of the home he'd prized as a reflection of their wealth and social standing. Jessie, unimpressed by material possessions, had always viewed their home as a big house for a small family – ludicrous and, at the same time, slightly sad.

The size of his family had been a source of regret to Donald, as was Magnus' decision to join the army instead of following his father and uncle into the family business. Jessie had cherished hopes that Magnus would try for university, but wasn't surprised when he made it clear he wanted to leave school and home at the earliest opportunity. In her heart, Jessie blamed Donald for Magnus' decision, though she knew she was also partly responsible. She'd tried to compensate for Donald's lack of warmth toward his son, but suspected Magnus found her love and loyalty oppressive. She had no idea how to deal with an angry and rebellious teenage boy, but wisely chose to respect his preference for solitude. As she dusted and hoovered the luxurious wasteland of her home, Jessie wondered at the loneliness contained within its four walls.

When Magnus left home, Jessie was full of plans. She wanted to get a job. She talked of moving to something smaller and more modern, perhaps a bungalow or a flat in Perth, but Donald would have none of it. There was no need for Jessie to work and if the house had become too much for her to manage, she could have paid help.

An only child and an only grandchild... Jessie liked to count her blessings, but even she had to admit her cup didn't exactly overflow with them. She nursed Donald at home until he went into a hospice, then six months after his death, she put the house on the market, gave a large proportion of the proceeds to Magnus and Fay and bought a tiny flat in Perth where she threw herself – with a passion – into the arms of the Open University. By the time Jessie graduated with a degree in History, Magnus had left the army and was able to attend her graduation, which he claimed was the proudest day of his life.

Addicted now to self-improvement and encouraged by Fay, Jessie bought herself a computerised sewing machine and made quilts for her favourite charities to raffle. She also took on the management of the local Hospice shop, developing the book department with a ruthlessly selective eye. Every so often, she would surreptitiously cull the chick lit and beach reads in favour of what she called "proper books", by which she meant biography, historical fiction and the classics.

With her reading group, her Tai Chi class and a large circle of friends, Jessie's life as a widow was active and happy. Fay kept in touch, even after the divorce, but as often as not, when she rang, she'd get Jessie's answer phone because her mother-in-law (popular as ever and still, at seventy, a pretty woman) was out, living her life belatedly to the full.

The telephone interrupted Fay's reverie.

'Fay? Hope I'm not disturbing you. Are you working?'

'No, Jessie, your call is very well-timed. I'm staring at my sketchbook, praying for interruptions.'

'You're sure now? The muse wasn't about to strike?'

'The muse is *on* strike. Either that or she's away on holiday.'

'Och, what you need is a rest! You must be exhausted after all the hard work for the exhibition. I heard it went very well.'

'Who told you?'

'Magnus. He said the gallery was packed and you sold quite a few pieces.'

'Well, yes, I did, actually. And people were quite complimentary. Even Magnus, in his backhanded way.'

'What did he say?'

'He said I was far too young for a retrospective, but that the range and quality of the work justified it.'

'My goodness, *Magnus* said that?'

'Yes. I suspect it was mainly for the benefit of a journalist standing close by. I think Magnus was hoping he'd be mistaken for an art critic. His hair really is impossible these days.'

'Aye, I know. The Wild Man of Borneo. I suppose Nina's too busy to cut it.'

'Well, it was good of him to do a bit of PR for me. Everyone liked *Root and Branch*, by the way. I'll get it to you at the end of next week, when the show's finished.'

'No problem, Fay. Whenever you can manage it. Now, I don't want to keep you as I'm sure you *are* busy, but I wondered if you'd give me some advice?'

'What's the problem?'

'It's not a problem exactly, but I feel a wee bit embarrassed talking about it. That's why I wanted to ask *you* rather than Magnus. I thought a woman would be more understanding.'

'Are you all right, Jessie? Are you keeping well?'

'Oh, aye, I'm fighting fit. I had my MOT at the surgery just recently and they were very pleased with me. No, what I wanted to ask you about was an invitation I've received. From a gentleman.'

'Ooh, Jessie! Do you have a date?'

'Aye, I think maybe I have. Except that I haven't accepted yet.'

'Why not? Are you playing hard to get?'

'Och, away with you! No, I pretended I'd left my diary at

home. I said I thought I might have a prior engagement. I was flustered, you see. It came out of the blue.'

'Tell me all, Jessie. I'm agog. What's his name?'

'Clive. He's a widower. He lost his wife a few years ago. Cancer,' Jessie said, lowering her voice. 'Like poor Donald. Very sad. That's how we got talking. About the Hospice, then about the shop. He and his wife had lived in Perth for many years. I knew them by sight. Clive started coming to the Tai Chi class a few weeks ago and that's when we got chatting. About Donald and Angela. That was Clive's wife,' Jessie explained, lowering her voice again. 'He seemed very pleasant. And easy to talk to. We got on to the subject of books and – well, you know me, once I get started, I just blether on. Anyway, Clive came into the shop this morning, looking for books. He said he'd heard we kept a good stock. I was there on my own and he was the only customer, so we got chatting again. Well, to cut a long story short, Fay, he's asked me to lunch.'

'Jessie, you pulled! You must go.'

'Well, that's what I wanted to ask you. *Should* I go, d'you think?'

'Why ever not? Although... if he's asked you to his home, that might not be such a good idea. I'm thinking of your personal safety.'

'Aye, I know you are. But Clive suggested we eat at the Italian opposite the Concert Hall. They have a nice lunch menu there.'

'Perfect!'

'But I can't allow him to pay for me, can I?'

'Offer to buy the wine. Or if you feel really strongly about it, accept the invitation on the condition that you go halves.'

'Aye, that's what I'll do! If you're *sure* you think it's a good idea?' she added uncertainly.

'Yes, I do. I think it's a great idea. I'm positively jealous.'

'The trouble is, Fay, I think he's *younger* than me. And by a good few years.'

'What does that matter? You look ten years younger than your age – at least! And he's interested, so age is clearly not an issue for him. It shouldn't be for you.'

'You think I should ring and accept then?'

'I certainly do. And I want to hear *all* about it. What you wore, what he wore, what you ate – the works. And whether you'll be doing it again.'

'Now promise me you won't tell Magnus. I don't think I could bear his teasing.'

'I rarely speak to Magnus these days and I only see him once in a blue moon. But your secret is safe with me.'

'Thanks, Fay. I'll let you know how it goes.'

'Can't wait. Have fun, Jess! 'Bye.'

Fay hung up and turned back to her sketchbook. Love is in the air, she thought. First Emily, now Jessie. Of late, Fay's own love life had been a desert, a desert in which she'd stumbled, parched and gasping, upon the oasis that was Freddie.

And now, like Jessie, she could do with some advice.

Fay

The thing about Freddie was, it was just sex.

Why do we say that? Why do we say, "just sex", as if attractive men, worth going to bed with, grow on trees? Why do we insist that sex is not sufficient reason to get involved with someone? I mean, how many people do you know who are having a) great sex? b) enough sex? And how many people do you know who'd give you an honest answer?

I've known plenty of marriages based on staying together for the children; a few based on the retention or consolidation of wealth; one that provided a heterosexual alibi for a lesbian celebrity. I even know of one married couple who stayed together as an act of reciprocal revenge. Yet we still apologise for getting involved in a relationship that is "just sex".

I should perhaps declare an interest here. And I don't mean Freddie. Well, not just Freddie. I lived with Magnus for sixteen years. Since many of them were unhappy, I was forced to ask myself if the glue that kept us together was "just sex". (As glue goes, it was pretty powerful stuff. Super-glue in fact. An instant bond formed on contact.) Other women have told me it's impossible to maintain any romance, any mystery in a normal marriage. Routine and familiarity are passion killers. By the time you've listened to him brush his teeth and watched him drop the boxers on the floor that you'll pick up and put in the laundry basket tomorrow, lust could not be further from your thoughts. Or so they said.

What I chose not to tell my girlfriends – one doesn't like to gloat – was, that when I used to drive to the airport to collect Magnus after a tour of duty, we sometimes didn't get home before conjugal relations were resumed. (There are a few deserted country lanes in the vicinity of military airports that I suspect have seen a fair bit of action over the years.) Was that "just sex"? I don't know and I'm not sure I really care. It was bloody marvellous.

Do I miss Magnus? That shambolic, uncommunicative, emotionally Neanderthal, partially deaf, wholly infuriating man? No, I don't. Not really. Life post-Magnus was unrecognisable. I felt born again. Since I stopped living with him, I've felt free — free to be myself, free to create. I've known less anger, less anxiety and I haven't had to waste energy trying not to lose my temper. I've known something resembling peace. So, no, I think I can honestly say I don't miss Magnus.

Do I miss sex with Magnus? You have no idea how much.

Fortunately, neither does he.

Chapter 5

Fay

We first laid eyes on the sad remains of Tully Tower in 2001 on a cold October's day. We'd driven up the hillside until the bumpy track petered out, then I pulled over, switched off the ignition and twisted round to look at Emily who'd fallen asleep in the back, listening to her personal stereo. At fourteen she had even less interest in ruinous buildings than I did, but she'd agreed – not very graciously – to come with us, rather than stay home on her own.

'There's no need to wake her,' Magnus said softly. 'Let her sleep.' He nodded in the direction of the ruined tower house. 'We'll be able to see the car from up there.' He got out and I followed, lunging to grab hold of the car door as the wind tried to rip it off its hinges. As he zipped up his jacket against the elements, Magnus looked round and said, 'You can see for miles... No surprises,' he added, smiling, then he walked up the hill, limping slightly. Magnus was much fitter than most men of his age, but he sometimes dragged his shattered leg, suffering silently in cold, damp weather. (I've known Magnus for almost a quarter of a century and in all that time I've never heard him refer to physical pain. Not his anyway.) As I watched, he began to clamber over piles of rubble, happily absorbed, like a child in an adventure playground. I trudged up the hill after him.

To begin with I wasn't worried. The tower – what was left of it – was clearly beyond restoration, both in terms of our budget and our expertise, so I just waited, keeping one eye on the car, shivering as rain started to fall. As I stood there, surveying the rolling Perthshire hills – a gaudy tapestry of reds, greens and golds – I could see why someone had built on this spot. As Magnus said, there could be no surprises. Approaching enemies would be visible for miles. If you were

36

prepared to live on this exposed and isolated site, you would feel safe. Maybe that was part of the attraction for my husband.

I perched on a bit of crumbling wall and, to warm myself up, thought about a pub with an open fire, serving hearty food. Magnus hobbled back over the stony ground and stood in front of me, his eyes shining, his dark hair corkscrewing in the drizzle.

'Well, what do you think?'

'About the site?'

'Aye! And the tower.'

'*Tower*?' I laughed. 'It's just a ruin!'

Magnus looked hurt. 'It's a Z-plan tower house. Well, it was. Come on. I'll show you round.'

Until the mid-seventeenth century tower houses were Scotland's basic architectural form. Something between a fortress and a manor house, they were built in lawless times by minor lairds. While the nobility lived in enclosed castles that could provide security for a whole community, tower houses were simple but solid family homes. (Many, now renovated, still are.) A tower house was defensible, not defensive. Sites were chosen for comfort and convenience, but in an age when war always threatened, feuds were rife and cattle were rustled, families built upwards with self-protection in mind.

Imagine a fortified vertical cottage, with one room placed on top of another. Rooms weren't large, apart from the Great Hall on the first floor. Windows were unglazed, with only wooden shutters to keep out the cold. The plain and windowless ground floor was used as a store and livestock could be gathered there in the event of a raid. Living quarters began on the first floor where cooking was done. Goods were hauled up through a hatch in the floor from the store below and there was no other access to the floors above except from the single doorway on the first floor, protected by an indestructible iron grille, something like a portcullis.

The laird's bedroom was on the second floor and there would have been smaller chambers above. All rooms were accessed by a stone turnpike stair (a spiral staircase) housed in a separate abutting tower. Windows were protected by iron grilles and as the tower house rose, the windows became larger and the exterior more complex. Spacious upper storeys would be corbelled out, with decorative brickwork supporting conical-roofed turrets known as bartizans; oriel windows provided panoramic views; gables were crow-stepped and chimneys were tall, creating an exuberant, fantastical building style that was peculiarly Scottish, but could have inspired Walt Disney. Some people – Magnus for one – regard the tower house as the finest achievement of Scottish architecture and on that cold and windy day, he was in his element.

He grabbed my hand and dragged me over to the remains of the tower, the only bit of ruin that looked as if it might once have been a building. I craned my neck to check on Emily and could see she was awake, but had wisely decided not to relinquish the warmth of the car. I gave her a wave which she didn't return. When I turned back, Magnus was pointing to holes in the walls and talking about gun loops, sketching in the air with his hands. I felt the first faint stirrings of panic. My husband was talking about this place as if it were a possible site for a home. He was appraising a collection of ancient stones as if it were a building. I watched, appalled, as he described doors and windows that weren't there, pointed to a staircase that led nowhere. But his face was animated, his eyes alive in a way I hadn't seen in years.

'Can you not *see* it, Fay?' he asked abruptly, his brow furrowed with impatience.

'No, to be perfectly honest, I can't. All I can see is... ruins. Destruction. Desolation. It's *awful*, Magnus. You can't possibly want to take this on.'

'Why not?'

'Because there's nothing here! You'd be starting from scratch!'

'That's better than taking on something where you've got to rip out nineteenth century "improvements". We'll just be building. Restoring. That'll be much simpler. And most of the stone's already here!' he said, indicating the piles of rubble scattered in every direction. 'And the site – well, it's fantastic!

Look at that view! And it will be even better viewed from the first floor.' He put his arms round me and pulled me to him. 'What's wrong? What are you so worried about?'

I laid my head on his chest, glad of a moment's shelter from the wind. 'I'm worried about *you*. And Emily. And *us*. How would we live here?'

'We'll have a caravan on site. I told you.'

'I know, but I thought you meant live in a caravan for months, not years!'

'A couple of years, maybe. Maybe less. It depends if we can get the grants. How fast we build will depend on cash flow. I'll be doing a lot of it myself, obviously, but it'll be much quicker if we employ skilled labour.' I lifted my head and looked into his eyes. They were glittering now and his breath was coming fast. Too fast. 'Someone told me about a local guy who's a bit of a specialist. We could maybe use him—'

'Magnus, stop it! You're talking about this as if it's going to happen!'

'Why shouldn't it happen?' He grabbed me by the arms and shook me. 'This will be *good* for us, Fay! Good for me. It will give me a *reason*...' He faltered and I detected the sudden shift in his mood, saw his shoulders sag as he let go of me, noted the tension round his mouth as soon as he stopped talking about his hare-brained scheme. I felt horribly guilty until I remembered that mine was the voice of reason.

'You surely can't be serious, Magnus. I mean, just *look* at it! It's hopeless!'

'Nothing is ever hopeless,' he said quietly. Plunging his hands into his jacket pockets, he turned his face up to the rain and stared into space, seeing a building that wasn't there. 'Nothing is ever *hopeless*. Not unless you allow it to be. It's a question of willpower. And sheer bloody-mindedness. Isn't it?' He looked at me and grinned suddenly, which frightened me even more than his visionary zeal. 'You didn't think I'd ever leave the house again, did you? You didn't believe I'd ever be right.'

'I never said—'

'No, you never *said*, but that's what you thought. You gave up on me.'

'I didn't! I never did that. I just... resigned myself. To what I thought was inevitable.'

'You thought I'd lost my mind. That I'd never come back.'

'Magnus, please – stop this. I think we should go back to Emily now.'

He wasn't listening. 'But I did come back, didn't I? I came back from the dead. You see? *Nothing* is hopeless. Whatever they say. Whatever you think.'

'Look, let's talk about this later. I think we all need some lunch.'

He grasped me by the shoulders, too hard, his powerful fingers digging into my flesh. 'We can do this, Fay. Please, believe me. And we'll all be happy again! Emily will be a princess in her own daft wee castle and we'll *love* each other again! We'll rebuild!'

He didn't wait for a reply, he just kissed me and there was never anything I could refuse Magnus when he kissed me. So we bought a mountainous heap of stones for an extortionate amount of money but I couldn't share Magnus' vision. I saw what was there. He saw what *had* been there. What *could* be there.

So he rebuilt the tower house that had once been Tullibardine Tower. It was meant to save our marriage.

It was the last straw.

Freddie was causing me sleepless nights. (Not, unfortunately, in any way you'd want to repeat.)

Magnus held the firm belief that if you ignored a problem, nine times out of ten, it would simply go away. If it didn't, then you had a problem. The Freddie problem wouldn't go away, so I thought about confiding in Jessie. Never one to judge, Jessie had offered me unstinting support over the years, even when I was technically no longer her daughter-in-law. I think she saw me as the daughter she'd never had, easier to talk to than Magnus and far more forthcoming. But it was sewing and silence that had bound us together. We'd sat together by the phone, or watching news bulletins on TV, or at Magnus' hospital bedside, waiting, stitching and saying nothing. We both refused to carry on regardless, in the time-honoured army wife tradition. We stitched to stop ourselves going mad, but we stitched in silence to honour the dead and the wounded.

I knew it would be far easier to talk to Jessie, but in the end I decided I had to speak to Magnus and it needed to be somewhere I felt in control, somewhere it wouldn't matter if he made a scene. Admittedly, that would be uncharacteristic of Magnus, but I just didn't know how he'd react to the information I was going to give him.

I thought he probably *would* make a scene. Or maybe he'd just laugh.

I didn't know which would be worse.

When I rang Tully Tower it was Magnus who picked up the phone. I plunged straight in.

'Hi, Magnus. I need to talk to you. In private.'

'Go ahead. Now's a good time. Nina's out at her mum's.'

'No, not now. It's not something I want to deal with on the phone.'

There was a long silence and I was wondering whether we'd been cut off when he said, 'You're not ill, are you?'

'No, of course not. It's nothing like that.'

There was another pause, then he said, 'You'd tell me, wouldn't you, if it *was* something like that? I mean, I'd want to know.'

'I haven't ever thought about it. As far as I know, I'm in the best of health.'

'Good, that's grand! So – what's the problem?'

I felt my patience ebbing away. 'I've already told you – I don't want to talk about it over the phone. I need to *see* you, Magnus.'

'OK, let's have lunch then.'

'Yes, that's what I'd like to do. If you think Nina wouldn't mind.'

'Do you want to go somewhere in Glasgow? I could drive down. Or if you fancy a change of scenery, we could go into Perth. There's a new bistro opened up. The food's good.'

'No, I don't want to go anywhere public. It's... it's a delicate matter, you see. And ... well, to be perfectly frank, I don't want you making a scene.'

'A *scene*? Is this something to do with me, then?'

'No, not at all. I just think you might be... angry.'

'Why would I be angry?'

'I've told you, I can't explain now! I'd like you to come here. To the flat. I'll make lunch. If that's all right with you.'

'Aye, no problem,' said Magnus sounding mystified. 'When?'

'Soon. Can you do Friday?'

'Aye, Friday's fine. You're sure you're OK?' he added, sounding distinctly worried.

'*Yes!* It's nothing to do with my health.'

'Are you in some kind of money trouble?'

'No! *Please*, Magnus – I promise I'll explain everything. On Friday.'

'What time?'

'About one?'

'OK. See you Friday then.'

'Thanks. I really appreciate it. 'Bye.'

I felt guilty about dragging Magnus down to Glasgow. He didn't cope well with crowds or traffic and was alarmed by sudden noises, all of which he found acutely embarrassing. The exaggerated startle reflex – symptomatic of post-traumatic stress disorder – was humiliating for him. People find it hard to understand why someone who was in bomb disposal should have a problem with loud noises. They don't realise that a car backfiring or even just the sound of breaking glass can propel a damaged man, one whom people think of as the epitome of courage and cool-headedness, into a panic attack. To the uninitiated, it doesn't make sense. How could a man that jumpy ever have dismantled bombs?

PTSD rendered Magnus prone to inappropriate responses. Gunshots on TV took him back to being under sniper fire. The sight and sound of falling rubble on a building site might drag his mind back to Belfast and exploding bombs.

Ambulance sirens could transport him mentally to scenes of horrific carnage. These weren't distant memories for him, even years afterwards. The nature of PTSD is that an event can play itself over and over in the victim's memory with the same intensity as the original experience, so in his head, Magnus would be literally re-living the worst days of his life.

There's not much in the way of treatment for PTSD and Magnus had little time for talk therapies. Talk therapy for Magnus meant getting paralytic with a bunch of his old army mates, cataloguing their bizarre practical jokes and laughing immoderately at various dire, even deadly situations they'd found themselves in. Recalling the death of one of their number was no cue for introspection. They would observe a short silence, agree the poor bastard was a great bloke, one of the best, then they'd order another round and resume their hilarious and macabre reminiscences.

It seemed to work for Magnus, to begin with. But eventually he had to admit he was finding it hard to cope as a city-dwelling civilian. Too much noise, too many people, too many explanations to be made. We stopped going to the cinema because he couldn't cope with the claustrophobia of queuing or the loud noises. (I saw half of so many films, one of the first things I did after I left him, was buy a dvd player. I binged on rented movies for weeks, as a form of closure.)

Magnus dealt with the problem of how to manage a pint when your hand shakes uncontrollably by ordering a half in a pint glass, but in the end we stopped visiting pubs because he always needed to sit with his back to the wall and a view of the door. We stopped going for walks because he thought people were watching him. Eventually he hardly left the house at all, spending his time reading books about castles, tower houses and other ancient Scottish monuments. Magnus found respite from his own past by burying himself in the distant past.

We joined Historic Scotland and spent our weekends working through the properties in their handbook. It brought him a kind of peace to be surrounded by tranquil, green places, ancient stones, birdsong. It was only in these surroundings that I ever saw him relax. (He said he relaxed drinking with his mates, but it was relaxation only in the sense that a pressure cooker could be said to relax when steam begins to escape through the lid. It wasn't relaxation, merely release.) So I shouldn't have been surprised when he announced he'd had enough of city life; that he wished to move to the country; that he wanted to spend his days and our money restoring a tower house. I shouldn't have been surprised, but I was. I was devastated.

But how could I object? Emily was miserable and under-achieving at her high school and we suspected she was being bullied. She was ready for a change. Magnus was using a combination of alcohol and sleeping tablets to cope with stress and insomnia. His mood swings were violent and in his profoundly depressed periods, I just couldn't get through to him. Worse than that, I feared he might take his own life, either deliberately or accidentally, with a combination of booze and pills.

Perhaps some women would have left then. Magnus said as much, so I knew he understood what he was asking of me. That was the problem. He was always sweetly reasonable when demanding the impossible, asking for more than anyone could possibly give. I gathered this was what had made him such a good officer and, like the men under his command, I was ready to follow him into Hell (or at least darkest Perthshire) if he'd lead the way. I was prepared to make more sacrifices, put my life on hold yet again. Was it loyalty? Or just stupidity? I liked to think it was love. So did Magnus.

It's much the same in the army. Don't ever fall for any of that "Queen and country" nonsense. Soldiers don't fight for monarchs, for political or geographical reasons. They fight for their regiment. When things get really rough, they fight for each other, for their officers and mates, because they love them, because they don't want to let them down, they don't want them to die.

Magnus knew what he was asking of Emily and me: to follow him into the unknown, cheerfully and without question. Devotion was what he expected of his men and he was used to getting it. It's what he expected of me and for

sixteen years he got it.
Then I deserted.

~

When Fay wakes, Magnus' side of the bed is empty. Instantly alert, she lies still, rigid, listening. She can hear nothing. She looks at the clock by the bed. Not even 4.00am so the central heating won't be on yet. Suppressing a groan – she thinks it unfeeling and disloyal – Fay throws back the duvet and steels herself against the cold air. She turns on a light, pulls on her dressing gown and sets off along the corridor. Passing Emily's room, she pulls the open door toward her and shuts it quietly.

Fay finds Magnus in the sitting room. He is naked and sits huddled under the dining table, mumbling and hugging his knees. She pulls a patchwork quilt off the back of the sofa and approaches him carefully, positioning herself so that, if he has his eyes open, he will see her approach.

'Magnus?'

He doesn't look up, but starts to pant, his face a hideous rictus of pain.

Fay sinks to her knees. Dragging the quilt, she crawls across the carpet toward him. 'Magnus, it's all right. I'm here. It's me. Fay.' She stops in front of him, just out of reach. She's learned the hard way not to surprise him. Her eyes are drawn to his feet and legs, a pitiful mess of livid scar tissue, a miracle of reconstruction. Fay says his name again, trying to call him back to the present, then crawls closer. He is shaking convulsively now. She raises the quilt slowly. 'Magnus, I'm going to put this round you, OK?' He doesn't appear to register her words or even her presence, but starts to mutter again. She passes the quilt behind his back and arranges it round his shoulders, tucking it round his body.

His words don't make any sense. It sounds as if he's giving orders or a set of instructions. Every so often he flinches, then writhes, as if in agony. Fay puts her arms around him and holds him, recoiling instinctively when her skin makes contact with his icy flesh. She continues to listen to Magnus' tortured litany, then realisation begins to dawn. She knows now where he is.

Not here in their Glasgow tenement. Magnus is in Londonderry. In 1994.

He'd been defusing a series of mortar bombs left in a van near a hospital. Although it would have been normal practice, he'd decided against the use of remote control equipment. There was too great a risk of launching one of the bombs. While dismantling each bomb in turn, by hand, one of them blew. Magnus had been thrown across the road by the force of the explosion. Although badly injured and in great pain, he'd refused to be evacuated until he'd briefed his assistant with details of the device, so the operation could be completed.

Fay cradles her husband's head. 'It's all right, Magnus. You're here with me. It's over, darling... It's over.'

But she knows that, for Magnus, it isn't.

Chapter 6

When they embarked on the restoration of Tullibardine Tower, one of the jobs Magnus and Fay tackled was the re-building of the barmkin wall – the wall that had originally surrounded the tower house, creating a secure enclosure and which now provided shelter for a productive kitchen garden. The patched rubble walls kept out the wind and retained the sun's heat, so despite the elevated and exposed position of the tower, it was possible to grow apples, pears and quinces, trained against the rough stone. The garden also produced vegetables and soft fruit and Fay had insisted that some ground be given over to shrubs and flowers, including some to cut for decorating the interior of the tower house.

When Fay finally left, it was the garden she missed – the pear trees in autumn with their flame-coloured foliage; gaudy chrysanthemums powdered with frost. Most of all she missed the birds and their song. Glasgow was blessed with many parks and gardens, but up on the eighth floor, behind double-glazed windows, Fay never heard birds. She rarely even saw them at close quarters. The few she did see (disconcertingly *below* her as she looked out of her windows) were sea and estuary birds: gulls, swans, cormorants, oystercatchers. Fay pined for ordinary garden birds that sang. She didn't miss the bitter cold, the back-breaking labour that had gone into the garden's creation, or the constant depredations of armies of rabbits. What Fay missed were the inhabitants of the Tully garden, especially the owls and foxes she used to hear when she lay in bed on sleepless nights, contemplating a future without Magnus.

Nina now tended Fay's garden, spending more time on the vegetables than the flowerbeds, for which she had little time or affection. Nina liked to dig and hoe. Her care of the garden was efficient rather than tender. Imposing order on chaos was Nina's natural bent and in that respect, Magnus said, Nina gardened like a man.

As he looked out of their bedroom window and watched Nina barrowing compost along the uneven stone paths, Magnus thought she would have made a splendid pioneer's wife. Strong, healthy, practical and blessed with childbearing hips, Nina would happily have set about clearing virgin forest, shooting and skinning rabbits, founding a dynasty.

Magnus shied away from this last thought and closed the window. He picked up his jacket and descended the turnpike stair, surefooted, familiar with every dip on the worn stone treads. When he reached the vaulted ground floor, he opened the yett, a latticed wrought-iron grille like a gate, mounted behind the massive wooden door and originally intended to provide extra fire-proof security.

Pulling on his jacket, Magnus strolled across the courtyard toward Nina, who was forking compost on to the vegetable beds.

'I'm away now,' he announced.

She looked up and tossed her long fair plait over her shoulder. 'To Glasgow?'

'Aye. I'm going to meet the guy from the BBC. The one who's interested in using Tully for some location work.'

'That could be pretty lucrative, couldn't it?'

'Aye, it could. If he makes it worth my while, I'll have to say yes. The roof needs some serious attention.'

'Are you having lunch with him?'

'I'll see how it goes,' Magnus replied, looking at his watch. 'I'm meeting him for coffee, but I don't really know when I'll be back. I'll give you a call.' He nodded in the direction of the wheelbarrow. 'Don't work too hard now. You're supposed to be on holiday.'

'Compared to managing a class of nine-year olds, this *is* a holiday.'

He shook his head. 'You're missing them already. I can tell.'

She laughed. 'Is it that obvious?'

He laid a hand on her arm. 'Och, Davy rang. I meant to tell you. He's going to drop by this afternoon and take a look at that leak in the roof. But he won't trouble you.'

'No, but I dare say he'd appreciate some tea and scones. The poor man always looks half-starved.'

'You spoil him, woman.'

'It's my maternal instinct. I'm drawn to waifs and strays.'

'And old crocks like me?'

'*Especially* old crocks like you.'

He grinned. 'Save me some home baking then.'

'You won't need it if you're being entertained on a BBC expense account.'

Magnus didn't reply, but ducked his head and kissed her. 'Take care now.'

'I always do. Do *you*?'

'Me? I'm the cat with nine lives.'

'But you only have one left, so look after it, please.'

He turned and headed toward the arched gateway in the barmkin wall. Nina watched fondly as he covered the ground with his loping, long-legged stride. Magnus opened the gate and turned back to wave. She waved back, calling, 'Be good!' He saluted her and was gone.

As she bent over her wheelbarrow, Nina couldn't help asking herself the question that had been hovering at the back of her mind for some time. She wondered whether Magnus would go and see Fay while he was in Glasgow. She wondered whether, in fact, that was the real reason for his trip.

As the sound of the Land Rover receded into the distance, Nina began to fork compost again, chiding herself for disloyal, even irrational suspicions. Magnus and Fay had been divorced for five years and the marriage had been unhappy for several years before that. But the fact remained, Nina hadn't asked Magnus if he'd be seeing Fay. She hadn't asked for two reasons. In the first place, she didn't want to hear that he *had* arranged to meet her. Secondly, if Magnus claimed he wasn't meeting Fay, Nina didn't want to have to ask herself if she believed him.

Nina liked to keep things simple.

The question of what to cook when entertaining your ex-husband was almost as vexed, Fay decided, as what to wear. You didn't want to look as if you'd gone to any special effort or expense, nor did you wish to suggest you lived on pizza and Pot Noodles. Something delicious but quick to prepare, the culinary equivalent of "smart casual" was required, which was also what Fay had aimed at when dressing for lunch.

Magnus would wear whatever clothes came to hand and he would eat – with relish and without comment – whatever was put in front of him, so the futility of taking trouble over food or her appearance did not escape Fay. She'd long ago accepted that fraternising with your "ex" entailed the transmission of various mixed messages from which, with luck, he would be able to draw no conclusions at all. But bearing in mind the nature of the news she had to impart, Fay wanted to make sure she wouldn't look like a sad, middle-aged divorcée. She wasn't. She had Freddie to prove it.

But, as Fay changed her outfit for the third time, it suddenly struck her that perhaps Freddie proved that she was.

At the last minute, Fay rejected heels in favour of comfort, so when she opened the door to Magnus, she felt a familiar sense of inferiority, a feeling mixed with surprise, that she could forget just how tall he was and how cramped her tiny hallway felt when it contained a man.

She took the flowers he proffered, her pleasure quite genuine and wondered whether they were a result of Nina's civilising influence or even Nina's suggestion. Fay was even more surprised when she relieved Magnus of his coat to discover he was wearing a suit, but this was soon explained when he began to talk about his meeting with a BBC location manager.

Fay offered Magnus a drink, which he declined, pointing out he'd driven to Glasgow. She arranged the flowers in a vase, then poured herself a glass of white wine. Pursuing the dull but safe topic of how easy it was to get around Glasgow in a car compared with the impossibility of doing the same in Edinburgh, Magnus remarked that he had no idea how anyone managed to live in a city and not go mad. Sensing a familiar minefield, Fay excused herself to prepare food: *spaghetti carbonara*, which had the virtue of being quick to prepare but not all that easy to cook. Served with a tomato salad, the dish would combine a hint of luxury with an air of rustic simplicity, thus presenting Fay's desired culinary paradox: a superb lunch on which she'd lavished no time, money or effort.

She was less happy with her outfit, but had given up at the third attempt and reverted to her first choice: faded, but well-fitting jeans and a cream silk shirt. She'd been pleased with the contrast, but as she sliced tomatoes and cracked eggs, she regretted having chosen to cook in such a light garment. She was damned if she was going to don an apron, so she handled her ingredients gingerly, instead of flinging them together in the nonchalant way she'd planned.

Oblivious to her performance, Magnus was engrossed in the study of a large print of *Root and Branch*, the textile wall hanging Fay had made for Jessie. Fay had framed the print and Magnus had spotted it leaning against the wall on her work table.

'The more you look at this piece, the more you see.'

'That's the general idea,' Fay replied, pleased with the comment.

'I didn't notice the handwriting in the background when I was in the gallery. Would that be transferred from real letters?'

'Yes. I asked Jessie to give me a selection of material to work from. I said I wouldn't use it all, but it would feed in to the final piece, somehow or other. She had old photos, greetings cards, letters – some of them love letters. I didn't get to read those, but she gave me the odd sheet. She also gave me some bits of old fabric from her scrap bag. She's quite a hoarder, isn't she?'

Magnus was still peering at the print. 'Would that be love letters from my *father*?'

'That's what she said. You sound surprised.'

'I am. D'you not remember Donald?'

'Not very well. We didn't meet that often. He wasn't

51

exactly the sociable type, was he? I thought of him as a typical dour Scot. I always assumed you took after Jessie.'

Magnus was thoughtful. 'I don't remember my parents even touching... And you say he sent her *love* letters?' He shook his head. 'What the hell went wrong?'

'Did you know they weren't happy? When you were a boy, I mean?'

'Must have done at some level. Though I can't claim to have been a particularly observant child. I was never home anyway.'

'Perhaps there was a reason for that. Jessie said you were always out playing – all hours, all weathers. And up to all sorts of mischief. She used to worry about you. And she said you and Donald didn't really get on.'

'Aye, true enough. My father thought a good skelping was the best way to sort out our differences. I, on the other hand, was always in favour of peaceful negotiation.' He straightened up and turned away from the print. 'It's a fantastic piece, Fay. Could I buy a copy of the print from you?'

'Good Heavens, you don't think I'd charge you, do you? You can have one.'

'No, I insist on paying.'

'They're pricey, Magnus. It's a small limited edition.'

'All the more reason for me to pay up. I'd like to frame it and hang it on the wall at Tully.'

'Yes, it would look well there,' she replied, reaching for the grater and parmesan cheese.

'Whereabouts d'you think? I don't have your eye for these things.'

'The Great Hall? One of the public rooms anyway. There's some prints in cardboard tubes over there, in a box under my desk. Take one. Get it framed in non-reflecting glass, otherwise you won't see anything but yourself when you look at it.'

'Was that not your intention?' Magnus asked with a smile.

'What do you mean?'

'That as a McGillivray, I *should* see myself. Where I've come from. What made me what I am. Is *Root and Branch* not

52

a kind of mirror in which my family can see itself?'

Fay looked up from tossing the pasta in its coating of creamy sauce. 'Oh, that was beautifully put! I should get you to write my press releases... Sit down, I'm about to serve up.'

As he wolfed down spaghetti, Fay asked politely after Nina. Magnus responded equally politely, then moved on to developments at Tully and current problems with the roof. Whenever there was a lull in the conversation, Fay felt Magnus' eyes on her, as he waited for her to explain why she'd summoned him.

After one such hiatus, he remarked casually, 'I think Emily might be getting engaged.'

Fay choked on a mouthful of wine and reached for her napkin. '*Engaged*? Who to?'

'Rick, of course. You met him at the gallery. Seems a nice guy.'

She sipped her glass of water. 'What makes you think they're getting engaged?'

'Em's general air of excitement. Something's afoot.'

'She could just be in love.'

'Aye, but she's been dropping hints. And she's inviting us both to dinner.'

'You and me?'

'Aye. Has she not spoken to you about it?'

'No.'

'That surprises me.'

'Well, Emily and I are not exactly close, are we? I rarely see her.'

'Maybe it's not definite, then. The dinner, I mean. She rang me and asked if it would be OK to invite me without Nina. She said she was inviting you too. It was to be a family affair. With Rick.'

'Emily's never invited me to dinner before.'

'Nor me. I didn't even know she could cook.'

'And you think this could be the big announcement?'

'Aye.'

'But she's far too young to be getting engaged!'

'It's no big deal, Fay. It's not much of a commitment these days. Maybe they're planning to live together and Em wants a veneer of respectability. She's an old-fashioned girl in some ways.'

'That's what I'm worried about,' Fay murmured.

'There's nothing we can do anyway. She's old enough to know what she's doing. Or *think* she knows what she's doing.'

'Couldn't you talk to her? Warn her about rushing in to marriage when she's so young? You're much closer to her than me.'

'I'd rather defuse a booby-trapped bomb. In the dark. *In the rain.* In any case, it's none of our business. I know what you're thinking: we married far too young and it didn't work out, but that's not to say Em and Rick will go the same way. At least they won't have the army to contend with. Or Tully.' Magnus raised his water glass. 'I say good luck to them. May they profit from our mistakes.'

Fay seized her opportunity. 'Speaking of mistakes... I asked you to lunch because I wanted to ask your advice about something.'

'*My* advice?' He looked surprised. 'Go ahead.'

Fay fixed him with a look. 'It's a very delicate matter, Magnus. Can I ask you to please spare me any facetious remarks? It concerns... a relationship of mine. A *casual* relationship.'

'Christ, Fay – you're not pregnant, are you?'

'Of course not!'

'Is the wife gunning for you?'

'It's nothing like that! Look, I'd just like to tell you what happened – *exactly* what happened – so that you... well, so that you'll understand.'

Magnus looked uncomfortable and began to fidget in his chair. 'What is this? Some sort of delayed revenge?'

'I know it sounds like that, but it isn't. Trust me, Magnus. You're going to think badly of me anyway, but please bear in mind the only reason I'm telling you is because I need your advice. About what to do.'

'Fay, I hardly think I'm an appropriate person to discuss your sexual indiscretions with. Don't you have girlfriends who lap up this sort of thing?'

'Oh, yes, and unlike you, they'd be deeply sympathetic.

But they wouldn't be able to tell me what to *do*.'

'And you think I will?'

'Maybe. Clear thinking and decision-making under pressure – isn't that what you were good at?'

'Aye, once. Now I'm not so sure... OK, let's get this over with. But spare me the clinical details, if you please.'

Fay

I always cry at weddings. It isn't that I believe anyone is likely to live happily ever after, it's more the investment of hope, *communal* hope, that two human beings can live in close proximity, for better but mostly worse, without ending up loathing each other.

I went to a wedding in the Lake District. The bride was an old school friend. She was forty-four and, unusually, this was her first stab at marriage. Dinah had devoted herself wholeheartedly to a teaching career and resigned herself to childlessness, but she'd got to know a widower with young children. They'd fallen in love and decided to marry. The reception was held in a hotel overlooking Lake Windermere, surrounded by misty fells. Even the constant drizzle couldn't dampen anyone's spirits or dispel the air of triumphant romance that permeated the whole proceedings. It was a joyous occasion and I'd cried.

There had been dancing to an excellent band, the food had been good and the champagne had flowed freely, but I hadn't over-indulged. I'd never turned to booze for consolation the way many army wives did, taking a bottle to bed instead of their man. I'd seen what happened to them. I'd also seen that it didn't really help. So I can truthfully say what happened that night had little to do with inebriation. But I was tired and emotional. I was also very angry with Magnus after a phone conversation we'd had the night before.

I was staying at the hotel and retired around midnight when the band packed up and people started to drift home or off to bed. It was one of those hotels where you had to swipe a piece of plastic to get into your room. I'd had trouble with mine earlier and, as I walked along the corridor, I hoped I wasn't going to encounter any more problems. I needed my bed.

I drew out my card and inserted it into the slot. As I did so, the door moved, swinging away from me slightly. Straight away my heart began to pound. After years of living alone, I was always security-conscious. I knew I'd left that door locked. I'd checked before going downstairs.

I must have stood staring at the card in its slot for I don't know how long, trying to decide what to do. I couldn't bring myself to walk into the room, but equally I couldn't face going down to reception and asking someone to come in with me. I wasn't even sure I wanted to go in. I wondered what I might find. Or *not* find.

I decided I was going to knock on the door and say in a loud voice, "Is anyone there?" I realised this wouldn't panic a mad axe-man into vacating the premises, but I couldn't think what else to do. I'd just lifted my fist to knock when I heard soft footsteps approaching along the carpeted corridor. Flustered, I waited for the man to pass, but he didn't. He stopped at the adjacent door and swiped his card. I could see his hands out of the corner of my eye, but I didn't look up, I was too close to tears. He paused with his hand on the door, then said, 'Excuse me – but are you all right?'

I looked up and registered a slightly familiar face, though I felt sure I hadn't been introduced to him at the reception. He was young, about thirty, dressed in a tuxedo. I remember thinking he filled it out well. Young men can rarely carry off a dress suit, but he looked quite at home in his. The silk bow tie, hanging loose round his neck, gave him an attractively raffish air, as did his obvious exhaustion, but I could tell he wasn't drunk, so I blurted out, 'Someone's been in my room. It's unlocked and I *know* I left it locked... I'm frightened to go in,' I concluded, feeling foolish.

The young man waved me away from the door and appeared to study it. I think he must have been listening. He turned round and motioned me to stand back, then he pushed the door open slowly. He didn't enter but stood on the threshold. I tried to see past him, but I'm not tall. Neither was the young man, but he was broad in the shoulder and obscured most of my view. Without looking at me he extended a hand, palm upwards, indicating I should stay put, then he walked in.

The room had a short corridor before it opened out and the double bed was mostly hidden, round the corner. I watched, feeling both frightened and ridiculous, wishing I'd sent for a security man. My rescuer stood at the foot of the bed, regarding it, then he looked up at me. I remember registering kind brown eyes and a thick mop of blond hair. There was something schoolboyish about the hair, but despite that, the steady look in his eyes filled me with confidence. I felt, if not exactly safe, then a little calmer.

He said gently, as if he was breaking bad news, 'Did you leave all your underwear on the bed?' He cleared his throat and added, 'Spread out?'

I swallowed and said, 'No... No, I didn't.'

He turned away and examined the bed again. I thought I saw him recoil slightly. He exhaled, his broad shoulders sagging. 'What's your name?' he asked, not looking at me.

'Fay.'

He turned to me again, his expression pained, and said, 'This isn't nice, Fay.'

I looked down and studied the geometric pattern of the carpet in the corridor. Teal and burgundy... I remember naming the colours in my head, precisely, as if it mattered. Then, in a strangled sort of voice I said, 'What's *your* name?'

'Freddie.'

I steadied myself with a hand on the doorframe. 'Freddie, I think I'm going to be sick, but I can't bear to come into the room. Would you mind letting me use your bathroom?'

He rushed past me without a word, opened his door, switched on the lights and ushered me into his *en suite*, where I threw up copiously.

I've always admired competence in men. And you have to like a man who holds your hand while you vomit.

I sat down on the edge of the bed while Freddie got me a brandy from the mini-bar. He folded my shaking fingers round the glass. 'I'll ring Reception and ask for another room. They can move your stuff. Or I'll move it for you if you like.'

I shook my head. 'The hotel's full. Because of the wedding. The bride's my friend. She had to put some people in B & B.'

Freddie thought for a moment, then said, 'Well, if that's the case, we can just swap rooms. Or if that seems like too much hassle, we can just swap beds. I'll sleep next door, you sleep in here.'

'You're being very kind. I do appreciate it.' Tears started to well and I looked round for my handbag.

'What do you need?' he asked.

'My bag. I didn't leave it in the corridor, did I?'

'No, you dropped it in the bathroom. Don't get up – I'll fetch it.'

He brought it to me, then sat down in an armchair. I rummaged in my bag and brought out a wad of tissues. 'I'm sorry to be such a wimp—'

'You're not being a wimp! What's happened is... *horrible*. Especially for a woman on her own.'

I blew my nose. 'It's someone on the staff, isn't it? It must be. Some pervert with a pass key who can check the register and see which rooms have single women. And he doesn't even lock the door when he's finished. He wants you to know you've been... *violated* from the moment you stand at your door. I suppose he left his calling card?' Freddie didn't reply or meet my eyes, just nodded his head. '*Jesus*, how can men be so sick!'

'Do you want me to call security?'

'No, I can't face it. I'm exhausted. And I'll only cry. They'll ask me to go in there and check my belongings to see if anything's missing.'

'I don't think you'll find anything gone. That type isn't into theft. Just thrills... Finish your brandy. It'll help you sleep.' I obeyed and he said, 'Do you want another?'

'Not unless you're going to join me.'

'That sounds like a good idea.'

He took my glass and, as he busied himself with the mini-bar I said, 'Freddie, why do I feel I know you? You weren't a guest at the wedding, were you?'

'No. But I was *at* the wedding.'

'In a tux?'

'I was playing the piano. You danced to my trio.' He handed me another brandy, then removed his jacket and tossed it on to the bed.

'Of course! I'm sorry, I didn't recognise you. Well, I wasn't really looking at you, I just registered the music. Which was very good, by the way. A real pleasure to dance to. Everyone was commenting.'

'Were they? That's nice to know. I'll tell the lads.' He picked up his glass and sat down again. 'We try to be self-effacing at weddings, so people don't tend to talk to *us* about the music, they just tell the hosts. It's good to get feedback from the punters.' He put his head on one side and regarded me. 'You look dead tired. Why don't you tell me what you need from your bathroom and I'll go and get it. Then I'll clear out and leave you to it.'

'I really can't impose on you—'

'Rubbish. It's no trouble for me to go next door. Do you want your... underthings left for the police? Or—' He coloured and looked down at his glass. 'Shall I just put everything in a bag and bin it?'

Another wave of nausea threatened to overwhelm me and I put a hand up to my mouth. Freddie moved across to the bed and put an arm round me. 'I'm sorry! I shouldn't have asked that. I was trying to be helpful.'

I composed myself and said, 'You *are* being helpful. You're being brilliant. *Thank* you.'

'Look, if there's anything I can do... Is there someone you could contact? Husband? Boyfriend?'

'No. There's nobody.'

'Really? You amaze me.'

'What do you mean?'

'Well, I'm just...' He shrugged. '*Surprised*, I suppose.'

'Surprised?'

'That such an attractive woman should be single.' He heard himself and pulled a face. It made him look very young. 'Oh, shit – that sounded like a line, didn't it? Like I'm trying to make a pass. Sorry. Nothing could have been further from my thoughts...Well, actually that's not *quite* true,' he added with disarming honesty. 'I meant, I wouldn't have dreamed of making a pass at you, under the circumstances. Highly inappropriate.'

There was an awkward silence and I was struck suddenly by the strangeness of my situation: sitting on a bed in a hotel room with a young man about whom I knew almost nothing, apart from the fact that he played the piano and I trusted him. Liked him, in fact. Liked him and his capable hands.

'Freddie...Would you mind staying with me? I don't think I can bear to be alone. I know he isn't likely to come back but... I just can't face being on my own. I could go and sit in the lobby, I suppose, but they'd ask questions. And I've drunk too much to drive home.'

'You mean, you'd feel happier with me in the room?'

'Yes.' I pointed at the armchair. 'And with *that* jammed up against the door.'

'There's a safety chain.'

'I know, but I'd like to go to sleep feeling as if I'm in Fort Knox.'

'OK, I'll get the duvet from next door and I'll sleep on the floor. In front of the door, like a guard dog. Nobody gets in without treading on me. Just let them try.'

I laughed and laid a hand on his arm. 'No, I couldn't possibly expect you to do that! I'll doze in the chair. I don't expect to get a wink of sleep anyway.'

'You're having the bed, so don't argue.'

I laughed again, starting to relax. Or maybe it was the second brandy. Freddie looked down then, at my hand still resting on his arm. I too stared at my ringed fingers, curving round his forearm. I wondered, if I lifted my hand, whether it would shake, so I left it there. Through the fabric of his shirt, I could feel the comforting, but unfamiliar solidity of a male body; sense the strength in an arm I wished would go round me and pull me toward him, so I could lay my head on that broad chest – gift-wrapped in a rumpled dress shirt – and let someone look after me, tell me everything was going to be all right.

Freddie lifted my fingers and held them gently, rubbing his thumb over the stone of one of my rings. He raised his other arm and put it round my shoulders. He didn't even need to pull. I leaned. I swear I was heading for his chest, but somehow his mouth got in the way. When we'd finished kissing, he did something rather wonderful. He slid one arm under my legs, another behind my back and scooped me off the bed. He carried me to the head of the bed and deposited me gently on the pillows. As he leaned over me his silk bow tie dangled in front of my face. I tugged and it slithered into my lap.

I looked up and saw that he was smiling, his eyes slightly unfocused. It wasn't the brandy. I knew that look and I remembered what it meant. As his capable pianist's fingers removed cufflinks, I watched, oddly fascinated. He dropped them on the bedside table, then whispered, 'Everything's going to be all right, Fay.'

And it was.

~

Fay regarded Magnus, seated across the table, profoundly ill at ease. His shoulders were hunched and his hands tightly clasped, as if he was arm-wrestling himself. Eventually he pushed his plate away and leaned back in his chair. 'So what was it you wanted to ask me? Why did I have to listen to... all that?'

Fay drained her wine glass and set it down again, her hand not quite steady. 'I wanted to ask you about Rick.'

Magnus frowned. '*Rick*? Emily's Rick?'

'Yes.'

'What about him?'

Fay took a deep breath and, avoiding Magnus' eye, said, 'Do you know if – well, if by any chance he... if he happens to have an identical twin?'

Magnus turned pale. Fay refilled her glass and braced herself.

'You've slept with... *Rick*?'

'Not if he has an identical twin called Freddie!' she

replied, unable to keep a note of desperation out of her voice.

'Well, if he does, I've not bloody heard about him!'

'I realise it's unlikely. I'm just grasping at straws. I suspect if you ask Emily – and I would like you to ask her, Magnus – what Rick is short for, she won't say Richard. I think she'll say Frederick.'

Magnus stared at Fay, his eyes wide with disbelief. As a soldier, his language sometimes consisted of strings of expletives linked with a few key words to convey meaning. Since quitting the army, he'd purged his vocabulary, but every so often – when stressed, for example – he would lapse into old habits. Still staring at Fay, he shook his shaggy head from side to side and said, 'Well, fuck me...'

Fay got to her feet and started to clear away plates. 'If only I had, Magnus. If only I *had*.'

Chapter 7

Magnus stood up and, walking like a condemned man, went to the cupboard where Fay kept alcohol.

'You're driving,' she said, as he poured a large whisky.

'Not in a state of bloody shock, I'm not.' He swallowed a mouthful, turned round and said, 'I just don't get it, Fay. *Why?*'

'Why Freddie?' She opened the dishwasher and began to load it with crockery. 'Because he was charming and attractive. Because he was interested in me.'

'No, I mean, why a guy that young? You're old enough to be his mother.'

She wheeled round, brandishing a salad server. 'No I'm not! He's nearly thirty.'

'Twenty-eight, according to Emily.'

'He told me he was thirty.'

'He told you he was called Freddie.'

'Maybe he is sometimes. They called you Gus in the army. People have different names with different people, don't they?'

'So you think Freddie's his name when he's seducing older women? Aye, come to think of it, "Freddie" sounds like a gigolo.'

'*Gigolo?* Oh, Magnus, for goodness' sake!'

'He's twenty-eight, Fay, and your daughter's twenty-two!'

'So's yours! And your mistress is twenty-seven.'

'*Mistress?*'

'If I have a gigolo, then you have a mistress.'

'Nina's not my mistress!'

'What is she then?'

'She's my... girlfriend.'

'Oh, that makes a difference does it? If she's your *girlfriend*, that reduces the lustful old goat factor, does it?' Magnus winced. 'At least what Freddie and I got up to was just a one-off, a mistake! You're involved in a long-term relationship with a girl not much older than your daughter.'

'That's different.'

'Why is it different? If it's unseemly for me to have sex with the younger generation, why isn't it for you?'

'I didn't say it was unseemly.'

'So what exactly *is* your objection, then?'

Magnus opened his mouth and closed it again, apparently at a loss. He drank another mouthful of whisky and loosened his tie. 'I just don't see what a guy like Rick would have to offer a woman like you.'

'Well now, let me see...' Fay enumerated Freddie's attractions on her fingers. 'Considerate behaviour. Compliments. A sense of humour. And – oh yes, it's all coming back to me now – a fit, young body. Women are suckers for attractive packaging, Magnus. Probably because sometimes, that's all there is.'

'But a one-night stand, Fay! How could you have got so desperate?'

'*Desperate*? I'll tell you how.' She took a step toward him. Craning her neck to look up into Magnus' face, she poked him in the chest with her forefinger. 'Because *you'd* made me feel like something the cat dragged in, thought better of, then dragged out again!'

'*Me?*' He gazed at her, aghast. 'When did I do that?'

'When Nina walked out on you. On your first anniversary.'

'Anniversary? We aren't even married!'

'Much to Nina's regret, I should imagine. She thought of it as your first anniversary, apparently. Anniversary of meeting, I suppose. Or maybe it was the first anniversary of going to bed together. Who knows? I certainly didn't want to!'

Magnus' puzzlement turned to concern. '*What* didn't you want to know?'

'All the stuff you told me. About you and Nina.'

'What stuff? What the hell are you talking about?'

'You. Ringing me up afterwards. Drunk. *Very* drunk.'

'When?'

'The night you and Nina went out to celebrate your first

year together.' With an angry rattle of crockery and cutlery, Fay slammed the dishwasher shut and switched it on. Ignoring Magnus, she strode across the open-plan room and sat down on the sofa. 'You told me she'd stormed out of the restaurant and gone home to Mummy. Then you asked me what you should do.'

Magnus followed Fay. 'I did?' He lowered his long frame into a small Art Deco armchair where he sat, cramped and uncomfortable, his expression perplexed. 'What did I say exactly?'

'Do you really not remember any of this?' Fay asked wearily.

'No, I don't. Well, I remember the meal. Unfortunately. But I don't remember phoning you.'

'Well, *I* certainly remember it.'

'And this is when I'm supposed to have made you feel terrible?'

'You *did* make me feel terrible!'

'So terrible you go and sleep with the first guy who asks you?'

'Freddie didn't ask me. He wasn't remotely pushy. He didn't need to be. He just... well, he just made his interest known to me... and we... well, we took it from there.'

'Tongue down your throat, I suppose,' Magnus sneered.

'The massive erection was more persuasive, actually.'

Magnus blinked, then swallowed more whisky. 'Tell me – what did I say?'

'You said Nina had got upset.'

'Aye, she did, I remember that... But I don't remember why. Did I say why?'

'Oh, yes. In some detail.'

'It was my fault, I presume?'

'Yes. Though you said she laid the blame partly at my door.'

'*You*? What did you have to do with it?'

Fay gazed at him in disbelief. 'You really don't remember, do you?'

'No, but I'm beginning to think I might have wiped all this for a very good reason. You're saying, I upset Nina so much, she walked out on me. Then I rang you and drove you into the arms of a total stranger.'

Fay nodded and said, 'It's quite a talent you have, Magnus.'

'Talent? For what?'

'Demolishing a woman's self-esteem.'

Fay

It was one of my riotous nights in. When the phone rang I was tucked up in bed with a mug of cocoa, re-reading *Persuasion*. It was gone midnight and, as I picked up the phone from the bedside table, I assumed it would be a wrong number, but it was Magnus.

'Fay?'

'*Magnus*? Is something wrong? Is Emily all right?'

'Fine. At least, she was last time I saw her. I wasn't ringing about Emily.' He hesitated, then said, 'I wanted to talk to you... About Nina.'

I suppressed a groan. Magnus had said enough for me to realise he'd had a lot to drink. He didn't sound drunk, but I knew he was, from the effort he was making to enunciate clearly. I tried and failed to suppress my irritation.

'Magnus, it's twelve-thirty! I don't want to talk about Nina in the middle of the night. I'm not sure I want to talk about Nina at any time, especially if you two have got problems.'

'She's left me, Fay.'

My stomach lurched. I set my mug of cocoa down carefully on the bedside table. '*Left* you?'

'Aye. She gave me a row, then said she was away home to her ma.'

'What on earth did you row about?'

'You.'

My stomach lurched again. I wondered if my cocoa was about to make a reappearance. 'Magnus, exactly how drunk *are* you?'

'Och, barely.'

There seemed no point in arguing, so I continued. 'Let me

get this straight...You and Nina fell out over *me?*'

'Aye. She doesn't understand, you see. She feels threatened. By the friendship that still exists between us.'

'Oh, is that what we are? Friends?'

'D'you not think so?'

'No, not really. My friends aren't rude to me. And they don't ring me up in the middle of the night to indulge in drunken binges of self-pity. Well, not often.'

'I think of *you* as a friend, Fay. A good friend.'

'Well, that's nice to know, I'm sure. Now, do you think you could tell me how I can help? I'd quite like to get some sleep.'

'Sorry, did I wake you? I won't keep you, I just wanted to know what you think I should do.'

'About what?'

'I want to know how I can convince Nina it's all over between us.'

'Between you and Nina?'

'No, between you and me.'

'Show her the divorce certificate! For God's sake, Magnus, we split up *years* ago.'

'Aye, I know, but Nina still seems to think there's something going on between us. You and me, I mean. She said there's an indissoluble bond.'

'That's quite difficult to say, isn't it?'

'What is?'

'*An indissoluble bond.* Especially when you're drunk.'

'She wasn't.'

'No, but *you* are.'

'Possibly,' Magnus conceded.

'So Nina wasn't drunk, but she said there was something going on between us? Tell me, which part of "Fay is my ex-wife" doesn't she understand? Has she never noticed that we can't spend more than a few minutes in each other's company without starting to squabble?'

'It's never me who starts it, Fay, you know that. I simply rise to the bait.'

'Oh, and you don't see your sarcasm as provoking? Or your jokes at my expense as demeaning?'

'I didn't think it was my sense of humour that drove you away.'

'It wasn't.'

'Why *did* you leave me, Fay?'

The wistful note in his voice sounded an alarm bell. 'Don't start, Magnus! We're not going over all that again. It's all water under the bridge.'

'Is it? I think of it more as a stagnant pool.'

Exasperated now, I inserted my bookmark and closed *Persuasion*. 'So what did Nina actually say?'

'That I'm not over you.'

'After five years? Oh, come on!'

'She thinks I'll never be over you, that I'm still in love with you, so there's no future for us. Me and Nina, I mean.'

'But *why* does she think that?'

'Because I'm never going to stop hoping. She says.'

'Hoping?'

'That you'll come back to me.'

'Nina thinks that's what you want?'

'Aye, she does. For some reason.'

'So what did you say?'

'I told her not to be so daft.'

'Oh, that was tactful! Very sensitive, Magnus. Well done.'

'She was making a scene! In the restaurant, then in the street. She was practically hysterical! Crying and shouting. I thought she'd taken leave of her senses.'

'Did she just start talking about me out of the blue?'

'No, she was talking about some friends of hers who were getting engaged. Or maybe it was married, I don't remember. I wasn't paying much attention. I couldn't see why she was telling me all this.'

'Oh, Magnus, you *idiot*.'

'What did I do?'

'It's not what you did, it's what you *haven't* done.'

'Which is?'

'Propose.'

There was a silence, then, sounding mystified, Magnus said, 'Why would I do that?'

'Oh, no reason. Unless you're in love with the girl and

want to make her happy by showing your commitment to a joint future. Apart from that, no reason at all.'

'You think she wants me to *marry* her?'

'I don't think, Magnus, I know.'

'Ah.'

'Ah?'

'I'm beginning to see now.'

'What?'

'I can see that what I said might not have been *exactly* what Nina wanted to hear.'

'What did you say?'

'I just said I thought marriage was an outdated institution. One that put intolerable strains on a relationship. And then—' He stopped speaking and I heard him breathing heavily down the phone.

'What did you say, Magnus?'

'I said, a lot of couples living together would be much happier apart.'

'And?'

'I cited us.'

'As a happy couple?'

'No, as a couple who are happier living apart.'

'But we're not a couple any more.'

'No, I know.'

I gripped the phone and counted to five. 'Magnus, did Nina understand the point you were trying to make? Because I'm not sure I do.'

'I don't think she can have done, because she went off the deep end again.'

'I'm not surprised! You trashed marriage, then told her you get on better now with your ex-wife. None of this will have been music to her ears.'

'Aye, I gathered that. But I think I made a good recovery,' he added cheerfully.

'How did you manage that?'

'I told her you were history. *Ancient* history. I said we no longer even fought because we no longer cared about each other.'

'You... said that?'

69

'Aye. I did.'

I sank back against the pillows. 'Go on.'

'I told her I'd come to terms *years* ago with you leaving me. Now all that existed between us was a shared past, the ruins of a relationship that had always been difficult—'

'Not *always*, Magnus,' I protested faintly.

'Och, I know, but that's what I told Nina. She was sobbing her heart out. I had to say *something*.'

'So you told her there was nothing left between us?'

'Aye. That cheered her up a wee bit. And then she seemed to calm down.'

'Because she believed I'm ancient history.'

He paused, then said cautiously, 'Well, I'm not so sure about that.'

'What do you mean? What did she say?'

'It was a trick question, Fay! I only realised afterwards.'

'What did *you* say, Magnus?'

'She threw me by being so suspicious! I couldn't see what she was driving at. She accused me of *using* her, using her as a temporary bedmate – that's the phrase she used! – while waiting for you to come back to me. So I told her that was a load of bollocks.'

'Oh, Magnus...Why do I not have a good feeling about what you're going to say next?'

'I said it would be a complete waste of time, waiting for you to come back, because a woman as attractive as you would have had a succession of lovers by now and wouldn't be giving me another thought.'

I swallowed hard and said, 'Is that what you think?'

'Och, no! But I was trying to get Nina to see she'd nothing at all to worry about.'

'Nothing at all?'

'No. Because we're history. Aren't we?... Fay, are you still there?'

'Yes, I'm still here. I'm history, but I'm still here... So I take it then your ploy didn't work? Nina wasn't reassured by the idea of your ex-wife being fully occupied with a troop of toy boys? You must have lacked conviction, Magnus.'

'Aye, but I thought if I agreed with *her* view, there'd be

more trouble.'

'Nina's view? Of me?'

'Aye. *She* said you'd be in bed with a mug of cocoa and a good book, not lovers.' I made an indeterminate sound, but Magnus carried on, oblivious. 'She said it was obvious you were lonely and had realised you'd made a big mistake divorcing me. None of your relationships had worked out—'

I gasped. 'How does *she* know?'

'I think Emily told her.'

'Emily knows nothing about my private life!'

'I thought that was because there was nothing to know?'

'Emily had no business discussing my private life with your girlfriend! Tell me, what else did Nina have to say about me? Oh, this is *fascinating!*' I said with a snarl.

'She said your career was a substitute for—' Magnus broke off, suddenly and uncharacteristically prudent.

'For?'

'For a fulfilling sexual relationship.'

'Nina said that?'

'Aye. She said it was a well-known fact that women of your age diverted superfluous sexual energy into creativity.'

'*Superfluous?* I'll give her superfluous! Did Nina have any more to say on the subject of me and sexual frustration?'

'She said you were playing a waiting game.'

'Oh, waiting for *you*, I suppose?'

'Aye.'

'*Ha!*'

'Well, waiting for me to dump her.'

'And when you did, I suppose I was going to crawl back? Begging for your sexual favours.'

'Aye, that was the gist of it.'

'So *that* must have been when you told her that an attractive woman like me would have men queuing at the door?'

'Aye, I did.'

'Thank you, Magnus, that was jolly decent of you – lying on my behalf.'

'Och, you're welcome. I thought Nina was being a wee bit harsh, but she was pretty upset at the time.'

'Poor Nina. My heart bleeds for her. But do I gather your gallant defence of my fading attractions didn't have the desired effect?'

'No.'

'Nina went home to Mummy?'

'Aye.'

'Best place for her, the silly cow! If she thinks I'm lying in bed night after night thinking about *you*—'

'I know, it's ridiculous, but what more could I say?'

'Oh, I think you said quite enough, Magnus. Now could you please tell me what it was you wanted? I've totally lost track of why you rang.'

'I just wanted to know...Well, I wanted to ask you...'

'What?'

'If there's any way...' He ground to a halt.

'*Please*, Magnus, it's very late and I'm tired.'

'I wanted to ask if you think there's any way I can convince Nina that I'm not still in love with you.'

'Oh, yes, I can think of a way all right.'

'What?'

'Marry her. She'd find that very convincing. So would Mummy. Goodnight, Magnus. And good luck. I think you're going to need it.'

With that I tossed the phone on to the floor, flung *Persuasion* to the end of the bed, pulled the duvet up over my head and howled.

Chapter 8

Fay sat on the sofa, her legs coiled beneath her, hugging a cushion. She'd barely looked at Magnus during her account of their phone conversation, but she regarded him now as he sat slumped in an armchair, his tie awry and his head bowed, his expression masked by his mop of greying curls.

'You were so emphatic!' she said, the anger gone from her voice now and replaced by sadness. 'So certain it was finished. So sure you felt nothing for me... I'd never expected that. That wasn't how I felt. We hadn't had one of those divorces where both parties are out for revenge. I thought we'd parted more in sorrow than in anger... So your words came as a shock. And a blow to my self-esteem. To find myself relegated like that, to ancient history. A woman's self-confidence is not a resilient thing at the best of times, Magnus. Especially if she's my age and single.'

He lifted his head and said, so faintly, Fay almost didn't catch his words, 'I'm very sorry. I was drunk.'

'I know. *In vino veritas*,' she added.

'I wasn't *that* drunk.'

'What do you mean?'

'I wasn't so drunk I couldn't lie if I had to. And lie convincingly it seems, since Nina came back to me. And you went off and shagged bloody Rick.' Rubbing at his chin, Magnus eyed his empty glass. 'Christ Almighty, I need another drink... You wouldn't happen to know the train times to Perth?'

'I'm sorry, you've lost me. Are you saying you *lied* to me?'

'Aye, I did. I lied to Nina, then I lied to you.' He spread his hands. 'It seemed the kindest thing. Kindest to Nina, that is. I said what she wanted to hear and eventually she decided she believed me. I didn't mean to hurt you, Fay. It never occurred to me you'd care what I felt! You left *me*, right? It was a reasonable assumption. It *was* all over between us. But not so over, I can commit to a future with Nina. Which I suppose is what she wants. So I said some things that... weren't true. Were *lies*, in fact. But I only said them because I was trying to convince her.' He looked away from Fay and murmured, 'Maybe I was trying to convince myself too.'

She clutched the cushion more tightly. 'You're not making any sense. Convince yourself of what?'

'That you're history. That *we're* history.'

She stared at him for a long time, then a hooter sounded, with a long and hideous blast that penetrated the double-glazing. Magnus shot forward and fell to his knees, his body arched, arrested in the act of flinging himself to the ground. Fay tossed the cushion aside and kneeled in front of him, her hands cupping his face.

'It's all right, Magnus! It's nothing! Just the hooter! It's tea time, over at the shipyard.' As she watched, his heaving chest gradually slowed and the terror in his eyes subsided. She let go of his face, suddenly self-conscious and smiled. 'You know, you're a lot better than you used to be. Once upon a time you'd have vaulted over the sofa and taken cover.'

Magnus screwed his eyes shut, swore violently, then said, '*Tea time*?'

'Yes.' Fay pointed to the wall of glass, overlooking the river. 'Over there. You can hear that hooter for miles... Would *you* like some tea?'

He got to his feet. 'I'll get it.'

'No, it's all right—'

'Let me, Fay. I need to be moving.' Without waiting for a reply, he headed for the kitchen area and filled the kettle.

She stood up and went back to the sofa. 'That's one of the worst things about living alone. No one ever brings you a cup of tea.' He didn't respond, so she turned and said, 'Why *did* you ring me that night? There must have been other people you could have rung. Why me?'

Leaning against the worktop, calmer now, Magnus appeared to answer a question of his own. 'She was crying in the street. Trying to be dignified and brave. And failing. I wanted her to *believe* me. Believe we were going to be OK.'

'Like you used to tell me *we* would be OK? That never worked in restaurants. Don't you remember? It only ever worked in bed, Magnus. You're more convincing lying down.'

Magnus nodded. 'Nina said that's why she'd raised the topic in a public place. So I couldn't... change the subject.'

Fay laughed. 'What a splendid euphemism! You know, despite all she said about me, I still rather like Nina.' The kettle boiled and Magnus turned away to make tea. 'I think I understand why you lied to her, but I still don't understand why you rang *me*.'

'I wanted to hear you tell me I was a lying bastard. And a coward.'

She stared at his back as he poured tea into a mug and said, 'If there's one thing you're *not*, Magnus, it's a coward.'

He brought the mug of tea and, casting a longing glance in the direction of the drinks cupboard, set it on the coffee table.

'You aren't having any?' Fay asked, looking up.

'No. But I could use another whisky.'

'You'd better not. Not if you're driving.' Magnus sank into the armchair again, his long legs extended. 'Why *did* you ring?' Fay persisted

'I wanted you to cut through all the crap.'

'Crap?'

'Aye. Make me face up to facts.'

'What facts?'

'Facts about you and me!'

'I don't understand—'

She was interrupted by his bark of mirthless laughter. 'I mean, if I'd any doubts *before*... what you've told me today, about you and Rick—' He dragged a hand through his hair and sighed, exasperated. 'And how I *feel* about that—'

'Magnus, are you saying—'

He leaned forward, his blue eyes blazing. 'I'm saying I'm *jealous*, Fay, that's what I'm saying! Jealous as hell and – pissed off! *Really* pissed off!' He leaned back again, scowling, and folded his arms. 'I mean, I didn't suppose you were living the life of a nun. But I bloody well *hoped* you were!'

Fay stared. Realising belatedly that her mouth was open,

she shut it. When she finally found her voice, she said, 'Are you saying... that you're still *in love* with me?'

'Och, what do *you* think?' He sprang up like a jack-in-the-box and headed for the drinks cupboard. 'I'm having another whisky.'

'No. I think you'd better leave. Leave now.' Fay sat quite still, her voice level, her expression neutral.

Magnus wheeled round and stared. '*Now*? But we haven't talked about Rick.'

'There's nothing to say. It's a private matter between them. If Freddie – I mean, *Rick* – thinks Emily should know about... what happened... then he'll tell her.'

'Maybe she knows already.'

Fay looked alarmed. 'How?'

'He could have told her.'

'Why would he do that?'

'Well, if he's the all-round nice guy and super-hero you say he is, wouldn't he have come clean?'

'Not necessarily,' Fay replied. 'He's a man.'

'Oh aye, I was forgetting.'

'If he loves Emily, he wouldn't risk it, surely?'

'How would I know? I'm just a man. But might I suggest – as a mere man – that you speak to him? Check your stories are the same?'

'I don't need to speak to him.'

'He might want to speak to you.'

'I suppose so,' Fay said doubtfully. 'Well, he knows how to get hold of me now.'

'Fay—'

'Please go, Magnus. You might not think it, but all this has been rather an ordeal for me, even before you – you said what you said. I'd just like to be on my own now.'

'I'm sorry if—'

'It's all right, you don't need to apologise.'

'Och, you can't really have been *surprised*, Fay!'

She looked up suddenly and he noticed how pale she was. 'Of course I was surprised! You're living with *Nina*! She expects you to marry her. She no doubt wants you to be the father of her children.'

'She's never said so. And I've certainly never told her I loved her. She's never even asked.'

'Don't you love her at all?'

Magnus was thoughtful for a moment. 'No, I suppose I don't. I really *like* her. And I feel very protective toward her. But I don't love her because I still love—'

Fay thumped the arm of the sofa and dust rose in a cloud. 'I'm *not* going to listen to this! By the time I wanted out, the only conversations we ever had were rows! We were sleeping separately and sex was just a distant memory!'

'Aye, but a fond one,' Magnus said quietly.

She glared at him, refusing to be distracted. 'The army broke you, Magnus. Then it broke our marriage... And then it broke me.'

He sat upright, a hint of the old military bearing about him now. 'Not the army, Fay. It was the job. The EOD.'

'*Everyone's divorced.*'

'Not everyone.'

'We are.'

'Aye, but just because you divorced me doesn't mean I stopped loving you.'

'You shut me out! And Emily! It was just you and your bloody castle and your bloody nightmares!'

He nodded. 'Aye, they were bloody all right.'

She put a hand to her eyes. 'I'm sorry, I shouldn't have said that. I know you couldn't help it. Believe me, I felt like a rat leaving a sinking ship. But I hung on for as long as I possibly could.'

'Aye, you did. And I was much to blame. I just didn't think you'd ever... have to leave me. That was a serious error of judgement on my part. I didn't think you'd want to live alone. Without Emily.'

'Neither did I. But she encouraged me to leave, you know she did. She was sixteen and fed up with seeing her mother crying and popping pills. It was best for her that we split up. But she chose to stay with you.'

'That was a vote for her friends and school, not me. Tully was her home. Em didn't stop loving you just because you weren't around any more. Neither did I.'

77

Fay stood up. 'I'm sorry, Magnus, but you have to go.'

'Aye, I'm going.' He set down his glass. 'I'm sorry if what I said came as a shock. I wasn't thinking of... the implications. I was just thinking about Rick. And you.'

Fay didn't reply but turned and left the room. She took Magnus' coat from the hall cupboard and stood by the front door, her arms full of the heavy old Harris tweed he'd always worn, a coat that had never been fashionable and showed no sign of wear, even though it had been owned by his uncle Lachlan, long dead. As she waited, Fay inhaled the scents of damp wool, heather and wood smoke that she'd always associated with Magnus and life at Tully. When he joined her in the hall, she handed him the coat, holding it up like a barrier between them. He took it and put down the *Root and Branch* print in its protective cardboard tube. 'I'll send you a cheque for that.'

'Please don't bother.'

'I insist.'

'You're family.'

'No, I'm just a customer now.'

Fay's resolve crumpled. Before he could see her tears, she turned away, reaching blindly for the front door handle. As he pulled on his coat, Magnus said, 'That letter.'

She swallowed, keeping her eyes averted. 'What letter?'

'The love letter. The one Jessie lent you.'

'What about it?'

'You say she wanted you to use it?'

'Yes. Well, she said I could. I think she wanted me to include it as part of the piece. Why do you ask?'

'My father didn't write it.'

'What do you mean? Jessie said it was from him.'

'She did?'

'Yes.'

'Then she was lying.'

'How do you know?'

'It's not my father's handwriting.'

'Then whose is it?'

'No idea. But it's not Donald McGillivray's. I understand he was no great letter-writer, but he wrote me a few when I was posted abroad and I read them many times. I know his hand.' He picked up the print. 'And this isn't it.'

'So... you think Jessie had a lover?'

'Maybe.'

'*Jessie?*'

'Why not? She was a beautiful woman. And she was unhappily married. Maybe she did what you should have done, Fay. Maybe if you hadn't been so damn faithful, I'd have seen some sense.'

Fay shook her head. 'I was an army wife. It was my duty to stand by you. And you never had the vaguest notion of failing to fulfil a duty. The concept was alien to you.' As he opened his mouth to reply, she said, 'I failed you, Magnus. I'm sorry. I really am. Now go. *Please.*'

She opened the door and stood aside. As he pushed past her in the cramped hallway, her cheek was grazed by the shoulder of his coat and, involuntarily, she inhaled. He stopped and looked down at her, concerned. When he didn't move, Fay lifted her head and, as he searched her eyes, she was unable to look away. Magnus dropped the cardboard tube and taking her face in both hands, he kissed her. Driven by the weight of his body, she fell back against the wall, but didn't struggle or respond. When he finally let her go, Fay stayed where she was, leaning against the wall, clutching at a radiator, her eyes shut tight. She heard Magnus pick up the print, then slam the front door. She stood quite still for a moment, then sniffed the air. A faint scent of wood smoke, nothing more.

With her back still pressed against the wall, she slid down to the floor, where she sat, unseeing, her cheeks wet, her closed eyelids no longer able to contain her tears.

Chapter 9

Fay

In the end I got up because I needed to pee. The call of nature answered, I went back into the sitting room and surveyed the untidy remnants of lunch. I poured myself another glass of wine (white, now warm and disgusting, but I was in a masochistic mood) then I walked over to the sofa where I sat at one end, facing the chair Magnus had occupied – my favourite, the Art Deco armchair I'd covered myself using a pair of old curtains and a staple gun. I hadn't made a very good job of it. The cushions sagged and still bore the imprint of Magnus' body, as if he was still sitting there, like the Invisible Man. I started to cry again. Turning away from the chair, I stared out the window at the helmeted matchstick men on the other side of the Clyde as they constructed more of their dragon.

By the time the bottle was empty, it was dark and I need to pee again. I got up, stumbled toward the door, hit the switch and flooded the room with light. Nothing seemed any clearer, apart from Magnus sitting invisibly in his chair.

When I came back from the loo, I went into the spare bedroom that served as my office and sat down at my laptop. I switched on and stared at the blank screen, trying to focus my eyes and mind.

I composed an email to Magnus. It took me hours. I think I deleted and re-typed every single word, rewrote, deleted again, then re-typed until finally I was satisfied. This was the email I wrote:

Dear Magnus
I'm finding it hard to make sense of what happened this afternoon. I had absolutely no idea you still felt something for me. If I'd known, I wouldn't have told you about Freddie. I know

I can be a bitch sometimes, but I would never want to hurt you.

I have no idea how we can possibly sort out this mess – Nina, Freddie and Emily, you living at Tully and me living in Glasgow – but I want you to know that I still love you, I have never stopped loving you and don't believe I ever will. If I was living only half a life with you, it was a damn sight more acceptable to me than the half-life I now live without you.

I want to come back, Magnus, but I don't know how.

All love,

Fay

And *this* was the email I sent:

Dear Magnus

I'm finding it hard to make sense of what happened this afternoon. I had no idea you still felt something for me. If I'd known, I wouldn't have told you about Freddie. I know I can be a bitch sometimes, but I would never want to hurt you.

I have no idea how you're going to sort this out with Nina but you must. You owe it to the poor girl. You must finish with her if your heart lies elsewhere.

But please don't cherish any hopes of a reconciliation between us. I remain very fond of you, but I have my own life here in Glasgow now – a career, new friends and my flat. There can be no going back for me. We went through too many different kinds of Hell together for us to make a new start. We both bear too many scars.

I think you know all this. I trust you'll not only understand, but spare me the pain of any more declarations.

With fondest love,

Fay

Oh, I know.

'How could you *do* that to the poor man?' (Not the first time I've heard *that* question, I can assure you.) Had she known, my loyal friend Morag – twice divorced, but an incurable romantic – would have said I needed a good slap. My ex-mother-in-law would have taken hold of Magnus and me and banged our heads together. My daughter would have rolled her eyes and snapped, 'For God's sake, Mum! Grow up!'

But none of them knew all that Magnus had put me through; what I'd put Magnus through; all that had come between us.

When we moved out of the caravan and into Tullibardine Tower, my first project was a wall hanging that I made for Magnus as a birthday present. It depicted Tully and a potted family history. I transferred a wedding photo onto the fabric, along with Emily's birth certificate and a favourite picture of her as a baby. There was a photo of the ruin that had once been Tully, one of Magnus in uniform and part of the wording of the citation that accompanied the medal he received "in recognition of most conspicuous gallantry in carrying out hazardous work in a very brave manner." These photos and fragments of text were faintly superimposed over a fabric representation of the restored Tully Tower, our new home. I wasn't sure it had worked – the semi-transparent figures looked like ghosts flitting between the ancient stones – but Magnus was thrilled with the piece and hung it proudly in the Great Hall on a wall he'd re-built himself, stone by massive stone.

The hanging is no longer in the Great Hall. It came down a few weeks later and was rolled up and put away, torn and stained.

The stains were blood.

The blood was mine.

And Magnus put it there.

~

Magnus gave up trying to sleep. Thoughts of the young man who might become his son-in-law making love to the woman who'd become his ex-wife ensured Magnus hadn't known a moment's repose since he'd slammed the door of Fay's flat. He got out of bed and pulled on his dressing gown and slippers. He stood for a moment, watching the sleeping figure of Nina, then padded downstairs to the Great Hall, the huge room that served as sitting and dining room.

Magnus ignored the light switch. His eyes had learned to function in the dark and he'd always preferred to see Tully lit by natural light or candles. Fay had complained about the perennial gloom, but Magnus had come to associate darkness and half-light with safety. Bright lights made him feel exposed and had been known to bring on one of his blinding headaches.

He crossed the uneven flagstoned floor, only partially covered by balding rugs, and flung himself onto one of three enormous sofas. He stretched out and gazed up at the tall windows, their heavy curtains undrawn. Moonlight fell in pale, silver shafts and illuminated the Hall. A vast stone fireplace formed the focal point of the room. Beside it stood an orderly pile of logs, stacked in an alcove. Above the soot-marked lintel hung two swords crossed behind a targe or circular shield, a copy of one originally made in Perth for Bonnie Prince Charlie's army.

To the right of the fireplace stood a long case clock, a wedding present from Magnus' parents, which had stopped many years ago and couldn't be induced to work again. Fay had insisted it should be retained for sentimental reasons and Magnus had dubbed it wryly, "the other Tullibardine pensioner."

All the furniture was large-scale: a dark oak refectory table with benches either side; massive carved chests; reproduction Jacobean chairs and sideboards. The fittings too were necessarily grandiose. Two circular wrought iron candelabra hung from the high ceiling and matching floor-standing candlesticks, the size of children, stood sentinel either side of the fireplace.

The thick, stone walls provided deep window recesses, their sills decorated with plants in brass and china pots and a selection of family photographs. Other photos showed Tully before its restoration and Magnus in various parts of the world, off-duty with his mates. (Some of the laughing young men were now dead, which was why Magnus chose to display their photographs, even though they caused him pain.)

The windows were framed by curtains Fay had made: tasselled patchworks of velvet, damask and brocade, the fabrics salvaged from old curtains found at auctions and junk shops. Each curtain was unique. When drawn across the windows and lit by flickering candle- and firelight, the fabrics glowed, bringing welcome warmth and colour to a room that was otherwise sparing in its creature comforts.

Fay had wanted to plaster the stone walls and whitewash them, to make the room lighter and less like a fortification, but Magnus had fought her on this, as on so many issues, insisting he wanted to be able to contemplate his own handiwork. In the end they'd run out of money and plastering a room the size of a small chapel had been a luxury beyond their overstretched budget.

There was only one door into the Great Hall, in the corner, leading to the turnpike stair that linked all floors. Magnus liked the fact that there was only one way into the room and he tended to sit facing that corner. He loved Tully because he'd restored it, but he also loved it because, within its walls, he felt safe. The feeling was illusory and he knew it. As a boy he'd witnessed his father raze derelict buildings to the ground with strategically placed explosives. He'd watched terrorists do the same. No wall was impregnable, no building indestructible. But Tully *felt* safe. A castle on a hill, in the middle of nowhere, its walls three feet thick – that was as safe as it got, Magnus reckoned. He'd quit the army and gone to ground in rural obscurity, but he knew he was on several terrorists' hit lists. Theirs was a revenge mentality and he'd personally thwarted many attacks or reduced the amount of carnage and destruction. So, out of long habit, Magnus sat opposite the door.

The log fire had gone out. As he lay on the sofa, brooding, Magnus was aware of the cold that constantly stalked his body at Tully, but he lay motionless. Numbness was what he craved now. Despite consuming industrial amounts of whisky, he'd managed to make love to Nina at bedtime, but still sleep had eluded him.

With fondest love.

What the hell was that supposed to mean? Why had Fay signed off like that? Was she hedging her bets? That wasn't like her.

Spare me the pain of any more declarations.

Well, that was pretty unequivocal. "Fuck off, Magnus," in other words.

We both bear too many scars.

Too bloody right. And Fay had given up trying to conceal hers. Was that a good sign? She used to wear a long fringe that covered the triangular scar on her forehead, the small pit gouged out of her flesh by a lump of stone.

Magnus swung his long legs off the sofa and walked over to the area of wall left of the fireplace. He stood and stared at it, as if he could see something other than stone, but the wall was bare. He extended his hand and laid his fingers on a stone at chest height. He pressed it, feeling how hard it was, how his fingertips were forced to yield and were grazed as he moved them over the stone.

Nausea made him suddenly dizzy. He had no memory of what had happened. No memory then, no memory now. All he could recall was Fay lying at his feet, blood pouring from her forehead. Since there was no one else present, Magnus knew he must be the culprit.

The room seemed to sway and he braced himself with both hands against the wall, leaning his forehead against the cold, unforgiving stone.

'Magnus?'

He spun round as Nina switched on the light. She stood in the doorway, clutching her dressing gown to her, blinking at him. 'Are you all right?'

'Aye. I'm fine,' he said absently.

'Did you have one of your nightmares?'

'No. I couldn't sleep.'

'Do you want to talk?'

'No.'

'Sure?'

'Aye, I'm sure.'

'Will you come back to bed then?'

'Aye, in a wee while. I just need... a moment, that's all.'

Nina gave him a long look, her brow furrowed with concern, then she turned to go. Magnus watched her retreating figure, the swinging curtain of blonde hair, tangled from their earlier lovemaking.

You owe it to the poor girl.

Magnus touched the wall again and called, 'Nina!'

She shuffled back into the room, yawning. 'What is it?'

'Would I be right in thinking that you'd like to get married? To me, I mean.'

She stared at him, wide-eyed. 'Magnus, is this a *proposal*?'

'Aye, I suppose it is... It's high time I made an honest woman of you.'

She launched herself across the room at him, squealing, and caught him off-balance. As he fell back against the wall with Nina in his arms, Magnus felt the hard protuberance of rock as it bruised his shoulder blade. As Nina kissed him, he made a mental note to get a masonry file and smooth the face of that stone.

It was a job he should have done a long time ago.

Fay

Anger had never come naturally to Magnus. The army would have trained it out of him but, given the nature of his work, I doubt it was ever there. If it was, it must have been buried at a psychologically subterranean level, at a depth where, like toxic waste, it could theoretically do no harm. Magnus' anger was an aberration induced by his extreme experience. Perhaps it wasn't even anger. There had been violence occasionally and constant fear, sometimes terror. That combination can look very much like anger, especially if you find yourself in the firing line, as I did.

These are things I know now, useless, bitter things I learned through painful experience. I didn't know them when I really needed to. By the time I was equipped to deal with the nightmare situation I found myself in, the damage had been done. I'd put my life on hold and, with no training or even any sense of vocation, I'd taken on the job of psychiatric nurse. Except that a psychiatric nurse is not on twenty-four hour call, seven days a week. And a psychiatric nurse has sedative medication at her disposal. She can call for heavyweight back-up and she tends not to be 5' 2" and small-boned. She might not even be a she – possibly some comfort when the patient takes a swing at you. Not that I think violence against women is necessarily worse than violence against men, it's just that for women it's a fine and sickening line between violence and violation. I doubt men ever feel that vulnerable. If someone hits them, or threatens to, even cowards know at some instinctive level that they could try fighting back.

As a small woman, I've never fought back, wouldn't *dream* of fighting back. I'd run – heels permitting – or I'd roll into a ball like a hedgehog and protect my vital organs. In any case, how do you fight back when the attacker is your husband, a sick and damaged man who has no idea what he's doing and will still have no idea when he's done?

I'd handle it all differently now. I don't know if I'd have given up and gone sooner, but I do know I would have sent for the cavalry sooner. I wouldn't have listened to Magnus and his habitual military understatement (which is just a clever form of whitewash. Or do I mean brainwash?) I wouldn't have accepted the destruction of our marriage as collateral damage. I would have cried out for help, instead of just crying. I would have hollered until someone heard.

In the end I found a rather drastic way of calling for assistance, but when help finally came, it was too late. At least, too late for our marriage.

Two weeks after my fateful lunch with Magnus I received an invitation in the post. I recognised Emily's handwriting on the envelope and opened the card with some trepidation, remembering what Magnus had said about Emily and Rick. If I didn't know my daughter well enough to be taken into her confidence about her engagement, I knew her well enough to know she was quite capable of springing it on me by post.

I opened the card, read it and was appalled.

Doubly appalled.

When he finally answered the phone, Magnus sounded tetchy, but I plunged in anyway.

'Magnus, I have to talk to you.'

There followed a silence in which I detected a long exhalation of breath, then he said, without enthusiasm, 'Hello, Fay.'

'Is Nina within earshot?'

'Not if you're going to speak at a normal level. But something tells me you're not.'

'Look, Magnus, when I said you needed to sort things out with Nina, I meant you needed to *finish* with her, not marry her!'

'So you'll have received your invitation, then?' he asked with mock geniality. 'It was Em's idea to have a joint celebration at Tully.'

'So I see. How very dynastic.'

'Aye, that's what we thought. Emily wanted a wee party but neither she nor Rick has the space, so Nina and I thought it would be grand to have a big family bash here. You'll be joining us, I hope?'

'Magnus, you can't do this.'

'I don't see why not. We've plenty of room and parking won't be a problem. Jessie said she'll give us a hand with the food.'

'I wasn't referring to the logistics, I was referring to the morality of your marrying Nina.'

He paused, then said softly, a warning hint of steel in his voice, 'It's none of your business, Fay.'

'I realise that. I'm appealing to you on humanitarian grounds. It just isn't *fair*! How can you do this to that poor girl?'

'The poor girl seems deliriously happy about it. As you so helpfully pointed out, it's what she wants. And expects. And I have no objections. We get along fine right enough. I'm very fond of her.'

'But you don't *love* her!'

'I love her enough to live with her. I've already proved that. And I feel... *responsible* for her.'

'Magnus, she's not a platoon! She's a woman and she loves you!' I took a deep breath and started to count to ten. I only got as far as three. 'It seems to me you're doing this for one of two reasons. Either you want to spite me, or you're acting out of a misplaced sense of duty.'

'You think the two are mutually exclusive then?'

'Magnus, *please!*'

'I'm not doing this to spite you, Fay!' He sounded angry and I knew I'd gone too far, further than I'd intended. 'I'm insulted that you think I'd use Nina as some sort of tactical weapon! I owe you no explanation for my actions, but for your information, I proposed to Nina because I want to make something meaningful of the rest of my life. Making a woman happy and proving I can make marriage work seem like worthwhile goals to me.'

'But you don't *love* her!'

'I heard you the first time!' he bellowed and, as he went on, I held the receiver a little distance from my ear. 'Loving you – being crazy about you, in fact! – didn't make our marriage work. And it didn't stop you leaving me, did it? So, in the words of the fucking song, what's *love* got to do with it?' I said nothing and Magnus resumed, mercifully at a lower decibel level. 'I take it you won't be attending our celebration then? Well, that's fine by me. Makes things a lot simpler. It might have been pretty awkward for you – guests asking what you thought of the strapping young man destined to become your son-in-law.'

Light began to dawn. A murky light. 'Is *that* why you're doing this? Oh, Magnus, how could you be so petty?'

'No, that's not why I'm marrying Nina. I may be cracked-up, washed up and impossible to live with, but I wouldn't have proposed if I didn't think I stood a chance of making it work, if I wasn't committed to *making* it work. It's what she wants. It's what she deserves. And I see no reason not to comply with her wishes.'

'Comply with her wishes? So you *are* marrying her out of a sense of duty?'

He hesitated, then said, 'Aye. In a way.'

'Does she know that?'

'No, I don't think so.'

'Tell her, Magnus. Or I will.'

'Go ahead! D'you think she'd listen to you? The vengeful

ex-wife who walked out on a war hero? I can think of no more certain way to seal our nuptials than for you to tell Nina she's making a big mistake! Just watch her stand by her man, Fay!'

Out-manoeuvred, I was silent and felt the stirrings of shame.

'Nina's a kind-hearted wee soul,' Magnus went on, calmer now. 'She loves lame dogs and lost causes. It'll be Christmas every day for her, married to me.'

It was as if I'd been slapped. I knew Magnus hadn't meant his flippant words to have that effect, but guilt suddenly overwhelmed me. 'I'm sorry... I've said too much. Far too much. It's just that – I just want you to be *happy,* that's all.'

'Thanks, but I don't aspire so high. I'll settle for being settled. So what shall I say to Emily? And Jessie? Or will you make your own excuses? Nina will understand. So will Rick, I imagine. But I don't know how you'll square your absence with Em. She won't understand. Or forgive you.'

'I know. I have to be there.'

'Aye, I think you do. I'm sorry.'

'Oh, don't worry about it. I promise not to be the spectre at the feast.'

'And I can trust you to say nothing about all this to Emily? Or Nina? It really is nothing to do with you any more.'

'Magnus, how can you *say* that? Two weeks ago you said you still loved me!'

'I can say it because you sent me an email saying – and I quote – "Please don't cherish any hopes of a reconciliation between us." That's exactly what I'd done, Fay. I'd cherished hopes. I realise now I was deluded about that and,' he added wearily, 'I want to draw a line. When you told me about Rick I had to accept – finally – that you'd moved on. Now I need to move on too. This is how I'm doing it. And I don't need your support or approval.'

'No, I know you don't. Well... you have my blessing. You and Nina. I hope you'll both be very happy.'

'Aye, but you don't think we will. Och, well,' he added cheerfully. 'We'll see you at the party then?'

'Of course. Though how I'll face Rick, I don't know.'

'My guess is, he'll be even more embarrassed than you.

And he has much more to lose if the truth gets out.'

'Which it *won't*. I'm warning you Magnus, just one of your cracks—'

'She's my daughter, Fay! No man could ever be good enough for her in my eyes, but I'll not make fun of her choice. What the hell d'you take me for?'

'A hero. A complete bloody hero. The kind that tilts at windmills, rescues damsels in distress and takes on the Powers of Darkness before breakfast.'

'You make me sound like Batman. Minus the tights. I just try to do the right thing.'

'And you really think marrying Nina is the right thing?'

'It feels right to me.'

'Does it? Or does it just feel like the lesser of two evils? Perhaps you think it'll be easier to marry Nina than dump her.'

'That's neither true nor fair. *Christ*, Fay! I didn't get blown to kingdom come in Derry taking the easy way out.'

'No, you didn't. I'm sorry, I'm judging you by my own cowardly standards of behaviour. But I'm not sure I ever really understood the demarcation line between courage and stupidity.'

'It's very simple. *Brave* is what the other guy is. *Stupid* is when it's happening to you.'

'Or your husband... I'll see you at the party. Please give Nina my congratulations.'

'I will. Thank you.'

There was an awkward silence after which I said, 'I do want you to be happy, Magnus.'

'Aye, I know.' There was another silence, then he said, 'Goodbye, Fay.'

Magnus' attempts at conciliation had always been both cack-handed and heartbreaking. Arguing with him on the phone about his engagement, I'd felt myself slipping back into my old nurse rôle, wanting to protect this fragile man who nevertheless felt protective toward his fiancée (who, as anyone could tell at a glance, was quite capable of looking after herself. Magnus too, probably.) Recognising the warning signs, I'd retreated in a hurry, but with retreat came the old, familiar feelings. Guilt. Shame. Defeat. And, inevitably, anger.

But for once I was angry with myself, not Magnus or the army.

After I'd finished speaking to him, I pursued the self-loathing theme and, leaning against the fridge, ate an entire tub of Häagen-Dazs pistachio ice cream. (There was a certain irony in this: I'd bought the ice cream for our lunch but, overtaken by events, we hadn't touched it.) The carton empty, my stomach uncomfortably full, I took stock.

I'd read in *Good Housekeeping* that faced with difficulties that threaten to overwhelm you, you should take an inventory of your life, then prioritise. Apparently this helps you maintain a sense of proportion and makes the problems seem more manageable. So I duly sat down with a pen and a sheet of paper. In no particular order, I listed my immediate problems:

1. *Emily is too young to marry.*

2. *I don't approve of her choice of husband because*
   a) she hasn't known him very long
   b) he's a music student with poor career prospects
   c) I've slept with him

3. *Emily is almost certainly unaware of 2c)*

4. *Rick and I need to consult a.s.a.p to check our stories agree.*

5. *I don't know how to contact Rick without asking Emily*

6. *What reason can I give her for contacting Rick?*

7. *Buy 2 engagement presents & cards.*

8. What to wear to party?

9. I'm possibly still in love with my ex-husband.

10. He's definitely still in love with me.

Reviewing my list, I concluded I was going to need more than a sense of proportion to deal with problems on this scale. *Good Housekeeping* hadn't expressly advised it, but I decided I would start praying for a miracle.

Chapter 10

Fay

Emily must have had second thoughts about dropping her engagement bombshell. In the next post I received a glossy 10" x 8" engagement photograph of her and Rick taken in the grounds of Tully. It was accompanied by a news cutting from the *Perthshire Advertiser* announcing the joint engagements of local hero Magnus McGillivray and his daughter, Emily. (Magnus, who still routinely checked under his car for bombs, would never have courted publicity like this, so I suspected the hand of Nina or, more probably, her mother.) The news item included a group photo taken in front of the ruins that Magnus had carefully preserved at Tully for the use of film crews and fashion shoots, which had provided a small income over the years. The girls looked windswept but lovely, the men handsome but awkward. Magnus in particular looked as if he'd had several teeth pulled and was afraid to smile.

The photo depressed me for the rest of the day, not because I was jealous, but because I realised I could no longer postpone a secret assignation with my daughter's fiancé.

~

Fay had chosen to sit at the back of the coffee shop, in a dim corner near the toilets, confident other customers would prefer tables near the window. Idly turning the pages of a magazine, she sensed rather than saw the man approach her table and braced herself. He stood at a slight distance and said, 'Fay?'

She looked up, still hoping it might be someone else, but it was Rick.

'Hello. Thanks for coming,' she said with a nervous smile.

'Sorry I'm late.'

'You're not. I was early.'

Rick set down his mug of coffee and sat opposite her. Dressed in jeans and a battered leather jacket, he looked even younger than she remembered. Fay's gloom deepened. 'I'm sorry for the summons.'

'That's OK. We do need to talk, don't we?'

'Yes.'

A silence ensued and Rick waited respectfully as Fay struggled to find somewhere to begin. Eventually she said, 'Why on earth did you tell me your name was Freddie?'

She hadn't meant it to sound like an accusation. From his hurt expression, Fay could tell she hadn't made a good start.

'My name's Frederick. Freddie's the name I've always been known by, but Emily didn't like it. She said it sounded like something out of P. G. Wodehouse.'

'But Emily *likes* P. G. Wodehouse.'

'Really?'

'Yes. Magnus used to read Wodehouse to her as a treat. In an excruciating English accent.'

'Well, Em said I wasn't a Freddie, and could she call me Rick?'

'Oh. I see. What's your professional name?'

'Frederick Hampton.'

'That sounds very distinguished.'

'Thanks.'

'I hear you're a baritone?'

'That's right.'

'Do you sing opera?'

'Given half a chance.'

'I don't know much about opera. I gather baritones never get the girl.'

'Not on stage, no.'

Fay shot him a look over the top of her mug and Rick looked down, abashed. She resumed. 'Are you planning a career in opera?'

'Well, that's what I'd like to do. And I've already done some performances with Scottish Opera. Just chorus and understudying, but it's a start.' He paused, then added, 'The money wouldn't be good. But Dad's a merchant banker, if

95

that's any consolation.'

'Oh, Freddie, I'm not here to check out your career prospects! Emily's twenty-two. Personally, I think that's too young to get married, but it's also too old to need your mother's approval.'

'Er... Hadn't you better start calling me Rick? I mean, that's how I was introduced to you. It would be tricky to have to explain—'

'Oh, yes, of course. You're right. I must try to remember. But you definitely seem more like a Freddie than a Rick to me. Honestly, fancy trying to change your *name*! My daughter's such a control-freak.'

'I think she was just joking to begin with,' he said affably. 'Then somehow it stuck.' He swallowed a mouthful of coffee. 'So if you're not checking me out as a prospective son-in-law, was there something you wanted to know?' Fay hesitated and he continued. 'We haven't set a date for the wedding yet. We want to save some money and sort out where we're going to live. That was the main reason Emily wanted to get engaged really. Because marriage seems a long way off.'

Fay smiled and leaned forward. 'Look, I'm not going to interfere, Fre— *Rick*. Emily and I aren't close and I don't suppose she gives a damn what I think anyway. But she'd be terribly upset if she found out that we... well, that we had a *history*.'

'Yes, I know.'

'I think she'd feel shocked and... extremely embarrassed.'

'I suppose so.'

'And there's no way she'd understand how... well, how such a thing could have happened.'

'No. Though I suppose she might feel encouraged by my consistency.'

'Consistency?'

'Well, you know – my taste in women. I mean, you're both very alike.'

'Are we? But Emily's tall and willowy. And really pretty.'

'Peas in a pod,' Rick replied. 'Only Em is, as you say, a lot taller. Taller than me in heels.' He smiled and dragged a hand through his thick fair hair in what Fay guessed was a habitual nervous gesture. 'When I met Emily the attraction was immediate. And she seemed strangely familiar. I felt I somehow knew her already, but I couldn't think why. She hardly ever mentioned you and when she did, she referred to you as "my mother", so I never caught your name. Not that you'd told me your surname anyway.' He ground to a halt and the conversation languished until he murmured, 'Billie Holliday.'

'I'm sorry?'

He pointed upwards, indicating a speaker on the wall. 'That's who's singing. Billie Holliday.'

'Oh.'

'Genius...' He shook his head. 'They don't make them like that any more.'

Fay laughed and felt her shoulders relax a little. 'Careful, you're sounding middle-aged.'

He studied her for a moment, then said, 'I'm sorry what happened between us has really complicated things for you, but I'd like you to be clear about two things.'

'Which are?'

'I love your daughter.'

'I'm very pleased to hear it. And the other?'

'I don't regret what happened between us. You and me, I mean. I don't think of it as a mistake. It was a meaningful encounter, not just sex. Though the sex was great,' he added with an involuntary grin.

Fay winced and closed her eyes. '*Please*. Can we not go there?'

'Sorry. I just want you to know, it was only a one-night stand because you didn't tell me how to contact you. Made it clear you didn't *want* me to contact you.'

'But... I sincerely hope you feel differently *now*?'

'Of course. A lot of water's passed under the bridge since then. I met Emily and ... I fell in love.'

'I'm very pleased for you both. Really, I am.'

'Em's the first woman I've met who seems to be... well, the *answer*.'

'Answer to what?'

He shrugged. 'All the questions, I suppose.' Fay looked

blank. 'The questions you ask yourself at 4.00am... All the questions you'll *ever* ask yourself at 4.00am.'

Fay stared at him in silence, then reached down to the floor for her handbag. She extracted a tissue and dabbed at her eyes.

'What's the matter?' Rick asked, alarmed.

'Nothing. It must be all this talk of weddings.' She sniffed. 'I warn you now, I *always* cry at weddings.'

'Was it something I said?'

'I suppose it must have been. What you said... about the questions. It made me realise, my concern for Emily is quite misplaced. I thought she was rushing into something foolish. A big white wedding scenario. I hadn't realised—' She swallowed.

'What?'

'What a very lucky girl she is. To have found the right man. And so soon! No multiple frog-kissing for Emily. Typically efficient of her.'

'But you were the same, weren't you? You found the right man, very young. Em said you gave up college to marry Magnus. And I gather the marriage lasted until a few years ago.'

Fay looked surprised. 'You think that means Magnus was the right man?'

'Well, yes, don't you? Just because something ends, it doesn't mean it wasn't *right*.'

'Doesn't it?' Fay asked doubtfully.

'Well, not in my book.' He peered at her face. 'Oh, no – I've upset you again, haven't I? I'm sorry.'

'I'm not upset. I was just... *moved*, that's all. By your eloquence. And your honesty. You have some very special qualities, Rick. That was clear to me when I first met you. I don't wonder Emily wants to snap you up. She'd be a fool not to.'

'Thank you.'

'Look, we don't need to prolong this, do we? I think we're in total agreement. Our story is, we never met before that night at the gallery. I can't see the point of telling Emily anything, can you? She'd die of embarrassment. And I think she might be angry with me. My daughter apparently thinks I live a sad, solitary life, reading pulp romance and scoffing chocolates. I'm not sure she'd be able to get her head round the idea of her mother taking an attractive young man to bed on a whim. So we say nothing. Right?'

'Right.'

'Thank you. I'm glad we've got that sorted.' She pushed her empty coffee mug away and stood up. 'I'm afraid I must go. I have to get a train to Perth.'

Rick got to his feet and helped her on with her coat. 'Are you seeing Emily?'

'No, I'm visiting my mother-in-law. My *ex*-mother-in-law, I should say, but I actually think of her as a friend. Have you met Jessie yet?'

'No, but Em's talked about her.'

'She's a splendid woman. She'll be at Tully for the party. On peace-keeping duty while the rest of us play toxic *Happy Families*. That woman missed a brilliant career with the UN.'

'Will you be bringing someone?'

She stared at him for a moment, then said, 'Oh, you mean a *man*. No, I don't think so,' she added vaguely.

'You haven't found the answer then?'

'To my 4.00am questions?' She looked down as she buttoned up her coat. 'I don't even ask myself the questions, Freddie. Not anymore.'

'*Rick*,' he said gently.

'Sorry. I promise I'll go home and practice. And I'll try very hard not to mess things up for you and Emily.'

'And I'll try not to mess things up for *you* and Emily.'

'Oh, don't worry – I managed to do that very thoroughly some years ago.' She looked at her watch. 'I really must go. Thanks for coming. I'll see you at Tully. Take care.'

Fay

If you're any kind of an artist or gardener, travelling through Perthshire in autumn is a visual treat. I don't know why the coloured foliage is so much more brilliant in Scotland than in England. It must be something to do with the indecent haste with which the short Scottish summer ends and autumn begins. The trees retract their sap in a hurry and the resulting bright colours must be a panic-stricken response to the sudden withdrawal of that life-blood. Because the sight's so beautiful, you forget what this gorgeous display actually represents. Decay and death. If only human death were so glorious.

So I sat back on the train, enjoying the scenery and my packed lunch. The sky was a cloudless blue and there was that particular quality of clear, northern light one never sees in England, however fine the day. Finally I began to relax. I'd sorted out my story with Rick and I could look forward to spending the rest of my day with Jessie McGillivray who, unlike her son, knew better than to ask awkward questions.

Jessie was kind and ever tactful. I'd always thought her consideration for others was the by-product of a good Scottish education and what had seemed, on the face of it, a quietly traditional marriage. Now I wasn't so sure. I was on my way to Perth to return my *Root and Branch* wall hanging to Jessie, together with one page of a precious love letter that, according to Magnus, had not been written by his father. The late Donald McGillivray's name and image appeared on the hanging but apparently his handwriting did not. The firm, artistic hand I'd transferred on to cloth was unknown to Magnus, yet Jessie had asked for it to be included and had misled me (deliberately?) about the author of the letter.

I knew Jessie well but I couldn't ask her about the identity of her lover. It was none of my business. Except that she'd said to me (had she made a particular point of doing so?) that the letter was from Magnus' father. Did she just want me to assume the letter was from Donald? Or was she actually telling the truth? That the letter was from Magnus' *father*? And was that why she'd requested its inclusion on the wall hanging?

Jessie's love life was no concern of mine, but the identity of my ex-husband's father - our daughter's grandfather - was of great interest to me. Jessie's mystery lover was a piece of the jigsaw of my family life. I knew there had been no love lost between Donald and Magnus and it was no secret that

Magnus had joined the army to get away from home. Was there a reason why the two men hadn't got on? Had Donald known Magnus wasn't his son?

Had poor Jessie been in love with one man, while married to another? Possibly. It was easy to forget that Jessie had been a young woman in the permissive sixties. From everything Magnus had ever said about his parents' marriage, it seemed it hadn't been particularly happy. Perhaps Jessie had tried to make her marriage work, but her heart lay elsewhere.

And now her son was about to try and repeat the exercise.

I knew Magnus would never listen to me, but if anyone could talk him out of marrying Nina, it might be Jessie. But what right had I to worry her with Magnus' garbled and graceless declaration of undying love for me? Jessie's discreet silence on the subject of my disintegrating marriage and subsequent divorce had always been a comfort to me. She hadn't taken sides and had continued to treat me as a daughter, long after the divorce. But I was now beginning to see her reticence in a new light. If my guesses were correct, Jessie had tried to make a loveless marriage work, but had almost certainly failed. And Magnus was about to do the same.

But what about me? Hadn't I also tried to supplant Magnus, with Rick and a few other kind, attractive men whose only shortcoming was, they weren't Magnus. Had I failed too? As I stared out of the train window, the scenery became a blur, as unclear as my thoughts and feelings. My wall hanging might depict the branches of my family tree with some degree of accuracy, but the roots were buried deep – unknown and likely to remain so.

A distant but familiar shape on the horizon caught me unawares: Tullibardine Tower, visible for miles on its hill, sticking up like a rude finger. Normally I braced myself for the sight of Tully and contrived to be reading or looking in another direction when the train passed, for whenever I saw my old home, I felt a pang. I was never quite sure what the pang was. I thought it was probably nothing more than the

101

dull pain a soldier might experience from an old wound – a twinge in damp weather, a jangling nerve, nothing more. If occasionally I felt I was missing Tully – the building or the life I'd lived there – I knew it must be mere sentiment. I missed Tully the way parents miss teenagers after they've left home. Life is transformed, mostly for the better, but you know that really, you loved having them at home. But you also know it was hell, like living in a war zone. The only way to survive was to collaborate with the occupying forces.

I'm not exactly speaking from experience here. I know that in some warped, self-indulgently sentimental way, I do occasionally miss Tully, but I don't know about missing teenage children after they've flown the nest. My teenage daughter didn't leave home.

I did.

~

Jessie throws her bicycle down in the long grass where no one will see it. She makes her way toward the door that was once the tradesmen's entrance at Drummond Hall. He'd said it wasn't locked, just stiff. If she leaned against it hard, it would give and she could get in. He'd told her to make sure she closed it behind her. They didn't want to be disturbed by tramps.

Jessie stands looking at the door, fighting panic and the nauseous excitement that threatens to overwhelm her. She wonders whether the lavatories still work – he'd said there was no electricity – and she worries what she'll do if she needs one.

Jessie's mother thinks she's at the pictures with friends, seeing Billy Liar. *Her friend Samantha summarised the entire plot of the film for Jessie in case her mother subjects her to one of her interrogations when she gets home. Jessie didn't tell Sam why she was so interested in the plot of* Billy Liar *and Sam, who likes to talk, didn't ask. No one knows why Jessie needs an alibi. He said no one must know anything. If anyone finds out about them, it will have to end and Jessie doesn't want it to end. She loves him. She knows she'll never love anyone else, ever, and tonight she's going to prove it to him. He hasn't pressured her, not really, but she knows what men expect, what they want. She knows why she's meeting him in this godforsaken place. At twenty-four, Jessie's no innocent. She knows what she's doing. She knows what he will do. The thought thrills and appals her in equal measure.*

Jessie pulls out a powder compact from her handbag and checks her appearance for the last time. There was nothing she could do about her unfashionably curly hair. She's tried straightening it many times, but nothing lasts more than a few minutes, even when she sellotapes her fringe to her forehead and dries it with the hairdryer. As soon as the tape is removed, her hair starts to kink and she just has a red face to show for her pains.

She checks her pale pink lipstick, reapplies it carefully, then powders her nose where it's begun to shine. She'd wanted to wear one of her short skirts but if you cycled through Perth in a short skirt and sling-backs, you'd draw attention to yourself. That's the last thing she wants. So she's compromised and worn a summer dress with sandals. He said he likes her in pretty, feminine clothes. But it doesn't really matter what she wears. It's not as if her clothes will be staying on for long. She feels sick again and shivers, although the summer evening is mild.

Jessie puts her compact away. As she leans against the door and pushes with her shoulder, she wonders if he will have brought a blanket for them to lie on. She knows there won't be a bed. All the furniture was sold at auction long ago. But he said he'd take care of everything. Jessie wonders if he will. She'd wanted to ask Samantha about taking precautions (Sam struck her as the sort of girl who'd know) but in the end Jessie's courage failed her. In any case, it was the man's job to see to all that.

The door gives way suddenly and Jessie half-falls into a dark hallway. She hears a fluttering aloft and the cooing of pigeons. The noise is oddly soothing. She chides herself for doubting her lover, her soon-to-be lover. Closing the door behind her, she peers along a dim passageway. There must be rats, but he said they wouldn't see any, not in daylight, so she walks forward, calling out his name, tentatively at first, then with more confidence.

She hears a distant shout, then footsteps running down a staircase. She follows the sound, feeling her way along the dark corridor, until she finds herself in a huge, hexagonal entrance hall into which curves a wide, stone staircase. Sunlight falls in shafts through the dirty, broken windowpanes, lighting the motes of dust dancing round her beloved, who stands on the bottom stair, his hand resting on the carved wooden banister. He looks pale but smiles, with something that looks like relief.

'Jessie! You're here.'

He doesn't move, just gazes at her. She feels awkward and wishes he'd stop staring and take her hand. Or kiss her. She gestures back the way she has come. 'I shut the door. Firmly, like you said.'

He descends the final stair, walks toward her across chequerboard tiles and reaches out. He takes both her hands and bends to kiss her pale mouth, then leads her up the spiralling staircase. They say nothing. Jessie studies her sandaled feet as they mount the stairs and realises she's counting. When the squawk of jackdaws makes her jump, he squeezes her hand, but they continue their slow ascent in silence. To her dismay, Jessie finds herself wondering – as a matter of some urgency – if there is a working lavatory and if she can possibly bring herself to ask.

Chapter 11

Fay

I needn't have bothered with my packed lunch. I arrived at Jessie's little flat in Perth to discover she'd baked scones and shortbread in my honour. When I said I was trying to cut back on the carbs she treated me to her *I'm-a-puppy-that's-just-been-kicked* expression.

'Don't do this to me, Jessie. I'm standing firm. I have a deadline now.'

'The engagement party?'

I nodded. 'I need to look good. Mother-of-the-bride-to-be *and* ex-wife. That's a lot of pressure. Especially when you consider the age of the *other* bride-to be.'

Jessie eyed her home bakes and sighed. 'It's very awkward for you, I admit. I suppose you do have to go?'

'Oh, yes. I have to be there for Emily's sake. I want to be there anyway. I just don't want *too much* of me to be there.'

Jessie laughed. 'Och, you're the size of a wee girl! Nina would make two of you. Sit down by the fire now and make yourself comfortable. I'll fetch us some tea.' She bustled off to the kitchen and I sat, as instructed, beside the gas fire which blazed in my honour. (Jessie said she never felt the cold having spent her married life in a draughty barn of a house that no amount of radiators ever seemed able to warm.)

I surveyed the quantities of books that lined the walls and was admiring my mother-in-law's eclectic taste when she called out from the kitchen, 'Will you be taking someone to the party? I'm sure Magnus wouldn't mind if you took a companion.'

'Well, that would have to be you, Jessie. There's no man in my life at the moment. Another reason I want to look my best.'

She appeared in the doorway with a tea tray. 'You've

nothing to worry about! You always look gorgeous.' She set the tray down on the coffee table. 'It's Nina who'll be wondering if she can get into her glad rags. The last time I saw her she was looking a wee bit... *tubby*.'

There was what you might call a pregnant pause while Jessie and I looked at each other.

'You don't think—'

'Och, no! I shouldn't think so. I can't believe either Nina or Magnus would be that careless.'

'No, you're probably right. Though from what Magnus said, getting engaged does seem to have been a spur of the moment decision.'

Jessie looked up from pouring tea, her eyes wide. 'You've spoken to him about it?'

'Well, yes. As it was a joint engagement party there were things we needed to discuss. About Emily and Fred— I mean, *Rick*.' Jessie blinked at me, confused, then handed me a cup of tea. 'His name's Frederick,' I explained. 'But he's known as Rick. Such an awful name! I much prefer Frederick, don't you?'

'I suppose so,' she replied vaguely. 'I haven't met him yet, but Emily assures me he's a lovely boy.'

'Hardly a *boy*! He's twenty-eight. And looks older,' I added firmly. 'But yes, he is extremely nice. And clearly very much in love with Emily.'

'That's grand! I'm sure it will be a wonderful evening. A double engagement party in a castle! What could be more romantic? The girls will be so excited!'

I smiled with as much enthusiasm as I could muster. 'I thought you and I could share a taxi to Tully from here. Do you think you could put me up for the night? Emily offered, but she only has a sofa bed and anyway, I'm sure Rick will stay over. They'll want to be on their own after the party.'

'Aye, you must come and stay in my spare room. It will be lovely to have you.'

'Thanks.'

'You know if you ever need a bed, Fay – or a shoulder to cry on for that matter – you can always come to me.' She shook her head. 'What that man has put us both through over the years has bound us together. Almost as close as mother and daughter.'

'I think of us as friends, Jessie. *Good* friends.'

'Aye, and so do I. Though...' She indicated the plate on the coffee table. 'If you refuse to eat even one wee morsel of shortbread, our friendship will be severely strained.'

'You're such a bully!' I said, reaching for the plate, not at all reluctantly.

'Aye, I know. I'm a holy terror!' Jessie chuckled as she refilled our teacups. The mischievous glint in her blue eyes reminded me of Magnus. It also called to mind her mystery love letter. I was debating whether or not our friendship would allow me to probe the identity of the author when she threw me by saying, 'I just hope Magnus and Nina will be happy.'

'You sound as if you don't think they will.'

'Well, do *you*?'

Jessie fixed me with a look that made lying difficult. Difficult, but not impossible. There was no way I was going to tell Magnus' mother what a prize pillock he was making of himself. 'I don't see why not. Nina's obviously in love with him. And she's of an age to want to settle down.'

'Aye, true enough,' said Jessie sipping her tea. 'But what about Magnus?'

'What about him?'

'Does he strike you as love-struck?'

I suddenly remembered Magnus' hands clasping my head, turning my face upwards, then the force of his kiss, a kiss that had left my mouth feeling bruised for hours. I stared down into my teacup. When I was able to look up, Jessie's sharp eyes were on me and her head was cocked on one side, like a bird's. I felt like a worm.

Clearing my throat, I played for time while I endeavoured to compose myself. 'I don't think he's *love-struck* exactly. But I'm sure he loves Nina. In his way,' I added lamely. Swallowing a mouthful of tea, I reached automatically for another piece of shortbread. The significance of this panic-stricken gesture wasn't lost on Jessie.

'I see. So it's no love match then. And we don't think it's a shot-gun wedding.'

'No. I'm sure it's not.'

'There can only be one other motive then,' said Jessie setting down her cup and leaning back in her armchair.

'Really? What would that be?'

'One nail drives out another,' Jessie replied cryptically.

'I'm sorry?'

'Magnus has struggled to get you out of his system for five years and he's failed. Now the big eejit thinks he can get over you by marrying another woman!'

'Oh, I'm sure it's nothing like that!'

Jessie leaned forward. 'Fay, has anyone ever told you, you're a terrible liar? "Transparency" should have been your middle name. For that reason I'll not embarrass you by asking if you're still in love with Magnus. It's none of my business. But my son's happiness is.'

It seemed pointless to argue, even more pointless to pretend she was wrong. 'I don't recommend you speak to him about it, Jessie. I have tried. He thinks he's doing the right thing. It's what Nina wants. And he wants another go at marriage. At making someone happy. He's actually quite convincing in his warped way.'

'So he's found another way to play the hero,' said Jessie, grim-faced.

'He thinks he's making the best of things.'

Jessie pursed her lips and looked thoughtful. 'A loveless marriage can sometimes work. A marriage of convenience only. I've seen that. But a marriage where one partner loves *outside* the marriage? How can that work? It's not just doomed to failure, it's morally wrong! And if my son can't see that, then I'm disappointed in him.'

'I think he sincerely believes it's the lesser of two evils. He thinks if he commits to Nina he'll abandon any idea of us getting back together again.' Jessie rolled her eyes and made an eloquent noise, conveying her impatience and disbelief. 'Yes, I know... But Magnus has always lived in a world of his own, hasn't he? A black and white world of heroes and villains.'

'Oh aye! Give him someone or something to rescue and

he's happy. That boy always had more courage than sense! Did you have any idea he wanted you to be reconciled?'

'No. I only found out recently that he still – that he had feelings for me. It came as a dreadful shock. I was already reeling from the news that Emily wanted to marry Rick. And then I heard Magnus was going to marry Nina. I'm still struggling to take it all in... Oh, why does life have to be so complicated? And why does Magnus think it *isn't*?'

Jessie got to her feet. 'I think we need a fresh pot of tea. Perhaps now you'll take pity on those poor wee scones, sitting there, going stale. I'm away to put the kettle on.'

The afternoon was growing dark and I suddenly felt chilly. I got up and stood in front of the hissing gas fire, warming my legs. Jessie's wedding photograph caught my eye and I picked up the wooden frame from the mantelpiece to examine the photo more closely. How pretty she'd been with her laughing eyes and dimples; how unprepossessing Donald had looked with his spectacles and Brylcreemed hair. He looked more like her father than her husband. I replaced the photo and picked up another: Magnus in uniform, solemn but proud, looking little more than a schoolboy. But then, he'd been a schoolboy before he joined up.

Jessie came back into the room with the teapot and I replaced Magnus' photo. As I turned away, there was a sliding sound and I looked back just in time to see the wedding photo topple over. I tried to catch it but wasn't quick enough. It somersaulted down, hit the top of the gas fire and bounced. There was a sound of breaking glass and the wooden frame sprang apart, the pieces tumbling on to the hearthrug.

Jessie cried out and hurried to set the teapot down. 'Leave it, Fay! Don't touch anything! You'll cut yourself.'

Taking no notice, I bent down to retrieve the photograph and shook it free of glass shards. As I did so, another photo detached itself and drifted to the floor, landing face upwards. The picture was upside down but I saw at once that it was a photo of Magnus, taken when he was much older, his mop of dark curls almost as wild then as it was now.

Jessie bent to pick up the photo of Magnus, then took the wedding photo from my hands. She pulled open a drawer in her bureau, dropped the two pictures inside and slammed it shut. 'Let's have our tea now. I'll clear up in a wee while.'

'I'm so sorry! I don't know how it happened. I must have put the photo back without checking it was stable.'

'Och, don't worry about it,' Jessie replied, a little breathless. 'It was always a shoogly frame. I've been meaning to replace it for years, but it was one Donald made me as a present. Now, will you just leave that glass alone! Pour us both a fresh cup of tea and sit down.'

'Please, let me—'

'I won't hear of it! Pour the tea and butter me a scone. Aye, and I'll have jam too, if you please! It's been one of those days...'

Faced with the daunting prospect of a party at which both my ex-husband and my ex-lover would be present with their much younger fiancées, I did what any woman would do in such an emergency.

I shopped.

I took Morag with me for moral support in my quest for the ultimate killer outfit. We went to Fraser's in Buchanan Street where you can get posh frocks to suit a variety of budgets. Primark would have suited mine better, but this was – I hoped – a once in a lifetime occasion: my only child getting engaged to my cast-off lover and my cast-off husband getting engaged to a girl not much older than our only child. This was not an occasion for penny-pinching.

I wasn't sure how I'd cope with a party in my old home. A decent outfit would go a long way toward shoring up my pulverised self-esteem. If necessary, I was prepared to eat lentils for months if it meant I'd look all right on the night. Morag didn't know anything about Rick's chequered past, but approved of my battle plan since I was *so* much older than Nina and lamentably still single. Desperate times called for desperate measures, according to Morag. In any case, I was footing the bill. She could afford to think creatively.

We may have agreed on tactics, but sadly we didn't agree on style. Morag is, shall we say, voluptuously built as well as very tall and she's never had children so there were times when I felt choosing outfits for me to try on was fulfilling some sort of doll-dressing fantasy for her...

~

'Don't even *think* about it. I'd never get into that.'

'Of course you would! It might be a wee bit snug—'

'I wouldn't be able to sit down. Or bend over. Walking could be difficult.'

'Well, I don't suppose you'll be Stripping the Willow,' Morag said grumpily replacing a tiny black dress back on the rail.

'Who knows? I might have to,' Fay replied. 'You're forgetting, this is a party organised by Magnus the Mad Scot.'

'By Nina more likely.'

'In which case we could be playing *Musical Chairs* and *Blind Man's Bluff.*'

'Miaowwwww...'

'Sorry. I shouldn't be so nasty, should I? I'm tired already. Can we break for coffee yet?'

'No, not yet. I think we should have a shortlist of at least three possibles before you're allowed coffee.'

'I had no idea you were such a sadist.'

'No pain, no gain, Fay,' Morag replied sweetly. 'And if you think a personal shopper would have been more lenient, you'd be wrong. What about this?'

Morag pulled a floaty silk chiffon number from a rail and dangled it in front of Fay, who wrinkled her nose in distaste.

'Tarty. I'm too old to get away with something as girly as that.'

'It's not a question of age, it's a question of size. You're a size 10. You can wear *anything*,' Morag said wistfully.

'But not sequins... or lace... or taffeta... or lamé,' Fay announced as she worked her way along a rail of flamboyant dresses.

'Well, what about this one?'

Fay studied the dress Morag held up. She was tempted by the fabric: a reproduction of a 1960s "Flower Power" design, bold, colourful and quirky. 'The sort of thing Twiggy and Lulu would have worn,' Fay thought ruefully, 'when they were thirty years younger than me.' She took the mini-dress from Morag, held it up against herself and looked in a mirror.

'Try it on!'

Fay shook her head. 'No point. It's wrong.'

'But it's so *you*.'

'Yes, it is in a way. And I do like it,' she conceded. 'But this would be trying too hard. It's a young woman's dress.'

'You've got a young woman's body.'

'You're very kind, Morag. I didn't realise you were also partially sighted.'

'Try it on!'

'*No*,' Fay said putting the dress back on the rail. 'It's gorgeous, I love sixties designs and it would probably suit me, but I know what I'm looking for and this isn't it.'

'So what is?' Morag asked.

'*This*, possibly,' said Fay as she selected a turquoise satin cheongsam. 'Now this I like. But will I look like an extra from a Bond movie?'

'Of course you won't! That colour's gorgeous. It will look great with your hair.'

'I've got some heels this colour,' said Fay examining the fabric closely.

'Stilettos?'

'No. You can't wear stilettos on Tully's floors anyway. They're too uneven. You can wear heels, but not real spikes. And stilettos would be over the top. I don't want to look as if I'm competing with the youngsters.'

'Though you are, of course.'

'Of course. Do you think I could get away with this?'

'Why ever not? To wear a dress like that you have to have a small arse, a waist and a flat tummy. And, damn you, you have. Try it on.'

'All right, I will. Then I insist we go for coffee. If I don't get a caffeine fix soon, you'll have a rebellion on your hands.'

'Let me see it on, even if you hate it.'

'OK. I'm going to take this in as well,' Fay added, picking up the retro dress. 'Just for a laugh.'

'Maybe it could be your Mother of the Bride outfit,' Morag called out as Fay disappeared into the changing room.

The cheongsam fitted perfectly, so perfectly Fay was worried it drew too much attention to her neat figure, but since the skirt stopped modestly on the knee and the only skin exposed was her arms and a glimpse at the keyhole neck, the fit was the only overtly sexy aspect of the dress. The fabric was satin but embroidered with chrysanthemums, which prevented it from looking trashy. The colour was intense but not eye-poppingly bright. Fay tried to find fault with the fabric, the cut, the length, the fit, even the price tag, but she failed on all counts. The dress had her name on it.

She didn't bother to try on the mini-dress but emerged from the changing room after only a few minutes, carrying both dresses. Morag recognised an air of decision when she saw it.

'Which one?'

'The cheongsam, of course.'

'You didn't show me!'

'Didn't need to. I knew it was right. I couldn't risk you not liking it. I'd made up my mind.'

'Brilliant! Coffee and cake?'

'No cake for me. Not till after the party. This dress is not remotely forgiving.'

Fay handed over her purchase and credit card to an under-employed sales assistant who was idly folding headscarves.

'Did you try the sixties dress?' Morag asked.

'No. I was tempted. I might even have succumbed,' Fay said as she keyed in her pin number. 'I've always wished I could have been a teenager in the sixties. It must have been such fun.' The assistant handed Fay her card, receipt and an ostentatious carrier bag.

'Oh, aye, the sixties were brilliant! Fantastic music... All those wonderful clothes... And all that hair!'

As they walked away from the counter, Fay suddenly stood still and stared into space.

'Fay? Are you OK?' As Morag watched, the blood drained from her friend's face, leaving her very pale. 'Fay, what's wrong? Oh hell, don't go and faint on me!' Morag took the carrier bag and waved at their sales assistant. 'Could you bring us a chair? I think my friend's going to pass out.' Glad of some excitement, the young sales assistant whipped a chair away from the wall and placed it behind Fay, apologising for the excessive heat in the store.

'No, really, I'm fine. I don't need a chair. I just... I just remembered something.'

'Something important?' Morag asked, puzzled.

'In a way. But it's nothing to worry about. It's just something about Jessie.' Morag frowned. 'My ex-mother-in-law,' Fay explained.

'Look, why don't you sit down for a bit? You're still white as a sheet.'

Fay caught the eye of the sales assistant who was hovering now, looking disappointed that no one had actually fainted. 'No, not here. Let's go and have a coffee in Caffè Nero. It's down a floor.'

'Well, take my arm then.'

'Really, Morag, stop fussing! I'm *fine*.'

'You could have fooled me, hen,' Morag replied, threading Fay's arm firmly through hers. 'You looked to me like you'd seen a ghost!'

Fay

In a way I had. When Morag was talking about the sixties I suddenly realised the picture Jessie kept behind her wedding photograph wasn't Magnus. That man had been young, perhaps thirty, no more. Magnus had never had long hair when he was young. I never saw him with long hair until after he'd quit the army. Up till then, I didn't even know it curled. The man in the photograph must have been his father, pictured in the 1960s, his hair looking much as Magnus' did now.

I'd seen Magnus' father, seen that he was the image of his son, but I had no idea who he was. Nor, presumably did Magnus.

Had Donald known? Had anyone, apart from Jessie?

~

There's always a way in. A door at the back left unlocked or hanging off its hinges. Or there'll be a broken window, the sash rotted, the frame so far gone you can just push it in. There's always a way in if you're twelve, resourceful and fear the structural instability of a condemned building less than the wrath of your father.

Magnus patrols the corridor, placing his feet, cat-like, on filthy varnished floorboards. An accumulation of dust, dirt and bird droppings deadens his footsteps. Piles of fallen plaster and dead leaves conceal rotten floorboards, so he avoids them, weaving a careful path through the empty rooms, testing the floor with his weight as he walks. "Step on the cracks and the bears will get you." That's what his father used to say when Magnus was small and they walked together along the High Street, each proud of the other. Obedient in those days, Magnus avoided the cracks, but not because he was afraid of bears. (There weren't any left in Scotland, his mother had said, scoffing at the little joke between father and son.) Magnus doesn't fear bears or any other creature, not even spiders. He doesn't fear anything except his father's temper and his mother's tears. He can mostly avoid those by keeping out of their way, slipping out of the house and cycling off to one of the secret places where he goes to be alone.

Drummond Hall is one, but won't be for much longer. Magnus has come to say farewell to the mansion he thinks of as a condemned prisoner awaiting execution, like Mary, Queen of Scots at Fotheringhay. He wants to walk round the derelict building one last time before it's completely destroyed by dynamite. By his father.

It was said that King James I destroyed Fotheringhay Castle because his mother was killed there, but the truth was less romantic. The castle fell into such disrepair, it had to be pulled down and the stones were taken to be used in other buildings. Almost four hundred years later, Scottish baronial halls, erected as status symbols by affluent Victorians, stand empty and unwanted, an architectural embarrassment and financial burden, worth more to their owners as building materials than as decaying country houses, too expensive to heat or maintain. Donald McGillivray, demolition agent to the Perthshire gentry, belongs to a fine tradition of thrifty, unsentimental Scots who have long seen the value of recycled materials.

Magnus has heard his parents talk about razing buildings to the ground, but he can't see how you can raise a house to ground level, not if it's three storeys high and built like a palace. Dynamite makes buildings collapse and sink to the ground. For as long as he can remember, his mother has taken him to watch his father at work, but Magnus notices she sometimes weeps a little. She says it's because the destruction of so much history makes her sad, but Magnus always wonders if there's more to it than that. He was glad when he grew big enough to stand on his own to watch the demolition. He hated to be held by his mother, hated to see the tears filming her bright blue eyes. He sensed a sadness in her that he couldn't understand. How could you feel sorry for a building? It was just bricks and mortar, wooden floorboards, slabs of marble. And dust.

Magnus pushes open a door on the first floor and walks into the middle of an enormous room with an ornate ceiling that resembles a wedding cake. Lumps of greyish-white plaster have broken off and lie on the floor. In front of the fireplace there's a hole in the floorboards through which he can see the room below. He lies on his front, spreading his weight over the rotten boards, sneezing as dust rises in a cloud. He looks down, then picks up a lump of damp plaster, drops it through the hole and watches as it smashes to pieces on the tiled floor below. He gets to his knees and crawls over to the wall where he studies the peeling wallpaper, embossed with gold and stained with black mould. Taking hold of a loose edge, he pulls gently, removing a large section. As he folds it to put in his pocket, the paper crackles, then crumbles to pieces. He decides to keep them anyway and shoves them into his trouser pocket.

Magnus gets to his feet and looks round the room, noting the pale rectangles on the wall where pictures used to hang. He wonders where they've gone and if they were portraits of the people who lived at Drummond Hall. He stands in the middle of the floor, legs apart, arms extended, as if he's trying to fill the room. Closing his eyes, he tries to imagine what the house will feel like when it's blown up. It will lift off its foundations and into the air – he'd seen that happen – then the house will crumple and fall and then there will be nothing, nothing but dust.

He tries to imagine the floor pushing up suddenly through his feet, lifting him into the air; tries to imagine the noise of walls cracking, wood splitting, the ceiling caving in on him, then taking him down, down to the ground, crushing him under tons of plaster, wood and stone.

He can't imagine it.

Instead, he leaps into the air as high as he can and yells, 'Bang!', bracing himself to fall through the floorboards onto the tiles below. But the boards hold and jar his ankles as he lands. In the roof, startled pigeons begin to fret and jackdaws protest in the chimney.

Taking a stub of black crayon from his pocket, Magnus approaches one of the walls where there is a pale rectangle of wallpaper he can reach. Instinctively, he looks over his shoulder then, reaching up, quickly draws a face with a scribble of curly hair and a big smile. Underneath he writes:

MAGNUS DONALD MCGILLLIVRAY
Age 12
1976

He stands back to admire his handiwork, then looks round the room a final time. There's an odd prickling sensation behind his eyes, as if he might be about to cry, so he turns and, forgetting to be cautious, runs out of the room, along the corridor and back down the wide, stone staircase. He charges through the hall, kicking up clouds of dust. Flinging himself at the unlocked door, he yanks it open and runs outside, gulping fresh air into his lungs. Not stopping to look back, he jumps on to his bike and peddles down the long drive as fast as he can, his eyes blind with tears and dust.

Chapter 12

Fay

On the evening of the party Jessie and I had fun getting ready together, advising each other about accessories. It was a hoot. She had the casting vote as to which of the three pairs of outrageous shoes I'd brought with me would go best with my dress. She chose the strappy, high-heeled, beaded satin pair, so glamour triumphed over comfort. That suited me. I was in for a difficult evening anyway and I'm of the school of thought that, if you're already feeling miserable, you might as well clean the oven. It can't make you feel any worse.

Jessie looked great in a fuchsia dress and jacket from M&S. I thought I detected Emily's guiding hand here, but decided to say nothing and give Jessie all the credit for her good taste. I told her she looked stunning and that her silver hair was the perfect foil for the fuchsia.

I took a last look at myself in Jessie's wardrobe mirror and cursed Morag for talking me in to such a strong statement of an outfit. But, as I examined my profile critically, even I had to admit I looked good. Looked good; felt crap.

Jessie and I shared a taxi to Tully and I was grateful not have to make my entrance alone. We arrived bearing gifts: home bakes from Jessie (dozens of sausage rolls and a haystack of cheese straws), plus two bottles of rather good champagne from me – one for each couple. I also had a homemade present for Emily and Rick in my bag: a small textile picture based on a nineteenth century Valentine's card, but I wanted to give it to them privately as I'd been unable to think of any sort of personal present I could give Magnus and Nina. John Lewis caters for most occasions, from gay weddings to the birth of triplets, but they hadn't been able to furnish me with either a card or present appropriate for the engagement of my ex-husband. I'd felt tempted to buy a *With*

Deepest Sympathy card for Nina but I didn't think she'd appreciate facetious humour on what must be for her a very romantic occasion. (Magnus on the other hand almost certainly would, but that might have upset Nina even more.)

The taxi struggled up the hill and deposited us outside Tully's massive wooden front door which stood open, spilling a welcoming light into the courtyard. I paid off the taxi and we went in. Nina had made the lobby area look attractive with bowls of chrysanthemums and trailing ivy, no doubt cut from the garden, but someone had had the bright idea of making bows out of Buchanan and McGillivray tartan ribbon, tying them on to twigs artfully arranged in pewter jugs. The colours clashed horribly (there's a lot of yellow in Buchanan) and the little bows looked twee against Tully's stark and uncompromising stone walls. I must have made some small noise of disapproval because Jessie looked at me, then followed my gaze. 'Och well,' she said softly. 'We don't all have your artistic talent, Fay. Nina's a primary teacher. You have to make allowances.' I laughed at my visual snobbery as we handed over our coats to a teenage boy on cloakroom duty and then the home bakes, which were gratefully received by two smiling female clones of Rick, one young, one not, who introduced themselves as his sister and mother. After an exclamatory conversation about family likeness – the female Hamptons assured me Emily and I could pass for sisters – Jessie and I ascended the turnpike stair to the Great Hall.

As we climbed to the first floor, the temperature rose as warmth from the hall permeated the chilly air. I smelled wood smoke, whisky and the heady scents of lilies and ripening fruit. I was already intoxicated and not a drop had passed my lips. Things were looking up.

Magnus, Nina, Emily and Rick were lined up in the doorway of the Great Hall, forming a reception committee. Magnus and Nina were talking to guests but Emily sprang forward and threw her arms round Jessie, hugging her tight. Rick leaned forward and kissed me on the cheek in a circumspect manner. I handed him one of my gift-wrapped bottles and, as he turned to show Emily, my eyes swivelled toward Magnus, now bending to catch something Nina was saying. Her head was close to his and I admired the cascade of blonde hair, dazzling against Magnus' silvered dark mane. He looked up and his gaze travelled over me for a moment, our eyes meeting finally. I turned away to greet my daughter.

Emily is tall, slim and dark and would probably look good in a bin liner, but she'd put together an outfit with her usual flair. Combing the vintage shops, she'd come up trumps: a flirty, cherry red *crêpe de chine* frock and shoes I'd have killed for, that miraculously matched the dress. She'd completed the outfit with a beaded black bolero and accessorised with an antique jet brooch and necklace that looked familiar. (I suspected Jessie might have raided her jewellery box for the occasion, or perhaps she'd given them as gifts.) Emily looked chic and festive – not an easy trick to pull off, especially in a freezing castle.

We embraced without speaking, not because there was nothing to say but because there was too much, all of it impossible to put into words. After a moment I placed my hands on Emily's shoulders and held her at arm's length.

'Let me look at you... Oh, darling, you look *wonderful*!'

'So do you, Mum!' Emily replied, laughing. 'You're definitely giving Nina and me a run for our money!'

'Is it too much?' I whispered.

'No, you look fab! Doesn't she, Rick?'

There was the slightest of pauses before Rick said, 'You're the second best-looking woman here tonight, Fay.'

Emily laughed and kissed him on the cheek. Without meeting my eye, Rick turned away to speak to Jessie.

'Show me your ring!' I exclaimed, changing the subject abruptly.

Emily extended her left hand and fluttered her fingers under my nose, giggling. The modest little diamond ring glittered against her dark outfit, like the first star in the sky. I made a squealing sound that would have spoken volumes to any woman and been incomprehensible to any man. Jessie cooed and Rick smiled tolerantly. Swallowing back a sob of pride, I turned to him and said, my voice fierce with emotion, 'I hope you realise what a lucky man you are!'

He grinned, took Emily's hand and raised it to his lips.

'Indeed I do.'

I heard laughter and footsteps behind me ascending the stairs as more guests arrived. I leaned forward and patting my bag, said, 'I've made you a little something for the occasion. I'll give it to you later.' Emily's eyes began to brim. 'No, don't start! You'll spoil your make-up! And so will I!'

'Mum, you really didn't have to go to so much trouble.'

'It was a pleasure. It's not every day my only child gets engaged. These milestones should be commemorated with something more romantic than a gift voucher and more lasting than champagne, don't you think?' Squeezing her hand, I said, 'We'll talk later,' and I moved away, dabbing at the corners of my eyes.

As the guests in front moved on into the Great Hall, Jessie stepped forward to embrace her son and his fiancée, leaving me at liberty to admire the elder of the two happy couples. Magnus was in full Highland rig. Tall and broad-shouldered enough to carry it off, nothing suited him better. His wayward hair actually looked less eccentric. Magnus was at home in a kilt and the McGillivray tartan (predominantly red with some bright green and blue) suited both his dark colouring and the festive occasion. I was aware of a very odd and uncomfortable mix of emotions as I regarded him, but the sight of my beautiful, happy daughter had already shredded my composure.

I'd only met Nina a few times but I'd heard a lot about her from Emily and Jessie. She looked lovely, in an untidy, pre-Raphaelite sort of way: her creamy skin, dusted with freckles, glowed with health and she had the pale permanent tan that comes with a love of the outdoors. She was wearing a strapless pale blue velvet gown that made the most of her opulent figure and youthful skin, but she'd ruined the effect with a silver organza stole. It no doubt warded off some of Tully's vicious draughts, but the effect was more Christmas tree fairy than elegant.

Nina and I greeted each other politely. I couldn't bring myself to kiss her and I certainly wasn't prepared to kiss Magnus, so we all just smiled at each other, mouthing appropriate platitudes. During this exchange, Magnus rotated an empty champagne glass as he listened, his long, agile fingers holding the stem while he beat a silent tattoo on the glass bowl with his other hand. The movements reminded me how he used to fidget, how he could never settle when home on leave. We'd joked he should take up knitting to keep his hands busy.

As we chatted, I studied Nina's eyes. Brown and long-lashed, they were striking but not, I thought, particularly intelligent. Her smile was wide but a touch perfunctory – the smile she reserved for women perhaps? I suspected men received a more dazzling version, but I may have been doing her an injustice. The lack of warmth in her smile might not have been because I was a woman. It perhaps had more to do with my being the *other* woman. I felt sorry for the poor girl and broke away as soon as it was polite to do so. Magnus pointed us in the direction of the drinks table and, as I turned away, Nina positively beamed with relief.

Tully comes into its own for high days and holidays. Decorated with flowers, bright with candles and the flickering light from the log fire burning in the inglenook, the Great Hall looked spectacular. I remembered when it had no ceiling and the only adornments were the remnants of jackdaw nests. Tully had come a long way. So, I reflected, had Magnus.

I averted my eyes from the (presumably) homemade bunting Nina had strung around the room and scanned the Hall for people I knew. I didn't expect to find many. Magnus – or rather his illness – had alienated many of our friends. Some we'd lost when he quit the army, others we'd lost touch with when we left Glasgow to move to Perthshire. Those who'd persevered were then divided by the divorce, the circumstances of which tended to make people choose sides. So I wasn't surprised to find there was no one in the room I knew well apart from Davy Campbell, our builder and handyman who'd helped Magnus shift tons of earth and rubble before they started to rebuild. They'd sorted the rubble carefully and classified it according to its usefulness. Wherever possible, every piece was re-used. This was the decree of *Hysterical Scotland* (as Magnus called the august body which had given him a generous grant to restore Tully) but recycling also saved having to buy and transport new stone.

Davy Campbell was a hard worker, fiercely loyal to Magnus and his vision of Tully reborn, but I'd soon discovered there was a limit to the amount of conversation you could have with a young man who got excited about rubble classification. Magnus used to say admiringly of his right hand man, 'What Davy doesn't know about machicolated walls isn't worth knowing,' which about sums it up really.

Turning to Jessie, I said, 'Do you need a sit-down after all those stairs? Why don't you go and settle yourself in that window seat while I get us some drinks. Look, there's Davy Campbell over there. Is that his mother, do you think? The large woman, bending his ear?'

'Och no, that's Mrs Buchanan, *Nina's* mother! And the wee fellow beside her is her husband, Willie. They're a very nice couple,' said Jessie. 'She's English, but they've lived here for years.'

I studied Magnus' prospective in-laws. 'I wonder how they feel about the engagement? Magnus isn't exactly what anyone would describe as a good catch, with his debts and money-pit castle.'

'No, I suppose not,' Jessie replied, looking a little crest-fallen.

'There again,' I added cheerfully, 'Not many grooms have been awarded the George Cross.'

Jessie brightened, but Willie Buchanan didn't look thrilled at the prospect of acquiring a decorated war hero for a son-in-law. He was a grey little man with thinning hair of indeterminate colour and eyes the colour of dishwater. His face bore an expression of such graven impassivity, he almost blended into Tully's stone walls. The same could not be said of his wife. They say if a man wants to know what sort of woman his wife will become, he should study his mother-in-law. Magnus is a brave man. I hadn't realised quite *how* brave until I saw Mrs Buchanan.

Nina is what some would describe admiringly as a big, strapping girl. Her mother, similarly proportioned, was built on a grander scale. *Wagnerian* was the word that came to mind. Fair and tall, she wore a voluminous green velvet kaftan that – fortunately, I think – left everything to the imagination. Her impressive height was exaggerated by an old-fashioned bouffant hairstyle which drew her greying blonde hair back into a French pleat from which a few wisps escaped, framing her face with corkscrews of hair, reminiscent of her daughter's fairytale locks.

I was prepared to concede that Mrs B might once have been handsome until she smiled, revealing a set of large, yellowing teeth that reminded me forcibly of piano keys. Guests were given ample opportunity to examine Mrs B's dentistry. She laughed loud and often, making a braying sound that carried easily from one side of the Great Hall to the other, as did most of her conversation. I wondered what she'd done for a living. Had I been responsible for her vocational guidance at school, I might have suggested that, with her operatic voice production and talent for attention-grabbing, she should consider a career as a town crier.

A buffet supper was set out on the fake Jacobean banqueting table in the middle of the hall. The table had been given to us after a film company had shot some of a historical drama at Tully. Magnus had hoped this would do for Tully what *Monty Python and the Holy Grail* had done for Doune Castle. The film company overran their budget and when they couldn't pay our fee, Magnus demanded payment in kind, or rather props. The table was a bargain, but at the time I questioned the usefulness of all the pewter jugs and horn beakers, but now they happily served a turn, holding bunches of asters and chrysanthemums.

The table was mercifully free of bunting and tartan ribbon. Someone – Mrs Buchanan perhaps? – had done a spectacular (but rather gaudy) arrangement of flowers and fruit as a centrepiece. I collected a few canapés on a plate and two glasses of champagne and took them back to Jessie who now had a little group gathered round her, which included Rick's father, Frederick senior, as genial and suave as I'd expected a merchant banker to be. He and Jessie were discussing patronage of the arts and I joined in briefly when Jessie mentioned some of my corporate commissions.

124

Frederick Hampton expressed an interest and surprised me by saying he'd checked out my website and admired my work.

It was turning into an evening for compliments, but apart from Hampton, who was perhaps being professionally polite, no one seemed very anxious to speak to me. What can one say to the ex-wife, other than, 'How brave of you to come'? So I sank on to the empty window seat in one of the deep alcoves that Nina had made comfortable with tart's boudoir cushions. (I didn't begrudge Nina putting her own stamp on the home Magnus and I had created, but I couldn't bring myself to admire her taste in furnishings.) I wondered what had happened to the cushions I'd made from faded velvets, old damasks and brocades. I hadn't taken them with me because I'd made them for Tully and thought they should stay. Magnus wouldn't have thrown them out, so I assumed they were mouldering away in store. I tucked myself into the window seat and from this relatively secluded vantage point, I was able to sit and sip my champagne, observing the party.

Magnus was a good host. As an army officer he was used to putting all sorts of people at their ease. As a soldier he knew how to have a good time under the most trying, even dangerous circumstances. As a Scot he waxed loquacious and sentimental the more whisky he consumed, but as a Scot he was still able to dance a (limping) reel with the best part of a bottle inside him. Magnus was always good fun at parties. He didn't get maudlin or aggressive, he didn't even get loud, so as I observed him across the Great Hall I was concerned to see that, whenever he wasn't actually speaking or listening to a guest, he looked oddly detached. He was conscientious in his duties as host, filling glasses and laughing at people's jokes, but I knew Magnus and I knew his ways. He never looks worried, even when he is. (You can't afford to look worried as an officer. It's bad for morale and suggests you aren't in command of the situation.) Magnus had developed a look of bland composure that I'd learned to recognise as his response to stress. He switches on some sort of facial automatic pilot that allows his brain to think very fast, while his inscrutable expression gives nothing away.

The trick was unnerving, but I'd grown used to it over the

years. It was a coping mechanism imposed by the demands of his job and sustained by his willpower, which was phenomenal. I think of myself as determined, stubborn even, but in a clash of wills, Magnus always won because he was prepared to sit it out, calmly and without rancour, until I caved, which inevitably I did. (Witness our purchase of Tully, which was entirely Magnus' doing.)

So when I spotted that calm, slightly absent look, as if part of his brain were elsewhere, grappling with an explosive device, I felt uneasy, as I used to when we lived together. Only now there was nothing I could do about it. It wasn't my problem anymore. But still I watched him. Out of habit, I suppose. And concern. Or maybe, if I'm honest, just because Magnus was still, at forty-five, the tallest and best looking man in the room.

I don't know how long I'd been watching him, lost in thought, when I realised he was looking at me. With that look. The look that meant trouble. Trouble for Magnus. I averted my gaze immediately and tried to find someone in my vicinity whom I could engage in conversation. Jessie was now listening to Mrs Buchanan (her glazed expression rather like her son's) and I thought it best not to interrupt what was probably a mother-of-the-bride monologue. When I turned back, my view of the room was occluded by Magnus' sporran. He was standing in front of me, clutching an open bottle of champagne.

'Your glass is empty. Allow me.'

When southerners of a salacious turn of mind used to quiz Magnus about what he wore under his kilt, he'd reply, truthfully, "An air of mystery". Before my thoughts started running in that old direction, I got to my feet. This still only brought my eyes up to the level of his shoulders which looked splendid in his fitted Prince Charlie jacket. I held out my glass and, as I watched him pour, noted that his hand wasn't quite steady. My concern increased. Magnus could build a house of cards under sniper fire. Was he experiencing one of his flashbacks? I peered up at his face. 'Are you all right?'

His eyebrows rose. 'Why d'you ask?'

'I wondered if you're OK with all this noise? The music's

quite loud.'

'Not,' said Magnus, raising his voice, 'if you're under thirty.'

'If you turned it down no one would notice. They're all busy chatting.'

Magnus surveyed the room. 'Aye, true enough.' He turned back and examined me. 'But you're not.'

I looked away. 'You know I have mixed feelings about the occasion.'

'Are they mixed? I thought they were one hundred per cent negative.'

'Magnus, please don't start. All this... Being here tonight... It isn't easy for me, you know.'

He nodded. 'I can see that. But I don't know why.'

'For Heaven's sake! I'm here as a singleton, watching my ex-husband celebrate his engagement to a lovely young woman half my age—'

'You're not fifty-six. Not unless you used to lie about your age.'

'You know what I mean.'

'No, I don't. And I don't know why you didn't bring a man. I didn't expect you to suffer all this on your own.'

'Thank you, but I don't have one to bring. At the *moment*,' I added hurriedly.

His eyebrows rose again. 'I apologise on behalf of my entire sex for their lamentable lack of taste.' He refilled his own glass and this time I avoided watching his hand. 'Or is it just that you're extremely picky?'

'As it happens, I *am* extremely picky—'

'Well, not *that* picky if you were prepared to go to bed with Rick on ten minutes' acquaintance. But I suppose you must have found him irresistible? Emily obviously does, so maybe it's a genetic thing. Or a reaction against me, perhaps? We could scarcely be more different, could we – Rick and I?'

'Magnus, I really don't think it's appropriate for us to be having this conversation. Presumably you came over to fill my glass. You've done that, so you can go away and circulate now. I may not have been able to rustle up a man for tonight, but I can fend for myself at parties, thank you.'

He was silenced by the snub, or so I thought until he spoke again.

'I didn't come over to fill your glass. I came over to tell you, in all sincerity, that there isn't a woman here tonight to touch you.' I stared at him, bracing myself for the punch-line, but it didn't come. He lifted his glass to me. 'I've never seen you look more alluring. And...'

'And what?' My voice was just a whisper.

'I thought on this special night, you might have spared me that.'

The room seemed to go suddenly quiet, then I realised it was because of a rushing sound in my ears. My heart also seemed to be thumping painfully against my ribs. 'You mustn't say things like that! Supposing someone *hears* you? They might tell Nina.'

He glanced round the room and shrugged. 'Who'd do that? These are her friends and family. Who'd repeat such a remark?'

'I might.'

He laughed. 'You're neither brave enough nor bad enough.'

I laid my hand on his arm. 'Magnus, you should call off this engagement.'

'Aye, probably. But I'm not going to. Och, I'll be sober tomorrow – at *some* point – and mental order will be restored. For now, I'm just indulging in an uncharacteristic bout of self-pity. And allowing myself the indulgence of making a pass at you.'

I laughed nervously. 'It's getting to be a habit!'

His eyes narrowed. 'You're referring to the kiss at your flat?... Never, never in my *life*, Fay, have I shown more restraint. Believe me, you got off lightly.' He looked down and appeared to study the contents of his glass. 'I can't handle wanting you that much. So I have to close the door. For good. And this is how I'm doing it.' He looked up again and gestured toward his guests. 'With a flourish!'

I watched as he emptied his glass, turned and strode across the Great Hall where he took up a position at Nina's side, in front of the roaring fire. She carried on talking but acknowledged Magnus by linking her arm through his in a comfortable but proprietorial way. He looked down at the floor and his curls fell forward, masking his face, but still I didn't take my eyes off him. Then suddenly he lifted his head and looked straight at me. The expression in his eyes propelled me, almost stumbling, from the room.

Finding myself at the foot of the turnpike stair, I kicked off my shoes and began to climb hurriedly, heading for a place where I knew I would be alone.

Chapter 13

Fay

The temperature of the cold stone under my stockinged feet sent me racing up the spiral staircase, past the room that used to be our bedroom and up again until I arrived at the top of the tower and the door that led out on to the roof walkway.

I hesitated as I heard far below me the muffled sound of violin and accordion. I wondered whether Magnus had been prevailed upon to dance and almost turned round to go back down again. But there was something I wanted to see more than Magnus dancing. The stars. The stars I never saw in Glasgow, constellations scattered like diamond dust across the black sky. I would freeze half to death on Tully's roof, but I was determined to watch the stars. Tonight of all nights.

There were hooks on the wall by the door and a few coats and scarves hung there, just as they had when I lived at Tully. On the floor stood two pairs of wellington boots. I slipped my feet into the smaller pair, noting how much bigger than mine Nina's feet must be. My hands hovered over her duffel coat, but settled instead on Magnus' old fleece jacket. As I zipped it up, my fingers found the hole at the front, made by a flying piece of burning rubbish, ejected suddenly from a bonfire. The fleece had melted, leaving a neat round hole. Afterwards I asked Magnus not to wear the jacket because the hole looked as if it had been made by a bullet and sat directly over his heart.

Clad in Nina's wellingtons and Magnus' fleece (which would have gone round me twice), I opened the door and stepped out on to the roof. The cold hit me like a slap in the face. In addition to the November-in-Perthshire factor, there was the on-top-of-a-tower wind-chill factor. For the hundredth time, I asked myself how I'd survived even two winters at Tully. Then I had to ask myself, why I was sensing a twinge of something that felt suspiciously like nostalgia. But starlight can do that to a person. Stars can render you insensible to a crick in your neck and the chill that creeps up through ancient stones right into your bones.

Magnus said no matter how cold he got at Tully, he would never be as cold as he was in the Falklands, lying in the mud and snow, disoriented, looking up at stars that were in completely different positions from the stars he saw in Scotland. He used to say the cold at Tully didn't touch him, couldn't touch him because of the Falklands. I think he derived some sort of perverse comfort from that thought.

I used to derive a form of comfort from the stars, but for a rather macabre reason. I knew the ways in which Magnus could die. There was the good, clean way – a sniper's bullet, for example – or the messy way: a bomb. A bomb might collapse and destroy his body internally with almighty shock waves, or it might turn him into human mincemeat, spraying him into the air, leaving me nothing to bury.

When I used to look up at the stars all those years ago, thinking how our very existence (and theirs) had arisen as the consequence of one unimaginable explosion, I would remember a quotation from Shakespeare's *Romeo and Juliet*, which I'd studied at school. I used to mutter some of Juliet's lines as a sort of consolatory prayer.

"And, when he shall die,
Take him and cut him out in little stars,
And he will make the face of heaven so fine
That all the world will be in love with night
And pay no worship to the garish sun."

Anxious and agnostic, I needed to know where I could find Magnus in the event of his messy death. I needed to know where I could go to feel his presence, to feel that his sacrifice had been worthwhile, that something of him somehow persisted. I tried to see him in Emily, but she favours me, not Magnus. I would study Jessie's features in the hope of seeing an older version of Magnus, but Jessie didn't resemble Magnus either, apart from her curly hair. (She once told me he was very like his father as a young man, but she didn't offer to illustrate her point with photographs. Now I knew why.)

I looked for Magnus and I found him in the stars. What could be more eternal, more beautiful or more glorious? Sentimental of me, I know, and irrational. But it got me through the night. A lot of nights. And when Magnus was away on a tour of duty it comforted me to think we both looked up at the stars; that however big the world was, we at least shared a sky.

As I searched for familiar patterns in the sky above Tully, my eyes began to water with the cold – I like to think that was the cause – and my craning neck started to complain, so I looked down at the courtyard garden, patchily visible in the light from the Great Hall's windows, then I looked beyond the barmkin wall to the Dule Tree, an ancient sycamore. According to local legend, if you stand beneath the Dule Tree's boughs, you can hear the sound of a corpse swinging.

Earlier inhabitants of Tully used the tree to hang wrong-doers and the merely troublesome. Into the latter category fell an unlucky fellow known as Gypsy Jack. He was supposedly hanged from this tree in the seventeenth century, after he'd abducted Isobel Moncrieffe, mistress of Tully. Isobel was very young and her husband very old. Since Jack was also known as The Black-eyed Gypsy, we can perhaps assume Isobel was not entirely unwilling. She might even have connived at her own disgrace.

Isobel and her lover were eventually apprehended and Jack was summarily hanged by her cuckolded husband from the Dule Tree (*dule* being an old Scots word for sorrow). Isobel was forced to watch. She was dragged, so the story goes, to the top of Tullibardine Tower, from where the Dule Tree is plainly visible. Her lover died to the accompaniment of her screams, which might have been a comfort to him I suppose, but not, I would have thought, a great one.

Jack's body was left to hang, putrefying, as a lesson to other lustful young men. Isobel was imprisoned in Tully and her husband decreed she would never leave the confines of its walls. But Isobel found a way.

She was allowed to exercise on the roof walkway and it was her custom to go up there to contemplate the Dule Tree and weep. One winter's day, when her minder was perhaps sheltering in the doorway, avoiding the scything wind, Isobel climbed onto the parapet wall and threw herself from the roof, flying through the air in the direction of the Dule Tree, calling out her lover's name. Or so the story goes. I'm inclined to think her stunned waiting-woman failed to take into account the wind resistance offered by Isobel's long robes. Ballooning layers of clothing might have slowed her descent, but eventually the poor woman hit the ground and died, like her lover, of a broken neck.

I used to wonder whether, when she leaped from the tower, poor mad Isobel was trying to touch the stars. She and Jack would have gazed up at them, navigated by them, perhaps slept under them, when they were on the run. Or perhaps she knew those words of Shakespeare's and was trying to join her true love, her black-eyed gipsy, without whom life was apparently insupportable. I preferred to think that's what she was doing when she dashed out her brains in the courtyard.

Of course Isobel's death leap might not have been made at night, but I'd always imagined she would have jumped into blackness, so she wouldn't see the ground coming up to hit her. And because perhaps the very last thing she wanted to see before she departed this life was the stars...

I shivered convulsively and turned up the collar of Magnus' fleece. This was what Tully did to me, with its old stones and stories, its blood and its ghosts. Magnus gloried in it and saw it as so much history, but I felt it as an accumulation of pain and sorrow. Magnus looked at the Dule Tree and marvelled that, after hundreds of years, it still stood. I looked at it and thought of that young woman, forced to watch her lover die. I never told Magnus, but whenever there was a storm at Tully, I used to hope a bolt of lightning would strike the Dule Tree and fell it, remove it from the horizon, because eventually, when I stood at the top of the tower, that's all I could see: the Dule Tree and a swinging corpse.

I plunged my hands deep into Magnus' fleece pockets and

tried to banish my melancholy thoughts. I stamped my feet up and down, but in the depths of Nina's wellingtons, numbness persisted.

'As I said earlier,' a voice announced, 'you've never looked lovelier.'

I wheeled round and saw Magnus silhouetted in the doorway, holding my shoes.

'Oh! You startled me.'

'What the hell are you doing up here?'

'Looking at the stars. I never see them in Glasgow.' I stared down at my feet. 'I hope Nina won't mind me borrowing her wellingtons.'

'Shouldn't think so,' said Magnus, stepping on to the walkway and closing the door behind him. 'She's borrowing your husband.'

'You're not my husband and Nina hasn't borrowed you. She's in this for keeps, Magnus. As you should be.'

He didn't reply but studied my ridiculous shoes, dangling from his fingers.

'How in God's name do you manage to walk in these things?'

'Hours of painful practice.'

'You never wore shoes like this when you were married to me. Have you become a shoe fetishist? Or do you now consort with men who are?'

'None of your business, Magnus. Not anymore. Let's just say I've developed other aspects of my personality since we split up. I've grown, I hope.'

Magnus eyed the shoes again. '*Taller*, certainly. Pity. I used to like you small.'

'Oh, being small is fine when you're young—'

'Except when they ask for proof of your age in pubs. That used to make you mad.'

'Young and short isn't so bad. You have a wider choice of boyfriends for a start. But old and short—'

'You're not old.'

'No, I know I'm not. But sometimes I *feel* old.'

'Aye, I know what you mean. "It's not the years, it's the mileage." Who was it said that?'

'Indiana Jones, I think. Hadn't you better return to your guests? They'll be wondering where you are. And even if Nina doesn't notice we're both missing, I'm sure her mother will. She's been giving me the evil eye.'

'Och, it's not personal!' Magnus exclaimed. 'Everyone gets that Medusa look. Have you not seen Willie Buchanan? Turned to stone years ago! Now showing signs of serious erosion.'

I smiled but registered that Magnus was building up to something. Whenever he went off on a riff like this, it was because he was softening me up. So I waited. And it came.

'Fay?'

'Yes?'

'You wouldn't lie to me, would you?'

I sighed. 'Is this going to be about Freddie?'

'*Rick.*'

I hugged the fleece around me, hunching my shoulders against the cold. 'I *know* he's called Rick. I just forget.'

'It isn't about Rick. Or Freddie. So... would you lie to me?'

I thought for a moment, then said, 'No. I wouldn't. I don't think I *could* lie to you. Not now.'

'Now?'

'Not now I know how you feel. About me, I mean.'

'So can I ask you a question? Two questions, in fact? Then I'll leave you to your stars.'

'Fire away,' I replied, with a growing sense of foreboding.

'Question number one... Are you OK? I mean, *really*. Are you OK?'

The question took me by surprise. 'Yes, I think so. Well, I'm not exactly *happy*, but, yes, I'm OK. Life is... *steady*, I suppose. I have lots of work and... well, there are men occasionally... What was your other question?'

There was a stiff breeze on the walkway now. It lifted Magnus' curls and blew them back from his face revealing furrows on his brow and deep lines around his mouth that ran from nostril to jaw. I thought he looked tense, but it might just have been a distorting effect of the moonlight.

'If you could turn back the clock,' he said softly, 'Would you still divorce me?'

I hadn't seen that one coming and tried to bluster my way out of it. 'We *can't* turn back the clock! What's the point of hypothetical questions?'

'Answer me, Fay. Remember, you said you wouldn't lie.'

'And I won't.'

'Well?'

'I don't know.'

He looked down and seemed to consider my words, then he said, 'As your answer wasn't exactly conclusive, can I ask another question?'

'For God's sake, Magnus—'

'Same conditions. Please tell the truth.' He stared up at the glittering sky. He looked very pale in the moonlight and I could see his Adam's apple moving up and down. When he looked back at me, his anxious expression had been wiped and replaced with that calm, abstracted look, as if he was only mildly interested in my answer. But I wasn't deceived. I never saw Magnus dismantle a bomb, but God knows, I'd spent enough of my life imagining it. In my waking nightmares, this was how he looked: alert, but not agitated.

After what seemed like a long time, he said, almost casually, 'Do you still love me?'

That one I did see coming. I resisted the temptation to turn away – he might have construed that as some sort of answer – and I continued to meet his unblinking gaze.

'Well?... Do you?'

I opened my mouth to reply, then shut it again.

'You work so bloody hard at conveying that you feel nothing for me,' he went on. 'Nothing more than irritation. Why d'you have to work so hard, Fay?' Watching me carefully, he added, 'You said you wouldn't lie.'

'I know.' I walked toward him and held out my hands for my shoes. 'But I didn't say I would answer.'

His eyes widened. '*That's* your answer?'

'Yes. That's my answer.'

He swore and thrust the shoes into my hands. 'You know what this means? The fact that you refuse to answer?'

'No, I have absolutely no idea what it means, Magnus. I wish I did.'

I opened the door to the stairs, stepped out of my successor's wellington boots, removed the jacket and hung it back on the peg. Then, still carrying my shoes, I wound my way downstairs toward noise, warmth and light.

On my way down I noticed a light under the bedroom door and could hear someone moving around inside. Nina, I assumed. I felt a momentary pang of something unpleasant – jealousy, I suppose – at the thought of another woman occupying the bedroom I'd shared with Magnus. I paused outside the door, not to eavesdrop, but because I suddenly had a vision of the interior of the room as I'd known it, with its huge fireplace, its moth-eaten wall hangings and the four-poster bed hung with the thick and very necessary curtains we used to keep out draughts and shut the world away.

Standing outside the room, exploring a hitherto unsuspected taste for masochism (my stocking feet had now lost all feeling), I heard the familiar crunch of a log being thrown on to the fire. Nina had come up to check. She was making sure there would be a good blaze when they went to bed. This was after all, her engagement party and nothing was more flattering to the naked human form than flickering firelight. Not that Nina had any need of flattering light, I reflected, as I peeled my icy feet from the stone floor and continued my descent.

At the foot of the stairs, I met Rick. As I bent to put on my shoes, he said, 'Fay, you haven't seen Emily, have you? She seems to have disappeared.'

'No, I've been up on the roof.' He looked surprised. 'Just getting a breath of air. The stars look amazing. You should get Emily to take you up there.'

'Oh. Yes, I will. When I find her... Actually, I wonder if I could have a word with you?'

'You mean now? What about?'

'It's about Emily.'

'Is something wrong?'

'Oh, no. Nothing's wrong. But I do need to talk to you.'

'Well, could we go and stand near the fire? I'm frozen.'

'Yes, of course.'

He held the door open for me and as we entered the Great Hall I saw Mrs B's beady eyes register my reappearance. As I headed for the fireplace, like a heat-seeking missile, I felt her eyes bore into the back of my head, but I ignored the uncomfortable sensation and stood facing the fire, my hands extended toward the blaze. It was throwing out a lot of heat and most guests had moved away. The accordionist and fiddle player were taking a break but there was a gentle hum of conversation. Rick pulled up a chair and a stool and waited for me to sit, but I was happy hogging the fire, waiting for sensation to return to my feet.

Warmth, alcohol and the emotional strain of talking to Magnus meant I was tired, but even if I'd been firing on all cylinders, I doubt I would have remembered about the Laird's Lug.

Chapter 14

Emily stood beside the log fire in her father's bedroom, shivering in her slip. She took her wet dress and spread it over the back of a chair, pushing it as close to the fire as she dared. She bent and threw another log on to the coals, but the big log all but extinguished the dying embers. Peering into the coalscuttle, she saw a few lumps at the bottom and tossed them on to the fire but, as the temperature in the room continued to fall, so did her spirits.

Should she just return to the party in her wet dress and tough it out? She'd decided to take off her champagne-soaked dress to dry it, but now she was very cold. She picked up a woollen throw from the end of the bed and put it round her shoulders. Resisting an impulse to cry, Emily swore mentally at Rick who was responsible for drenching her. It wasn't like him to be clumsy, but he'd been on edge all evening. This was understandable, she supposed. It was only the second time he'd met his future mother-in-law and Fay hadn't exactly been cordial the first time. Emily had assured him Fay wasn't normally so frosty, it was just "the Magnus effect". Individually her parents were delightful, but as a couple they brought out the worst in each other, like a couple of fractious children. Rick had laughed and said he liked both her parents enormously. That hadn't stopped him gesturing awkwardly when chatting to Magnus, knocking Emily's glass and emptying the contents down the front of her dress.

Emily cursed herself for not having the foresight to bring an alternative outfit and she cursed Nina for being two sizes larger. Staring at the feeble flames as they licked the edges of the log, she suddenly thought of a hair-dryer. Nina must have one to dry all that long hair and she'd surely keep it in her bedroom.

Emily went into the *en-suite* Magnus had installed in the

tiny ante-room at the corner of the tower. She opened a cupboard door and as she began to rifle through Nina's toiletries and towels, the sound of voices drifted up from the floor below.

The Laird's Lug.

Emily smiled as she remembered the hole situated in the inglenook fireplace below, connecting it directly to the small room above where, in troubled times, the laird of Tully could have sat, concealed, eavesdropping on his possibly disloyal family and friends below. Magnus had shown Emily how the Laird's Lug (or ear) worked when he was restoring the tower. He'd positioned her in the corner of the bedroom, beside the hole, then he'd gone downstairs. After a few moments, Emily had heard her father's voice, pitched no louder than a conversational level, reciting *Tam o' Shanter*. Listening at the hole, she'd heard every word.

Now, as she pulled a hairdryer triumphantly from the cupboard, she caught her own name and realised she recognised the voices below. Her mother was talking to Rick. To judge from her tone, Fay still wasn't making any effort to be friendly. Irritated, Emily overcame her moral scruples and decided to eavesdrop.

'I really don't think we should be discussing this now, Rick. It's neither the time nor the place. Where is Emily anyway?'

'I don't know. I think she went off with Nina to change her dress.'

'*Why?*'

'I spilled drink down it.'

'Well, she could be back any minute then. In any case, I don't feel at all comfortable talking about this.'

'How do you think *I* feel? And how will Emily feel if she finds out?'

Transfixed by the disembodied voices below, Emily clutched the hairdryer to her chest. She was shivering, but there was no way she was going back to the fire now.

'There's no reason why she ever *should* find out,' Fay replied, sounding exasperated. 'I appreciate that you think being totally honest is the best way to deal with it, but I'm her mother and I'm telling you it would be a big mistake. It's not the kind of thing she'd ever forgive me. Daughters *aren't* very forgiving. Nor are they renowned for understanding their mothers' sexual frustrations. Believe me, it's best forgotten. What happened was just... well, it was just a stupid *mistake*! I must have been out of my mind. Sorry, Rick – no disrespect intended! But I was feeling vulnerable. And terribly lonely.'

'I know. You were in a bit of a state... Which was understandable under the circumstances.'

'Oh, I was just being pathetic! And I was upset because of something Magnus had said – *lots* of things Magnus had said – the night before. But you weren't to know that. So you really shouldn't feel guilty. As I recall, you didn't exactly have to drag me into bed.'

Emily dropped the hairdryer and clapped her hand to her mouth.

'Well, no, I didn't,' said Rick. 'My conscience is clear on that score at least.'

'So can we please just let it go? If we both keep quiet about it, there'll be no consequences.'

'But it feels so... *dishonest*. I really think I should make a clean breast of it to Em. Surely I owe her that?'

'If you do, she'll be incredibly hurt! She might even break off the engagement. Had you thought of that? If you want to keep her, don't tell her. I'm not just saying that to protect myself, though I realise it must look like that. I'm actually thinking about you and Emily. Your future happiness. What happened between you and me was – well, it was very nice, but it was just...'

'Sex?'

'Yes, it was. Some of the nicest sex I've had in a long time, but that's all it was. Let's not kid ourselves. It surely isn't worth Emily *suffering* for it?'

'No, I suppose not. I just dread her finding out.'

'She *won't*. If you're careful and I'm careful, she need never know.'

Stifling her sobs with her hands, Emily slumped against the cold stone wall, struggling to grasp what she'd just heard... Her fiancé had betrayed her. Quite casually, it seemed. And with her *mother*!

'Was it really?' Rick asked.

'Was what really?'

'Was it really some of the nicest sex you've had?'

'Yes, it was,' Fay replied briskly. 'Now can we please stop the ego massage and get on with our allotted roles in life? I'm your mother-in-law-to-be and our sexual history is now precisely that. *History.*'

'If you insist.'

'I do. Trust me, Rick, it's all for the best. In my experience, coming clean about sexual indiscretions is completely disastrous. People don't understand. They get very hurt. And they don't forgive. I know honesty is supposed to be the best policy, but it's definitely not the kindest.'

Emily grabbed a towel and sank to the floor. Burying her face in its folds, she screamed, no longer able to bear her anger and pain in silence.

After Fay had abandoned him on the roof walkway, Magnus spent some time looking up at the stars and then down into the courtyard below, thinking about his ex-wife, his future wife and his concept of duty. He was unclear as to his duty toward Nina; equally unclear where his duty lay as a man still in love with his ex-wife, but he was in no doubt about his duty as host, so he descended the turnpike stair, his mind deeply troubled.

As he passed his bedroom door, he heard the sound of stifled sobs. His first thought was of Fay, then he realised it must be Nina. He opened the door and found Emily sitting on the floor of the *en suite*, her face buried in a towel. She appeared to be in her underwear, so Magnus hung back in the bedroom, resisting an impulse to put his arms round his grief-stricken daughter.

'Emily, what's wrong? What are you doing up here?'

Startled into silence, she lifted her head. Magnus saw red, swollen eyes and cheeks stained with mascara. She'd evidently been crying for some time. He kneeled down beside her.

'What's wrong?'

Making an effort to control her spasmodic breathing, Emily said, 'Rick spilled champagne down my dress.'

Magnus stared at her, uncomprehending. 'Is that *all*?'

'And he—' She broke off and started to whimper.

Magnus took her hand and squeezed it. 'Try to tell me, Em.'

She took a deep breath and said, 'Rick's been sleeping with Mum!'

Magnus let go of her hand and reeled back on his heels. '*Christ*... Who told you?'

Emily stared at him in horror. 'You *knew*?'

Magnus tried to think quickly, but the cold had dulled his faculties. Shock was now adding to his difficulties and he blustered. 'Of course I didn't know!'

'But you said, "Who told you?". '

'No, I didn't!

'You *did*!'

'I meant, who told you this *lie*?'

'No one.'

'So how do you know? I mean, why do you think that—'

'I *heard* them!'

'You heard them *shagging*?'

'No, I heard them talking about it.'

'When?'

'Just now!'

'They were in *here*? In my bedroom?'

'No, downstairs! They're downstairs now. Talking about their affair.'

'*Affair*? Bloody hell, she said it was a one-night stand!'

'So you *did* know!' Emily turned away from him and began to sob again. 'How could you not tell me, Dad?'

'Now, look, Emily, calm down. I know this *looks* bad – really bad – but it isn't as bad as it seems.'

'How could it be any *worse*? My mother's been sleeping with my fiancé and they're downstairs discussing it at my engagement party!'

'Discussing having sex? Are you sure?'

'Oh, yes! I heard all the gory details. Mum said sex with

Rick was the best she'd ever had. The *bitch!*'

'She said that?' Magnus asked in a small voice.

'Yes.'

'She actually *said* that?'

'Yes!'

'I'll kill him! I'll fucking kill him!'

'Dad, my life is in ruins! Please be serious!'

'I *am* serious! Just say the word, Em. I'll tear the bastard limb from limb and throw the bits off the roof for the bloody crows.'

Emily stared at her father, her blackened eyes wide. 'Oh... my... God.'

'What?'

'You're *jealous!*'

'Jealous? What d'you mean?'

'You're jealous of Rick!'

'Bollocks!'

'You *are*. You're jealous of Rick sleeping with Mum! So that means... Oh, God! *You're still in love with Mum!*'

'Don't be ridiculous, Em! We've been divorced for five years!'

'You still love Mum, but you're marrying Nina! How could you *do* that to her? How could you be such a heartless bastard?' She began to cry again. 'I hate men! You're all the same!' she wailed. 'I wish God had made me a *lesbian!*'

There was a knock at the door. As Magnus got to his feet, they heard Fay's voice outside. 'Emily, can I come in?' The door opened before Magnus reached it and Fay entered. 'Oh! Magnus... I wasn't expecting – actually, I was looking for Emily.'

'She isn't here,' said Magnus, standing in front of Fay in an attempt to block her view of the *en suite*.

'Yes, she is,' Emily called out, her voice leaden with exhaustion.

Fay glared at Magnus, pushed past him and saw her daughter huddled on the floor, wrapped in a blanket. 'What's on earth's the matter? Are you ill?'

She was about to kneel beside her when Emily snapped, 'Don't you dare touch me!'

Fay looked up at Magnus, shocked and confused. He shook his head and said, 'I think you'd better leave.'

'Why? What's going on?'

'Just go, Fay.'

'Not before you tell me what's happened.' She turned back to Emily. 'Why are you crying? Has Rick done something awful?'

'Ha!' was Emily's scornful response.

'Leave now, Fay' said Magnus. 'You'll only make things worse. I'm dealing with it.'

'Well, clearly you're not! Look at her. She's in a dreadful state. What have you done?'

'What have *I* done? You've got a nerve!'

Fay sighed with exasperation. 'Will somebody *please* tell me what's going on?'

Emily staggered to her feet, clutching the woollen throw. 'Go away, Mum. I don't want to speak to you.'

'Oh. I see... Or rather I *don't*. Well, I just came upstairs to give you this.' She held out a small gift-wrapped parcel. 'It's just a little textile picture. Based on an old Valentine's card... Victorian,' Fay explained superfluously. 'I made it as an engagement present. For you and Rick.'

Emily stared at the gift, then took it from her mother's hand as if it were coated in poison. She stood motionless for a moment, still staring at the parcel, then hurled it into the fire where it landed on top of a burning log. Magnus darted forward and bent to retrieve it.

Fay grabbed his arm. 'Magnus, don't! It doesn't matter!' He picked up the gift, which now burned at one edge where the paper had caught fire. He dropped it on to the hearth and stamped out the flames.

Fay looked down at her crushed and charred present, then covered her face with her hands. After a moment, she looked up and said wearily, 'This is about Rick, isn't it?' She glared at Magnus. 'You bastard! How could you do such a dreadful thing? I *trusted* you!'

Magnus' jaw dropped. 'I didn't tell—'

'How could *he* do such a dreadful thing?' Emily cried. 'How could *you*? How could you betray your own daughter?'

'I *didn't*!'

'Don't lie to me! Dad didn't need to tell me, I *heard* you.'

'What do you mean?'

'I heard you and Rick! Talking just now.'

'Talking?'

'About your affair.'

'It wasn't an affair, it was just—'

'Don't lie! I heard you! I was in there,' Emily said pointing to the *en suite*, 'and I heard every word!'

'Oh, God,' said Fay sinking on to the bed. She looked up at Magnus. 'The Laird's Lug?' she said faintly.

'Aye. The Laird's sodding Lug.'

There was another knock at the door. Three heads turned and heard Rick's disembodied voice.

'Emily? Have you dried out yet? I've brought you up another glass of champagne. Thought you might be needing it.' The door swung open and Rick stood smiling in the doorway holding two glasses. As he surveyed the haggard faces of the McGillivrays, his expression turned to dismay. 'Oh... I didn't realise it was a family conference. Sorry to disturb you.' He was backing away when Emily called out.

'Rick, don't go. I want to ask you something. And I want you to tell me the truth.'

Hearing these ominous words, Rick resisted the temptation to look at Fay, knowing it could incriminate him. Instead he smiled again and said, in what he hoped was a casual manner, 'What do you want to know?'

'Have you slept with my mother?'

Rick's smile vanished. He averted his eyes from Emily's scrutiny and registered Magnus' thunderous expression. When he finally looked at Fay, her tear-filled eyes seemed to plead with him. He searched those eyes for guidance, trying to remember all the excellent reasons she'd given for lying to Emily. He could remember only one: Emily would be hurt by the truth. Rick faced his fiancée, his mind blank with panic.

'Please tell me the truth, Rick. Have you slept with Fay?'

'Of course I haven't, Em! She's your *mother*! For God's sake,' he added, with an ill-considered laugh, 'she's twice my age!'

Seated between the two men, Fay saw Magnus move and knew what he was about to do. As he swung his fist, she sprang up. '*No*, Magnus!'

The punch caught Fay on the jaw and Emily screamed. As Fay dropped like a sack of potatoes on to the stone floor, Emily ran from the room, screaming for help. Magnus looked down at Fay's unconscious body, appalled. Without looking at Rick, he said, 'Get out.'

Transfixed with horror, Rick found himself unable to move.

'Get out!' Magnus bellowed. 'Get out before you get what's coming to you!'

Rick fled without a word, spilling champagne as he ran.

Magnus dropped to his knees beside Fay. He gathered her body carefully into his arms, lifted her as if she weighed no more than a child, then carried her over to the bed where, with infinite gentleness, he deposited her lifeless form. He could hear footsteps on the stairs and female voices raised in consternation, undercut by the magisterial tones of Dr McKay. Magnus felt a brief sensation of relief. It would be all right... Someone would look after Fay. Someone would take her away and care for her. Like they did before...

When Dr McKay entered the room, followed closely by Emily, Nina and Jessie, he found Magnus sitting on the edge of the bed, his head bowed, Fay's limp hand held to his lips.

Chapter 15

Fay

I don't remember anything after Magnus' fist made contact with my jaw. Well, I remember the pain. And the stars. You do see stars when someone punches you, just like in the cartoons. It was all quite spectacular, like a firework display, or it would have been if it weren't for the equally spectacular pain. But that was only momentary. Then the stars went out and everything turned black.

Jessie told me what happened afterwards. She got the short straw. Everyone agreed she was the only person I'd want to see at the hospital, but Magnus came anyway and paced up and down in the waiting room like an expectant father, conspicuous not only for his height and hair, but also his full Highland dress. He sat with Jessie while someone wired my teeth together, rendering my fractured jaw immobile. Jessie said later, however much I'd suffered – first being punched, then manhandled by the doctors – she thought Magnus had probably suffered more.

I don't think she was trying to make excuses for him. She was thoroughly ashamed of him and made no bones about saying so, to me or to him. I think she just wanted me to know he'd really suffered as a consequence of what he'd done; that there was no painkiller strong enough to touch his guilt and anguish. I suppose she thought that might give me some sort of satisfaction.

It didn't. I knew Magnus hadn't meant to hit me. It had been a stupid accident. If anything, it had been my fault for getting in the way. I'd sensed him simmering away for some time and I saw the blow coming. But I was glad I'd stopped it. I knew once Rick had explained what had really happened, there was every chance Emily would forgive him. (I wasn't quite so confident her generosity would be extended toward me.) But I couldn't see how Emily could ever have forgiven her father for punching her fiancé. For once I thought I'd done the right thing. The thought of Magnus' suffering didn't in any way diminish mine.

Someone – I suspected Nina's mother – must have informed the police. A kind and terribly young WPC came and sat at my bedside and asked if I wanted to press charges. I was still groggy with anaesthetic and, with my teeth wired, I was reduced to writing on a scrap pad. The WPC pointed out gently that this wasn't "a domestic" as Mr McGillivray and I were no longer married so, she assured me, the police would take the assault very seriously. I scribbled on my pad that I had no wish to press charges. The blow had been accidental, the result of a stupid misunderstanding. She gave me what I thought was a pitying look, shut her notebook and wished me a speedy recovery.

When Jessie came in later I showed her what I'd written. She fished in her handbag for her reading glasses and when she'd read the message, I wrote underneath, PLEASE TELL MAGNUS. She raised an eyebrow and said, 'Och, he can stew for a wee while. It'll do him good.' I took back the pad and wrote, NO. PLEASE TELL HIM.

Jessie sighed. 'Well, if you insist. Did you want to see him? He's still out there in the waiting room, prowling around like a wounded tiger. He says he'll not be leaving till you've seen him.'

I'd no idea what time it was. There was hardly any noise coming from the corridor outside and I suspected it was now very early rather than very late. They'd put me in a small side ward with only one other occupant: an elderly woman whose thunderous snoring could have wakened the dead, but not, apparently, her. I didn't expect to get much sleep, even though I was groggy with painkillers.

I looked at Jessie sitting by my bedside. She was obviously exhausted. I wondered if anyone had told her what really happened. And what did poor Nina make of it all? Was there any explanation Magnus could have given that didn't incriminate him in some way? If he lied and said the punch was meant for me, it made him a wife-beater. If he said the punch was meant for Rick, what reason could he give that would account for such violence? Fathers don't normally thrash two-timing boyfriends, especially not at their engagement party and I doubted Magnus would have told Nina that Rick had slept with me, for the simple reason, she'd jump to conclusions about Magnus' feelings for me.

It was a complete mess and a mess of Magnus' making. Trying to see things from Nina's point of view, I couldn't help concluding that she'd think her cracked-up war hero fiancé was not only more cracked up than she'd bargained for, but also violent. Not exactly the sort of man you want to father your children. And that was before you factored in her suspicion that Magnus was still in love with me.

As if she'd read my thoughts, Jessie said, 'It looks as if it's all over between Magnus and Nina.'

I looked up so quickly, my head spun with the pain. I widened my eyes to indicate enquiry.

Jessie needed no further prompting. 'Nina insisted he stay at Tully with her. Folk were very upset. The guests, I mean. But no one explained. Well, Rick tried, but he didn't make any sense. He said Fay had fallen downstairs, but that didn't account for the state poor Emily was in, or why she was running around in her underwear! Magnus said nothing. He just hung on Dr McKay's every word. You know,' said Jessie lowering her voice, 'I think Magnus thought he might have *killed* you... Then Mrs Buchanan decided to have hysterics, so Nina – och, the silly wee besom! – she started ordering Magnus about.' Jessie shook her head. '*Never* a good idea. He just stood his ground and said he was going to the hospital with you. He said it was his duty. So Nina gave him an ultimatum.' Jessie paused for effect. 'Magnus said, "So be it," and got into Dr McKay's car. I don't think he'll find Nina at Tully when he gets back,' said Jessie, shaking her head. 'But it's probably all for the best. The poor lassie had no idea what she was taking on.' Jessie got to her feet and said, 'I'm away home now, in a taxi. Will you see Magnus? He refuses to come home with me and I doubt he'll go back to Tully. Not yet.'

I reached for my pad and wrote, IS HE STILL ANGRY WITH ME? I DON'T WANT TO SEE HIM IF HE IS.

I handed the pad to Jessie who put her glasses back on to read my scrawl. 'Och, no! He's not angry, he's *mortified*. He'll likely grovel at your feet. If he still feels any anger, he's directing it at himself,' she added sadly.

My heart heavy with apprehension, I wrote, SEND HIM IN.

~

Magnus opened the ward door and it swung shut behind him. He looked around and saw Fay in the far corner, propped up on pillows. She looked smaller than he remembered, but it was a long time since he'd seen her lying down. Even at this distance, he could see her face was a mess. Slowly, his brogues squeaking on the rubberised floor, he approached her bed.

He carried his jacket over his shoulder. His waistcoat was unbuttoned, revealing a crumpled white shirt which now looked the worse for wear, as did Magnus. He'd mislaid the bow tie that had been hanging loose round his neck and now only the pleats of his kilt looked fresh.

Fay turned her head gingerly and watched Magnus. His bearing was upright and his steps measured. He was approaching her bed as she imagined he'd approached many an explosive device. With extreme caution. With a sense of a job that had to be done. And with no idea of the outcome.

Magnus stood at Fay's bedside. She was unable to lift her head far enough to meet his eyes. Instead, she examined his hands. Fay had always loved Magnus' large, agile hands with their sensitive, long fingers. She liked to think how many lives those hands had saved. Her eyes settled on the livid bruise that spread across the knuckles of his right hand, inflicted by contact with her jawbone. She wondered what her face must look like. The nurses had failed to locate a mirror for her and she now thought perhaps they were being kind.

'Are those *wire cutters*?' Magnus asked, indicating the pair strategically placed on Fay's bedside table. 'For if you vomit unexpectedly?' he said, answering his own question. 'Aye, well, I'm your man for that. I used to be a dab hand with wire cutters.' He sat down in the chair recently vacated by Jessie. As his face finally came into view, Fay was shocked to see how pale he was. Strain was etched in deep lines round his mouth and eyes. His chin was dark with stubble now and she realised he must have been in the waiting room for hours.

He gazed at her for a moment, then said, unsmiling, 'On a scale of one to ten, how much does it hurt?'

Fay reached for her pad and, with two firm strokes, wrote, '11'.

As she handed him the pad she saw his eyes fill with tears. Snatching it back, she scribbled quickly, I KNOW YOU DIDN'T MEAN TO HURT ME.

He composed himself and said, 'Did you get in the way to stop me hurting Rick? Or to stop me making a complete arse of myself?'

She wrote, BOTH.

'Can you nod?' Magnus asked. 'Or does that hurt? Knock three times for "Yes".'

Her mouth twitched and she wrote, DON'T MAKE ME LAUGH. THAT HURTS TOO.

'Och, not much chance of that! It's a long time since I made you laugh, Fay. Or even smile.' Eventually he said, 'I'm very sorry. For hitting you, I mean. I'm sorry. From the bottom of my heart. For... *everything*.'

Fay wrote, DID YOU WANT TO PUNCH RICK BECAUSE HE'D INSULTED ME?

He read her words and said, 'Aye. And because he'd slept with you. And....' He shrugged. 'Because it was the best sex you'd ever had.'

Fay emitted a strangled noise, which, if it had included consonants, might have sounded like, '*What*?'

Misinterpreting her protest, Magnus explained. 'Emily heard you tell Rick. Then she told me. I'm not sure *why* she told me,' he added, bemused. 'I suppose she thought I was past caring.'

He looked down at the message Fay had been scrawling in large letters and read, I NEVER SAID THAT!

'You didn't?'

She shook her head, then immediately moaned in pain.

Magnus reached instinctively to cradle her battered face in his hands. 'Don't! Write it down. Or we could try telepathy. You always said we had that kind of a connection.'

Fay wrote, THE BEST SEX I EVER HAD WAS IN THE LADIES' TOILET AT BRIZE NORTON. WITH YOU, she added as an afterthought.

His face lit up. 'Oh aye, that was fun! Did you enjoy that more than the time we did it in the back of the Land Rover in the B & Q car park?'

She thought for a moment, then wrote, TOUGH CALL.

Reading upside down, Magnus laughed out loud. Fay looked up, strangely moved, wondering when she'd last heard him laugh. She turned over a new page and wrote, DOES NINA MAKE YOU LAUGH?

Staring at the pad, Magnus said, 'Not a lot, to be honest.' He ran a hand through his tangled mass of hair and, without meeting Fay's eyes, said, 'It's pretty much over. You probably gathered from Jessie... I've fair blotted my copybook with young Nina. Even if I managed to talk *her* round, Medusa's unlikely to be swayed.' Seeing Fay's frown, he added, 'My future ma-in-law. As *was*. She'll have decided I'm not good breeding stock. Tainted blood. Temperamental head-banger.' He sat back in his chair and folded his arms. 'She was only in it for the George Cross anyway.'

Fay frowned again and wrote, NINA?

'Och, no! The estimable Mrs B.'

They were both silent for a while, then Fay wrote, DID YOU LOVE NINA?

Magnus stared at the words, then without raising his eyes from the pad, said, 'Not as much as I loved you. *Love* you.' Fay looked away and started to write again but he placed his hand over hers, enclosing it completely. 'Fay...' He appeared to struggle with the words. Avoiding her gaze, he took a deep breath and said, 'I want you to read something... Something I wrote. It was written for you, but you've never read it.'

He let go of her hand, unfastened his sporran and withdrew two envelopes – one sealed, the other dog-eared with use. 'I used to carry one of your letters with me at all times. I still do. Force of habit... This one you sent me when I was in the Falklands. It was very special and I always carried it with me. Except for some reason, the day I was blown up in Derry, I didn't have it on me. So I've carried it ever since. As a sort of good luck charm. I convinced myself the letter had magical, life-preserving properties.'

Magnus looked at the other envelope for a moment, then appeared to come to a decision. He handed the letter to Fay. 'This one I wrote for you. You never received it because... well, because I never died. But I'd like you to have it. I don't think I should have had to die for you to know the contents. And I'd like you to read it now. If you would.'

She looked at the inscription: *Fay McGillivray*. The name she hadn't used in years. Handing it back to Magnus, she picked up her pen and began to write on her pad.

Misunderstanding, he said, 'Please, Fay! Then we can draw a line. I want you to know how I—'

She held up the pad and he read, I WON'T BE ABLE TO READ IT WITHOUT CRYING AND THEN I WON'T BE ABLE TO SEE THE WORDS. PLEASE READ IT TO ME.

He looked at her for a long moment, then took the envelope and tore it open. He pulled out two sheets of handwritten notepaper. As he opened them up, Fay noticed his hands were shaking. Magnus cleared his throat and started to read.

December 31st 1993

My dearest Fay
This is not going to be easy for you. If you're reading this, it's because I'm no longer with you. This is the letter I hoped you'd never receive. I know it will be no consolation, but in time I hope you'll be able to read my words and draw comfort from knowing how I felt about my death and how I felt about you.

I loved you more than you ever knew, more than I could ever say. I loved you more than my job (and that's saying something) but I never found a way to give up a job I believe I was born to do. So I'm sorry, really sorry that it ended this way.

Don't ever think of mine as a life that was wasted, even though it was cut short. I lived life to the full and I was bloody happy for most of it! The worst bits weren't the long walks down to a booby-trapped device, they were the goodbyes at airports, wondering if I'd ever see you and Emily again, feeling sick to my stomach with guilt about what I was putting you through, time after time.

I want you to know I died happy, doing a job that needed to be done. I think I did it well. Even if I was alone at the end, I always had the back up of a brilliant team of mates and the best army in the world. (Please don't blame the Army, Fay. If it was the ending of me, it was also the making of me.)

I had so much to be grateful for. I was proud to serve my country and if I made the ultimate sacrifice, it was one I was ready to make. My life was one of calculated risk, so I was always prepared for the worst. I've been able to leave my affairs in order and I know you'll be given this letter in which I have the priceless opportunity to try to console you and tell you one last time, how much I loved you.

If I'd lived, I would have had to give up the job one day. Then what would I have done? Taught other guys how to do it? Become a security consultant for some political bigwig? Written my memoirs? Bugger that for a game of soldiers! I was never going to retire and grow roses, was I? I'd have died piecemeal doing that. Instead I went out on a high. And that's what I'd have chosen, if I could choose.

I know I wasn't the best of husbands, Fay, but you've been the very best of wives. No man could have wished for a more loyal, understanding or forgiving wife. (You're beautiful, too! I really had it all, didn't I?) I could only do that job because you gave me the balls to do it. You believed in me. You stood by me – for better and for a lot of worse.

I loved you with all my heart and I died loving you. I don't want you to be lonely or unhappy and I want you to have support as a single mother, so just as soon as you're ready, find someone else you can love. Now I know you, you'll think that's disloyal, but one day it will feel right for you to move on. And that's what I want you to do. My life has ended, but yours mustn't! If one day you're able to find happiness with another man, then believe me, I'll be the happiest dead guy in the world.

What is there left to say? Everything and nothing.

If you're a dead Scot, you can perhaps be forgiven for quoting Burns. (Perhaps.) I was never one for poetry, but whenever I heard these words sung or spoken, I always thought of you.

> "And I will love thee still, my dear,
> Till a' the seas gang dry.
> Till a' the seas gang dry, my dear,
> And the rocks melt wi' the sun,
> O, I will love thee still, my dear,
> While the sands o' life shall run."

My sands have stopped running, Fay, but I'll find a way to love you still. Hell, did you think a wee bitty thing like death was going to stop me?
Yours forever,
Magnus

Ignoring Fay's muffled sobs, Magnus folded the sheets of paper, pushed them back into the envelope and then dropped it on to the bed saying, 'I thought you should know... Because I don't think I ever told you.'

He stood up and, as he turned to go, Fay lunged across the bed, caught hold of a handful of his kilt and tugged. Magnus steeled himself, then turned and looked into her imploring eyes. Tears ran freely down her cheeks but he couldn't read her expression. He bent suddenly, as if to kiss her, but she raised a warning hand and put it in front of her mouth. He gazed at her helplessly. Fay grabbed the pad and, in a wild scrawl, wrote, DRAW THE CURTAINS.

He looked up and stared, uncomprehending. She reached behind her back and began to undo the ties of her hospital gown. As realisation began to dawn, Magnus grinned. Fay's bruised lips twisted in response.

In a dazzling display of manual dexterity, Magnus drew the curtains round the bed while shrugging off his waistcoat and undoing the buttons of his shirt. When he turned back to face Fay, she was sitting wide-eyed and naked on the edge of the bed, shivering, but not with cold. Magnus stood in front of her, speechless. With a strangled laugh, Fay began to haul at the buckles on his kilt. Magnus threw off his shirt and unclasped the chain of his sporran, which hit the floor at precisely the same moment as eight yards of worsted. He reached for the wire cutters on the bedside table and, with two deft strokes, snipped the long laces of his brogues that wound up and round his calves. He kicked off his shoes and, as he pulled at his white stockings, he said, conversationally, 'The Duke of Argyll was once heard to remark that white kilt socks are strictly for pipe bands and music hall artists. I'm inclined to agree.'

Fay threw her arms round his neck and, turning her head to one side, pressed her body against his naked chest. As her thighs parted, Magnus moved forward and, bending his knees, he gently lifted and – not quite so gently – entered her. Fay clutched at his hair and moaned, suppressing a raging instinct to kiss him. As she wrapped her legs around his hips, Magnus thrust deeper and whispered, 'Fay, this isn't something I want to rush... but if a nurse comes in, or the old lady wakes up, we're fucked... Or rather, we're not.'

Fay made an urgent noise which he construed as both encouragement and assent. He leaned forward, laying her down on the mattress, then vaulted on to the bed. As she wriggled into position, Magnus gazed down at her and shook his shaggy head. '*Till a' the seas gang dry*, Fay,' he murmured softly as he lowered himself, entered her again and began to thrust. '*Till a' the seas gang dry...*'

When, some time later, a nurse appeared on the ward to check up on her two patients, she found Fay fast asleep, with her bedding in disarray. Her hospital gown lay on the floor. Suspecting a fever, the nurse laid a solicitous hand on her patient's forehead and was relieved to find her temperature was normal, even though her breathing was heavy (though not as heavy as Mrs Mackenzie's who, the nurse remembered, had the good fortune to be deaf.)

Bending to retrieve Fay's gown, the nurse was surprised to see two envelopes on the floor. She picked them up and examined the inscriptions. Both were for McGillivray. The patient's name was Austin, but the nurse decided to leave the letters on her bedside table.

Then, as she straightened the bed curtains, she noticed a pair of wire cutters on the floor and what looked like a piece of shoelace. She picked them both up and put the cutters beside the letters.

Satisfied that the ward was tidy and her patients comfortable, the nurse left them to sleep on. As she dropped the shoelace into a waste bin, she made a mental note that someone should have word with the cleaners.

Chapter 16

Fay

And so they lived happily ever after... That's what you're thinking. That's what should have happened next. But it wasn't quite that simple.

I tried hard to persuade myself that love would conquer all, but the trouble was, I wouldn't listen to myself. The cynical girl-about-town who'd learned to live and sleep alone knew she'd succumbed to a potent, possibly toxic sex-and-sentiment cocktail, served up by Magnus with his inimitable panache. Of course, he hadn't done it deliberately, nor had he tried to exploit the situation. He'd read his letter to me because he thought we'd reached the end of the line. (A reasonable assumption. He'd hit me before, but never hospitalised me.) I knew he'd been trying to engineer a good, clean ending, not a reconciliation. The fact that things had got passionately out of hand was entirely my fault and my choice.

But it had been a big mistake.

Why?

Because now I was scared.

Scared of what?

Well, what have you got?... Scared of how much I loved Magnus; how much my body wanted him; how much he wanted me; how I might fail him; how he might fail me; how much Nina might want him back; how hard she might fight; how much I loved my independence; how much I'd hated life at Tully. I was scared of how ill Magnus was and how ill he'd always be, but most of all I was scared of losing him. Again.

As I sat up in bed, sucking baby food through a bendy straw (no wonder babies are so crabby, living on a diet of Pears & Rice), I concluded my fears were contemptible and my love overwhelming. So I gave myself a good talking to...

You're making a big mistake.

But he loves me! And I love him.

Sexual charisma. That's all it is and Magnus has it in spades. You've always known that. It's not love. It's lust and need and sexual frustration.

Not on his side. He's had Nina. To judge from her smug little expression, he's had her a lot.

Yes, but she's not part of that whole sex'n'death scenario you and Magnus have going on.

What on earth do you mean?

Oh, spare me the wide-eyed-innocent routine! You know what I mean. The intensity of what you felt for him—

Feel! What I feel for him!

Don't interrupt. That intensity has always been tied up with the fear of losing him, the fear of that glorious body being mutilated or completely destroyed. It was sick. It is sick.

No, it wasn't like that! That was always part of it, I suppose – the desperation – but that wasn't what made him write that beautiful letter to me. He was giving me his blessing to find happiness with another man.

You didn't need his bloody permission! He's a control freak. It was a cynical manipulation from beyond the grave.

It wasn't, it was written from the heart! And he read it from the heart. He was saying a last goodbye.

Exactly. And that's what he wanted. To end it. Then you went and offered yourself on a plate. Well, he could hardly say no, could he? But it doesn't mean he wants you back. On your back, possibly.

I didn't say I was going back.

Who are you kidding? You know you want to.

I don't! I mean, a part of me does, but just because I've accepted I still love him, doesn't mean I'm going back to Tully. I just couldn't! Too much happened there. Too much that was... unbearable.

Like I said. The whole sex'n'death thing.

Oh, shut up! You don't understand.

Yes, I do. You won't go back to Magnus because you're scared.

Of course I'm bloody scared!

Scared it will happen again.

Stop this, please. It isn't helping.

I mean look at you, for God's sake – talking to yourself! How sane is that?...

The thing is, you see, I haven't been entirely frank about why I left Magnus. Why I had to leave Magnus. The fact is, I have a confession to make.

About just how much I *owe* him.

~

Magnus shuffled along the hospital corridor, reeling with exhaustion. His progress was impeded by the makeshift bows he'd tied in what remained of his laces. Sinking to one knee, he re-tied a lace, then wondered if he'd ever find the strength or willpower to get to his feet again. He summoned up both and staggered out of the main doors of Perth Royal Infirmary, into the freezing air. It was still dark but hunger told him it was morning. He located a taxi and gave the driver an address in the centre of town. Climbing into the cab, he selected a number on his phone.

'Ma? It's me. Did I wake you?... Sorry about that... Och, no, I'm fine!... No, she's fine too. I left her sleeping like a baby... Aye, that would be the painkillers right enough... Ma, listen – get the kettle on. I'm coming round to cook you breakfast.'

A grim-faced Jessie opened the door in her dressing gown and for a moment they regarded each other in silence. She looked older than Magnus remembered. He imagined he looked older than she remembered. It had been quite a night.

Jessie stood aside to let him in. Glancing down, she exclaimed, 'What happened to your *shoes*?'

'It's a long story. Can you make us some coffee?'

'I thought you were cooking me breakfast?'

'Aye, that's the deal. But I'll let you make me some coffee first.'

Jessie looked at the dark shadows under her son's eyes and registered that, beneath the stubble, he was very pale. She shut the door and followed him into the kitchen. 'Has

Nina thrown you out?'

'I haven't been home. I've come straight from the hospital.'

'You've been talking to Fay all this time? She must have writer's cramp!'

Magnus dived into the fridge, emerging eventually with a packet of bacon. 'I sat with her a wee while. After she fell asleep. Where d'you keep your eggs?'

Jessie noted her son's studiously averted face, then pointed to a box on the worktop. As he cracked eggs into a jug, she shook her head. 'Last night was a right stooshie, Magnus.'

'Oh aye,' he replied cheerfully. 'It was *biblical*. Was there anyone there I didn't upset? I'd hate for them to feel left out.'

'Not that I'm aware. You were pretty thorough.' Jessie filled the kettle and switched it on. 'Well, look on the bright side. You'll not be needing to buy many Christmas cards this year.'

'Thanks, Ma,' Magnus said with a weary grin. 'I knew you'd think of something.'

As Jessie cleared away their dirty plates Magnus stood and examined Fay's wall hanging, *Root and Branch* which hung on the wall in the sitting room. When Jessie re-appeared with fresh coffee, he turned to her and announced, 'I want your advice, Ma. That's why I came. Tell me what to do.'

'Do?'

'About Fay. And Nina.'

Jessie set down her tray beside the hissing gas fire. 'And what makes you think *I'd* know what you should do?'

'Because I think you know about unhappy marriages,' Magnus replied, turning back to the hanging. 'About passion... And impossible love. I think you know about trying to do the right thing. And it not working out.' He looked down at his mother, seated now in her fireside chair, her attention seemingly occupied by the box of artificial sweeteners she was shaking over her cup.

'I can't seem to make this thing work... Don't tell me it's

162

empty already.'

Magnus continued, undeterred. 'I didn't understand while I was living with it. I was too young. But that letter—'

'What letter?' Jessie asked, suddenly alert.

'The one you gave Fay. To include in *Root and Branch*. It wasn't from Dad, was it?' Magnus touched the lettering on the hanging. 'This isn't his writing. But you told Fay it was from my father.'

Jessie tossed the plastic container on to the tea tray. 'Och, I'm sweet enough!' She picked up her mug and sipped her coffee while Magnus waited patiently. She regarded him over the rim of her mug, then said, 'I knew if I asked for that letter to be included it could lead to... repercussions. And I might have known *your* eyes would miss nothing. But it didn't seem right to have something so beautiful made about our family and have it enshrine a lie. I decided I could at least *hint* at the truth.'

'So the letter *was* from my father?'

'Aye. From the only man I ever loved. And I'm afraid that wasn't Donald McGillivray.'

'Thank Christ for that!' Magnus exclaimed. Jessie looked up, her eyes wide with surprise. 'It's not a gene pool I'd have chosen for myself, Ma. I'm pleased to hear you had better taste in men than I gave you credit for.' He settled into the other armchair. 'I think it's time for a wee story. That's what you used to say when you put me to bed. "Time for a wee story..." But I suspect this one is a *long* story. Well, that's just grand,' he added, helping himself to more coffee. 'You used to be good at telling stories. Go ahead, Ma. I'm all ears.'

Leaning back in her chair, Jessie rearranged her dressing gown, smoothing the quilted fabric over her knees. 'I did my best, Magnus. I'll say that much in my own defence. I did my best to make my marriage work, but Donald wasn't an easy man to please.' She waved her hand in a dismissive gesture. 'Well, you know that.'

'Oh, aye. "It is never difficult to distinguish between a Scotsman with a grievance and a ray of sunshine." '

Jessie couldn't suppress a smile. 'P G Wodehouse?'

'Of course.'

'Donald was… deeply disappointed in life. In his family.'

'I tried to make him proud of me, Ma.'

'He wasn't disappointed in *you*, he was disappointed you weren't his *son*. And he was disappointed again when you didn't follow him into the family business. He'd always hoped you'd do that. But once he'd adjusted to the idea of the army, he was very proud of you. He just wasn't good at conveying it, conveying *any* kind of emotion. But that doesn't mean he didn't feel it.'

As she leaned forward to adjust the setting of the gas fire, Magnus gazed at the photographs on the mantelpiece: Jessie's wedding photo, flanked by one of himself in uniform and another of the dour, implacable man he'd known as his father. Magnus recalled that the photo in pride of place used to be of a different wedding: his and Fay's. That had disappeared one day, to be replaced with the older photograph. He wondered whose feelings Jessie had wished to spare: his, Fay's or her own.

'Are you warm enough?' Jessie asked.

'Oh aye. I'm toasty. Will you finish your story?'

Jessie drank a mouthful of coffee, then said, 'I'm wondering, did you always know? About the marriage, I mean?'

'No. I think maybe I sensed it. Sensed you weren't exactly happy. But I had no idea why. I think I pieced it together after I'd left home. I saw a lot of marital breakdown in the army, especially in the EOD. The lads talked and I got to hear about the symptoms. The effects on their kids. It set me thinking about you and Dad. Then I got a ringside seat, didn't I? Saw Fay trying to hold it all together. And failing.'

'She didn't fail, she went under. And she had the sense to get out before she went under for good.'

'Aye, I know. I didn't see it as failure, but she did. I never felt she'd let me down. Never. And by the end I knew it was me who'd let her down.'

'Neither of you was to blame. Mental illness is a wrecker of marriages as well as minds. But minds are more resilient. They mostly heal, given time. And love.'

Magnus regarded his mother. 'She really admired you.'

'Fay?'

'Aye. She saw you as a model wife and mother. Tried to live up to your example.'

'If she'd known the truth about my marriage, she'd have seen there was little enough to admire. And it's not as if I had any real choices. I was economically dependent, with a young child. Things were very different for Fay. Emily was almost grown and Fay was still young enough to start over again.'

'And she had your support to do that, Ma. If you weren't a model wife, you were certainly a model mother-in-law.'

'Och, away wi' you!' Jessie scoffed. 'Fay's been as good a friend to me as I was to her. But I will say this, Magnus – and I hope I'm not speaking out of turn – I think you've maybe had a lucky escape.'

'Would you be referring to Mrs Buchanan now?'

'Aye. I'm thinking you and she would not have seen eye to eye.'

'Not without me turning to stone, that's for sure. I imagine Mrs B is saying much the same to Nina right now.'

'About a lucky escape?'

'Aye. From the desperate clutches of Mad Magnus McGillivray. Hell, it's not as if I actually *killed* anyone! I just broke my ex-wife's jaw and rendered her unconscious for a wee while.' He spread his hands. 'What family doesn't have its little differences?'

Jessie wasn't deceived by her son's sarcasm. 'Don't worry. Magnus. Fay will be all right. It was an accident. She'll forgive you. She always has. I think she always will.'

'Her generosity of spirit doesn't make me feel any better about my lack of it.'

'I know. And that's how I felt about Donald. I should have found it in my heart to love him. But I didn't. I just *couldn't*.'

'You must have been pregnant when you married.'

'Two months gone. But it didn't show. I'd been sick right from the start and I hadn't put on any weight.'

'Did Donald know you were pregnant?'

'Aye, he did.'

'Did you tell him it was his?'

'There was no chance of that – he'd barely kissed me! So I

had to tell him the truth. I might have been damaged goods, but I was honest. With Donald, at least. He'd been after marrying me for a while and I'd already turned down a proposal from him.'

'Because your heart lay elsewhere?'

'Aye... Then I found myself pregnant.'

'The father wouldn't marry you?'

'He couldn't. He was already married... I didn't know what to do. I wouldn't consider an abortion, but I didn't have the sort of parents who'd stand by me. So I decided to confide in Donald. Our families had always been friends and we knew each other well. I'd always looked up to him as a sort of older brother. That was why I couldn't take his proposal seriously. And he was so much older than me. Anyway, Donald and I, well, we came to an understanding. And we married. In a hurry. Nothing was ever said, not to our faces anyway. Maybe folk thought I'd finally come to my senses! Donald was regarded as a good catch financially. And he was a highly respected member of the community.'

'He must have loved you, Ma. To take on another man's child.'

'Aye, he did. And he hoped I'd love him for it. God knows, I tried.'

'Is my father still alive?' Magnus asked gently.

'No. He died many years ago.'

'Did I know him?'

'Aye, when you were very young. I have a photo of you together,' Jessie said with a sad smile, her voice unsteady. 'It was taken when you were just a wee bairn. He's holding you in his arms.'

'I'd like to see that.'

'Aye, of course you would! I'll let you have it,' she replied, not moving from her chair.

Magnus looked down and was silent for a moment, then he raised his head and said, 'Who was he, Ma?'

Jessie clasped her hands tightly in her lap. 'This isn't easy for me, Magnus. I've never talked about it to anyone apart from Donald. And we never, ever discussed it after – after your father died.'

'Ma, I'm forty-five. D'you not think I have a right to know who my father was?'

'Aye, you do. I know you do. And it's what I want. It's just not easy for me to talk about him. After all these years!'

Seeing his mother's distress, Magnus set down his mug on the coffee table. 'Maybe some other time then.'

He was about to get to his feet when Jessie said, 'Do you remember, when you were a wee boy, the big explosion?'

Magnus frowned. 'There were lots of explosions. That was Dad's job.'

'Aye, but this one was different. But what am I thinking? Of course you wouldn't remember! You were only three... It was the first time I'd taken you to see Donald at work. It was a big event. There was almost a party atmosphere. Folk had come from miles around to see the old place come down. But that day... there was a terrible accident. And someone died.'

Magnus sat up straight in his chair, his eyes wide and alert. 'My father?'

'Aye.'

He looked away and appeared to study the wall, as if it might yield the answer to his father's identity. 'I think I can remember you crying,' he said softly. 'And clouds of dust... Folk running about, yelling... and I can remember *fear*... It must be my first memory.'

Jessie nodded her head slowly. 'I didn't tell you he'd died. Not then. I told you later. Much later... I said he'd had an accident. A bad motorbike accident.' Jessie didn't see the colour drain from her son's face because she couldn't bring herself to look as he closed his eyes and leaned back in his chair. Instead she stared fixedly at the flickering gas flames. 'You believed me, of course. Why would a child not believe his mother? But you didn't really understand. How do you explain death to a three year-old? I told you your father had gone to Heaven and that he would be very happy there. I said... he'd be safe for ever now.'

'Only you didn't say, "Your father", did you?' Magnus asked, his voice hoarse with emotion.

'No. I wanted to. But I couldn't.'

'You said..."Uncle Lachlan".'

167

'Aye,' Jessie replied, her voice breaking finally. 'I lied to you about how your Uncle Lachie died. And I never told you he was your father. Perhaps I might have told you one day, if he hadn't died. I like to think I would. But once he was gone, I couldn't see the point. Not even when you were a young man and had a right to know. I couldn't do that to Donald! And I didn't want you to know *how* your father had died because—' Unable to continue, Jessie reached into her dressing gown pocket for a handkerchief.

'Because I faced a similar death myself every day,' Magnus replied, his voice matter-of-fact. Jessie nodded briefly, her face half-hidden by her handkerchief. 'Lachlan was Donald's younger brother, wasn't he?'

She nodded again and, with an effort, said, 'Younger by eight years.'

'Will you tell me something about him?'

Jessie crumpled her handkerchief and pushed it back into her pocket. 'Lachie was the golden boy. The one with the charm. The talent. The looks... You're the living image of him.'

'I don't suppose Donald was too happy about that.'

'He never mentioned it, but I think it *was* hard for him. Especially after Lachie died.'

'What sort of a man was he, Lachlan?'

'They said he was a ladies' man. That women were always throwing themselves at him. But I didn't. He was a friend. Someone I'd always known. A boy, then a man against whom I measured all others. It wasn't until he married that I realised how much he meant to me.'

'And that's why you turned Donald down.'

'I think I had some daft idea I was going to be an old maid schoolteacher, nursing a secret love. Like Charlotte Brontë! That was until I discovered Lachie felt the same way about me... To begin with, I was very shocked and I tried to keep my distance. But... Well, you can't reason with the heart. Or the body... So we used to meet in secret.'

Magnus looked at the small, elderly woman seated opposite him, her face sagging with tiredness, her pale, papery skin creased in tiny folds. He tried to imagine the brave and passionate young woman who'd met her married

168

lover for illicit sex. The task defeated him and he resorted to a random question. 'Where did you meet?'

'Your old haunt. Drummond Hall.'

'You're kidding me!'

'You were conceived there, Magnus. Amidst the dust and mouse droppings and the withered leaves. We knew such *happiness* there!' Jessie's eyes shone as she smiled and Magnus was granted a vision of the woman his mother had been. He bowed his head, overcome by the weight of memories.

'I remember you crying when Dad – when Donald blew up Drummond Hall.'

'Aye. You cried too.'

'I loved that place! It always felt special to me.'

'It *was* special. It was where you began. And I'm glad you know now. Know why I cried when that place came down.'

'Did Donald know—'

'Och no! I spared him the details. His idea of me as a good, wee lassie had already taken a hammering. He preferred to think Lachlan was a heartless seducer of silly girls. But he was nothing of the sort!' Jessie snorted. 'He was just a good-looking young man and popular. Then when he trained as an architect, he became a very good catch. Lots of girls were after him.'

'Did he marry for love?'

'Not really. He said he married his wife because she said she was pregnant. He never knew if it was just a scare or maybe a ploy. There was no baby anyway. Which is why you were so precious to him. You were his only child.'

'And you and Donald didn't have a child either.'

'Not for want of trying. I wanted to give Donald his own son. I could at least do that for him. But I never conceived again. Donald had to assume it was his fault. That was hard for him too. When he took on Lachie's child, he never thought he'd have none of his own. It was all very sad.'

'I wish I'd known. Known some of this while he was alive. I might have understood the way he treated me. Why he was so... remote.'

'Donald was a disappointed man. Even if you'd been his

own flesh and blood, he was still saddled with a wife who didn't love him. Things might not have been very different.'

'Why didn't you tell me after he died?'

'I wanted to, but you and Fay had your own problems by then. And you had so much responsibility in the army. I didn't want to burden you with anything else. And it wasn't something I could just put in a letter. I needed to tell you in person. But I could never find the courage. The right words. Every time we said goodbye, I never knew if I'd see you again. It wasn't a time to be rattling skeletons in cupboards! And – it's hard for me to admit this, Magnus – I didn't want you to think any the less of me. I didn't want you to think any the less of Donald either. He'd been a hero in his own way and sorted out the terrible mess his brother had made. Donald saved my reputation and gave my baby a father. His only condition was that the relationship with Lachlan must end. Which it did. I didn't stop loving him, not even after he died, but the affair ended and I did my best to be a good wife. I gave Donald everything except my heart.'

'And he never forgave you for that, did he? And he never forgave me for not being his son.'

'He *tried*. I believe he tried very hard. But he didn't have an easy life, even before the accident.'

'Was that his fault? Lachie's death?'

'No, but he blamed himself. He'd always prided himself on his safety record. But these things happen with explosives. You know that. They're unpredictable. No, Lachie was to blame. He was much closer to the site than he should have been.'

'Can you bear to tell me what happened?'

Jessie cast her eyes down. Staring at her clasped hands, she fixed her gaze on her wedding ring. 'They'd spent weeks setting up the demolition. Everything had been done very carefully, with safety in mind. Donald was in no way to blame. That was the official verdict... Lachlan wasn't standing anywhere near me. We kept our distance, especially in public. Out of deference to Donald,' Jessie explained, lowering her voice. 'Lachlan and his wife were at the front of the crowd, but off to one side. This was Donald's big moment, his chance to be the centre of attention. He was in charge of demolitions and Lachlan was responsible for the sale and recycling of the building materials. That's how they ran the business... Donald had insisted I should stand well back. He was worried you'd be frightened by the noise of the explosion. So I was standing well back in the crowd, with my mother-in-law.' Jessie began to fidget with her wedding ring, rotating it nervously. 'I didn't see what happened. I only heard afterwards... The building was wired up, all ready to go. They were going to take it down a section at a time. The wings first, then the main part of the building. It was going to be quite a show. The Laird was there with his family and his factor and Donald wanted to impress... I remember, they had a fine day for it – not a cloud in the sky – and just before the detonation there was an odd stillness in the air. Anticipation, I suppose. Afterwards folk said, everything had happened at once. They could just *see* what was going to happen, but nobody moved... Apart from Lachlan.'

Magnus knew if he put an arm round his mother, she would lose the battle to maintain her composure, so he simply said, 'Take your time, Ma. There's no hurry.'

Jessie swallowed and said, 'Just before Donald gave the signal to detonate, some rats came running out of the building. They say animals know, don't they? Rats leave a sinking ship... They ran out of the wing that was about to come down. There was a boy near the front of the crowd with a terrier on a lead. That dog shouldn't have been there! If Donald had known, he'd never have allowed it. When the dog saw the rats, it jerked the lead from the wee boy's hand and went chasing after them. The boy followed. Worried his dog would be hurt, I suppose. He ran after him, frantic, calling him back. Everyone was horrified. They knew Donald was about to give the signal for detonation – perhaps had already given it. So nobody moved. Except Lachie. He ran after the boy. He was a fast runner. He had long legs like you, Magnus, and he'd run for his school... Eyewitnesses said he caught up with the boy in a matter of seconds. He grabbed him and pulled him against his own body, spinning round, away from the blast, then he threw himself flat – or maybe the blast threw him flat

– so that the boy's body was completely covered by his own.'

'Did the boy survive?'

'Aye. But Lachlan didn't. He was killed by a small piece of masonry that hit him on the back of the head. Death could have been instantaneous. Maybe he was dead before he even hit the ground. But folk didn't realise... There was so much dust! You couldn't see. And everyone was deaf temporarily. They must have assumed Lachlan was unconscious. It wasn't until they saw the blood seeping from the back of his head—' Jessie faltered, then said 'He had such fine hair, Magnus! Thick black curls, just like yours. They wouldn't have seen the blood. Not at first...'

'Ma, you don't need to go on.'

'No, I want you to know. About your father. How he died a hero.'

'Was the boy OK?'

'Aye. He had a broken nose and he was very shaken, but otherwise he was unharmed. He was very lucky... By the time I realised what had happened, folk were swarming round Lachlan's body. His wife was on her knees beside him. Donald too. And a doctor... So I just stood by. There was no place for me at Lachie's side. Not with his poor wife there... And then I remembered you. I could hear you crying. I'd left you with Granny when I pushed my way through the crowd. The poor woman must have put you down and gone running after her sons. I found you, screaming fit to burst. I picked you up and I ran, away from Lachlan, away from Donald. I held you close, Magnus, and I ran. I don't remember where or when I stopped. But Donald found us eventually... He told me Lachie was dead and how he'd died. And then he took us home.'

After a while Jessie got to her feet and walked over to the window where she drew the curtains and stood, watching the apricot glow of a winter dawn deepen and spread.

'It's a new day, Magnus... Another one.' Jessie cinched the belt of her dressing gown tightly round her waist and said, 'I'll get that photo for you now. The one of you and Lachlan.' As she passed his chair, she laid a hand on her son's shoulder, bent down and kissed the top of his unruly head. 'I know he'd have wanted you to have it.'

172

Chapter 17

Fay

Confined to a hospital bed with my teeth wired, I had a lot of time to think after Magnus' quasi-conjugal visit. Which was just as well. I had a lot to think about. But mostly I thought about Magnus. And worried. From the moment I'd arrived at the party, I'd seen him reacting badly to all the old triggers: the noise; the press of people; memories crowding in on him; the anger he couldn't control. The omens weren't good.

I worried on Nina's account too, but she was a sensible girl. I felt sure she wouldn't have hung around at Tully while Magnus spent most of the night at the Infirmary, attending – one way and another – to his ex-wife. For Nina's sake, I hoped she'd gone to stay with her parents. For Magnus' sake, I hoped she hadn't. I didn't like to think of him on his own.

I could have texted Emily to ask her to check up on Magnus, but I had no idea how things stood between us. The future of my relationship with my daughter rested on Rick's capacity to talk himself out of a tight spot (which I thought might be considerable), so I decided it would be best to wait for Emily to make the first move. She and Rick would need time to sort themselves out. In any case, I didn't actually want to explain to Emily how worried I was about her father. She might have already guessed from the way he took a swing at Rick, how Magnus really felt about me, but so far, Emily didn't know my true feelings for *him*. It occurred to me, I could reassure her about the insignificance of my liaison with Rick by declaring my undying love for Magnus.

Undying love? For once the corny cliché was true.

After I'd left Tully, living alone was terrifying, but not as terrifying as living with Magnus when he was ill, or living without him when he'd been posted to a war zone. I worried myself sick about Magnus and Emily after I'd left, but I knew

Jessie was there most days and I often spoke to her or Emily on the phone. Magnus rang a few times, but eventually I asked him to stop. I found it too upsetting. He'd never been much good on the phone and whatever the topic of conversation, all I could hear was the ache in his voice, willing me to come home. But after a while – a long while – I had a growing sense that I was becoming my own person, perhaps for the first time in my life. To my parents' utter dismay, I'd dropped out of college to become an army wife. From then on, my life had been lived in the service of Magnus and his regiment, so my new sense of freedom was exhilarating.

We still owned a small flat in Glasgow, which we let out to augment our meagre income. We gave the tenants notice and I moved in. Morag was lonely after her second divorce, so I invited her to share the flat, telling her I could do with some company and extra cash. It was only a stop-gap for her, but flat sharing eased me into my new single life.

I got my first ever job at the age of thirty-eight. I waitressed part-time, then took on another job, serving in a shop. Slowly my confidence grew, but I refused to date men, even though Morag tried hard to set me up with a few. I just wasn't interested, even though at times I thought I'd die of sexual frustration. It was even worse than the years when I used to count the days till Magnus came home. It's one thing coping with celibacy when you have a man who will (you hope) eventually come home. It's quite another, thinking you've possibly had your last experience of lovemaking and don't even remember when it was.

By the time I felt ready to see other men, sex was just a distant memory. But not distant enough. Memories of Magnus sabotaged my tentative sexual forays, probably because I was only attracted to men physically like him – long, lean, athletic types. My body occupied itself with a selection of pleasant and attractive men, but my mind was full of another. I wasn't prepared to do that to a man twice, so my lovers were taken aback when I finished our relationship abruptly and for no very clear reason. I'm sure they must have thought I was very fickle. The problem was, I was *faithful*.

Morag said it was a phase and I'd get over it. (She'd never

had children and although only a few years my senior, treated me in those early days as the teenage daughter she'd never had.) She claimed I'd get over it quicker if I actually slept with my ex, as apparently most women do at some point, but as Magnus and I became more and more distant, there was little chance of that. I heard his news – a censored version – through Emily and Jessie. Neither of them told me about Nina, but Emily let the cat out of the bag one day. Taking my elaborate show of mild interest at face value, she was happy to gossip.

Like Morag, I thought my Magnus fixation was just a phase, albeit a long one, and after my encounter at the hotel with Rick, I dared to think I was finally over it. Rick was nothing like Magnus, physically or temperamentally. Although I didn't exactly *select* him as a partner, when I found myself responding to him sexually, I thought perhaps I'd finally abandoned the quest for a Magnus-clone.

But I hadn't. Rick's enthusiastic lovemaking just served to remind me how much I'd missed the male body, the fun and intimacy of lovemaking. Rick awoke my dormant sexual self, but that self wanted Magnus; *craved* Magnus.

After Rick, I effectively gave up on men. In theory I was still looking, but attractive men seemed increasingly thin on the ground (a dearth also bemoaned by Morag). I kept myself busy with work and it became my habit to stay up late so I'd fall asleep soon after I turned out the light.

But I didn't always stay asleep. Sometimes I'd be woken by dreams and often they were dreams of Magnus. I'd wake remembering things I couldn't recall in my waking life: the feel of his springy curls under my fingertips; his long, bony spine; the smooth undulations of his muscular arms; the sad, scarred wreckage of his legs. I would wake after one of those dreams, sweating, breathing heavily, unable to believe Magnus wasn't actually beside me in the bed; desolate that he wasn't.

I felt the lack of him like a physical pain – a familiar one and one I'd lived with for many years as his wife. It hadn't occurred to me I might continue to suffer that pain when I was no longer his wife, like the "phantom limb" experienced by amputees. After all, they say time heals all wounds, don't they? That memories fade. Well, they lied. But by the time I'd made that discovery, Magnus was shacked up with Nina and it was far too late to admit I'd made a mistake.

Had I?...

I asked myself the question again and again. Each time I came up with the same answer: I'd had no real choice. The marriage seemed to be over. I was exhausted, sick, incapable of caring for a mentally ill husband. Was my first duty to care for him or to look after myself? I still don't know. But I don't think it was a mistake leaving Magnus. I still think it was the best thing to do. The *only* thing. It's just that, in my enfeebled, irrational state, I had no idea I was still so much in love with him.

And if I'd known? Then what?

I don't know.

What I do know is, if I'd been aware Magnus still loved me, would apparently always love me, even when he was in bed with the woman he intended to make his second wife, I would have stayed. I would have stayed and taken my chance. But I was convinced our love had died. I thought only if Magnus and I still loved each other could we survive his illness and another bloody freezing winter at Tully.

But our love wasn't dead. Not quite. It was on life support and the prognosis wasn't good, but it wasn't actually dead. There was a tiny pulse, but neither Magnus nor I could feel it. So I pronounced the patient dead.

The call sign for the EOD is "Felix", the cat with nine lives. The EOD had given Magnus several dramatic opportunities to demonstrate he wouldn't just lie down and die.

Nor, it seemed, would our marriage.

As I feasted on baby rice and puréed cauliflower cheese, I acknowledged that my life was descending to the level of soap opera. I sought to calm my mind by sketching new ideas for textile pictures. A nurse provided me with a pad of paper and brought some felt tips and pencils from the children's ward. As I doodled, I remembered Emily hurling my engagement gift on to the fire at Tully... And Magnus putting his hand into the fire to retrieve it... What a *horrible* evening it had been, especially for Emily and Nina. If I hadn't gone to the party, Emily would still be happily engaged to Rick, Nina to Magnus and my jaw would be in one piece.

And Magnus and I would not have made love. After – what must it be now? – six years. Longer. Toward the end of our marriage, we'd slept separately. Prior to that, we'd always slept together, in so far as it was possible to sleep with a man who woke up several times a night – sometimes screaming – and frequently got up to check every door bolt and window catch, after which he'd return to bed, frozen and shaking.

After the onset of Magnus' PTSD, not much sleeping went on in the marital bed. Nothing else happened in it either. Whenever we found ourselves in bed together, we both craved sleep, not sex. I even gave up cuddling Magnus in bed because if I fell asleep in his arms, I might find myself thrown out of bed or given a black eye as he surfaced from one of his hideous nightmares. I learned to keep to my side of the bed and we both kept our hands to ourselves.

When, out of consideration for me, Magnus suggested we resort to separate bedrooms I could have wept with relief (but made sure I didn't.) It was merely formalising the gulf that already existed between us, physically and mentally. I was too depressed and exhausted to feel anything other than grateful for his suggestion, but sleeping separately severed the last tie. As we became strangers to each other's bodies, we became oddly distant, almost formal. We had at least occasionally held each other in bed, especially after the nightmares. Sometimes we just lay side by side, holding hands, like effigies on a tomb, a living memorial to our dead marriage. It wasn't much, but it was all we had left in the way of physical intimacy; the only comfort we could offer each other.

Looking down at the doodles on my pad, I saw an attenuated, mop-haired cartoon figure that bore a passing resemblance to Magnus. It was hardly a fitting tribute to the man to whom I owed my career, for I'd become interested in art, especially its therapeutic power, when I saw how learning

177

to express what he'd experienced not only released Magnus from the grip of unimaginable horrors, but actually began to heal him.

His recovery would only ever be partial and it was a long and very painful process. Various people put him back together when he was invalided out of the army: surgeons and physiotherapists worked their magic on his body and a counsellor and an art therapist worked on his mind. When reassembled, Magnus didn't much resemble the man I'd married, but the abject raw material they'd had to work with hadn't resembled the man I'd married either: that bright-eyed, smiling boy who'd gone off to fight in the Falklands.

Once Magnus was diagnosed with late-onset PTSD and the severity of his condition acknowledged, he was sent several times a year to stay at Hollybush House in Ayrshire, a residential home for veterans run by the charity, *Combat Stress*. Sometimes I was allowed to stay too. At other times, I visited. Occasionally I observed the veterans' recreational activities. These were life-changing, for them and for me.

During his first stay, Pauline, the art therapist showed Magnus round the art room, pointing out the various materials. She invited him to paint or draw. He was pretty unresponsive at first, but after a lot of good-humoured teasing and encouragement from the other patients, he picked up some brushes and "messed around with them", as he put it. When Magnus said he didn't know what to paint, Pauline encouraged him to paint what he saw in his head and, with a lot more encouragement, that's what he did. Not surprisingly, he painted scenes of devastation – rubble, ruins, explosions, even bits of body flying through the air. Magnus was no artist and his efforts resembled a particularly nasty comic book. He painted derelict houses with shattered windows like blinded eyes and doors hanging off their hinges, like tongues lolling out of mouths. Sometimes a small, solitary figure would be standing in the foreground, looking at the ruins. I couldn't tell if this was meant to be a child or a man and I didn't like to ask.

These pictures were the stuff of nightmares, Magnus' nightmares. They were horrific, even though they were executed in a naïve, child-like style. (Perhaps they were all the more disturbing because they looked like something painted by a child.) Magnus must have produced scores of these pictures, compulsively, almost automatically. As soon as he finished one painting, he'd start another. Pauline rarely commented on his work, other than to encourage, but she made sure he was kept supplied with paper and paint.

Then one day Magnus did something different. He drew a sketch using a charcoal pencil. It appeared to be the usual ruinous building, but I noticed there was something different about the way he was working. He seemed calmer and more methodical. Instead of the usual flurry of brush and paint, he was taking care over what he drew and every so often he would stop, look up and stare into space. Pauline, who just happened to be passing (I noticed she often contrived to be on hand when one of her student-patients was experiencing difficulties) glanced down at his picture and said, 'Can't you see it, Magnus? In your mind's eye?'

He shook his head. 'No. It's not there... *I'm* not there. But I remember it.'

Pauline looked alert, but her voice remained dispassionate, only mildly curious. 'Is it something you want to remember?'

'Aye,' he replied, unable to keep the wonder from his voice. 'It's a place I used to play as a boy... A place I loved.'

Pauline looked down at his sketch. 'What happened to it?'

'My father blew it up. Razed it to the ground... It was a big house. *Huge*. A mansion called... Drummond Hall. Aye, that was it! *Drummond Hall*. It'd been empty for as long as I could remember. Years and years... and I watched it gradually decay.'

'How did you feel about that?'

He struggled to find the right words, then said, 'Helpless... There was nothing I could do. Rain got in. And birds. It became a sort of refuge for all sorts. Tramps. Lovers... Then one day my Dad blew it up. Reduced it to rubble. Sold it off as building materials. All that was left was just this great big *gap* in the sky... where Drummond Hall had been.'

As he stared into space at something that wasn't there,

something he'd known and loved, tears ran down his cheeks. His body sagged forward and I thought he might collapse, but he placed his palms flat on the edge of the table and propped himself upright, his head bowed, his shoulders hunched. Tears dropped onto his charcoal sketch making little puddles as he spoke, the angry words almost choking him.

'Pieces! That's all there was! Lumps of stone and plaster. Bricks. Tiles. *Dust.* There was nothing left. And it had been home to a grand family... And jackdaws. And Christ knows how many rats!... And *me.*' Magnus looked down at his damp sketch, grabbed hold of it and screwed it up, crushing it into a ball with both hands. He hurled the paper across the room, sat down and buried his head in his arms, sobbing like a child.

The army deals with loss and grief in two ways: ceremonial ritual and the consumption of prodigious amounts of alcohol, the one often followed by the other. Neither method has much to do with facing up to reality; everything to do with boosting morale.

If there was a point when Magnus began to heal, it might have been then, when he drew Drummond Hall, when he finally got angry, consciously angry. I don't doubt that Pauline's encouragement to paint – and paint obsessively – was what brought his anger to the surface. Then finally Magnus allowed himself to grieve for all he'd seen and all he'd lost.

It was high time.

~

Magnus took a taxi home from his mother's flat and paid the driver in a daze. He pushed open the front door, stood at the foot of the turnpike stair and listened.

Silence.

Silence, but for the distant sound of squabbling jackdaws.

'Nina? Are you home?'

He called again, louder this time and waited for the sound of footsteps. None came. He wasn't surprised.

It was colder inside Tully than outdoors, where wintry sunshine took the chill off the air. He couldn't smell wood smoke either, so he assumed no fires were alight, the central heating was off.

Nina was gone.

Relief overwhelmed him. He turned and bolted the door, top and bottom, then headed for the kitchen in search of a bottle of whisky.

The kitchen table was piled with plates of leftover food and the draining board was covered with dirty glasses. His mind full of apprehension, Magnus scanned the kitchen looking for a note from Nina. He didn't want to find one, but if he did, he hoped it would say she'd thought better of her engagement and had decided to emigrate. With her mother.

He found no note and, feeling a little better after his cursory search, he opened the door to the drinks cupboard. There, propped up against a bottle of Lagavulin, was an envelope addressed to him. The firm, clear hand was unmistakably Nina's. Magnus picked up the note and the whisky bottle, took them to the kitchen table, then hesitated. He found himself unable to recall where glasses were kept. Disdaining a dirty glass on the single malt's behalf, he unscrewed the cap and put the bottle to his lips. When the fire in his belly had abated, he tore open the envelope.

His eyes moved over the dancing words but he couldn't decipher them, so he screwed up the note and lobbed it across the room. He snatched up the envelope, repeated the exercise and was about to drink again from the bottle of Lagavulin when he froze, the bottle in mid-air. A tiny movement barely registered in his peripheral vision. His body became still, an instrument for listening. He could hear nothing. He risked moving his head, imperceptibly, widening the range of his sight.

Nothing.

But it only looked like nothing. Nothing often meant there *was* something. *Look for the absence of the normal, the presence of the abnormal.* That was the golden rule, if you didn't want to get killed.

He saw the movement again, dropped the whisky bottle and upended the massive oak table. Before the plates and cutlery had hit the floor, Magnus was crouched behind the table, his eyes raking what he could still see of the room.

A mouse skittered over the flagstones and vanished under the sink. Magnus watched it go, then listened again. He could hear nothing but his own breathing, which he tried to slow, so he could hear better.

Still nothing.

Look for the absence of the normal...

Nina. Where *was* she?

The presence of the abnormal...

The note. Read the bloody note...

Magnus waited another two minutes, then, when he was satisfied he wasn't being watched, he ran across the kitchen, head down, bent double, till he reached the discarded ball of paper. Turning, so his back was against the wall, he unscrewed the note with trembling hands.

Nina was safe. But she sure as hell wasn't happy.

Magnus' laughter was immoderate. It stopped abruptly and he got to his feet. Staggering a little, he attempted to re-orient himself. Finding the kitchen table upended, he set it to rights, heaving it back on to its legs. Surveying the floor, he couldn't account for the pile of shattered crockery and glass and concluded it must have been quite a party.

He looked round and saw a chair on its side, halfway across the kitchen. He fetched it and tucked it neatly under the table, then went to the drinks cupboard in search of the Lagavulin. It was gone. *Definitely* some party... As he searched the cupboard, his hand fell on a bottle of Famous Grouse. It would do. He grabbed a dirty glass from the draining board and set bottle and glass on the table. Arranging his chair so he had a good view of the only door into the kitchen, he sat and poured himself a large whisky. As he drank, his shaking grew less. Eventually, when sleep overtook him, it stopped altogether.

Magnus gradually surfaced, aware of a pounding noise. He assumed he was being shelled and slid rapidly under the kitchen table where he lay face down and prepared to die. Recognising Tully's cold flagstones, he reviewed his situation and decided someone was banging at the front door. He got to his feet, wondering idly what day it was. He felt his chin. From the length of his stubble, he guessed no more than a few hours could have passed since he'd left Jessie's flat.

As he approached the door, the banging stopped and someone began to shout his name. A woman. A flicker of animation crossed his face but died as he recognised the voice. He slid back the bolts, turned the huge key and swung open the oak door. He stood, blinking at the daylight, then, with neither enthusiasm nor surprise, said, 'Nina.'

'For goodness sake, Magnus! Who on earth were you expecting?'

He shrugged. 'The IRA... Al-Qaeda... Your mother.'

'She's in the car.'

'Does she have a gun?'

'Don't worry, you're quite safe. She says she refuses to have anything to do with you.'

'She does?' said Magnus, brightening a little.

'Will you let me in please? This is supposed to be my *home*.' Magnus swung the door wide to allow Nina to enter. As she stepped over the threshold, she looked up into his bloodshot, unfocused eyes and said, 'If I don't emerge within fifteen minutes, my mother has instructions to ring the police.'

Magnus closed the door and, to Nina's consternation, bolted it again and turned the key. She headed toward the kitchen, but Magnus called out, 'I wouldn't if I were you. I haven't cleared up yet. Since the party. It's a wee bit... squalid.'

Nina sighed and mounted the stairs to the Great Hall, where she was dismayed to find her homemade bunting still hung, looking tawdry in the sunlight that now entered through the big windows. Someone – she doubted it was Magnus – had made an attempt to clear the room of plates and glasses, but the floor still needed sweeping and the fire wasn't lit or even laid. Nina thought she'd already cried herself out, but found she was close to tears yet again.

She turned to Magnus, hoping to see the man she thought she loved; who she'd believed loved her. Instead she saw someone resembling a vagrant, his clothes filthy, his long hair

183

uncombed, his face dark with stubble and his expression oddly vacant. With exhaustion? Alcohol? Nina sniffed the air discreetly, but could detect no fumes. She wasn't prepared to get close enough to Magnus to be certain. Under strict instructions from her mother, Nina was taking no chances.

She glanced at her watch and said, 'Please don't get upset, Magnus and *please* don't be angry with me. I have something to say that I don't think you'll want to hear.'

Magnus looked at her, his eyes wary now. 'You're pregnant?'

'No, of course not! Why – would that have been bad news?'

'The worst.'

'I see. Well, this won't come as quite such a shock then. But promise me you won't shout or swear at me.'

'I don't swear.'

'You swear like a trooper!'

'That's because I was!' he said, suddenly angry.

Nina took a step back. 'You know what I mean. I forbid you to swear at me. I don't stand for it in my classroom and I won't stand for it from you.'

'*I won't bloody swear!*' Magnus yelled. Nina treated him to the basilisk stare with which she quelled wayward ten year olds. It had its usual effect. 'I won't swear,' he mumbled.

Nina took a deep breath and, fixing her eyes on a stain on the floor, said, 'It's over, Magnus.'

'Oh.'

'I'm leaving.'

'Oh.'

'I think it's for the best. I know you probably think we could patch things up—'

'I don't.'

Nina blinked at him in astonishment. 'I see.' Departing from the script she and her mother had prepared, she said, 'Are you trying to be deliberately offensive?'

'Och, no! It's just coming out that way. It's a knack I have. Sorry.' He leaned forward and ran both hands through his hair, dragging it back from his face, then he held his head, cradling it as if he feared it might split, or topple from his shoulders. 'I'm sorry, Nina. Take that as an across-the-board, all-inclusive, global apology.' He dropped his hands and let them hang loosely at his sides. 'I apologise for existing. And for fucking up your life.'

'Please don't swear, Magnus.'

'Sorry. But look at it this way. You've had a lucky escape. Why should a lovely young woman like you saddle herself with a... a *wreck* like me? And a ruin like Tully.'

'That's just what Mummy said.'

'She did? Bloody hell!'

'*Magnus!*'

'Sorry. Well, she's right,' he said, calming himself. 'An astute woman, your mother. Aye, you could do much better for yourself. Marrying me – ach, you might as well take a part-time job as a psychiatric nurse! It's no life for a young woman. You should talk to Fay about that.'

'I'd rather not, thanks.'

'No. No, of course.'

'Is she... all right?'

'Fay?'

'Yes.'

Magnus gazed at her blankly.

'The last time I saw her,' Nina explained, 'she was unconscious.'

'She's in the Infirmary. Fractured jaw.' Nina gasped but Magnus appeared not to notice. 'Contusions. They don't think there's any concussion, but she's under observation. Apart from that she's... fine. Aye, she's fine right enough...' Magnus suddenly ground his fists into his eye sockets. When he removed them Nina noticed his bloodshot eyes were wet. 'I need a fucking drink. A *big* fucking drink. Will you join me? For old times' sake?' His sudden grin was macabre. Nina took another step back.

'No, thanks. Mummy's waiting.'

'Oh aye, mustn't keep Mummy waiting! So, you'll be leaving Tully, then?'

'Yes.'

'Soon?'

'Immediately. Well, as soon as I've packed up my stuff.

185

Davy's going to move it for me in his van.'

Magnus looked pained. 'I'd have done that for you!'

'I know. But... well, I'd just prefer Davy to do it. And he did offer.'

'Aye. Davy Campbell has a soft spot for you.'

'Does he?' Nina asked, surprised.

'For your baking, certainly. He often mentions it.'

'He's never said anything to me.'

'Aye, he's shy. But a great wee bloke. Hard worker too.' They maintained a moment's awkward but respectful silence, as Magnus contemplated Davy's encyclopaedic building skills and Nina reconsidered his eligibility. 'You should bear him in mind maybe,' Magnus continued. 'Talk it over. With your mother, I mean.' Nina gave him a withering look and he quickly changed the subject. 'So you're going back home then?'

'Yes. Mummy's always kept my room for me.'

'Aye, she was always one for looking on the bright side.'

'She's a realist, Magnus.'

'Is that what she is? I've often wondered.'

'Let's face it, things were never going to work out for us, were they?' Nina said bitterly. 'You just won't look to the future! Your heart and mind are rooted in the past.'

'I thought that was one of the things we had in common!'

'I love the past, but I've no desire to *live* there.'

'Is that what you think I do?'

'Yes. But I also understand that it's your way of moving forward, from your own past. But...'

'But?'

'I don't think I can wait that long, Magnus! I'm twenty-eight. I want to settle down. Have a family.'

'Aye, and I agreed that we—'

'I know what you *said* and I think it's what you *believed*, but the fact is, mentally, you're still married to Fay.'

'*What*? We divorced five years ago!'

'I know, but you're as married to Fay now as you ever were. You just don't *live* with her any more.' Nina looked at her watch. 'I must go or Mum will be ringing the police. Look, I'll come back later with Davy to collect some of my stuff. You

186

don't need to wait in. I've still got my keys.

'Nina, I—'

'Goodbye, Magnus. I hope you manage to work something out with Fay. I suspect you're meant to be together. Even if,' she added gently, 'you're not meant to be *happy* together.'

He stared, struggling to absorb the meaning of her words.

She looked away and said, 'Fay looked gorgeous at the party, didn't she? I felt like a cart horse next to her!'

'Och, no,' said Magnus, his voice unsteady. 'Fay's just... *wee.*'

'And from the way she tried to avoid you all evening, I think you can assume she still feels something for you. Perhaps more than she cares to admit.' She laid a hand on his arm. 'Go for it, Magnus! What do you have to lose?'

He shook his head. 'You don't understand.' He looked down, suddenly ashamed. Staring at his feet, he tried – and failed – to remember what had happened to the laces of his shoes. 'I can never ask Fay to come back... I drove her away. I drove her mad.'

'You drive *everyone* mad! You're the most exasperating man I've ever met! God knows why we all love you!' Nina laid a hand on his chest, went up on tiptoe and kissed him on the cheek. 'I have to go now.' Magnus didn't reply. At the door she turned and said, 'Look after yourself.'

He nodded, then watched her go, his body braced, as if huddling against a wind only he could feel. After some minutes had passed, he went back down to the kitchen and poured himself another whisky. He took both glass and bottle to the corner of the room opposite the door and squatted on the floor with his back against the wall. He drank the whisky down, then took his mobile out of his sporran and selected Fay's number. He pressed *Call* and waited, his eyes shifting back and forth, scanning the kitchen for mice, rats, snipers, insurgents, the IRA. Even before Fay's voicemail told him she was unable to answer her phone, he remembered her jaw was wired together. Then he remembered *why* her jaw was wired together.

With a savage cry, Magnus hurled his mobile at the stone wall. It shattered on impact and the pieces fell to the floor, joining the remains of the best dinner service.

It had been an expensive day.

Fay

Magnus and I used to talk about fear, its crippling and corrosive power. I wanted to know how he managed it, how *I* could manage it – the fear of his being maimed, the fear of losing him altogether.

He said his fear of madness was much greater than his fear of death had ever been. He'd always managed not to dwell on the fear of death, at least while he was doing the job, because the technical demands were so all-consuming. He said there wasn't time to be afraid, but he admitted it often hit him afterwards. Sometimes it hit him badly.

When he no longer lived in fear of death or injury, he began to fear madness – with good reason since he frequently retreated into states that the average person would call madness. Magnus said the fear of madness was much harder to manage than the fear of death. He claimed that in his job, death would probably be instantaneous. (He used to say this was one of the perks of the job.) There would be no consciousness of the imminence of death. There would be no suffering. One minute you're alive, the next you're not. But he said the madness of PTSD *stalked* you. You always knew it was there, even on a good day. It lay in wait like a sniper. A bullet could come hurtling out of a cloudless blue sky, any time, any place. It wasn't so much "if", but "when". It was possible, Magnus said, to live defying death, ignoring its statistical probability. But madness was different.

He knew only too well what it was to be conscious of the threat of madness and the sudden descent into it. He said there was nothing more terrifying than to be conscious that he was possibly losing his mind.

Nothing, except perhaps his realisation that I was losing mine.

Chapter 18

Fay

I was surprised when Magnus didn't contact me. I wasn't sure what the etiquette was with regard to making contact with your ex after a sudden and frenetic resumption of sexual relations. (I dare say Morag could have set me right on that one.) I expected a text, if only because Magnus knew I couldn't speak to him on the phone. I'd discovered it was actually possible to talk with my teeth wired together and to my surprise, the nurses were able to understand me, but I didn't think my limited conversational ability would be up to a morning-after-the-night-before telephone conversation with Magnus.

When I hadn't heard from him after twenty-four hours, I thought of texting him myself, but it occurred to me he was probably trying to sort things out with Nina. I thought it best to leave him alone. He had enough problems as it was. Even if Nina forgave him (which seemed unlikely) Magnus would never go ahead with the wedding. Not now. He hadn't wanted me to leave and now I knew he'd spent years waiting for me to go back. Whatever I said now, he'd never believe there was no chance for us. He knew I still loved him – passionately – and Magnus didn't give up easily. He'd read me that heartbreaking farewell letter to demonstrate that the only way he'd be getting out of this marriage for good would be by dying. (And even then I wondered. I could just imagine him haunting Tully as a ghost, moping about like a lovesick teenager, indulging in pointless, irritating poltergeist activity.)

By letting Magnus make love to me, I'd undone the work of years spent feigning indifference; years dating men who weren't worthy, intellectually, conversationally or sexually, to touch the hem of Magnus' kilt. Had it all just been an elaborate ruse, designed to convince myself (and Magnus) that I could live without him?

Well, I'd proved that, actually, I *could*.

But I'd discovered that, actually, I didn't want to.

~

Emily found Fay in a corner of the day room, a sketch pad on her lap, her fist full of coloured pencils. Engrossed in her work, she didn't notice Emily's arrival until she spoke.

'Hi, Mum. How're you doing?'

Startled, Fay looked up and smiled awkwardly. She hoped her wired jaw would account for both her embarrassment and inability to respond immediately. Straining to articulate through her wired teeth, she said, 'Thanks for coming. I didn't really expect you.' She wondered if Emily would be able to understand, given the competition from the day room TV, but she just smiled, sat down in an adjacent armchair and handed Fay a carrier bag.

'I thought you'd prefer magazines to flowers, so I got you copies of *Selvedge* and *Fabrications*. Hope they're OK.'

'Thank you! What a treat.'

Emily grinned, then put a hand up to her mouth. 'Sorry, Mum – I'm not laughing at you. It's just that you look as if you're snarling at me, baring your teeth like that. Is it OK for you to talk? I don't mind if you want to write on your pad. Or just listen and nod.'

Fay shook her head. 'I'll talk till I get tired. Or my jaw starts to hurt.'

'Are you still in pain?'

'It's not that bad now. The worst thing is not being able to lick my lips. It's driving me crazy.'

'Do you want some lip salve? I think I've got some in here,' said Emily, rummaging in her handbag. 'You're welcome to have it.'

She handed Fay a small tin and watched while she smeared some cream on to her bruised lips, which then formed an ecstatic smile.

'*Bliss!*'

In the conversational lull, mother and daughter regarded each other and attempted to assess the damage. Fay thought Emily looked tired. Puffy eyes suggested she'd been crying, or perhaps not sleeping, but for now she was smiling bravely.

'I wasn't sure you'd want to see me, but... well, I was worried about you. And in any case,' Emily added looking down at the worn, floral carpet, 'I wanted to apologise.'

Fay felt flooded with relief but resolved to ration her words. She wouldn't be able to talk for long. 'Rick explained?'

'Yes.'

'And you believed him?'

Emily looked surprised. 'Of course. That's why I've come to apologise. I wanted to say, I'm sorry I jumped to some really stupid conclusions. But it was such a shock, hearing you and Rick talking like that... And I think I was a bit drunk. I'm not used to champagne. It slips down really easily, doesn't it?' Fay nodded. 'And Dad didn't exactly help matters. In fact he made everything worse. He jumped to the same conclusions as me.' Emily hesitated before adding, 'And for the same reason.'

Fay raised her eyebrows in enquiry.

'I love Rick,' Emily said simply. 'And Dad loves you,' Fay looked away, but Emily went on. 'You do realise, don't you, Mum? I mean, I know he's supposed to be in love with Nina, but I think he's still in love with you! He *must* be, otherwise why would he have tried to punch Rick?' Emily paused to let her mother reply but Fay said nothing and appeared to study the sketch on her lap. 'Dad shouldn't marry Nina,' Emily declared. 'It would be very wrong.'

'I'm sure he won't,' Fay said. 'Not now. But he needs time. Time to sort things out. In his own mind.'

'Has he been in to see you?'

'Yes.'

Emily waited for further information. When it wasn't forthcoming, she sighed and said, 'Is there anything you need while you're in here?'

Fay shook her head. 'I'm going home soon.'

'Back to the flat? Will you be all right on your own? I think Granny was hoping you'd go and stay with her. She's been so worried about you. Worried about Dad too for some reason.'

Fay looked uncomfortable. 'I don't want to go to Jessie's.'

'Because you think Dad might show up and ask to see you?'

Or because he might not, Fay thought as she stared at her reflection in the day room window. It was dark outside and she couldn't tell if the distortion of her face was a product of the harsh day room light or Magnus' blow. She turned back to Emily and said, 'I think Magnus and I need to keep our distance. For the moment anyway. He feels terrible about... what happened. And he needs time to sort things out with Nina.'

Emily shrugged. 'Whatever you think best. But considering how he's made you suffer, I think you're being very generous.'

'It's difficult to rant with your teeth wired together.'

Emily laughed and appeared to relax a little. Fay wondered just how much it was costing her daughter to be angry with the father she adored. The crying might not have been entirely on Rick's account.

'Will they unwire you before they let you go home?'

'No, not yet.'

'You'll have to stay on a liquid diet then?'

Fay nodded. 'And I won't be able to chew properly even when they do unwire me. I shall be eating goo for weeks.'

Emily pulled a face. 'Poor you.'

'How many flavours of Häagen-Dazs ice cream are there? I'm thinking of working my way through the complete range. Thought that might keep me sane.'

Fay regretted her last words as Emily's face clouded over. She wasn't surprised when her daughter voiced her concern again.

'Couldn't you go and stay with Granny without letting Dad know?'

'I can't let him know anyway. He's not answering his phone.'

'Well, that's hardly surprising when you think what he did. I haven't heard from him either. Not since the party.'

192

'I don't suppose he knows what to say. Grovelling wouldn't come easily to Magnus. Jessie would be the one he'd ring.'

'I'm not so sure. Granny said she'd had a long talk with Dad after the party. She said he'd found it a bit... unsettling. I think that's the word she used.'

'What did they talk about? Not me, I hope?'

'I don't know. Granny was being a bit mysterious. But I think she wanted me to back off. Not put the boot into Dad about how he'd behaved at the party.'

'Perhaps she read him the riot act about Nina. How is Nina, do you know?'

'I rang her about some stuff I'd left at Tully – things we used for the party – and she said she'd been back briefly and it was still chaos. Dad hadn't cleared up or anything.'

'She's gone back to her parents then?'

'Must have. She said it's all over with Dad. I think she's moved her things out.'

'So Magnus is at Tully on his own... Will you go and check up on him?'

'No, I won't, Mum! He ruined my engagement party! Totally trashed it. Finding out about you and Rick was embarrassing enough, but at least our row wasn't public. Not till Dad punched you. He should apologise to me – for ruining my day, embarrassing my guests and worst of all, for assaulting you! And he hasn't even *called*.'

'He didn't mean to hit me.'

'No, he meant to hit *Rick*! Do you think that makes me feel any better? And what about poor Nina? How am I supposed to look her in the eye? We were friends! Now she can't even talk to me about what's happened because the man who's broken her heart is my father. It's a complete *mess*. And it's up to Dad to sort it out. The very least he could do is apologise! So, no, I am *not* rushing up to Tully with a nice hot casserole and some home bakes. I'll leave all that to Granny.'

'She's angry with him too.'

'I should think so! He's behaved *appallingly*, Mum.'

'I know. He knows too. I'm not trying to make excuses for him. But he *is* really sorry.'

193

'Well, he needs to say so. To those he's hurt.'

'I'm sure he will. I just think he's very confused at the moment.'

Emily studied her mother's expression. She sensed there was something Fay wasn't telling her and a familiar anxiety twisted her gut. 'Is Dad – I mean, do you think he's going to be ill again?'

'No, I don't think so,' Fay replied, with more confidence than she felt. 'He seemed fine when he left the hospital. In good spirits.'

'Did he apologise to *you*?'

'Oh yes,' Fay said, unable to repress a small smile. 'Handsomely.'

'So you've forgiven him?'

'Yes.'

Emily was silent. She looked across at the television screen and wondered why it was on when no one was watching it. A group of actors were simulating a bitter family row in Cockney accents. When it became clear one of the protagonists was about to throw a punch, Emily got up, strode across the room and turned off the TV. The few patients and visitors looked up, astonished, as silence settled on the room like a blessing.

Emily sat down again. Eventually she said, 'You still love Dad, don't you?'

'Yes, I'm afraid I do.'

Emily sighed, reached out and took her mother's hand. They sat without speaking for several moments, until Emily said, 'So... will you be getting back together again?'

'I don't know. I don't see how we can. I could never ask Magnus to leave Tully. He wouldn't. And I could never go back. There are just too many memories.' Fay swallowed and reached into the pocket of her dressing gown for a tissue.

'Don't get upset, Mum. You don't have to talk about this now. I shouldn't have asked.'

Fay wiped her eyes, put the tissue away, then reached for her pad and pencil. She wrote, LOVE ISN'T ALWAYS ENOUGH.'

'I know. I think I understand. *Sort* of.'

Fay wrote again. SO MUCH GOT IN THE WAY FOR US. THE ARMY. PTSD. TULLY. THERE'S A GULF BETWEEN US NOW AND NEITHER OF US KNOWS HOW TO BRIDGE IT.

'Maybe we should just let the dust settle for a while. We've all been through the mill – you especially. I'm really sorry for my part in it. I could kick myself for being such an *idiot*. I should have known I could trust Rick. And you.'

Fay squeezed Emily's hand. 'It's me who should be asking for forgiveness.'

'Please don't worry about it! Rick explained everything.'

Fay's expression was grave. 'I didn't mean Rick. I've put you through a lot over the years. And I'm very sorry.'

'But *that's* what made me the wonderfully balanced and mature individual I am now!' said Emily with a bright smile at odds with the catch in her voice. 'Mum, you and Dad are total heroes to me and always have been. I couldn't have wished for better parents.' She got up and put her arms round her mother's neck. '*Saner* parents, possibly... Look, I need to go. I hope you and Dad manage to get something sorted out. I do so want you to be happy. Together or apart. Don't mind which.'

'Try not to worry about us.'

'But I *do*.'

'It doesn't really help, you know. And worry will wear you down. Look what it did to me.'

'That's why I worry.'

'There's no need. I think Magnus and I are probably indestructible.'

'Together or apart?'

Fay smiled. 'I'll let you know. Just as soon as *I* know.'

'Well, I wish you luck.' Emily bent and kissed her mother carefully on the cheek. 'I'm rooting for you. For *both* of you.'

Fay

Emily had good reason to be worried. We'd become the owners of Tullibardine Tower in the winter of 2001-2. Despite the fact that the purchase probably constituted grounds for declaring Magnus insane, it was the by-product of a healing process that had started some years before. Restoring Tully became Magnus' therapeutic project, intended to heal his mind and the growing rift between us. It was also supposed to provide a beautiful and spacious home for us.

Space had become an issue in Glasgow. I'd taken up my own artistic pursuits, inspired by what I'd seen the veterans do at Hollybush House. Looking after Magnus and Emily, I found it hard to make time to go out and see my friends. Magnus wasn't keen on me going out anyway and his moods and weird outbursts had taken their toll on our friendships. Living on the top floor of a tenement, I'd felt increasingly isolated by my role as nurse and minder, but I'd taken over the spare room and turned it into a bit of a studio. It was a cross between a den and Aladdin's cave and the space was precious to me. I signed up for adult ed. classes in painting and into textiles and took me to a few exhibitions. As soon as I saw the possibilities of working with fabric and thread, I was hooked. I started off with patchwork, then moved on to fabric collage. Morag talked me into signing up for a City & Guilds course with her and I found once I'd got over my initial terror and sense of woeful inadequacy, I loved it.

All my spare time was spent on projects for the course. The work was satisfying and absorbing, but it wasn't something I could share with Magnus, who anyway wasn't interested. Tower houses had become his obsession and he devoted his time to studying history, reading building textbooks and writing to Historic Scotland, badgering them about grants. He was delighted when I started to sell a few pieces at craft markets, but only because it added to the fund that might one day allow us to buy a ruin and bankrupt ourselves restoring it.

I never stood up to Magnus, not until it was too late, because I assumed the worst would never happen. I saw no reason to discourage him from pursuing his dream. Although he appeared to be making a good recovery, we both knew PTSD was for life. We also knew how vulnerable veterans could be, long after the fighting stopped. (256 British servicemen died in the Falklands war. At the last count, more than 300 had committed suicide since they'd returned home.)

So I wasn't prepared to rock the boat, not until Magnus actually started talking about buying Tully. Even then I thought we were safe. I couldn't believe restoration was practical, nor did I think Historic Scotland would give us a huge grant. I certainly couldn't have anticipated that once Historic Scotland had come through, Jessie would decide to give Magnus a large part of his inheritance while she was still alive, so he could realise his dream.

I still don't know if I should have said no. Our marriage was already in difficulties. Magnus was physically fit, mentally far from well, but he was a lot better than he'd been for years and his Tully obsession seemed to be a major factor in his recovery. Emily hated her school, was constantly falling out with her bitchy, bullying school friends. She would in any case have wanted whatever Magnus wanted. They both saw Operation Tully as a romantic adventure. He wanted to rescue the tower house and Emily wanted to rescue Magnus. When I put forward my very reasonable objections, I found myself out on a limb and my resistance didn't last long. How could I possibly begrudge Magnus this new start?

For me personally, the move from Glasgow was a disaster. It meant moving away from my friends and giving up my workroom. Magnus assured me I'd have a room at Tully for my personal use, but it was a long time coming. When I did finally get a room in which to work, it was too dark because the small single window faced north and the stone walls reflected very little light. To Magnus' purist horror, I whitewashed the walls, but I still pined for the big south-facing windows of our old flat.

I had to let go of all the things that had kept me buoyed up in Glasgow and find the energy to build a new life, focussing on my marriage and an eccentric and uncomfortable new home. I thought I'd be able to manage it, especially as Magnus seemed to make great strides forward as soon as we quit Glasgow. But it's apparently often the case that when one partner has to look after the other, the health of the carer breaks down as soon as the sick partner begins to recover, almost as if recovery gives the carer "permission" to weaken. (Alternatively, it could just be the cumulative effect of intolerable strain and exhaustion.)

I didn't know what was happening to me and I didn't seek help. How could I go complaining to my GP about feeling tired, low, isolated, when my war hero husband was struggling to rebuild his life piece by piece, the way surgeons and psychiatrists had rebuilt his body and mind? The old army wife ethos prevailed and I soldiered on. As you do.

It was in any case unthinkable that I was becoming ill. I was the one holding it all together for Magnus and Emily. I was the buffer zone between a mentally ill father and his moody, adolescent daughter. There was simply no *room* for me to be ill.

Instead, I gradually shut down. I stopped socialising altogether. It was just too much effort. I didn't answer emails because I found I had nothing to say. Eventually I didn't even pick up the phone. I left the answer phone on as often as possible, then failed to return calls. Eventually there weren't any calls for me.

I thought of it as conserving energy. Since I felt permanently exhausted, this seemed like a good idea. I continued to function as wife and mother and kept us all supplied with regular meals and clean clothes. I spoke when spoken to, but rarely initiated a conversation. When I could summon up the enthusiasm, I tended my garden, but the rampant weeds and voracious rabbits defeated me. In the end I let the garden go, just like everything else.

I even stopped working on my fabric pictures in my gloomy den. I took up some simple hand–sewing again, which I found comforting. It taxed no part of my brain to sew random patches of fabric together and the repetitive, soothing activity left me free to think. Or rather brood.

As I pieced together my fabric mosaic, I formulated a plan. An escape plan. It wasn't a plan I would ever implement, but all the time I had a plan, I felt less trapped. I felt I still had choices. My plan was a sort of security blanket, something I hugged to myself in secret.

I believe I actually thought it would stop me cracking up. I didn't realise that by the time I formulated my precious plan, it was too late. I'd already cracked.

~

As the light begins to fade, Fay stands on the roof walkway at the top of Tullibardine Tower, staring out toward the leafless Dule Tree. It looks stark against the setting sun, almost black. Autumn has become winter. She can smell it in the air. A deadness. A coldness, colder than Tully's dank air, colder even than its stones. A grave cold, that rises up out of the hard, ancient earth.

Fay looks down and gazes without interest at the garden she created. Nature is reclaiming it now. From this height she can still see the grid of paths, the shapes of flowerbeds. At ground level all she sees are weeds, dead asters, chrysanthemums burned and blackened by frost. Death. Decay. Everywhere she looks.

Fay starts to feel dizzy. When the ground rears up to meet her, she raises her eyes to the sky, now livid as a bruise, to where she knows the first star will appear. She closes her eyes, only for a minute or two, but when she opens them again, it's dark and the sky is littered with stars.

Fay knows she should feel cold, but she doesn't. She doesn't really feel anything, not any more. She thinks that's probably a good thing. When she used to feel things, it was painful. And so tiring. But now she doesn't notice the cold at Tully. And she's no longer angry with Magnus. She's stopped hoping he'll get better, that they'll be happy again. She feels calmer for it. Things are simpler now. Clearer.

Fay longs for only one thing.

Sleep.

She'd like to sleep for a long time. A very long time. A long, undisturbed sleep, with no nightmares, without Magnus screaming. In fact, she wouldn't mind if she never woke up. What is there to wake for? She isn't needed. They all get by, in their own way, their paths rarely crossing. Magnus hardly seems to notice her. Emily has good friends now and a nice boyfriend. She has Jessie too, Jessie who's like a second mother to her. A proper mother.

Fay knows she wouldn't be missed. They'd cope. Perhaps they wouldn't even notice she'd gone. No one has noticed she's been on the roof for a very long time.

Has she?... She thinks it must be hours. It was light. Now it's dark. Very dark.

Or is it? Are her eyes playing tricks? Sometimes her eyes do play tricks. She sees things she knows can't be there. She's so tired these days, she can hardly keep her eyes open. Perhaps they're actually shut. Maybe that's why it seems so dark.

But she can see the stars. She can see the Milky Way spilling across the sky, above her head. And she can see the woman in the shadows, by the door.

Isobel Moncrieffe.

Isobel only appears to Fay after dark, when she's alone. Isobel is just a shape looming in the shadows, but Fay can feel her presence, the power of her will.

It's not a bad feeling. It's comforting in a way. Fay feels less alone when Isobel is present. Isobel understands. Because she can't sleep either. Sometimes Isobel accompanies Fay along the walkway. They stroll side by side, as if they were friends. Or sisters. Sisters in sorrow. Isobel lost her love a long time ago. So did Fay.

They stand and gaze out over the barmkin wall, toward the Dule Tree. Its ugly, twisted branches creak in the wind and Isobel starts to weep softly as she remembers. Fay has tried many times, but she knows there's nothing she can say to console Isobel for her loss. In any case, she's too tired, even to speak. If only she could sleep...

Isobel tugs at her mind, like a child pulling at her mother's hand. Fay knows what Isobel wants. Isobel says it's what they both want.

There is *a way they can sleep. Sleep forever. Isobel knows a way.*

She takes Fay's hand. Her grip is firm and they move forward. Isobel looks up at the sky and points to the stars. Fay stares, uncomprehending. Isobel smiles. Fay doesn't see her lips move but hears, quite distinctly, the words, 'Don't look down...'

Chapter 19

Fay

When I hadn't heard from Magnus after forty-eight hours I began to worry, not just about him, but about whether I'd read too much into our reconciliation. My spirits had crashed from a post-coital high to a recuperative low. The hospital had also reduced my dosage of painkillers, so I wasn't sleeping well, nor was I eating much. (My tolerance of liquid food already exhausted, I fantasised about crunchy baguettes, crisp apples and – bizarrely – meringues. Food with sound effects.)

Eventually I decided to text Magnus. I sent him a message asking how things were and sending him my love. I panicked and deleted the love bit, then keyed it all back in again. I sent the message before I could think better of it and lay back on my pillows to wait – far too eagerly – for a response.

For all his faults, Magnus had always been pretty good about the phone. He liked and understood technology and he always had his mobile on him. Tully was too large a home to be served adequately by a landline and anyway, Magnus was often outdoors, doing maintenance work. So when he didn't reply, I was surprised. And then I was peeved. It wasn't until a few more hours had passed that I started to worry. That I'd misread the signs. Or – what seemed more likely – that Magnus just wasn't coping.

~

As he finished his whisky, Magnus wondered if it was possible to die of guilt. Or shame. He sincerely hoped so. It would certainly solve a lot of his problems. He wouldn't have to apologise to Emily for a start. Or Rick. Or Nina. Or her mother. And he wouldn't have to suffer Jessie's disapproval or – far worse – Fay's forgiveness.

Death offered other benefits. He wouldn't have to choose between Fay and Tully. It was a no-brainer – Fay would win, obviously – but that begged the question of what he would do with the remaining fifty years he might still live, a question which only served to illustrate the desirability of his premature demise. The more Magnus thought about it, the more it seemed like a good idea. He wouldn't have to make sense of how he felt about Jessie, Lachlan and the poor bastard he'd always called Dad. That would be a relief. Because he couldn't work out why he felt guiltier now for treating Donald badly, than when he'd thought he was his father. And how come every time he thought about his *real* father, a lump came into his throat and tears welled up? He had no memory of Lachlan apart from dark-trousered legs walking toward him and a pair of enormous hands lifting him high into the air, so he could see over the heads of all the grown-ups. Magnus wasn't sure whether the choking sensation at the back of his throat was a result of what he could remember, or what he *couldn't*.

There was no doubt about it, his mind was a mess, a complete bloody mess. And so was Tully. Magnus got to his feet and picked up the empty bottle of Famous Grouse that had fallen on to its side. The contents must have spilled on to the floor. And dried. He sure as hell didn't remember drinking the best part of a bottle. Lurching sideways, Magnus grabbed a chair to steady himself as the room swam. Suddenly disoriented, he blinked, unsure now of his surroundings. When did it get to be so dark?... He should put the light on.

His feet crushed plastic on the stone floor and he froze. Looking down in the failing light, he could see what looked like pieces of electronic equipment and bits of broken plastic. Perhaps the makings of an IED. Or maybe it was a booby-trap. If he bent down and picked up a piece of this crap, would it set off a hidden explosive device?

Magnus stood still, every nerve strained to hear something in the silence, see something in the dark. He reached automatically for his rifle, but it wasn't there. He felt naked, suddenly vulnerable. His eyes were dry with staring into the dark and they were losing focus, so he decided to risk blinking. As his eyelids fell, the scene changed. What had been dark and unclear became vivid, surreal. A man he didn't know – a young soldier, just a boy – lay at his feet. He wasn't dead. His breath formed clouds of vapour in the freezing air. Magnus peered at the boy's face to see if he recognised him. His features seemed unfamiliar, but it was difficult to tell what lay beneath the crusts of mud and dried blood. The boy ignored Magnus and pulled up his army jumper. He stared down at a hole in his abdomen, through which something protruded. A piece of his stomach.

Magnus knew what he should do. He knew the drill. Any protruding parts should be pushed back inside the wound to reduce the chance of further damage to internal organs. Easier said than done, especially when the poor wee bastard was conscious. Magnus looked at the boy, no older than himself. Despite his exhaustion, despite the freezing cold and the waves of nausea that threatened to overwhelm him, Magnus managed to summon up enough anger, enough hatred of the Argies to do what had to be done. Steeling himself, he kneeled down and, swearing continuously under his breath, removed his gloves and began to poke at the wound. The boy glared at him and Magnus stopped. They locked eyes but said nothing. The wounded boy gave a curt nod, looked away and Magnus set about finishing the job.

With a queasy sense of both pleasure and disgust, Magnus noted how warm the boy's bleeding body felt to his frozen fingers. He tried to remember if he'd felt warm since they'd landed in the Falklands. He didn't think so. He'd got used to being numb with cold. That was why the feel of the wounded soldier's blood had surprised him. Magnus was shocked, nauseated that he was able to draw any comfort, however small, from the boy's suffering. It was obscene. But when you thought about it, war was obscene. Especially this war.

Magnus stared at the boy's eyes, dull with pain and exposure, then said, 'I haven't got a field dressing. Used them all. Sorry.' The boy shook his head, as if he didn't care. Magnus watched as his eyelids began to droop. 'You have to stay awake! You can't go to sleep. Not now.' The boy's eyelids flickered, then fell.

Magnus opened his eyes. He wasn't in the Falklands. He was in his moonlit kitchen. Bloody hell, he had to keep his eyes *open*! If he didn't shut his eyes, he wouldn't see things. If he stayed awake, he wouldn't have the nightmares. That's what Fay didn't understand. If he sat up all night or patrolled the grounds, it kept him awake, kept his eyes open and so long as he didn't shut his eyes, he wouldn't see his gruesome visions.

He needed coffee. Strong, black coffee. That would do the trick. His hand groped for the kettle and he took it to the sink. He thought of turning on the light but decided against it. He felt more comfortable in the dark. Safer. No sense in advertising your position. You don't want to make it easy for some bastard sniper to pick you off. With a palpable sense of relief, Magnus moved away from the moonlit window and switched the kettle on.

As he moved across the kitchen, his feet crushed another fragment of plastic, but this time he knew exactly what he was treading on. The remains of his mobile phone. He remembered hurling it at the wall. But why? Who had he been trying to phone? Jessie?... Fay?... Why would he be ringing Fay?... He thought there'd been a reason. An important reason.

Magnus felt a cold sweat begin to trickle between his shoulder blades. He didn't know where Fay was. He hadn't known of her whereabouts for several hours. She could be anywhere.

And that was bad.

He couldn't remember why, but he knew it was bad.

The kettle switched itself off but Magnus ignored it. He strode out of the kitchen and up the turnpike stair. He looked into the Great Hall and called Fay's name but there was no reply. He braced himself and switched on the light. A scene of celebration, strangely tawdry, greeted his startled eyes: tartan bunting, dirty wine glasses and arrangements of wilted flowers. He couldn't recollect what had been celebrated... His homecoming? If so, where was Fay?

Panic rising now, Magnus carried on up the stairs. He

didn't pause at their bedroom door but hurried on, up to the roof walkway, where he hesitated before opening the door to the exterior, suddenly overwhelmed by guilt, shame and nameless dread.

He'd been here before.

~

Magnus thinks he sees a ghost on the walkway: a small, pale figure blotting out the moon. As his eyes adjust to the darkness, he recognises the shape. Fay has climbed on to the low wall and stands with her back toward him, looking up at the stars. There's nothing between her and the drop to the courtyard below. A cold wind stirs her long, thick hair, which falls down her back in a tangled cascade. She raises her arms, as if preparing to fly and the sleeves of her loose shirt fill like sails. Then she looks down.

Magnus fights all his body's impulses to cry out, to leap forward or simply empty the contents of his stomach on to the stone floor. Instead, he stands very still and assesses the situation, as he was trained to do, in a matter of seconds. He releases the tension in his body, but remains preternaturally alert, like an animal stalking prey.

'Fay?' His voice is little more than a whisper. 'Don't look down.' He sees her spine stiffen and knows she's unsure, thinks perhaps she imagined his voice. She lowers her arms, then wraps them round her body. Slightly louder, he says, 'Please, Fay.'

She stands quite still on the parapet. 'Magnus?'

'Aye. I'm here.' He estimates the distance to the wall, then surveys her clothing, looking for handholds. Watching her feet closely, he starts to talk, assuming a jauntiness he doesn't feel. 'Christ, it's Baltic out here! Will you not give me your hand and come away inside now?'

She doesn't turn, but says, 'Don't come near me, Magnus. Don't touch me.'

'No, I won't. I won't touch you. I just want to come closer.'

'Stay away! I've made up my mind. This has to end!'

'I understand! I won't touch you and I won't come near

205

you, OK? But will you not even look at me?'

'I don't want to see you. You'll try to make me change my mind.'

'I won't.'

In the silence that follows he senses her astonishment. 'You won't?'

'Not if your mind's really made up. But I'd have to point out – in all honesty – that jumping won't necessarily kill you. You'll break both legs for sure, and possibly your back, so I wouldn't rate your chances of ever walking again. And serious head injury would be likely. But not necessarily fatal.'

His tone is matter-of-fact, but his eyes scan her whole body for the slightest move that will indicate her intentions.

'What are you saying?'

'I'm saying, if I wanted to kill myself – and I've given that a fair bit of thought over the years – I wouldn't throw myself off Tully's roof. I've no desire to end my days as a vegetable – och, a crippled *vegetable! I'm enough of a bloody burden to my family as it is. No, you'd be better off with pills and booze. That would be prettier too. For the family, I mean. Speaking as someone who's picked up bits of body and put them into plastic bags, take it from me – you really want to keep your insides* inside. *It's where they belong.'*

Fay doesn't move or reply. As Magnus steps forward, silent as a cat, he lowers his voice so she remains unaware of his approach. 'You could try jumping in front of a train, I suppose. Though some poor folk have survived even that. Lying down on the track is your best bet. Lying down and waiting for an express. Aye, that'd do it…Not nice for the family, but you're probably beyond such considerations by now. Believe me, I understand. I've considered your course of action many times. Weighed it all up carefully, the pros and cons. Risk assessment. That's what I used to do. What I'm good at. And I rejected suicide. D'you know why?'

Fay realises he isn't going to continue until she responds, so she says, 'Because of Emily?'

'No.'

'Me?'

'Hell, no! You'd be better off without me – financially,

emotionally, in every way.' He pauses. Still she doesn't turn. He watches her back as she waits for him to go on and observes the hesitant turn of her head as she tries to look at him over her shoulder, then thinks better of it. Magnus continues. 'I've never topped myself, Fay, for one simple reason. My analytical, unemotional brain won't let me ignore the bloody great flaw in the suicide argument.'

'What do you mean, flaw?'

She turns her head again and tries to bring him into view. He takes one slow, soundless step to the left, so she's able to see him in her peripheral vision. He knows he's judged the distance correctly when he sees her start and turn away. Shivering uncontrollably now, she lifts her head and looks up at the stars again.

'Why did you decide not to die, Magnus?'

He pauses, then says, 'Because of my dreams.'

'Your nightmares?'

'Aye... The real horrors of my life ended years ago, when I quit the EOD and then the army... I thought that would be it, after a period of... adjustment. But it's never ended... It's never-ending! Every single night for years, I went back. Every time I went to sleep, in fact. I was there, in my head. And it was all just the same. Exactly the same as when it was happening to me. I couldn't escape. Not even in sleep. That made me want to die. You see, I thought death would be like some Grimm's fairy tale, with a happy-ever-after finale tying up all the loose ends. Then one day I realised.'

'I – I don't understand. You're not making any sense.'

'Why d'you want to die, Fay? Why are you prepared to do this to Em and me?'

She holds herself again and through chattering teeth says, 'Because I can't take any more! I just want to go to sleep... and never wake up.'

'And you think death is the answer. The end.'

'Yes.'

'Aye, it's funny that. We all do... But who says it ends?'

There is a long silence while Fay struggles to absorb his words. Magnus waits, judges his moment, then repeats his question.

'Who says it ends, Fay? You assume you'll sleep peacefully forever and not be troubled by guilt, despair, exhaustion, responsibility – all those things you want to get away from. You tell yourself, that when your heart stops, when your skull's smashed, when your body's been bisected by a train, you tell yourself that's it, it's all over. But what's the evidence for your cosy wee hypothesis?... There's none. But you believe there's nothing more to a human being than the body. That with the termination of the body's contract, all suffering ceases. Well, that would be nice if it were true. And it may be true. But I don't know it's true. For all I know, everything gets worse! I mean, folk used to believe you went to Hell and fried in perpetual agony. Well, maybe we do! Personally, I find it all too easy to believe the torment goes on for bloody ever. That there really is no escape. In fact – answer me this, will you, Fay, before you jump? – how d'you know your post mortem life won't be even more hellish than this one? Who says death is the end? And what are they selling?'

Magnus allows a few moments for his words to sink in, then resumes. 'Just supposing this is as good as it gets, Fay? This night. Those stars. That moon. This life. Supposing after this, it's downhill all the way? What would be the point of your suicide? All that pain... Yours. Emily's. Mine... All the guilt. That I drove you to it. That I didn't save you... And that's if you die. If you just break your back, you'll spend the rest of your life in a wheelchair and I'll spend the rest of mine pushing it. Well, rather you than me, Fay! I decided I'd take my chances here, in this life. Better the devil you know... And if sometimes you can't hack it, well, there's always drugs. Or booze. Or drugs and booze. They hit the spot. For a while. So does getting angry. Though you want to try and stay this side of GBH if you can. Beating up your relatives is pretty bad for morale, I can tell you. And they don't like it either.' He takes another silent step forward. 'It's whatever gets you through the night, Fay. But don't go falling for that "rest in peace" bullshit. It's what we want for our loved ones, what we want for ourselves. It's how we manage to stagger through this vale of tears, telling ourselves, this is it. Death will be the end of all our travails and what follows will be everlasting peace. But it could just be a load of bollocks.'

He's getting tired now but knows she probably won't jump all the time he's talking. She'll be within arm's reach in a few paces, but if he moves any further forward, she'll hear how close he is. He stands still, poised, his eyes moving over her constantly, and continues in his mock-conversational tone.

'Me, I've had enough of dealing with unknown quantities. Snipers. Suicide bombers. Booby-trapped corpses filled with explosives. Mates who run amok because they've seen too many dead women and children... I'll stick with my nightmares, thanks very much. So far, I've always woken up. And that's the bottom line for me, Fay. It's bad – it's fucking terrible! – but it passes.' His tone changes suddenly and his voice softens. 'This will pass too! You're tired. You don't have any fight left and you've lost the meaning. But all that will pass. Especially if you go away.'

She stirs, starts to move a frozen foot and Magnus steps forward, his arms raised.

'What do you mean, "Go away"?'

Ignoring the pounding in his chest, Magnus maintains his quiet, even tone. 'Leave Tully. Leave me. Get some help and start over, away from all the bad stuff.'

'I can't do that!'

'Of course you can! Christ almighty, which d'you think I'd rather live with? Your suicide or our divorce? Which d'you think Em would prefer? And let's not forget the vegetable-in-a-wheelchair option! Because we're not dealing with racing certainties here, Fay. You're playing Russian roulette. With all our lives.'

He registers the slight sag in her body, hears the small sounds he's been waiting for. A sniff. Uneven breaths. The familiar whimpering sounds of his wife trying not to cry. He knows now that her respiratory system will be making more noise than his feet moving stealthily across the walkway. He also knows that, since he shifted back to the right, she can no longer see him unless she turns right round. In any case, he's fairly certain her eyes are closed now, because he knows how she cries. He's seen it often enough. He knows she'll be concentrating on staying upright on the ledge. Alternatively –

*his stomach lurches and he has to steady his breathing again –
she'll be engaged in the final psyche-up to jump. Either way,
there isn't a second to lose.*

*Magnus slows his heartbeat and commands his body to
move forward, relaxing the muscles of his hands and arms, so
that every scrap of energy can be channelled into the moment,
the exact second when Fay decides to jump or he's close enough
to grab her.*

*In the end, she falls. Perhaps she faints. As her legs start to
buckle, Magnus leaps forward. He grabs a handful of her long
hair and yanks it back, jerking her head violently toward him.
At the same time, the fingers of his other hand claw like talons
at the waist of her jeans. When he has a grip on her belt, he
releases her hair and feels her slide momentarily away from
him. He throws his arm round her neck, taking her weight in a
headlock. Staggering, he drags her backwards, scraping the
backs of her ankles and feet on the stone ledge, loosening her
shoes which drop, first one, then the other, down to the
courtyard below.*

*Magnus falls hard on to the stone floor, with Fay on top of
him. He doesn't release her but rolls on to his side, his arm still
imprisoning her head. His other arm circles her waist and he
holds her, pressed against his body, speaking calmly into her
ear until she stops sobbing. When finally she's silent, he guesses
from her muscle tone that she's unconscious or asleep. He
releases her, gets to his feet, then gathers her inert body into his
arms and carries her down to the Great Hall where he deposits
her in an armchair beside the fire.*

*She doesn't stir. Magnus checks her pulse, then arranges a
woollen throw around her. He removes his thick jumper and
wraps it round her shoe-less feet, then pulls up a chair and sits
opposite her, never taking his eyes from her lifeless form. He
reaches into his back pocket for his mobile, but it's no longer
there. As his eyes sweep the Hall, looking for the phone, missing
from its stand, he hears the front door bang and Emily's light
footsteps ascending the stairs.*

*He doesn't look up as she enters the room. He gives her
only a moment to take in the scene before saying, as if issuing
orders, 'Ring Dr McKay. Your mother's unwell. I don't know*

where the phone is. Try the kitchen. I can't leave her.'

Open-mouthed, Emily stares at Fay who hasn't stirred at the sound of Magnus' voice.

'Is she—?'

'She'll be fine. Just get Dr McKay... Now, Em!'

Startled by the urgency in his voice, Emily gallops back down to the kitchen to look for the phone. Only then does Magnus allow himself to lean back in the chair and close his eyes.

But still he sees.

Chapter 20

Fay

I was admitted to mental hospital and I went voluntarily. I thought at the very least they'd give me something to make me sleep. They did, which was just as well. The nocturnal repose of inmates was frequently disturbed by bouts of noisy sobbing, hysterical laughter and the occasional violent and profane outburst. It was just like sleeping with Magnus.

I went voluntarily because even I could see I'd reached the end of the line and needed help. Although he'd saved my life, I knew Magnus wasn't the one to help me. Magnus was the problem. I agreed to be admitted to hospital to save my family the trouble of looking after me and because I couldn't face them. I was ashamed. I'd been put to the test and failed lamentably.

My family was my life and I'd let them down, all of them. I'd let the army down too. I'd gone mad doing my duty, trying to look after my poor husband and my life had almost ended in an act of crazy, pathetic melodrama. I was already in debt to Magnus – as we all are – for his unstinting service to his country, for the sacrifices he'd been prepared to make for the causes of life, liberty and peace, but when that debt became personal, I couldn't handle it. I also knew if I went back, there were no guarantees it wouldn't happen again.

As I lay doped in my hospital bed, I formulated another plan, one that would allow me to live with myself. That plan entailed living alone. Call it damage limitation if you like. If I was to be of no use to Magnus, Emily and Jessie, I would at least be no burden to them. I still had my pride. Just.

So I decided to break with the horrors of Magnus' past and mine. I resolved that I would finally live without fear: fear of going mad; fear of being struck; fear of being blown up by a vengeful terrorist with a short list and a long memory; fear of getting to the end of my life and realising I'd done very little living, only preparation for a death and receiving the letter Magnus finally read to me in Perth Royal Infirmary.

I was scarcely saner when I formulated my new plan than when I decided to end it all by flying to the stars with the ghost of Isobel Moncrieffe, but as I couldn't face going back to Tully, I had to go somewhere else.

Magnus didn't try to fight me. He didn't have a leg to stand on. There was nothing he could have said to convince me (or anyone else) that things would be any different. Jessie actually told him that the marriage might stand a better chance of survival if we lived apart. This was true, but it was a terrible indictment of both Magnus and our marriage. He'd found it hard enough to accept he'd sometimes hurt me physically during flashbacks, but to be regarded as partly responsible for driving me to attempt suicide – well, I couldn't begin to imagine how bad he must feel. He really had no choice but to allow me to take my chance, living alone.

So we evicted our Glasgow tenant and I moved in. I made an attempt to appease my monumental maternal guilt by asking Emily if she'd like to join me in the city. I wasn't at all surprised when she opted to stay with her father, grandmother, friends and boyfriend in Perthshire. In fact, I was relieved. (More grist to the self-loathing mill.) I was walking away from my only child, but she was sixteen, sensible and fiercely independent. Any remaining qualms were set aside when Jessie announced she'd be staying at Tully for an unspecified period, to make sure things ran smoothly. So I found myself indebted all round, but free to rebuild my life and sanity.

Jessie stayed for a couple of months, then when she moved back to her flat, she still dropped by several times a week to check up on Magnus and Emily. Things settled down generally, but Magnus began to ask when I was coming back. I told him I'd never go back to Tully. I said I knew what I wanted and it certainly wasn't Tully. I wanted light and warmth. People. A job. Perhaps a career. I wanted to devote as much time as possible to my textile work, to my picture-histories. I thought they might help me come to terms with my marriage, my family, my illness and my guilt. To his credit, Magnus understood and suggested the compromise solution of living at Tully while trying to develop my career.

I said no.

I asked him if we could please sell Tully and start again in Glasgow, if not straight away, then when Emily finished school.

He said no.

Magnus said it would be mad – that was his word – to sell Tully in its unfinished state. In any case he was committed to Historic Scotland to do the work as agreed. He feared if he didn't, they'd ask for their grant back. I could see the sense of his arguments. I was also aware that Tully had been bought with a substantial amount of Jessie's money; that Tully was my daughter's home and inheritance and she loved it. I could, I suppose, have compelled Magnus to sell up when we divorced, but I don't know how I'd have lived with myself. He'd made the tower house his life and it was helping him to heal.

There wasn't really any way I could force the issue. I had no right. I had access to a flat in Glasgow that I could live in or sell. Eventually I sold it and made a tidy sum, which enabled me to buy a flat in a modern block overlooking the Clyde. The walls were white, the windows were huge, it was warm, cheap to run and there were no mice, bats or jackdaws. (I did miss Tully's barn owl.)

So gradually Magnus got better.

And gradually I got better.

The writing was on the wall. Clearly we were bad for each other. We needed to move on, to the next stage of our lives, so I decided we should get a divorce. Emotionally and mentally exhausted, I was convinced I no longer loved Magnus. I didn't bother to ask if he still loved me. The question no longer seemed relevant. He was living safely and apparently contentedly at Tully. It never occurred to me he might be playing a waiting game, waiting for me to come to my senses, waiting for me to come home. When I didn't go back, when I wouldn't even *talk* about going back, I assumed he'd finally accepted I no longer loved him.

And so we let go. Or appeared to. We set each other free, free to prove we could live without each other. In that we succeeded. What we failed – *utterly* – to prove was that we could stop loving each other. But then, as Magnus (and Tina Turner) said, what's love got to do with it?

Everything, apparently.

~

Magnus was playing a waiting game. He knew the sniper was out there, waiting for him. Waiting for him to fire. Or move. Do something that would betray his position. So he stayed put and waited. Magnus was a patient man.

He was also cold and stiff. His rifle rested in one of the gun loops, the defensive slits on Tully's ground floor through which he had a limited view of the enemy, but not as limited as the enemy's view of him. Magnus had extinguished all the lights as soon as he realised there was a gunman outside. He didn't know how he knew. There'd been no noise, no tell-tale signs. He'd just known. It was combat intuition, something you can't explain. A presentiment that something's wrong. And dangerous.

So Tully was dark and silent. 'As the tomb,' Magnus thought, then wondered, not for the first time, why under extreme pressure you thought in clichés? Was that the purpose of military understatement and euphemism? To avoid the ludicrous banality of clichés?... His mind was wandering. He needed to stay focused, but he was worried about falling asleep. It was hard to stay awake when you were cold and immobile. And hungry.

It was probably just one guy out there. If he'd only move, or do something stupid like strike a match, he'd have the bastard.

But maybe there was no one there... There'd been no sign for hours. Had Magnus actually seen or heard anything? He couldn't remember... He'd been up on the roof when he'd heard a scream and then he'd looked down. There'd been something on the ground... A body. A woman's body. He'd run downstairs and out into the courtyard, but he hadn't found

215

anyone. Then it occurred to him, it was probably a trap, designed to draw him out. The woman was just a decoy. She'd got up and run away. Probably wasn't even a woman. And he'd fallen for it.

Magnus had run back inside, bolted the door and fetched his rifle, which he kept cleaned and loaded. He took up a position at one of the gun loops and peered out into the darkness.

Look for the absence of the normal, the presence of the abnormal.

The barn owl... That had been normal. Flying out of the doo'cot, then swooping down over the courtyard. The squeal of something small and animal in pain, just before it died.

Death is normal. As normal as life. The flip side of the coin.

Magnus could face death, had faced it many times, had made friends with it almost. Death wasn't the problem. Not for him. Just for those left behind. Women crying. Howling. Like animals.

His mother...

He remembers her crying. Not for him. He was there, but he was just a wee boy. She was crying for someone else.

His father?

Magnus blinks and sees the man he knew as his father. There's a boy sitting beside him. Almost a man. It's 1979. Monday night. They're watching TV. His mother's in the study with her head stuck in a book. She doesn't like this programme. Says it's too noisy. And too sad.

Danger UXB.

Magnus is fifteen and he's sitting on the sofa with the man he's always believed to be his father. They're watching *Danger UXB*, a programme about ordinary men who become heroes, saving people from terrible deaths, by defusing unexploded bombs. Magnus longs to tell his father that this is what *he* wants to do. He wants to join the army and become a hero, like Lieut. Brian Ash, so his parents will be proud of him. So everyone will be proud of him.

But he and his father don't talk much. Donald's not one to sit around, enjoying a blether. Not like Jessie. So Magnus says

216

nothing. Anyway, Donald expects his son to follow him into the demolition business. Why would the lad do anything else? Donald doesn't understand that a bright boy might want to see the world and have adventures. Be a hero. Get away from an unhappy home.

Magnus blinks.

He doesn't know how much time has passed. He thinks perhaps he might have dropped off. He wriggles his toes and shuffles his feet in an attempt to get his circulation moving. Looking through the gun loop again, he sees a derelict building that he didn't register before. That will be where the sniper's hiding out. Unless of course it's just a come-on, what he *wants* Magnus to think. Maybe the building's booby-trapped. Oh, *shit...*

Abandoned cars and derelict buildings. Magnus hates them. Because the bombers only have to be lucky once. He has to be lucky every single time. But no use complaining. There's a job to be done. As some Republican bastard scrawled on a wall in Derry, *Every night is gelignite.*

'Not if I have anything to do with it', Magnus mutters under his breath.

As he sets off on another of those long walks, he offers up his version of every bomb technician's prayer.

If I die, let it be quick.
If I'm hurt, don't let me crippled.
But most of all, please don't let me fuck up.
Magnus walks.

Fay

Magnus didn't ring and he didn't text. I told myself he wasn't replying to texts because he'd lost his mobile and that he wasn't ringing me on the landline because he knew I couldn't really talk. I clung to these theories for as long as possible, then finally admitted to myself, I had doubts. Alternative explanations for Magnus' silence occurred to me. He could, for example, be in the delicate throes of working out a reconciliation with Nina. Maybe Nina was already back in the fold. Neither of these scenarios calmed my agitation, nor did

217

they diminish my sense of having been misled by Magnus. Used, even.

Yet at some level I felt I must be wrong. I knew my ex-husband, in sickness and in health. For years his damaged psyche had been showing him that horrific memories and primitive emotions governed his life, awake and asleep, yet still he'd persisted in his delusion that he could control, or at least suppress these malign influences. Failing all else, he believed he could simply ignore them. In this context, his actions, though bizarre at times, had made a sort of sense. They were the product of a male, military mind that thought one failed relationship could simply be replaced with a newer model, like changing a tyre. Nina – cheerful, attractive and uncomplicated – had fitted the job description, so she'd been appointed to the vacant post.

I don't mean to sound superior. God knows, I'd ignored some pretty primitive emotions too. Like fear, jealousy and lust. Magnus and I had both indulged in the fantasy that we were in control. Now one of those emotions – fear – prompted me to text Emily to ask if Magnus had been in touch and if he'd apologised to her yet. I received a one-word reply and it wasn't the one I wanted. That put paid to my idea of asking Emily if she'd go up to Tully to check up on her father.

Instead, I texted Jessie to ask if she'd heard from Magnus. Her reply was longer, but no more reassuring: *'No word from M. Havnt been 2 Tully since party. Am not well. Dizzy spells & a wee fall. Resting in bed. How r u? x '*

I was dismayed. Stoicism being something of a family trait, I knew Jessie's "wee fall" could actually entail broken bones. Although she had a network of friends who would rally round, I was still concerned. It wasn't like Jessie to have dizzy spells. Who knew what toll the party fiasco had taken on her? If she'd berated Magnus about his treatment of me (not to mention Nina, Emily and Rick), I didn't like to think who would fare worse in the argument.

I texted Magnus and Emily to tell them about Jessie's indisposition. I had a feeling she might not have told either of them. Emily replied immediately saying she'd drop round after work to see that all was well. Nevertheless, I lay back on my pillows feeling helpless and frustrated that I couldn't visit Jessie myself or build bridges between Emily and Magnus. I was furious with him for his various derelictions of duty. I could understand that he might not want to speak to *me*, but why this shameful neglect of his mother and daughter? I could no longer ignore a creeping and sinister suspicion that there was a third, much simpler explanation that would account for his inexplicable behaviour.

Magnus was mad. Or dead.

There was no way I was going to ask Emily or Jessie to deal with either of those eventualities, so I buzzed for a nurse. When she finally arrived I presented her with a piece of paper on which I'd written, in firm, large letters: FAMILY CRISIS. I WISH TO DISCHARGE MYSELF. NOW.

Two hours later, I was reeling down the hospital corridor, unsteady on my party heels, improbable in my blue satin cheongsam. Still dopey with painkillers, I clutched my pad of paper to my bosom, like a mascot. On it I'd written, I HAVE INJURED MY JAW AND CAN'T SPEAK. On the sheet underneath I'd written, PLEASE TAKE ME TO THE STATION. I brandished these at a taxi driver who looked bemused, then drove me to Perth station in tactful silence.

Sitting in the cab, my mind teemed with dramatic and colourful scenes, ranging from finding Magnus dead or deranged, to finding him *in flagrante* with Nina. I tried to order my thoughts. I decided that after I'd been home and changed my clothes, I would check the post. Magnus might have sent me a *Dear John* letter, or even (there's a first time for everything) a fulsome apology. After I'd checked my email, answer phone and watered my dying houseplants, I would rest up, then, if I hadn't heard satisfactory news of both Jessie and Magnus, I would get the train back to Perth early the following day, then a taxi up to Tully. If Nina happened to be there, I would wish her and Magnus every happiness (through unavoidably clenched teeth), then decamp to Jessie's to nurse my wounds and hers.

Sorted.

My head ached, but after taking another couple of painkillers on the train – and hey, one for luck! – I felt ready for anything. But not, as it turned out, a phone call from Jessie.

I was wading through my Inbox when my mobile rang. I pounced on it, but the screen told me it was Jessie. Stifling my disappointment, I answered as clearly as I could, hoping she'd be able to understand me. Her voice sounded hesitant, almost frail.

'I know you can't speak, Fay, but I wanted to say something to you, if you'll just listen. It wasn't something I felt I could put into a text.'

Feeling like a bad ventriloquist, I said, 'What's the matter? You don't sound too good.'

'I'm not so bad, thanks. How are *you* feeling now? I hope they're not thinking of discharging you just yet.'

'I discharged myself. I'm at home now.'

'Och, *no*, Fay! Was that wise?'

'I couldn't lie there any longer, doing nothing. It was driving me crazy. What was it you wanted to tell me? Was it about Magnus?'

'Aye, it was.' She cleared her throat and I heard her take a deep breath. 'I think I know why he's gone to ground. Why he's not contacting anyone. And I think...' Her voice wobbled. 'I think it's all my fault.'

'*Your* fault?'

'Aye! He came to see me. After he left you at the Infirmary. He turned up in the early hours of the morning. He was in a strange mood, but he seemed happy enough. *Considering*,' Jessie added vaguely. 'So we shared a cooked breakfast and... well, I told him something. Something I think might have upset him.'

'Sounds as if it upset you too.'

'Aye, it did.' The wobble again, but she got it under control. 'It did upset me, but it needed to be said.'

I waited for her to go on, but the silence grew, so I prompted. 'Was it something about the marriage?'

'Not yours, Fay. Mine.'

'*Yours?*'

'Aye. I told Magnus my marriage hadn't been happy. That things weren't quite what they seemed... And that he wasn't who he thought he was.'

Realisation slowly penetrated my stupefied brain. 'The letter. The one you gave me for *Root and Branch*—'

'Aye. That's why Magnus came. To ask me who'd written it. He knew it couldn't be Donald. So I had to tell him... That it was his father who'd written it. A father he doesn't remember. A man he hardly knew because... he was killed. When Magnus was three.'

'Oh, *Jessie.*'

'Killed... In an explosion, Fay.'

I think I must have made some sort of noise, then my hand flew to my face which I found was suddenly wet. I could hear Jessie weeping on the other end of the line. I gripped the phone and said, 'I'm on my way. Try not to get upset! I'll sort this out. Trust me. You're not to worry about Magnus. He can handle this, you know he can! What *can't* that man handle? But maybe he went on a blinder. He's probably still in bed with the mother of all hangovers! That's why we haven't heard from him.'

My jaw ached with the effort of speaking while trying not to cry. Swallowing hard, I said, in as bright a voice as I could muster with my teeth wired together, 'I'll be with you in a couple of hours. Don't worry, Magnus will be fine! He's the cat with nine lives, remember?'

As I hung up, I avoided doing the calculation that would tell me if Magnus had any left.

Chapter 21

The night was cold and clear. Visibility was good, which was bad for Magnus. He could have used some fog or rain for cover, but there was an almost full moon and constellations of stars. He didn't even need to look up to identify them. It was November. He knew Orion would keep him company all night, moving silently, almost imperceptibly across the sky, disappearing at dawn. It was a comfort of sorts. Made him feel less alone. But Magnus would have preferred cloud.

Avoiding the moonlit open spaces, he kept to the shadows as he advanced toward his objective: a derelict house on a piece of scrubby waste land. Was it a house? He couldn't really tell. Sometimes it looked more like a ruined bothy, just bits of crumbling wall and stones. But then he'd see square black holes, like eyes – windows where men sat, watching. Waiting for him. House or bothy, he knew that's where they were. He had an instinct for these things. So that's where he was going.

The terrain was uneven, unstable at times, but Magnus didn't use his flashlight. For all his painstaking stealth, stones still slid and twigs cracked underfoot. He told himself this worked both ways. If they heard his approach, he'd hear theirs. Except that they were sitting pretty, holed up in the ruin, just waiting for him to come into range, so they could pick him off.

Unless of course they had something more spectacular planned for him.

Remember, remember, the fifth of November.
Gunpowder, treason and plot.
Not just the fifth of November.
Every night is gelignite.

Fay

By the time I'd finished speaking to Jessie on the phone, I felt light-headed with shock, hunger and exhaustion. I'd lost weight in hospital and I didn't have much to lose in the first place. It had been hard for me to consume enough liquid calories and, eventually I'd refused the various kinds of sugary slop offered as high-calorie meal substitutes. I'd discovered, to my surprise, that there's only so much ice cream you can eat before you get sick of the sight of it.

Feeling pretty wobbly, I managed to find an over-ripe banana lurking at the bottom of the fruit bowl and a past its sell-by yoghurt in the fridge. I whizzed these up in the processor with some frozen raspberries and added a dollop of honey. *Voilà!* A fruit smoothie. How could I resist? Then I realised I had no straws. I carefully spooned the smoothie into the space between my cheek and jawbone, then sucked it quickly through my wired teeth before it could trickle out of my mouth. Mopping up pink dribble, I was tempted to take the hospital-issue scissors out of my handbag and cut myself free then and there, but I told myself the pain would be unspeakable. I might pass out and poor Jessie was waiting for me in Perth.

I poured the rest of the smoothie into a plastic container to take with me, changed my clothes and packed a few overnight things in case I spent the night at Jessie's, or even (hope springs eternal) with Magnus. I rang Emily and told her Jessie was all right, then I rang for a taxi and arrived at Queen Street Station with time to spare, so I stocked up on a few jars of baby food, plus a bar of chocolate which I slipped into my coat pocket.

I handed the man in the ticket office a slip of paper requesting a return to Perth, then boarded the train and collapsed into a corner seat. Unwrapping the chocolate, I broke off two squares, placed one inside each cheek and sat waiting for them to melt, looking, no doubt, like a hamster. The sugar hit lifted my spirits and galvanised my fuddled brain. Thanking God for the miracle of chocolate, I settled back to do some serious worrying about Jessie and Magnus.

It was a short walk from the station to Jessie's flat. She took a long time to answer the door and when she finally appeared, I didn't immediately notice her walking stick, I was so startled by her Technicolor black eye. If my jaw could have dropped, it would. I'm ashamed to say, my first thought was, is this what Magnus did when told about his real father? Then I remembered Jessie saying she'd had "a wee fall".

Struggling to articulate, I said, 'What have you *done* to yourself?'

'Och, you should see the other feller,' Jessie replied, with a grim smile. She stood aside to let me in. 'I'm just a bit shaken and bruised, is all. I had a dizzy spell when I got up, then I keeled over.' She chuckled and shook her head. 'I should take more water with it!'

'But... your eye!'

'It's grand, isn't it? All the colours of the rainbow now! I caught my face on the dressing table stool. Could have been a lot worse. Could have been the dressing table. At least the stool was padded. Och, look at us, Fay – we're the walking wounded! Come in and sit down.' She ushered me into the cosy fug of the sitting room where the gas fire was turned on full in my honour. 'What can I get you? A hot drink? Or something stronger? Are you managing to eat?' Jessie gave me an appraising look and pursed her lips as I removed my coat. She didn't like what she saw. 'My, but you've lost some weight! There's nothing to you now!'

I hitched up my sagging jeans and said, 'Do you have any straws?'

Jessie frowned as she tried to interpret my ventriloquial speech. 'Any what?'

'Straws. Big, plastic, bendy ones. I've brought some food with me.' I produced my plastic container from my overnight bag.

'I *might* have some. Left over from Christmas.'

She was about to head for the kitchen but I said, 'Sit down! Tell me where they are and I'll look. And I'll put the kettle on. Unless *you'd* like something stronger?'

'Och, maybe I will. If I'm to tell you about Lachlan.' Her face clouded over and she swallowed hard before explaining softly, 'Magnus' father... I might need a wee dram. Maybe two.'

I squeezed her hand. 'If I can find those damn straws, Jessie, you won't be drinking alone.'

Well, life is full of surprises. Did you know that whisky goes down very well with a banana/raspberry/past-its-sell-by-yoghurt smoothie? Or that getting tipsy with your (ex) mother-in-law isn't necessarily a bad idea?

With very little prompting, Jessie told me the story of Donald and Lachlan and then she had a little weep. I put my arms round her and gave her a hug, assuring her Magnus would take it all in his stride. Paternity issues were unlikely to faze him, especially as Donald and Lachlan were both long dead. Jessie agreed reluctantly and poured us both another dram.

I looked up to where *Root and Branch* hung on the wall and contemplated the work that had brought all this family history out into the open.

'I'm glad you gave me Lachlan's letter.'

'Aye, so am I.'

'And I'm glad Magnus knows now. One day you must tell Emily. I'm sure she'd want to hear about her grandfather. He was a brave man.'

Jessie nodded. 'Like her father.'

'Yes. Like her father.'

Jessie's speech soon became as indistinct as mine and I felt less like Frankenstein's monster, especially as her black eye outclassed my yellowish-purple jaw. We sat slumped in our armchairs, staring into the gas fire like a couple of old Labradors, pondering the enigma that was Magnus. The combination of single malt, strong emotion and the pain of my aching jaw meant our conversation became almost telegrammatic.

'He's back with Nina,' I said, trying to sound as if I didn't care. 'Must be.'

'*Possible*,' Jessie conceded. 'But not likely.'

'Why?'

'He loves *you*. Always has. Always will.' Jessie waved a

hand as if swatting an invisible fly. 'Just pretends!'

'Why hasn't he rung?'

'You can't talk.'

'I can text.'

'He's ill.'

'Or drunk.'

Jessie nodded slowly and sighed. 'Aye, very likely.'

I set down my glass with its ludicrous bendy straw. Placing my hands on the arms of the chair, I heaved myself upright. 'I'm ringing him. Now. Don't care if Nina *is* there.'

Jessie blinked at me in my new position, trying to focus. 'You're sure?'

'Yes! I refuse to be pissed about by that man any longer! Oh – sorry, Jessie.'

Jessie swatted the invisible fly again. 'Och, don't mind me! You've the patience of a saint, Fay. Magnus needs a good kick up the arse!'

She watched as I stood and stared at the phone, keeping my distance, as if it might suddenly leap off its cradle and bite me.

I turned to face her. 'If he doesn't answer—'

'Could be a fault on the line. We'll ask BT to check.'

'He could be in bed.'

Jessie's eyes swivelled toward the clock on the mantelpiece. '*At eight o'clock?*'

'With Nina.'

Jessie made a dismissive sound, then swallowed another mouthful of whisky. 'Even if he wanted her back – and he *doesn't* – she'll not have him. You should have seen her face when they brought you downstairs, unconscious! Magnus was beside himself. Ignored Nina. And things were said, Fay. By Magnus. *And* Nina... There'll be no going back. She might not be *Brain of Britain*, but the poor lassie's not stupid.'

'Then if Magnus doesn't answer, it means he's ill. Or drunk.'

'Or just not at home.'

'Where could he be?'

Jessie thought for a moment. 'Emily's?'

'No. He's avoiding her. Owes her an apology. Big time.'

'Och, he'll be drunk then!' Jessie said with a triumphant smile. I glared at the phone again and she said, more gently, 'Would you like *me* to ring?'

'No, thanks. I'm doing it,' I announced, steeling myself.

'Good. Get it over with! Then we'll have another dram.'

I punched the Tully number into the phone. Jessie and I locked eyes while I listened to the dialling tone. After an eternity, I replaced the phone on its cradle. Neither of us spoke. Then shifting uncomfortably in her chair, Jessie said, 'He'll be *fine.*' I don't think she convinced even herself.

'Should I go up to Tully now?'

'On your own!'

'Well, you can't come.'

'Could you ask Emily to go with you?'

I shook my head. 'She's very angry with him.'

'Aren't we all?... Ring again later. Perhaps he's... just popped out.'

'Where?'

'He could have taken it into his head to go out and walk off his hangover. He always was one for solitary walks. Especially when he was unhappy or needed to think things over.'

'You really think he's OK?'

'Oh aye. He'll be fine right enough,' Jessie said, giving me what was meant to be a reassuring smile. 'What could happen to him at Tully?'

~

Something was wrong. The derelict house never got any closer. Magnus had been moving forward steadily for some minutes now, but he still couldn't see the house in any more detail. Sometimes it disappeared altogether – he supposed when a tree or shrub got in the way. Disoriented, he had to glance up at the stars to be sure of his direction.

It must be the cold getting to him. He was feeling sluggish now and his feet were so numb, he kept stumbling. When he looked down, he could see what looked like a brick path. It seemed vaguely familiar, but he couldn't place it, nor could he figure out why there were neat brick paths running across this godforsaken piece of waste land. Something was wrong...

He emerged from the scrub and trees and found himself in some sort of clearing, almost like a garden. Again, it looked familiar, but he still didn't recognise it. His feet were sinking now into recently dug soil and he was aware that his new surroundings provided little or no cover, so he headed for a dense thicket of bushes and worked his way to its centre where he proposed to take stock and get his bearings. Picking his way over tree roots, stones and rubble, Magnus noted a change in the air. Now he was no longer out in the open, there was a strong, earthy smell of vegetation, rotting wood and – it was indefinable, but he was sure he could smell it – a source of water. But he could hear nothing. No river or burn.

Magnus stood still, his senses suddenly sharpened by a sense of imminent danger. He felt dizzy – hunger and tiredness, he supposed – and it seemed as if the earth beneath his boots shifted slightly. He repositioned his feet, finding his balance again, but as he moved, he sensed something odd. He wasn't standing on soil any more. At least, one boot wasn't. He crouched down and, risking his flashlight briefly, peered at the ground. Just soil and stones, but the smell of rotting wood was much stronger. He scraped at the soil. Before his eyes could see, his fingers identified what lay underfoot: wooden boards. An old floor? Out *here*? Something was wrong.

Magnus stood up. As he did so, there was a loud creak. Instinct and training drove him down again, hard and fast, as he raised his rifle. There was another creak as the boards strained, then gave way with a groan, first snapping and splintering, then falling away beneath him.

Magnus didn't expect to fall far – into a cellar maybe – and his highly trained body prepared to hit the ground rolling to avoid breaking bones. But as he kept falling, he realised it was more a question of which bones he would break and how badly.

He seemed to fall in slow motion, finding time to deduce that he'd fallen down a well, a well concealed by the ruins of its wall, a rotten cover and decades of vegetation. Magnus wondered why they'd never found it when they were renovating Tully. He'd always known there should have been a well in the courtyard and he enjoyed a fleeting moment's satisfaction that he'd been right. That satisfaction was swiftly supplanted by the knowledge that he was about to hit the bottom of the well; that he'd be lying, injured, in cold water until he died of hypothermia, his injuries or both.

As he hit the water, rubble and mud that lay at the bottom of the well, a foul stench rose into the stagnant air. He felt an ankle shatter, then the shock waves passing upwards through his body. Howling in agony, he struggled to maintain consciousness, but the sickening pain overwhelmed him. Just before he passed out, Magnus opened his eyes and looked up at the sky, where stars glittered, then he sank into the freezing water.

Light years above him, Orion looked down, then moved on, inexorably and without pity, leaving Magnus to die.

Chapter 22

Nina hunched over the wheel of her mother's Volvo as she inched the car up the winding, rutted track to Tully. She'd rung Magnus several times to inform him she'd forgotten to clear out the clothes she kept under the bed, but he hadn't answered, so she assumed he wasn't there. Nina wondered if he'd gone running back to Fay, though from what Emily had said, this was by no means a foregone conclusion. In any case, Nina didn't care. If Magnus wasn't at home, so much the better. She'd also forgotten to return her keys, so she'd be able to get in and out quickly, taking the last of her stuff without further wrangling or embarrassment.

Nina parked the car in the courtyard. As she killed the lights, darkness descended, a darkness that seemed all the more profound as not a single light showed at Tully's windows. This was unusual. Ignoring Nina's green convictions (which didn't prevent her from borrowing her mother's fuel-guzzling car), Magnus had always chosen to leave one or two lights on at Tully – to discourage intruders, he said, but also because he liked his home to look inhabited and welcoming. He'd spent many months living with Tully's cold, dark shell and his preference was for blazing fires and lights. None was in evidence this evening.

Nina let herself in, calling out, even though she knew Magnus wasn't at home. She always felt a little nervous when Tully was dark. She'd never lived alone and was used to company, the chatter of the classroom, the noise of TV and radio. Silence made her anxious. So did darkness. It didn't help that Magnus had told her (he must have been teasing, surely?) that Tully had a ghost, a woman who'd committed suicide in despair at being parted from her lover.

This defeatist attitude was not one with which Nina could readily sympathise. She believed a lot of so-called depression could be attributed to poor diet and lack of exercise. It was a question of taking oneself in hand and keeping busy, which is what Nina intended to do. Nevertheless, when she arrived in her old bedroom and saw the chaos, she felt immediately depressed. Magnus' crumpled shirt and kilt lay in a heap on the bed and an empty bottle of whisky stood on the bedside table. There wasn't even a glass. In an automatic gesture, Nina picked up the bottle and dropped it into the waste paper bin, then she switched on the clock radio. It was still tuned to her preferred station, Classic FM, and soothing strings poured forth in a major key. Nina felt a little better.

Averting her eyes from Magnus' discarded clothes, she got down on her knees and pulled out a large zip-up bag from under the bed. She undid the zip and began to remove her summer clothes, packing them into a holdall she'd brought for the purpose.

She'd finished packing her bag and was about to switch off the radio when the phone on the bedside table rang, making her jump. Nina was momentarily confused. This was no longer her home and she felt she shouldn't answer. Friends would have rung her mobile and she knew the caller couldn't be Magnus – why would he ring his empty home? – so she was certain the call couldn't be for her. She decided to ignore it and zipped up her bulging holdall.

But the ringing persisted and curiosity was getting the better of her. Who needed to speak to Magnus this badly? Perhaps it was Emily. Emily in some sort of trouble. Nina dumped the holdall on the bed and grabbed the phone.

'Hello?' She heard an intake of breath at the other end of the line, but no one answered. 'Hello?' she repeated. 'Is anyone there?' Irritability masked her nervousness. Nina recalled that sometimes, when he'd had a few drinks, Magnus would talk about the patient, vengeful men who held a grudge against him, who might wait years before striking him down. Was this one of them? Or just a nuisance call? As Classic FM's sobbing strings reached a crescendo, Nina rammed the phone back on its cradle. She turned the radio off, flicked the bedroom light switch and hauled her bag downstairs.

She locked the front door, and was about to post her bunch of keys through the letterbox, when it occurred to her that, if she did, the door might not open properly. She decided to post the keys back to Magnus with, perhaps, a final dignified note and a request to forward her mail.

She hurried back to the car and threw her holdall into the boot. Only when she was behind the wheel, with all the doors locked, did Nina begin to feel safe again. She gazed through the windscreen at Tully's imposing outline silhouetted against the night sky. Her old home... Beautiful. Romantic. But in the end, just not practical.

Rather like Magnus.

Nina turned the ignition and drove away.

Suddenly sober, Fay replaced the receiver but continued to stare at the phone.

'Did he answer?' Jessie asked.

'No.'

'But someone did?'

'Yes. Nina.'

'*Nina*?' Jessie stared in disbelief.

'Yes. I couldn't bring myself to speak to her. What would be the point? And like *this*,' Fay added, pointing at her mouth.

'What was *she* doing there?'

Fay shrugged. 'She sounded a bit annoyed... There was music on in the background. Maybe they were having a candle-lit dinner. I was obviously interrupting something.'

'Well, that's not what I expected *at all*!' Jessie exclaimed, dismayed.

'Me neither. But I suppose it means we can stop fretting about Magnus. He's obviously OK. And now we know why he hasn't been in touch. He's been otherwise engaged.' Even with her wired jaw, the bitterness in Fay's voice was unmistakable.

Jessie eyed her from her chair, then got to her feet. 'I'm going to put the kettle on. I think we need a cup of tea.'

'Thanks, Jessie, but I'd better be on my way.'

'Och, will you not stay over? It's late.'

'I'd prefer to sleep in my own bed. First night out of

232

hospital... And I've got a lot to do tomorrow. I've got a work deadline looming and I'm really behind schedule.' Jessie said nothing. Fay looked down at the floor. 'I'm giving too many excuses, aren't I?'

'I understand. You just need to get away. I should have realised.'

'If I leave now, I've got time to catch the last train back to Glasgow.'

'Off you go then,' said Jessie, following Fay out into the hall.

'Now I know he's all right, I'll be able to sleep. It was bothering me, not hearing from him. I kept thinking something awful must have happened. But obviously he's fine.'

'Oh aye. If not in his right mind,' Jessie added with a sigh.

'No, he's OK,' said Fay, arranging her aching facial muscles in the semblance of a smile. 'The madness has passed...'

When Magnus regained consciousness, he couldn't remember how he'd become detached from his platoon. He remembered the order to fix bayonets. The blades had glinted in the moonlight. Then they'd waited behind a rocky ridge. And then?... Then the order to charge, forward into enemy fire, taking cover where they could, pressing themselves face down into the cold, wet earth, trying to make themselves as small a target as possible, while rounds zipped over their heads. And then?... Then silence. And darkness.

Magnus found himself lying in a shallow pool of freezing water. To judge from the pain, his leg was wounded, though he didn't remember stopping a bullet. He couldn't see any of the others. Couldn't see anything at all, in fact. He wondered if he'd been shot in the head. He put a muddy hand up to his eyes to check they were both still there. Appeared to be.

He wondered if he was in fact dead. He considered the possibility for a moment, then rejected it. It seemed unlikely death would involve such acute consciousness of pain and cold. No, he was alive, all right, unless this was the Almighty's idea of a joke. Magnus resolved that if he ever got out of this hell-hole, he'd go home and spend the rest of his life sitting on his arse by a roaring fire in an overheated room with every bloody light in the house blazing. *If* he ever got out. Which didn't seem likely.

He called out his mates' names, but there was no answer. No groans from the wounded. No one calling for assistance. Just silence. It was eerie. His platoon must have moved on and left him for dead. Fair enough. He soon would be.

The coast seemed clear, so Magnus tried to raise himself out of the bog he was lying in. As he did so, the agonising pain in his leg made his gorge rise and he had to fight to stay conscious. He reached for the dog tags round his neck, searching with clumsy, numb fingers for the morphine syrette supplied for personal use, but burrowing beneath his wet clothes, he found nothing.

One of his mates must have removed the tags, thinking he was dead. They'd be sent home to his family. To Fay.

Fay...

How long was it since he'd thought of her? Tears sprung into Magnus' eyes and their sudden warmth startled him. *Jesus*, he was cold... He patted his body, trying to locate the pouch in his webbing where he kept the letter she'd sent him, that beautiful letter he never tired of reading, the one he'd carry in its waterproof packet till the day he died. There was no light to read it by, but he knew it by heart. He just wanted to hold it. Touch a bit of home. A bit of Fay, his beautiful wife.

But the letter wasn't there.

His *webbing* wasn't there.

Magnus knew then that his mind was going. Maybe he *had* been shot in the head. He must be close to the end now because he was losing it altogether. Looking up at the sky, all he could see was a small patch of light, like a window. A circle of stars. Just bits of constellation. Why couldn't he see the whole sky? Why this tunnel effect? His vision must be impaired. Is this what happened at the end?... Well, so be it. Magnus stared up at the stars, defiant, and waited to go blind.

But something was wrong. He *recognised* that pattern. And out here in the godforsaken bloody Falklands, he didn't recognise any stars, because they were all upside down!

Something was wrong.

Something was *very* wrong.

The realisation hit him like a piece of shrapnel. *He wasn't in the Falklands.* That's why he couldn't find his dog tags. Or Fay's letter. Or his bloody webbing.

So where, in the name of sweet Jesus Christ, *was* he?

Magnus threw back his head, glared up at the stars in the cold, clear Perthshire sky and screamed his wife's name. When the echo finally died away, he knew exactly where he was. To his everlasting shame, Magnus began to weep.

Fay

"Gutted" doesn't begin to describe it. Appalled. Outraged. Disillusioned. Disgusted. That's getting close. I was mad as hell.

I'd been in such a hurry to leave Jessie's flat, so scared I would dissolve into angry tears, I'd ended up at the station far too early, so I found myself standing on the platform with time to kill, contemplating killing Magnus. The train wouldn't arrive for another fifteen minutes, so there was nothing for me to do but just stand there, plotting how I would succeed where the IRA had failed.

So I just stood there.

Aching for him.

Because my anger wouldn't dispel my longing. I'd hoped to find some excuse to venture out to Tully, some reason to forgive his dreadful neglect of me and I'd failed. So then I'd done my best to avoid a doormat scenario by working myself up into a lather of bitter resentment. But my efforts were sabotaged at every turn by my knowledge of Magnus' character, which was basically honourable and kind. I tried to believe he'd behaved like a self-serving scumbag, but I just *couldn't*. His behaviour was at odds with the man who'd sat at my bedside, reading the letter he wanted me to receive after his death; at odds with the man who'd treasured a love letter sent to him in the Falklands, a letter he regarded as a talisman, protecting him from bombs and bullets for nearly thirty years.

As I recalled those letters, my thoughts congealed into an icy fear. Magnus no longer had his letter. The letter he believed had kept him alive. They were both in my handbag. He'd left them at the hospital after we'd made love. I knew he hadn't meant to leave both and I'd intended to return mine when I saw him.

I panicked. It was ridiculous, just *nonsense*, but I panicked all the same, on Magnus' behalf. How upset would he be? Would he remember where he'd left it? Supposing he'd gone to pieces when he found he no longer had it? God knew what that letter – or the loss of it – meant to him. For all his matter-of-fact heroism and reliance on high-tech wizardry to save lives, including his own, Magnus was as superstitious as the next man who risks his life on a daily basis and wonders why he's so damn lucky and the other guy isn't. Rituals, mascots and good luck charms are what human beings use to create an illusion of control, to mitigate the randomness and sheer loneliness of a dangerous job. Every "long walk" Magnus had ever done, he'd done with me, my words, close to his body, a body that might at any moment be blasted to oblivion.

I stood freezing on the platform, paralysed with indecision. How could I go up to Tully and return the letter? Nina was there. At best, she'd think I was mad. Well, maybe I was. Did I care what Nina thought? No, not really. I just wanted Magnus to have the letter back. More than that, I wanted to see him, see that he was all right – safe, sane and whole – because what my pounding heart kept telling me was that Magnus *wasn't* all right. He wouldn't treat me like this. He loved me. I knew he did. I didn't use to know, but now I did and I knew he wouldn't ignore me like this. Which meant that something was wrong.

But, my sane mind pointed out, *Nina* was there. She'd picked up the phone and I'd heard her voice. Unmistakable. There'd even been music on in the background. So it was apparently business as usual.

But what if Magnus *wasn't* there? Supposing Nina was waiting for him? Waiting, like me, for a call?... I'd assumed he was at Tully, but no one had actually heard from him for three days now. He hadn't answered the landline or his mobile. No one knew where he was, even if he was alive.

I took my mobile out of my bag, resolving once and for all to speak to whoever picked up the phone. If Nina answered, I would just tell her I'd found an important letter that belonged to Magnus and would return it to him by first class post. She'd think I'd taken leave of my senses, but I didn't care. It would put an end to this madness once and for all.

I called the Tully number.

No answer.

I rang again, but still there was no answer. I checked my watch. 10.25. If they were already in bed and asleep, they must have made quite a night of it. But if Nina was there on her own, she would have answered the phone, thinking it could be Magnus. So either they were *both* there and fully occupied, or *neither* of them was.

I hung up and stood shivering, clutching my phone. Fighting back tears of frustration, I stamped my cold feet and looked up at the sky. The stars formed a brilliant crystalline display, strung out like jewels on black velvet. Magnus had taught me to identify bright Sirius and massive Orion but, instead of distracting me, the stars simply reminded me how, as a young army wife, I used to gaze up at them, knowing Magnus might be doing the same. That connection had sustained us, would always sustain us.

> *"...And, when he shall die,*
> *Take him and cut him out in little stars,*
> *And he will make the face of heaven so fine*
> *That all the world will be in love with night..."*

When he shall die...The words reverberated in my head as I became aware of an ominous rumbling in the distance, like thunder. The train.

He shall die...

The Glasgow train was approaching. Decision time. This was the last train. If I didn't catch it, I'd have to go back to Jessie's or stay in a hotel. As the train wheezed to a halt, I heard a distant, blood-curdling shriek, an almost-human scream that turned my innards to water before I realised it must be a fox, a vixen's unearthly cry for a mate. Then as doors opened and a few passengers alighted, I felt a familiar presence. It was almost as if she'd tapped me on the shoulder. I didn't need to turn round. I knew who it was and I knew why she was there.

Isobel leaned close and whispered in my ear. 'He *shall* die.'

Doors banged. There was a short blast on a whistle. I stood, immobile, watching as the train pulled out of the station. When it had gone, I looked up at the stars again. Seeking what? Guidance? Perhaps their approval.

I turned and headed for the taxi rank. 'Hang on,' I murmured to my husband and the ghost of Isobel Moncrieffe; to Orion and countless galaxies of stars. 'Hang on, Magnus. I'm coming...'

Chapter 23

Fay

The taxi drew up outside Tully and I told the driver to wait. There was no sign of any light. That told me Magnus wasn't at home. Unless he'd changed in the intervening years, there would have been lights on somewhere. But if Nina was home alone, waiting for him, she could have turned them all off and gone to bed. It was only 10.50. If she was up waiting for Magnus, would she have gone so early? It seemed unlikely. Could she have given up and gone back to her parents?

I got out of the taxi and headed for the front door. I couldn't see the Land Rover, but Magnus sometimes parked it round the back. Lifting the wrought iron knocker, I banged on the door. (Magnus had always refused to have what he called "a poncey, *Avon-calling* doorbell" disfiguring Tully's fine oak door.) Silence followed and no one appeared. Given the lateness of the hour, this wasn't surprising if Nina was in on her own. I looked up at the windows, to see if a light had come on.

Nothing.

I took out my phone and rang Magnus' mobile yet again, then the Tully landline. I could hear the phone ringing on the other side of the door, so I knew there was no fault on the line. It seemed no one was at home and I'd had a wasted journey. I withdrew my old letter to Magnus from my bag and was about to leave it in the letterbox when I had second thoughts. This letter was too precious to leave lying around. Supposing Nina saw it and destroyed it in a fit of pique? I decided to return the letter to Magnus personally, so I turned away, intending to get back into the taxi.

Then I remembered the spare key.

When I'd lived at Tully, we'd kept a spare key hanging on a piece of string that was accessed through one of the gun loops, the holes in the wall at ground level originally used for Tully's defence. Magnus had retained and restored them with loving care. The spare key had been mainly for Emily's benefit. In her teens she was an inveterate loser of keys and the Tully front door key had been an expensive one to replace. She'd continued to live at Tully after I'd gone and moved out only a couple of years ago, so it seemed possible the spare key could still be hanging where we used to keep it.

I told the driver I was just going to have a look round the back, to see if any lights were on. He nodded and returned to his newspaper. I walked round the corner, finding my way in the dark with difficulty, but the moon shed some light, enough to spot the Land Rover. So Magnus ought to be at Tully. I followed the wall round till I came to the gun loop where the key used to hang. Taking a pen from my bag, I poked it into the deep hole and waved it around. The pen met some resistance. This must be the string on which the heavy key hung.

I came to a decision.

I walked back to the taxi and paid the driver. He seemed reluctant to leave me in a remote, unlit spot, but I told him I'd finally located my key at the bottom of my bag and would be able to let myself in. He drove away and as the taxi headlights swept the courtyard, then disappeared, a deeper darkness descended on Tully. I looked up at the sky and was relieved to see there were still no clouds. Once my eyes adjusted to the dark, moonlight would be sufficient for what I needed to do.

It was fiddly drawing the string through the gun loop. Emily used to carry a large crochet hook for the purpose. I had a long-tailed comb which eventually did the job. I drew the key through the hole and started to grapple with the knot, but my fingers were cold and tired. I gave up and took out the scissors I now had to carry at all times and cut the string.

I walked round to the front door and let myself in. As I entered, I felt I should call out to announce myself, but the best I could manage was an indistinct "Hello", uttered as loudly as I could without being able to open my mouth – which wasn't very loud at all. I reached for the hall light, my hand finding it automatically, then I listened for a sound that would tell me someone was at home.

Nothing.

I decided to go in to the kitchen. If Magnus was at Tully, or had been here recently, there would surely be signs of activity or food in the fridge.

There were signs of activity all right. The floor was strewn with broken crockery, glasses and bottles, as if there'd been a fight. As I picked my way through the debris, I spotted the shiny plastic remnants of a broken phone. I had no idea how it came to be smashed, but the wreckage explained why Magnus hadn't responded to any of my texts. Even more worrying were the signs of him "camping out". The kitchen table had been turned on its side and pushed up against the wall. Behind, I found a sort of den, with sleeping bag, torch, an alarming selection of sharp kitchen knives, a mug half full of black coffee and a plate smeared with what might have been (to judge from the smell) tinned sardines. Beside the sleeping bag were a can opener and a neat stack of food tins.

I was horrified. It was clear Magnus had been here, perhaps was still here, holed up somewhere, possibly hiding. What was equally clear was that he'd totally lost it.

Dreading what I might find, I went upstairs to the Great Hall. I switched on the light and saw another chaotic scene, but chaos of a different kind. I wasn't really surprised to see lingering signs of the engagement party – the awful bunting, dirty glasses, a few unopened cards and presents addressed to "Nina and Magnus" – but I was puzzled by the almost empty bookcase. Photographs had disappeared from the window recesses, as had the cushions. Had Nina cleared out all her stuff? Had she left Magnus?

I hurried upstairs, then stood outside their bedroom door, hesitating. I knocked, waited a few seconds, then went in. The first thing I saw was Magnus' kilt lying on the bed. The sight of it, abandoned again, gave me such a pang of longing for him, I thought my legs would give way. Holding on to the door handle for support, I looked round. It was only a few days since I'd stood in this room – been *knocked out* in this

241

room, actually – but it now looked very different. The TV was gone. So was a full-length mirror. A man's dressing gown hung on the back of the door, but there was no sign of a woman's. Resigned now to feeling like Glenn Close in *Fatal Attraction*, I went into the en-suite and checked the back of the door.

Nothing. There was nothing in the drawers either and nothing on the shelves, apart from sticky rings in the dust where Nina had kept her toiletries. There was no sign of any female presence in the bedroom or the en-suite. Nina had gone and she wasn't coming back.

It was over.

A tidal wave of relief swept over me. As I sank down on to the bed, my hand fell on Magnus' crumpled and discarded shirt. I grabbed it and pressed it to my face, inhaling his scent. I lay back on the bed – the bed that had been *our* bed – and remembered him removing this same shirt in the hospital. Thoughts of Magnus' naked body and what he'd then done with it distracted me for a moment, but the room began to swim as my brain engaged belatedly with the new information. Casting his shirt aside, I sat bolt upright, my heart thudding.

If it was all over with Nina, Magnus had had no reason to be out of touch for days. Even if his mobile was smashed, he could have rung me on the landline or come to visit me again. Why had I heard nothing from him? And why *was* his phone smashed?

As my fears multiplied, I began to feel nauseous. Nausea turned to panic when I realised I'd left my handbag in the kitchen. If I vomited with wired teeth, I could choke to death, which was why I was supposed to keep scissors on me at all times. Running out of the bedroom, I hurtled down the turnpike stair and into the kitchen. I grabbed my bag and, with shaking hands, extracted the scissors and a small mirror.

As soon as I had them in my hand, the nausea subsided and I felt calmer. I replaced the emergency kit in my bag, which I then slung across my body. Pulling myself together, I systematically checked every other room at Tully. I even looked inside the larger cupboards. When I was satisfied

Magnus wasn't in the building – dead or alive – I went back to the kitchen. I picked up the torch and, for reasons I didn't really care to examine, I also took one of the smaller kitchen knives, which I dropped into my pocket. Leaving all the lights on, I went outside to look for my demented ex-husband.

I don't know what I was looking for, but there was nowhere else left to look. As the Land Rover was still at Tully, Magnus couldn't have gone far.

Unless he'd been kidnapped.

Feeling panicky again, I told myself he could be camping out. During flashbacks, he'd been known to patrol Tully's grounds with a shotgun, convinced he was living in a war zone. Perhaps I'd find him on a stakeout in the ruined dovecote. I hoped that would be the worst I'd find. There'd been no note left conspicuously indoors, so I'd ruled out suicide, even though I knew the absence of a note didn't prove Magnus was alive. The horrendous nature of PTSD was that victims could be suddenly overwhelmed by unbearable memories and feelings. In a flashback, anything could happen.

I checked the garden shed, then the greenhouse. Once I'd been to the dovecote, there was nowhere sheltered left to look. If Magnus was still at Tully, he must be out in the open somewhere.

Was he actually watching me? I stood still and tried to feel his presence, sense if his eyes were on me. I couldn't feel anything. I was frightened, but didn't feel as if I was being watched. I thought of calling out (or rather *mumbling* out) but there didn't seem to be much point. My torch beam announced my presence and I was making plenty of noise moving round the garden, accidentally knocking over flowerpots. I'd had to kick the shed door to get it to shut. If Magnus was in the grounds, he must know I was here, so either he *wasn't* here, or he didn't want me to know he *was*. Neither scenario was remotely encouraging.

It was bitterly cold and I began to think about giving up and going indoors to make a hot drink. I was chilled, tired and hungry. Heating up one of my jars of baby food in the microwave began to seem like a tempting option. I was heading back when I heard an unearthly cry, like the one I'd heard at the station. It sounded like an animal in pain, but I knew it was probably just a healthy fox. The weird noises they made often used to disturb me when I lived at Tully. In the early days, the deafening silence of the countryside used to keep me awake at night, then, as I lay there sleepless, the cries of foxes, owls, and assorted ambushed and expiring mammals used to scare the daylights out of me.

Spooked by the fox, I had a sudden horrible thought. There was one place I hadn't looked. If you were going to hide a body (and I'd admitted to myself, shaking, that it might be Magnus' body I'd eventually find), you could do worse than hide it in the huge wooden compost bin he'd built for me. Once the thought had occurred to me, I couldn't get it out of my head, so I turned my back on warmth and light and headed for the vegetable garden. As I approached, it became obvious Nina had no idea how to make proper compost. A smell of vegetable decay pervaded the air. (Good compost, properly made and aerated, doesn't smell.)

I located the bin, but not, as it turned out, by smell. The lid was off and the bin was empty. It didn't smell unpleasant, nor did the vegetable beds where compost had been spread. I'd done poor Nina an injustice. Yet there was still a nasty, dank smell in the air, of something rotting. As I set off back toward the house again, the smell got stronger, so I stood still and looked around, puzzled. I was standing beside an uncultivated part of Tully's grounds that, tongue-in-cheek, we'd dubbed, "the wildlife reserve". It was a piece of ground so overgrown and strewn with rubble, we'd decided to leave it alone. Years later, it was now almost impenetrable, dense with weeds and brambles.

But this was where the strange smell seemed to be coming from. It was an odd mixture of damp and decay that took me right back to the early days of renovating Tully, when we seemed to do nothing but clear barrow loads of rotting wood, jackdaw nests and the remains of countless dead birds and animals who'd made Tully their final resting place. I assumed the thicket must be some sort of animal den or graveyard. Feeling more spooked than ever and shivering violently now, I headed back to the house.

I sat in the kitchen, sucking up a warmed jar of *Cow & Gate* Chocolate Pudding. (Not bad if you lace it with brandy, which I did, availing myself of a bottle I'd found in the cupboard). With no straw to hand, I was making heavy weather of a cup of coffee when another thought struck me. I hadn't been up to the roof. Magnus could be up on the walkway, "keeping guard". Or unconscious. Or dead.

I was furious with myself for not making a thorough search. I put down my pudding, picked up my handbag and torch and climbed the turnpike stair again. This time, I carried on up until I got to the door that led out on to the roof.

~

In and out of consciousness, Magnus was surprised to find, each time he surfaced, that he was still alive. Not for much longer, he supposed. He'd lost all track of time. For a while the patch of sky above him had been grey instead of black and he believed Orion was coming round now for the second time. Despite the low temperature and his sodden clothes, he'd stopped shivering long ago, so he knew he was suffering from hypothermia. He also knew, in a detached sort of way that didn't seem at all alarming, that he should be dead by now. He assumed his level of fitness and a working life that often entailed being cold and wet had extended his life expectancy by a few hours – for which dubious blessing he could summon little in the way of gratitude.

Magnus had eventually yelled for help, even though he knew no one would hear him. He'd been conscious when the Postie arrived in his van. Magnus had felt the vibrations of the vehicle through the earth, but as usual, Ewan had left the engine running and was doubtless plugged into his iPod. Magnus yelled anyway until he knew Ewan must have driven away. Later he'd yelled just because it went against all his training to sit passively, waiting for death to take him. He was still, at heart, a British soldier and he'd go down fighting. But his vocal cords had given out and the utter futility of the exercise had overwhelmed him.

For something to do, Magnus tried to move, even though he knew the pain from his ankle would probably make him pass out again. As he put his hands down into the mud to shift his body weight, his frozen fingers found a piece of cord. He tugged at the cord, which appeared to be attached to something heavy. Magnus dragged the object out of the water and, using his hands rather than his eyes, identified it as the flashlight he'd been holding when he was patrolling the grounds. He'd forgotten all about it. It was supposed to be waterproof, so he switched it on. Magnus was dazzled as it cast its powerful beam on to the slime-covered walls of the well.

So now he had some light. His death would at least be illuminated, if not illuminating.

He directed the beam upwards, examining the sheer brick walls. Climbing out would be impossible, even with two working ankles. There were no footholds that he could see, no crumbling bricks. Magnus was no quitter, but he had to admit, even Houdini wouldn't be able to get out of this one.

He switched off the flashlight and suffocating blackness enveloped him. He thought of turning it back on again, then wondered idly how long the battery would last. Longer than him, probably.

Magnus looked up at the stars and felt slightly better for their company. He remembered the many times he'd looked up at them and thought of Fay, knowing she'd be doing the same thing. What was it she'd called it?... *Sharing a sky*. She'd said, however far apart they were, they could always share a sky.

God, he loved that woman...

She wasn't very far away now – only in Perth. At the Infirmary. A matter of miles. He wondered what she was doing; if she could see any stars from her hospital bed. He could *feel* she was near. Not like when he was in the Falklands or even Northern Ireland. She'd seemed a world away then. Magnus looked up at the stars and thought of Fay, thought of the last time he'd seen her. Moving cracked lips, parched with thirst, he mouthed the words, 'I love you.'

When he closed his eyes, Magnus was disgusted to feel the warmth of tears trickling down his cheeks. He dashed them away with a muddy hand, reminding himself that, with his level of de-hydration, he could ill afford the luxury of blubbing. But he was past caring. All he wanted now was to commemorate his own death and his undying love for his wife, so he positioned the flashlight in his lap, switched it on and tilted it upwards. He watched the beam as it raked the black walls of the well, then he adjusted its position until the light found the hole at the top.

As if he'd hit some target, Magnus laughed, then began to weep again. His arms and shoulders relaxed and his hands fell loosely at his sides. As he lost consciousness, his body slumped to one side and the flashlight toppled off his lap, back into the noisome water.

Chapter 24

Fay

I opened the door and stepped out on to the walkway, bracing myself, not just for finding Magnus, but for the avalanche of memories I knew would engulf me. It was here Magnus had demonstrated how much he loved me – not just when he saved my life, but when, at his own engagement party, he'd made it clear he was only going through the motions; that his heart still lay with me and always would.

There was no sign of him on the walkway, so I stood looking up at the night sky, enthralled as ever by the display. I don't know if it was being up there, or staring at the stars, but I felt close to Magnus then, closer than I'd felt at any point since arriving at Tully. Did that mean he was alive? That he was here?

Searching the stars wasn't going to provide me with an answer. Placing my hands on the parapet wall to steady myself, I looked down into the blackness of Tully's courtyard. A few shafts of light from the windows illuminated the area around the house and moonlight picked out the reflective surfaces of the Land Rover. Otherwise, everything was dark. No light or sound betrayed any human presence apart from my own. A pale shape swooped silently across my field of vision, like a diminutive ghost. Just a barn owl on its nightly rounds. Why did I keep kidding myself? Magnus wasn't here. I just *wanted* him to be here.

I decided I had to give up, but before going downstairs, I took a last look at the stars, the stars that had brought me here in the first place. Closing my eyes against tears of exhaustion, I leaned on the cold, heartless stones of Tully, which had refused to yield up Magnus. When I opened my eyes again, there was a column of light before me, rising up out of the ground. Clutching at the wall, I blinked several times, but the light was still there, thin and straight, pointing up into the air.

My mouth moved instinctively to call out, but as my muscles met resistance, I remembered my padlocked mouth. Galloping down the turnpike stair, I told myself, it was nothing; I was hallucinating; the ghost of Isobel Moncrieffe had taken up practical jokes; Magnus *couldn't* be here, right under my nose – I would have found him. I hauled open the front door, ran out into the courtyard and round to where I'd seen the beam of light. I stood panting, my eyes straining to see in the darkness.

Nothing.

The light – if it had ever existed – was gone.

The sane part of my mind told me I'd imagined it. It was just a passing car, a passing UFO, a cut-down version of the Northern Lights. But the *insane* part of my mind said this was Magnus. Somewhere, somehow, this was Magnus and he was in trouble. Because if he wasn't, he would be here now, with me, in my arms, in that bed upstairs, because the only things that were going to keep us apart now were madness or death.

I switched on my torch and raked the ground yet again, looking for footprints, equipment, blood, bits of body, *anything*. I couldn't work out where the light had come from – it had seemed to appear from the middle of nowhere – but I knew I must be in the right general area. I stood still and waited for the light to reappear.

Nothing.

As loudly as I could, I said, 'Magnus?' and waited for a response.

Nothing.

I took stock. There were just two things I could do now. One was sit it out at Tully, wait for daylight, then mount a proper search. I shone the torch on the dial of my watch. Not even midnight.

So I did the other thing.

~

Fay cursed Magnus' lack of personal vanity as she searched

Tully for a mirror. She gave up and propped her handbag mirror against a teapot, switched on the kitchen worktop lights, pulled up a chair and sat down. She angled the mirror until she had a good view of her mouth, then extracted from her bag the small pair of scissors. With trembling fingers, she lifted them to her bared teeth, trying to remember the instructions she'd been given at the hospital. *Don't panic,* they'd said. *Keep breathing. Just snip the elastic bands to free your jaw, lean forward and let any vomit fall out...*

The nurse had assured Fay she wouldn't have to open her mouth very wide to avoid choking. But she *would* have to open her mouth wide to yell "Magnus". And she'd have to do it twice. Two syllables: "Mag-" and then "-nus". The important thing was not to faint after the first or even second syllable, because if Magnus heard her, he might give some sign of his whereabouts.

It's only pain, Fay told herself as she snipped the first band. It can't be any worse than childbirth... She snipped another band. It's not going to *kill* me. So get on with it.

When she'd finished, Fay put down her scissors and stood up. She parted her jaws very slightly to check she'd cut all the bands. The pain was so severe, she had to sit down again and rest her head on the kitchen worktop. When the faintness had passed, she stood up again, picked up the torch, pocketed her phone and, as an afterthought, grabbed the bottle of brandy. With jaws clamped shut, she went outside.

Fay walked back to the area of the garden where she thought she'd seen the strange light. She shone the torch round once again, then pointed the beam upwards at her head, so she was illuminated. If Magnus was watching he would be able to identify her easily. Standing with her back to the "wildlife reserve", where, if she passed out, she'd fall on to long grass, Fay set down the brandy, planted her feet firmly on the ground and cleared her throat. Paralysed with fear, she brought to mind an image she'd never seen: Magnus in Londonderry, lying in a pool of his own blood, his legs shattered, giving clear and precise instructions to his No. 2 so he could finish the job. 'It's only pain,' Fay muttered, barely moving her lips, then, filling her lungs and dropping her jaw, she yelled, 'Magnus!'

She sank to the ground before the second syllable had passed her lips. Dropping the torch, she screwed up her eyes in agony, then forced them open again, looking for the light, a movement, *anything*. Kneeling, she held her face in both hands, as if the bones might disintegrate. To judge from the pain, they already had.

Fay groped for the torch, then located the brandy bottle. She unscrewed the cap and held the bottle gingerly to her lips. Keeping her teeth clenched and her head back, she upended the bottle so brandy trickled into her mouth. She swallowed and, as the fire hit her stomach, she opened her mouth again and screamed, 'Magnus!' Sobbing now, she struggled to her feet and shone the torch round once again.

Nothing.

Stumbling, she took a step toward the house, then another. She'd have to give up the search. There was nothing more she could do.

The fox cried out again, behind her, only this time, it didn't sound like a fox. But it was definitely an animal in pain. As she turned, Fay knew what she would see, so the thin column of light rising up impossibly from the middle of the dense thicket didn't surprise her. As she plunged into the undergrowth, clutching her torch, her other hand was already reaching for her phone.

When Magnus' flashlight picked out a pale face at the top of the well, he switched off. A torch beam circled the top of the well, then descended. He heard a sound like a gasp, then a muffled voice. He tried to reply, but the only noise that emerged from his mouth was a wheezing cough. Willing numb fingers to move, he switched the flashlight on, then off again.

The faint voice said, 'Magnus? Can you hear me?'

He flashed the torch, on and then off.

'I'm ringing for an ambulance. Hold on!'

251

He flashed the torch on and off, quickly, several times. 'What's wrong?'

Forcing his lungs and diaphragm to work, Magnus parted bleeding lips and called out, 'Ring... mountain rescue... Better gear... for... vertical... rescue.'

Fay rang Emergency Services, requested an ambulance and asked them to call out Tayside Mountain Rescue. Then she rang Emily and said, 'Come to Tully. *Now. Please.*' At the sound of Emily's voice, Fay burst into tears. After a brief and emotional exchange, she hung up, blew her nose thoroughly and swallowed a generous amount of brandy. She screwed the top back on tightly, then removed her coat, scarf and jumper. She wrapped the brandy bottle in her jumper, then secured it with her scarf. Leaning over the crumbling edge of the well and rationing her words, she called down to Magnus.

'Ambulance is coming. So's Mountain Rescue. I'm dropping some brandy. Wrapped in my jumper and scarf.'

The flashlight acknowledged and Fay dropped her parcel. She didn't hear a splash, so she assumed Magnus had caught it. 'I'm dropping my coat now. Try and get it round you. There's chocolate in the pocket. Right hand.'

Fay thought she heard a laugh, but it could have been a sob. She bundled up her coat, dropped it down the well, then settled down, shivering, to wait for help.

An hour later, Fay was lying in Emily's arms, semi-conscious, wrapped in thermal blankets. Rick's smiling, floodlit face hovered above them.

'They've got him out! He's got a broken leg – ankle, I think – and he's suffering from exposure, but they say he's going to be all right.' Emily stifled a sob of relief and squeezed her mother tight, but Fay was already struggling to her feet. Swaying like a punch-drunk fighter, she shed the blankets, ignored Rick's offer of a steadying arm and staggered toward the ambulance where a stretcher was about to be loaded into the back.

Fay bent over Magnus, afraid to touch him in case of broken bones. He appeared to be unconscious. As the paramedics manoeuvred the stretcher into position, light from the interior fell on to his gaunt and filthy face, dark with mud and stubble. As she lifted a hand and gently scraped back curling tendrils of wet hair, Magnus opened his eyes. Fay was startled to see how blue they were. She thought, as long as she lived – as long as *Magnus* lived – she would never cease to be amazed by the blue of his eyes.

His lips were moving, so she lowered her ear to his face. His words came slowly, but were quite distinct.

'What... took... you... so... long?'

Fay gasped, then laughed and then she began to cry. As the stretcher slid into the back of the ambulance, she started to clamber inside. One of the paramedics said, 'Are you his wife?'

Fay looked the young man in the eye and, barely moving her aching mouth, said, 'Yes. I am. I'm his wife.'

'OK. Hop in.' As he handed Fay into the ambulance, the paramedic cast a professional eye over her swollen jaw. 'I'm thinking, your face is in need of some medical attention.'

She nodded.

'Assault?'

She nodded again.

'Who did it?'

Fay pointed at Magnus' unconscious form.

The young man looked down at his stretcher case, then gazed at the pale, diminutive woman sitting beside him. Unable to keep a note of admiration out of his voice, he said, 'Throwing him down a well and *leaving* him there – och, was that not a wee bit harsh?'

Epilogue

Fay

I stitch memories. That's what I do.

Emily married Rick in the spring of 2010, at Tullibardine Tower. (It was such a joyous and successful occasion that Emily suggested hosting weddings would be another way Tully could earn its keep.) Once the day and the venue had been decided, I set about making a commemorative wall hanging to represent the history of Tully and all the people who'd lived there or been associated with it.

I made a historical patchwork of births, deaths and marriages, transferring both words and pictures, embroidering the names of every person I could find who'd contributed to Tully's history, from the family who'd built the tower house, by way of Isobel Moncrieffe and her lover, Gypsy Jack, to the most recent custodian, Magnus. Even our builder and handyman, Davy Campbell was included. He's pictured – much to his delight – beside an orderly pile of rubble.

Tully itself was depicted under a night sky, full of glittering stars, which I embroidered with silver threads. I used the motif of a tree again – the Dule Tree this time – and I corrected the error contained in *Root and Branch*. Magnus' father was named as Lachlan McGillivray and faint, ghostly images of both men were transferred on to the linen. The likeness was so marked, the men looked like twins, not father and son.

Everyone pictured on the wall hanging was linked by threads that wove in and out, in front and behind the images, rather in the manner of an endless Celtic knot. The natural world was included too: the Tully garden, the Dule Tree, the foxes, the barn owl, even the pestilential rabbits. There's a sense of all things being connected, sharing a sky.

I spent many hours on the hanging, working against the

clock, trying to get it finished for the wedding in May. I was often very tired and tiredness can lead to accidents. One night, my rotary cutter skidded and slashed my finger. As I reached to get some tissues to staunch the flow of blood, some dripped on to the almost completed wall hanging.

I was distraught. It might have been possible to remove the blood with professional cleaning, but that process could also damage some of the delicate fabrics, threads and dyes I'd used. In any case, time was running out.

Magnus said I should leave the blood. He pointed out that any amount of blood must have been shed at Tully over the years – if not in battle, then in the execution of summary justice, in sickness and in childbirth. What Magnus didn't say – he didn't need to – was that blood had been so much a part of his life, it seemed only fitting that the wall hanging should depict bloodshed – and quite graphically. So I left it. To make the stains look slightly less conspicuous, I embroidered a date over the top: the date of the Londonderry explosion, when Magnus' active career ended.

On Emily and Rick's wedding day, I presented them with a Double Wedding Ring quilt made by my great grandmother, which has been handed down from mother to daughter ever since. On that same day, I presented my new wall hanging to Magnus, when he married me, for the second time, at Tully.

At the bottom of the hanging, in the centre, there's a large and complicated knot, which gives the work its name, The Gordian Knot. (Magnus' irreverent nickname for it is The Gay Gordian Knot.) In Greek mythology, the Gordian Knot was an extremely complicated knot tied by Gordius, king of Phrygia. According to legend, Gordius was a peasant who, when he became king, dedicated his ox-cart to Zeus and fastened it to a pole with the Gordian knot. Although the knot was supposedly impossible to undo, an oracle predicted it would be untied by the future king of Asia.

Many men attempted to undo the knot, but all failed until, one day, Alexander the Great visited the city. After trying unsuccessfully to unravel the knot, he became impatient, took out his sword and simply sliced through it. He went on to conquer Asia, thus fulfilling the oracle's prophecy.

The large knot at the bottom of my wall hanging is made from two fibrous, hand-spun threads, one dark and one light. One represents Magnus and the other represents me. The two threads have been tied and twisted many times, so that the knot can't be untied, only severed with a blade ('and a blade wielded by Alexander the Great,' Magnus always hastens to point out.)

It's our intention that every year, on our wedding anniversary, we shall tie yet another knot in those long threads to make the symbolic task of sundering us ever more difficult.

Impossible, in fact.

ACKNOWLEDGEMENTS

I would like to thank the following people for their help and support while writing this book:

Tina Betts, Jill Broderick, Freda Brooks, Nicola Coffield, Gregor Duthie, Amy Glover, Philip Glover, Miles Mack, Jan Marlowe, Erica Munro, Bert Mackenzie of *Stirling Astronomical Society*, Judy Spencer of *Historic Scotland* and Diane Will.

For more information about post-traumatic stress disorder visit the website of the veterans' mental health charity COMBAT STRESS – **www.combatstress.org.uk**

Other books by **Linda Gillard**...

EMOTIONAL GEOLOGY

A passionate, off-beat love story set on the bleak and beautiful island of North Uist in the Outer Hebrides.

Rose Leonard is on the run from her life.

Haunted by her turbulent past, she takes refuge in a remote Hebridean island community where she cocoons herself in work, silence and solitude in a house by the sea. A new life and new love are offered by friends, her estranged daughter and most of all by Calum, a fragile younger man who has his own demons to exorcise.

But does Rose, with her tenuous hold on sanity, have the courage to say "Yes" to life and put her past behind her?...

REVIEWS

"Haunting, lyrical and intriguing."
ISLA DEWAR (Keeping up with Magda)

"Complex and important issues are played out in the windswept beauty of a Hebridean island setting, with a hero who is definitely in the Mr Darcy league!"
www.ScottishReaders.net

"The emotional power makes this reviewer reflect on how Charlotte and Emily Brontë might have written if they were living and writing now."
NORTHWORDS NOW

A LIFETIME BURNING

Flora Dunbar is dead. But it isn't over.

The spectre at her funeral is Flora herself, unobserved by her grieving family and the four men who loved her.

Looking back over a turbulent lifetime, Flora recalls an eccentric childhood lived in the shadow of her musical twin, Rory; early marriage to Hugh, a handsome clergyman twice her age; motherhood, which brought her Theo, the son she couldn't love; middle age, when she finally found brief happiness in a scandalous affair with her nephew, Colin.

"There has been much love in this family – some would say too much – and not a little hate. If you asked my sister-in-law, Grace why she hated me, she'd say it was because I seduced her precious firstborn, then tossed him on to the sizeable scrap heap marked 'Flora's ex-lovers'. But she'd be lying. That isn't why Grace hated me. Ask my brother Rory."

REVIEWS

"An absolute page-turner! I could not put this book down and read it over a weekend. It is a haunting and disturbing exploration of the meaning of love within a close-knit family... Find a place for it in your holiday luggage!"
www.lovereading.co.uk

"Probably the most convincing portrayal of being a twin that I have ever read."
STUCK-IN-A-BOOK's blog

"Disturbing themes, sensitively explored... An emotional avalanche."
LOCHCARRON READING GROUP

STAR GAZING

Short-listed for *Romantic Novel of the Year* and *The Robin Jenkins Literary Award*, the UK's first environmental book award.

Blind since birth, widowed in her twenties, now lonely in her forties, Marianne Fraser lives in Edinburgh in elegant, angry anonymity with her sister, Louisa, a successful novelist. Marianne's passionate nature finds expression in music, a love she finds she shares with Keir, a man she encounters on her doorstep one winter's night.

Keir makes no concession to her condition. He's abrupt to the point of rudeness, yet oddly kind. But can Marianne trust her feelings for this reclusive stranger who wants to take a blind woman to his island home on Skye, to "show her the stars"?

REVIEWS

"This was a joy to read from the first page to the last... Romantic and quirky and beautifully written."
www.lovereading.co.uk

"A read for diehard romantics with a bent towards environmental issues."
ABERDEEN PRESS AND JOURNAL

"A story of love, music and nature, with touches of the supernatural and a very engaging and believable heroine."
ADÈLE GERAS (Facing the Light)

HOUSE OF SILENCE

Selected by Amazon UK for their *Top Ten BEST OF 2011* in the Indie Author category.

"My friends describe me as frighteningly sensible, not at all the sort of woman who would fall for an actor. And his home. And his family."

Orphaned by drink, drugs and rock'n'roll, Gwen Rowland is invited to spend Christmas at her boyfriend Alfie's family home, Creake Hall – a ramshackle Tudor manor in Norfolk. Soon after she arrives, Gwen senses something isn't quite right. Alfie acts strangely toward his family and is reluctant to talk about the past. His mother, a celebrated children's author, keeps to her room, living in a twilight world, unable to distinguish between past and present, fact and fiction.

When Gwen discovers fragments of forgotten family letters sewn into an old patchwork quilt, she starts to piece together the jigsaw of the past and realises there's more to the family history than she's been told. It seems there are things people don't want her to know.

And one of those people is Alfie...

REVIEWS

"HOUSE OF SILENCE is one of those books you'll put everything else on hold for."
CORNFLOWER BOOKS blog

"The family turns out to have more secrets than the Pentagon. I enjoyed every minute of this book."
KATHLEEN JONES (Margaret Forster: A Life in Books)

THE GLASS GUARDIAN

Ruth Travers has lost a lover, both parents and her job. Now she thinks she might be losing her mind.

When death strikes again, Ruth finds herself the owner of a dilapidated Victorian house on the Isle of Skye: *Tigh na Linne*, the summer home she shared as a child with her beloved Aunt Janet, the woman she'd regarded as a mother. As Ruth prepares to put the old house up for sale, she discovers she's not the only occupant. Worse, she suspects she might be falling in love.

With a man who died almost a hundred years ago.

REVIEWS

"As usual with Gillard's novels, I read THE GLASS GUARDIAN in almost one sitting. The story is about love, loss, grief, music, World War I, Skye, family secrets, loneliness and a ghost who will break your heart."
I PREFER READING book blog

"A captivating story, dealing with passionate love and tragic death... An old, crumbling house, snow falling all around, and a handsome ghost... Curling up with this book on a dark night would be perfect!"
THE LITTLE READER LIBRARY book blog

"The ending? Beautiful and completely satisfying. I cried tears of joy."
AWESOME INDIES book blog

18068285R00161

Printed in Poland
by Amazon Fulfillment
Poland Sp. z o.o., Wrocław